# PROJECT AZALEA

## By J.E. Conery

D1114062

This book is a work of fiction. Names, characters, places and
incidents either are the product of the author's imagination or
are used fictitiously, and any resemblance to actual persons,
living or dead, events, or locales is entirely coincidental.

Printed in the United States of America
Print ISBN: 978-1-953910-08-0
eBook ISBN: 978-1-953910-09-7
Hardback ISBN: 978-1-953910-60-8

Library of Congress Control Number: 2021905080

Published by DartFrog Plus, the hybrid publishing imprint of DartFrog Books.

Publisher Information:
DartFrog Books
4697 Main Street
Manchester, VT 05255

www.DartFrogBooks.com

Join the discussion of this book on Bookclubz. Bookclubz
is an online management tool for book clubs, available
now for Android and iOS and via Bookclubz.com.

*Artwork by Claire Conery*

This is a rendering of Mamaw's house as we envisioned it. Prudence was raised here after she was abandoned by her mother. It is a modest house in a small, quiet neighborhood that straddled the poverty line between the city and the suburbs. It was a tight-knit community founded in the 1950s, where everyone knew and supported one another. All were colorblind, even during the racial upheaval of the civil rights era, and it was in this context that Prudence's values were shaped.

After being gone ten years, Prudence and Theo moved back to take care of Mamaw. When she passed away, this house became Prudence's solace, her respite, and her source of strength. It was a place for her and Theo to retreat to during troubling times. The house is Prudence's anchor, and is omnipresent throughout the story.

We initially thought that this illustration would be on the cover of the book, but after much deliberation, and with my daughter Claire's guidance, we agreed on a different design that seemed to capture the overall feel of the book a bit more, and not just one small element of it. However, we fell in love with this depiction, and wanted to preserve and share it with our readers.

*This book is dedicated to my wife, Eileen, who gave me the encouragement I needed to finally start writing and then see this effort through to its completion (and for suggesting that I write her into the storyline). I love you deeply and could not have gotten this far without you.*

*Special thanks to my children, Ian and Claire, who gave me support and inspiration, and provided valuable input. Ian provided insight on the content, and Claire influenced the simplistic, yet elegant, cover and created the illustration inside the book.*

*I'd like to thank my parents, siblings, in-laws, as well as countless other family members and friends. Their consistent interest, patience, and encouragement helped sustain me throughout the process. Finally, I can say that my book is published!*

*Lastly, I'd be remiss if I didn't acknowledge the following:*

*Brian Baiamonte for the excellent photography shot under the shade of the Evangeline Oak in St. Martinville, LA, that is featured on the back cover of this book; more of his work can be found at www.brianbaiamonte.com.*

*Nick Gachassin III and Kenneth Johnston for taking the time to review and provide feedback from their legal perspective and experience.*

*Andy Winchell for wanting to be written into the story and providing the inspiration for the creation of Ti Pop.*

*Melanie Johnson from Elite Online Publishing, who provided me with great advice and insight over the last few years.*

*And finally, la Madeleine on Westheimer near Gessner, where I wrote the overwhelming majority of this book. The restaurant provided great ambience, white noise, as well as outstanding coffee and pastries!*

## Project Azalea Author's Notes

It's just human nature…we all dream of one day writing the next *great American novel.*

*Project Azalea* was in development in one form or another for more than twenty years. It started with the idea of a young misfit who was wise beyond his years, and who knew that education was the key to overcoming life's obstacles. Over the years, I toyed with different plot lines, characters, and other ideas, but it wasn't until a sudden change in employment in 2016 when pen was finally put to paper—or rather, fingers were put to keyboard—and the journey began.

I think it is important to note that I didn't start this effort with the intention of becoming a published author. I was simply a guy who idly toyed with a story idea for years, and when I was suddenly presented with unplanned free time, I needed to do something to occupy myself while I tried to find other employment. At that point, I was simply writing for my own sanity and amusement. Never did I dream that I would actually finish it, and never in a million years did I think it would ever see the light of day.

On that fateful day of the unplanned change in my employment, my wife, Eileen, told me not to feel sorry for myself, pick myself up, start making connections, and get that story written that I had talked about for so many years. I knew she was right, but I didn't start right away. After existing in an office setting for more than twenty-five years, I felt lost and didn't know what to do with myself at eight every morning. I was driving Eileen crazy. What I didn't know was that over the years, she would find scraps of paper I had left strewn about the house: stuffed in drawers, on counters, tables, literally everywhere. A character name here, a plot line there, even whole chapters. She had been collecting them in my nightstand drawer and eventually put them in an envelope once the drawer became too cluttered. When the envelope eventually became too full, it gave way to a folder, which she gave to me when it was clear that I was going to write this book.

I decided I would write the book, but I had no idea how to start. There were too many distractions at home; I needed time out of the house, and I no longer had an office to go to. Additionally, I'd picked up a couple of clients, one of whom is a fabricator in Louisiana, and the other a high-tech startup in Colorado; I had to find a workable solution. And so, the project started in earnest in October of 2016. I would take the kids to school in the morning, and on the way home, I'd stop at la Madeleine. I chose a table in the back by the coffee urns and decided that it would become my de facto office. Each morning I would write, do client work, network with colleagues, or apply for jobs. I thought about giving up a few times, and if I had found a full-time job quickly, I might have done just that. The flexibility I had doing client work allowed me to get into a groove, though, and I decided that even if I got a new job while in the middle of writing, I would finish the book. That presented a new conundrum. Would I complete it and stick it in a drawer, satisfied that I'd finished what I started, or play the long game and put it on a shelf for someone to buy someday? While it was Eileen who suggested that I start *writing*, an interview I saw with the famous author, Sidney Sheldon inspired me to start the *writing process*. The two, I learned, are dramatically different, though both require focus and discipline. Anyone can start with an idea and write in a stream of consciousness, but taking a story and turning it into a novel is an entirely different story (pun intended). In the interview, Sheldon spoke a lot about how personal his characters are, and that it took a year or two to develop them. On writing *Tell Me Your Dreams,* he noted that the book was written in only six months because the characters completely took over. *They* told the story.

My experience was not too dissimilar. In *Project Azalea*, Theo was initially the focal character, and I had a loose plot in mind. After a few fits and starts, it made more sense for Prudence to take over since her story was more compelling. I had already come to that conclusion, but it wasn't until I saw that interview with Sheldon that I had the idea to let her tell the story instead of having her follow a script. Once I did, it just flowed naturally. It was a lot of fun to develop the characters this way and see where they took me.

Eileen had been asking me for months to show her where I was in the process, and if I was comfortable letting her read the manuscript. I decided that I didn't want to show it to anyone until I'd decided how the story would end. The moment I finally presented it to her, she became (and remains) my editor-in-chief. She saw the makings of a great and compelling book, and she dedicated an incredible number of hours editing and molding the story. She suggested new characters and plot lines, added chapters, deleted paragraphs, combined chapters, and checked for continuity—just to name a few of her many contributions. We plugged away, and over the course of the next few months, we got to the point where we were both happy with it. She even *strongly suggested* that I write her into the book, which was a very good thing since that character came to have a pivotal role.

Sometimes, when something is so personal, it is hard to imagine that someone else might find what you are doing as interesting as you do. Eileen was instrumental in making me realize that I had something that other people might enjoy reading. So, I persisted. She came to this understanding early on and printed out the manuscript old-school style so she could begin reading it in a quiet local bookstore. She read for hours and took copious notes. Ironically, she finished reading *Project Azalea* a week or so later in the same la Madeleine where I started the story. She was more impressed than she thought she'd be—not because of my ability as a writer, but because she wasn't expecting a storyline with so much potential.

Then came the gut check. A couple of friends of mine had been interested in the effort for quite some time. I decided to let them look at it and tell me what they thought. These were two guys I'd known since high school (one since we were babies), who would be brutally honest and tell me whether I should press on or bury the thing in the back yard, never to see the light of day. When I asked one of those friends what he thought, he answered, "My wife wants to see the movie."

That was enough for me to keep going. As I continued on, something interesting happened along the way. As opposed to writing and publishing a book for sale, I became more interested in getting the *story* out there. I think there is room in the legal thriller genre for Prudence, and she provides an avenue for a whole new audience.

My writing influences are James Lee Burke, John Grisham, James Patterson, Michael Connelly, Patricia Cornwell, Greg Isles, and countless others. Collectively, their protagonists share similar traits: older cops/detectives, lawyers, professionals, tortured souls, strong women and men who are savvy, resourceful. Their backstories are interesting, and the situations in which they find themselves are always compelling. Otherwise, I wouldn't have read so many of their stories.

While Prudence's character is dramatically different from those protagonists, there are some situational similarities: crimes, mysteries, danger, law firms, and investigations. The differences in the *characters*, however, are stark, and make Prudence stand out in a familiar landscape; she's young, black, a single mother, not formally educated, naïve, and vulnerable. She is decidedly not like Dave Robicheaux, Alex Cross, Kay Scarpetta, Lindsay Boxer, or Harry Bosch, who are all in the middle or nearing the end of their careers. Those characters are experienced enough to handle dangerous situations. Prudence, on the other hand, is at the beginning of a new career and is painfully unaware of the danger in which she finds herself. She has no experience with legal matters, sleuthing, or the criminal justice system as a whole, and when she finds herself trapped, she must rely on her faith, her instincts, and her sphere of family and friends. She's a transitional character who can learn from her experiences and grow in her career as a paralegal, and perhaps even beyond. I have a lot of ideas for her, and hopefully one day I'll have the time to write a couple more books or even pursue other mediums to get her out there.

As for *Project Azalea*, it is a cornucopia of contrasts: good/evil, rich/poor, country plantation/urban city, greed/piety, love/hate. I wanted to highlight the importance of education and bring further attention to race relations, as well as the good that people can do together regardless of race or background. I also wanted to emphasize that a young woman with difficult personal circumstances was more capable of helping her own situation than she realized. Lastly, I wanted to present Louisiana from a different vantage point, one that paints a picture of more than just Mardi Gras, the French Quarter, and Cajun country. It is a rich palette with real people and real problems. Prudence could have been anyone from anywhere, but everyone knows that New Orleans is definitely unique from the rest of the country, so it made for the ideal setting.

I grew up in Cajun country, surrounded by bayous, swamps, sugar cane, rice, crawfish, duck hunting, fishing, as well as the oil and gas industry. Some of my fondest childhood memories are from the times I spent in St. Martinville with my cousins from my father's side, and friends from my hometown of Franklin. I went to middle school in Lafayette, and high school at St. Stanislaus in Bay St. Louis, Mississippi. I went to college and law school at Loyola University New Orleans, where I also spent the early part of my adult life, building my career. Though she was not born in Louisiana, my mother moved to New Orleans with her parents and younger sisters in the 1950s. Therefore, much of my mother's family is from there, or has at least lived there long enough to feel like a local: my grandparents, aunts, uncle, and cousins. My wife and her family are also from New Orleans—generations deep—so I know the city inside out. Friends and family from all of those places continue to influence me, and I wanted to incorporate those experiences into the story.

I know the positives and negatives of New Orleans, from the world's best food and the never-ending party in the French Quarter, to the government housing projects that are rife with drugs and unemployment—or at the very least, underemployment. It is a place where the national minority is the local majority. Its elegant façade eclipses rundown areas where the uneducated are hidden; out of sight and out of mind.

I've seen it. I've lived it, and thought it was important to show the city from Prudence's perspective and drop in little glimpses of the city and state along the way.

After I finished the story and felt satisfied that I had a new goal for Prudence, the next phase began: publishing. There are so many options for independent authors, and the search was overwhelming. Early in the process, I built a rapport with a publisher in New York who was kind enough to read some of the manuscript and give some great advice. Ultimately, they decided to pass and felt more editing was needed since a lot of the book was *telling*, rather than *showing*. I then looked at self-publishing options. I had already looked into this route at one time, and in order to put a book out there with the best chance of exposure, I knew I couldn't do it alone. Consequently, the interest and the effort slowed down. During the newfound free time we all experienced in this era of COVID-19, the perfect opportunity presented itself to give the effort additional serious consideration, so I continued to search for alternatives.

Still, we were all but resolved that this would be a self-published book, which was fine. We knew, however, that it would be a long haul: final editing, formatting, eBook and print production, cover design, social media, marketing, and public relations. I knew all of those things were part of the process, but it is an overwhelming effort requiring time, creativity, and money. I considered a crowdfunding campaign to help me purchase the services needed. Ultimately, I decided against that for fear that if I wasn't successful, I'd disappoint my benefactors. I would rather someone buy the book and not like it than take someone's money and risk double dissatisfaction by not having a successful or even readable book. I also didn't want to rush the timeline since I would be the project manager. I've spent enough time in the oil patch on some of the world's largest projects to know the kind of dedication a project manager needs to bring in a project on time and under budget, and I could not make that commitment without shirking other responsibilities.

While researching options, Eileen happened upon a website designed for independent authors that included publishers, editors, artists, and other services. I submitted the manuscript to a few of the publishers and was passed over for one reason or another. I eventually came across DartFrog Books. I had a great conversation with the owner, Gordon McClellan, and after his team reviewed a portion of the manuscript, he gave me the good news that they were interested in publishing my book under their hybrid program, DartFrog Plus, which is where this journey ends—or rather, begins again. Gordon and his team started right away, and Katelynn Watkins was assigned as my publishing coordinator responsible for final edits and serving as a point of contact for engaging the rest of the team in cover design, video trailer production, social media campaign ideas, and distribution. She's been great to work with and has kept me on point throughout this process!

While it was my love for the books my literary heroes wrote that *influenced* me, and the Sheldon interview that *inspired* my writing style, it was Eileen's constant and firm encouragement that made this a reality. She is the true protagonist to this story, because without her, none of this would have happened. She kept the notes over the years, encouraged me to start writing, helped me complete the story, and helped see it through the publishing process.

I authored the book, but it was her hard work and editing that shaped and molded it to a point where a publisher would seriously consider it. Without her, I wouldn't have started the project, finished writing, found a publisher, or stuck with the publishing process. To use an apropos metaphor, this book is my baby; she delivered it, and together we raised it to the novel you now hold in your hands.

My fervent hope is that you take from this book the messages I intended to proffer. Louisiana and New Orleans are beautiful places with beautiful people; education and life experiences are essential keys to success and advancement; the support of family and friends is crucial when faced with overwhelming odds; good trumps greed; love is more powerful than hate; people of different races and stations in life are successful when a common purpose is their motivation. I take the blame for any flaws or shortcomings, and I give Eileen all the credit for everything else. We hope you enjoy it.

# Table of Contents

# Prologue

The federal government's takedown of the New Orleans mafia in the '80s and '90s created a power vacuum. For more than twenty years, random violence and gangs ruled the streets, and the city was mired in a hapless holding pattern of fear and hopelessness. Growth and prosperity were stymied, and the citizens resigned themselves to the reality that fear, chaos, and murder was the daily norm.

In the wake of Hurricane Katrina, an opportunity presented itself. Over a few short years, the United Aryan Knights (UAK) quietly reconstituted on the north shore of Lake Pontchartrain—its primary base of more than forty years—with a new purpose and focus, and made the rundown, ragtag group of white supremacists more powerful than ever. The time was ripe to take back the streets, and the Leadership, a closed cabal of businessmen who were all but forgotten by their colleagues after the last Gulf of Mexico oil bust, slowly infiltrated the UAK.

While UAK traditionalists were still loyal to its founding *cause*, a new breed of management had taken over and surreptitiously fostered a cause of its own right under the noses of the very people they were controlling. A cause rooted in greed, which is an ideology, albeit one of a different color: green. The Leadership used the UAK to stockpile money in the name of whites' rights, but for the perverted purpose of a subtle *re*gentrification of the city. A campaign was underway to fundamentally reshape New Orleans, by force if necessary.

Project Azalea was as elegantly simple as the colorful bushes after which it was named. Beautiful azaleas dotted the yards of the stately Victorians that adorned the city's famous Saint Charles Avenue streetcar line, stretching from uptown to the Garden District, to downtown. The architects of Project Azalea wanted to create equally beautiful properties in depressed yet desirable areas, constructing an infrastructure for business and diversifying the revenue stream. The scheme would be repeated throughout the city until they either cornered the market, or controlled those who would survive. Police and politicians would be bought along the way to smooth out any obstacles. The Leadership had the vision, the ability, and the will, but lacked the money necessary to bring the project to fruition. To solve that problem, the Leadership brought to bear its organizational skills and business acumen, set its sights on the UAK, and began to build it into a force never before seen in The Big Easy.

The UAK Troops were well trained, equipped, and organized in a military fashion: rank, chain of command, pay grades, mission-based, focused, fearless. New Orleans' organized crime activities were owned by a white supremacist group that was deafeningly quiet in its activities, yet ferocious and efficient in the execution of its mission. With cash flowing into the coffers, the Leadership began to execute its flagship project, hidden in plain sight from those under its command. Other than the criminals they controlled, no one in The Big Easy noticed, and those who had couldn't have cared less.

# Chapter 1

### Dr. Japonica Is in the House

*B**AM!!** Thwacka, thwacka, thwack.* The tattered, screened porch door slammed and wobbled in its rotting wood frame and loose hinges. The rusted spring stretched and screeched like a tired Cajun accordion, playing in time with a *chank-a-chank* backbeat. A crying Theodore rushed through the door. He wiped his eyes and tracked gumbo mud all over the floor. Covered in dirt and grime—and God knew what else they threw on him—he collapsed face-first onto the couch and right on top of the royal blue, black, and forest green afghan his great-grandmother knitted for him in the last days of her life, which tragically ended a few months ago.

Obviously, Japonica would not be blamed this time since his paws were clean. Besides, he was curled up on the floor all day in his favorite spot, just as he was most of the time. Excited to see his master return, the mutt blew right past Theo. Despite a slight limp from an old leg injury, he darted out of the kitchen and squeezed through the small hole in the screen door to freedom, eager to play as they did most days after school. Theo didn't follow him this time, though, so Japonica raced back inside through the now larger hole. Japo joined Theo on the couch, and his paws and nails became entangled in the muddied and now torn afghan.

"Damnit, Japonica, get off the couch! You *stupid* dog, look what you've done! Mamaw made that afghan for me! Now it's torn and dirty and she's not with us anymore to fix it and Mom's too busy and I… I just can't take it anymore!"

Japonica jumped off the couch as commanded. Theo dropped to the floor and broke down, bawling as tears ran down his dusty, bloodied face. Japo cowered with his ears pulled back and his tail between his legs, where it wagged back and forth like dogs do when they are afraid or guilty because they'd violated house rules. Although he was in trouble for ruining the afghan, he dutifully stayed by Theo's side. Theodore Le Moyne Jean-Batiste needed him today more than he could ever know.

Theo knelt beside Japo and hugged him tightly around his neck, begging his forgiveness. After all, he's just an ol' cayoodle doing what dogs do and didn't intend to damage anything. Besides, he was the only real friend Theo has. In fact, Japo was the only friend Theo had ever had, and since Mamaw's passing, Theo's sense of loneliness, emptiness, and self-loathing was unending. You see, he was different from other kids his age, and seemed much older than his fifteen years on this earth. Mamaw was his great-grandmother and now she was gone. With his mom at work all day, and then only at home for what seemed like seconds before she headed to the Antioch most nights, he was, for all intents and purposes, a man on his own. He missed his Mamaw so much and thought of her every time he passed her chair with the wooden arm stained by the oils of her lilac hand lotion. He could still smell it throughout the house; it was comforting, like she was still there. In a way, she always would be.

Caring for Japo wasn't a duty at all for Theo, but more like therapy. Japonica was the best psychologist in the world, and Theo would do anything to keep that dog safe; Lord only knew how many times Japo had pulled him up from out of a funk. Dogs had an uncanny way of knowing what their owners needed, and sometimes Theo couldn't decide whether it was him or Japo that was the real rescue.

"I'm so sorry for yelling at you, boy. You know you're a good dog."

Japonica, likely sensing he no longer was in trouble, gave Theo's cheek a few wet, forgiving licks. He gingerly walked back over to his spot on the floor between the couch and the threadbare armchair and lay down. Mamaw used to sit there for hours rocking back and forth, humming her favorite church hymns, and knitting afghans for her relatives or whomever might need one on a cold, dark night.

Theo sat in the rocker and scratched behind Japo's ears, which calmed them both. He bent down, held Japo's face in his hands, and nose-to-snout, looked at him eye-to-eye. "I couldn't help myself. Those jerks pushed me over the edge this time and I just snapped. We're better than that, though, aren't we? Won't happen again, I promise."

Japo, of course, quickly absolved Theo of his sins, so they were free to resume normalcy—whatever that was these days.

About a year and a half ago, his mom finally relented and agreed to bring a dog into the family on the conditions that it was a rescue, that Mamaw agreed, and it was understood that Theo was to be its primary caretaker. Theo immediately agreed to the terms, so one day they visited the historic shelter in New Orleans on Japonica Street. He saw the ol' mixed Catahoula Leopard Hound and black Labrador Retriever lying defeated in his steel cell. He was backed up against the furthest wall, confused, shivering, frightened, and clearly hoping that one day soon he'd be either put out of his misery or freed to again roam the uptown streets that had been his home for so long. He had been beaten, scarred, and left for dead on the side of an empty two-lane, blacktop road when he was found by animal control. He was due to be euthanized the day Theo and his mother went to the shelter, a demise that surely would have been humiliating for a once free spirit.

When Theo looked into the dog's eyes—one a piercing, crystal, frost blue and the other a warm, yellowish-brown—peeking from that distinctly square Labrador head, he saw the pain and emptiness he recognized in himself. They made an immediate connection, and each seemed to silently agree to take care of the other forever.

"Okay, boy, you go on and wait on the porch for me. I'll clean up this mess and stuff the afghan under my bed. Mom never will think to look there."

Once that was done, they would play their favorite game: "hide the stick." Theo would break a stick from a tall pine tree, let Japo smell it, and, while Japo was still in the house, hide it somewhere in the neighborhood close to Mamaw's house. With his Catahoula Hound instincts and a Labrador's desire to retrieve, Japo would scour the area with his nose to the ground looking for the treasure, and usually found it within a few minutes. His record was twenty seconds.

Theo loved watching Japonica use his working dog instincts, and Japo obviously loved the game, which allowed him to stretch his legs and get much-needed exercise. Even old dogs needed to run every once in a while.

"Now, don't you escape through that hole in the screen again. It's plenty big already, and we need to fix it soon. With all the rain we've gotten lately, the mosquitos have been swarming something fierce."

It had been an early spring, the rainiest in recent history, and Louisiana mosquitos were like old WWI bi-wing dive-bombers looking for the right target. Night raids were the worst, with endless, high-pitched buzzing and stings that rendered one itchy, sleepless, and zombie-like during daylight hours. Made it real tough to pay attention in class, and Theo's grades reflected this.

Mamaw's home was a small, thinly insulated, but immaculately clean house with a postage stamp of a backyard right off Airline Highway in one of the poorest sections just outside New Orleans. Even though the jet engine noise never ended and the windows in the house shook when planes flew overhead, it was still viewed as a palace by most of those left stranded in the inner-city projects.

Summer humidity was brutal and damp, leaving the neighborhood with a swampy, pungent odor that was only deepened by the ever-growing algae carpeting sidewalks and wooded areas alike without discrimination. Winters were no less forgiving, with frigid and unfaltering winds that whistled through the windows and blew right through the clapboard siding. Sometimes, it was as if there were no walls at all.

It wasn't much, but it was tidy and a safe refuge for Theo. He often ran home from school, crying and with a bruise… or three… administered fiercely by schoolyard bullies, who, with each punch, grew more entitled. The beatings became somewhat ritualistic, like the whippings his forefathers endured for hundreds of years that were usually administered for no reason other than to serve as an example to others who might dare disobey the dehumanizing orders of massa's field sergeants.

Those who bullied Theo did so in a similar vein, though not to make an example to others, but because he was different, and therefore a threat. The truth was that he was a threat to no one other than himself. In their tiny minds, though, the schoolyard was their territory and they weren't about to let some half-breed ruin it for them. In their world, Theo needed to be constantly reminded of his place: the bottom of the pecking order.

That fateful day was the last straw, and Theo fought back to restore his dignity, which was so often splattered on the ground in red droplets after the normal 3:15 pounding. It was bad enough that the same group of thugs called him every name under the sun on a daily basis, (high-yellow, mulatto, Sambo, etc.). That day, they had to bring his mother into the fight by calling *her* all sorts of names and saying what terrible things they would do to *her* if they were fortunate enough to "catch" her. It was all talk, but talk could be as hurtful as a punch to the gut.

Enough was enough, and the sinewy kid fought back against the pudgy, doughy-faced redneck with a vengeance. All his pent-up rage came to the fore and he pulled the thug to the ground and knelt on top of him, pummeling him ferociously and fearlessly. He bent down just inches away from his face and yelled, "Don't...you...ever...say...that about *MY MOTHER,* you cracker son of a bitch!"

It was a beautiful effort. His fists landed like sledgehammers, each stroke perfectly timed and as accurate as those of the convict rail workers of old, who pounded spikes into the thick Louisiana gumbo mud, releasing hundreds of years of pain with every swing.

The skinhead wannabes standing nearby exchanged nervous glances until one finally yelled, "C'mon man, he's had 'nuf. You're gonna kill him."

Theo was in a zone, though, and he didn't care if this subhuman lived or died. Finally, he jumped off what was left of the almost unrecognizable thug with the swollen and bloody face. Enraged, but standing eerily still, Theo stared at all the kids surrounding the fight circle, and they stared right back at him with their mouths agape, stunned by the violence they'd just witnessed at the hands of such an unassuming boy.

One of them finally broke the deafening silence and yelled, "Somebody call for help!"

Theo ran home as fast as he could, satisfied that he'd finally stood up for himself, frightened to death that they would eventually come for him for what he'd done, and somewhat remorseful that he'd beaten the boy so savagely.

He normally took a circuitous route home, never going the same way twice for fear that his classmates would one day find out where he lived. That day, he ran straight home in a daze, not realizing until months later that he was followed closely enough that someone could have determined which of the row houses was Mamaw's. In the coming weeks and months, things would only get worse. He should have taken the circuitous route.

# Chapter 2

## Prudence

Theodore's mother, Prudence Jean-Batiste, was a thirty-year-old, single, black mother who carried herself with the same grace that generations of New Orleans ladies of color had before her. One such lady was Theo's great-great-grandmother—or, as she preferred to be called, *Grand-m*ère—who was the epitome of the 1820s southern gentleman's twisted fetish, the quadroon—hence Prudence's fairer skin, which was more of a café au lait color. Mamaw possessed that same beauty and grace, and she passed it on to her daughter, who then passed it along to Prudence. Every family had its outliers, though, and while his grandmother inherited Mamaw's physical beauty, the inheritance was squandered. Prudence was abandoned as a baby and raised by Mamaw in the same house in which she and Theo currently lived. Prudence tried her hardest to pass along life lessons to Theo, instilled in her by Mamaw; lessons which sustain her and steel her character.

Despite the great guidance from Mamaw, and every opportunity to make a good life for herself, Theo's grandmother left the house at an early age and ran with the wrong crowd in the inner city. She quickly became another drug-addled product of the projects, a tragic victim who spent her last years working the streets. Despite her many shortcomings, and rather than taking the easy way out, Theo's grandmother carried her baby to term, and Mamaw was happy to take Prudence in and raise her as her own.

At the time of Prudence's birth, the neighborhood looked quite different. Though it was never a neighborhood of *poor* people, it was still considered a *less affluent* part of the city. Its racial makeup back then was the opposite of what it was by the time Theo came along; whites made up about seventy percent of the residents, and there weren't many young black girls who were the same age as Prudence. She usually found herself playing around the block with a white girl who became her best friend: Evelyn "Evie" Cormier. Luckily, most children were still color-blind. Prudence and Evie did everything together, just as sisters might: playing dress-up in their mothers' clothes, having tea parties, and spying on Evie's brothers. Evie's upbringing wasn't as difficult as Prudence's, but there were plenty of times when both girls dreamed of nothing more than escaping the city and heading to greener pastures in cities like Baton Rouge or Lafayette.

While Prudence had a home with Mamaw, she didn't have siblings, so without Evie, she would have been quite lonely. Similarly, while Evie had four brothers, she had no sisters, so it was only natural that the two would form an unbreakable bond. They told each other their deepest secrets, and there was nothing one wouldn't do for the other. However, that friendship would eventually be tested with its most difficult trial yet—one with a secret that couldn't be kept.

Prudence dropped out of high school, ashamed and pregnant at seventeen years old. It wasn't the fact that she was a pregnant teenager that made her feel ashamed; there were, unfortunately, many young girls in similar situations, some of whom saw teen pregnancy as a badge of honor and a quick way to get government money after dropping out of school. For Prudence, the shame came from being perceived as a victim who was taken against her will one fateful day. She always knew there was evil in the world, but she'd never experienced so much violence and hate—hate for hate's sake. There seemed to be no other logical reason for what happened to her.

It was dusk on a hot spring day, and she was walking home from school after a long day of classes made longer by a math tutoring session. On her way home, she made a slight detour and stopped at a gas station for a candy bar and a Coke: the South's word for a soda or pop. She finished the snack while sitting at a table on the sidewalk outside the store, then continued on the detour. She cut through an undeveloped part of a neighborhood that contained newly built sidewalks that framed small, weed-filled lots. Trees that were soon to be felled were each marked with a prominent X. It was a perfect place for schoolboy stoners to hide from the police.

Prudence tripped on the buckled sidewalk, which was caused by the alternating searing hot Louisiana sun and rain-soaked gumbo mud. She'd dropped her books, and when she stood up, she found herself staring into the red, glassy eyes of three older boys she recognized from school. Two of them grabbed her by the arm and dragged her across a muddy ditch and through the weeds, stopping behind a cluster of old pecan trees. The third picked up her books and purse and joined the others. They spat on her, repeatedly punched her in the stomach, and violently pulled her to the ground by her hair. The devils pinned her shoulders down, pushed her face in the dirt, and ripped her shirt open, which exposed her breasts. Then they pulled up her skirt and took turns with her, each thrusting more violently than the last. It was as if they were playing a game to see who could best the last.

At first, she struggled to escape, but to no avail. So, she closed her eyes and gave herself to her fate. Further struggle would have undoubtedly been met with even more ferocity.

While to her it felt like hours went by, the vicious attack took just a few minutes. When it was over, the cowards hightailed it into the woods, whooping it up and high-fiving each other. One even twirled her torn bra in the air like a victory banner.

It might have been over for them, but the events of that afternoon would forever define Theo's family. They defined him. He was the one that kept the attack alive, and he ached because of that. Theo was the daily reminder to his mom that there was evil in their time, just as there was in times before, and that there surely would be when they were all long gone.

Prudence sat alone with her books strewn around her and wailed, hoping the pain would escape. She pulled her shirt together with a couple of the remaining buttons, then gathered her things and ran home as fast as she could, praying no one would be there. Her prayers were answered; Mamaw had gone to her weekly *bourré* game and she had the house to herself. She quickly took a shower in a feeble attempt to wash away the pain and the filth she felt clinging to her like a second skin. She changed her clothes and threw the old ones away, burying them at the bottom of the trash bag that she quickly stuffed into the trash can out on the curb for pick-up the next day. She knew she'd never be able to report the attack to the principal of her school for fear of reprisal. It would be her word against theirs, and the boys held the ultimate trump card—they were white.

The next day, Evie supported her friend as best she could. After the attack, Prudence was filled with self-loathing. Her fear was that if news of the attack spread, everyone would view her as weak. News of the attack, however, would soon be announced by the pregnancy. Prudence was not overly active in school, but she was well-respected. When it became obvious that she was pregnant, no one mentioned it—despite the rumors spread by the monsters who committed the atrocity. When she finally mustered the courage to tell Mamaw, she simply said she'd been attacked, and she didn't want anything to be done about it since it would only make matters worse. Respecting her wishes, Mamaw asked no more questions and instead chose to focus on the impending arrival of her first great-grandchild.

Rumors and stares were short-lived. Mamaw was the matriarch of the neighborhood and all respected her family's privacy. If Mamaw had something to say, she'd have said it. Otherwise, not a word was spoken about Prudence and her condition. There were some who gave a few curious looks here and there when she and Prudence were out and about, but not one single person directly asked them what had happened. No judgment passed, and no questions asked; there were only prayers for a safe delivery and a healthy baby.

Fortunately for Theo, the support from Mamaw and Evie, as well as the wise counsel of the right Reverend Dr. Honoré Drummond of the Antioch Faith Church—known simply as the Antioch—ensured that Prudence never gave a second thought to aborting the pregnancy. For her, there was no *choice* to make. Whenever she felt sorry for herself, she clasped her hands over her belly and said, "The Lord chose this for me, and this child will be loved." It was her way of moving beyond the hurt and focusing on the joy that was to come. She reminded Theo of this whenever he had a bad day. "Put your trust in God," she said. "After all, He brought you to me."

Prudence decided to stay in school until the end of the pregnancy. One day, after the bell rang, she just left, never to return. She didn't *drop out* in the traditional sense; she just stopped going.

When Theo was born, she gave him her last name and saw him as God's gift to her despite her pregnancy being the result of a vicious attack. In fact, the name Theodore was derived from the Latin *Theodorus*, which comes from the Greek *Theodōros*: a compounding of the elements *theos* (god) and *dōron* (a gift). "God's gift to the world," Prudence told others. "This boy will one day be very special indeed."

Despite the physical attack and the mental scars it left behind, Prudence maintained her faith, which was as solid as a rock, and a heart bigger than the Antioch, where she still regularly prayed for the souls of the damned and the lost. It was Mamaw who took her there at an early age to hear Reverend Drummond speak and to expose her to a good man, a man of God. Through the years, Prudence found him to be a very loving, caring man who constantly looked for ways to help others. It was Reverend Drummond who inspired Prudence to always help those in need, and it became a way of life for her, just as natural as eating or sleeping. She'd done her best to instill those same values in Theo. He hoped he could live up to her expectations.

# Chapter 3

## Chookie

Other than his mother, and Mamaw before her passing, the only person Theo talked to on a normal basis was his unique neighbor, Charles "Chookie" Jackson. Chookie had the mind of a four-year-old due to a head injury he sustained from a savage beating he took a few years ago at the hands of some Northshore neo-Nazi thugs.

Nowadays, Chookie passed the time by taking his daily walk around the little neighborhood block. On Sunday mornings, though, like clockwork, he would think he'd won Saturday night's lottery drawing and had grand plans for the winnings.

"I'M RICH, I'M RICH! I gots me *plennie* money now!!" he would gleefully say to the neighborhood kids sitting on their front porches, holding back their laughs, waiting to see what ol' Chook would say *this* week. "G-g-gonna buy me a *brand-new* foh-doh Cadillac and a new suit and g-g-gets me a *girlfriend*. You watch now, it's g-g-gonna happen soon. Yeah, you right!"

Chookie never disappointed. The neighborhood kids doubled over with gut-busting laughter—not *with* him, but *at* him—tears running down their brown, dusty faces, satisfied with that week's episode of *The Chookie Show*. One of them said, "Chook, you know you could buy you some gold bahs and plant 'em in yo back yawd and grow you some gold trees."

Chookie got so excited and stuttered, "Yeah, yeah, that's a g-g-goood idea. *Good* idea! Gonna buy me some gold bars t-t-tomorrow and g-g-grow, grow me a gold t-t-tree. Gonna get plennie money, you watch. Gonna plant me a *gold* tree." He laughed out loud to no one in particular, slapping his knee and yelling at an inappropriate volume, "Now you know *dat's* right!"

Poor Chookie. Kids could be so cruel, but these kids were good-natured at heart and weren't really hurting ol' Chook, just blowing off a little steam and having a bit of sport at his expense without him even realizing it. No harm, no foul, right? They had his back, though. He was *their* Chookie, the heart and soul of their otherwise lifeless neighborhood, and they would never let anything happen to him.

Theo saw it as bullying nonetheless, and whenever he saw the kids messing around with Chookie he'd remind them that those who could not care for themselves should not be the subject of ridicule or scorn, lest others be influenced and perpetuate the injustice. The kids, though, were young, and while Theo knew they weren't mean-spirited, he was still sensitive to Chookie's plight and made them stop.

He wasn't always Crazy Chookie, though. At six foot six and weighing three hundred pounds, Charles was an imposing figure, but was also good-natured and always up for a laugh. He was the big brother and father figure that a lot of the kids in the projects never had, and just an all-around nice guy looking to help whoever was in need. A few years ago, while walking to his home in the projects one night from his second job as a dishwasher at one of those fancy restaurants in the French Quarter, Charles Jackson came upon a small group of scraggly white thugs in the middle of a drug deal with some local gangbangers at the corner of Dumaine and North Rampart. They were obviously on the wrong side of town, but had the numbers and the firepower to handle trouble if it stumbled upon them.

The nervous meth-head Neos, though, saw him as an immediate threat and a witness to their crime. "You lookin' for some trouble, boi? Hey, boi, I'm talking to ya. I said, are you lookin' for some trouble?"

Not knowing what else to do, he froze, which they took as an indication that he was *indeed* looking for trouble. However, Charles wanted no part of trouble. This was his part of town and he was just walking home, minding his own business. Just an ordinary sultry summer's night in The Big Easy.

Even the local street gangs paid Charles no mind, mostly because of how he looked after the kids in the projects—kids who, the gangbangers secretly hoped, might break the deplorable cycle of poverty and government dependency. Maybe one day the kids would get out of that godforsaken place and win at least one battle in Lyndon Johnson's decades-long *war on poverty,* which he declared in his 1964 State of the Union speech—the last official year of Jim Crow.

Charles broke out in a cold sweat, paralyzed by fear. He knew this would end badly. Forcibly taken to the ground, viciously beaten, and left for dead in the streets of New Orleans, mere steps away from his home, Charles Jackson was never the same after that night. Just another life senselessly wasted in the city that care forgot.

At thirty years old, he stayed just a few houses down from Mamaw's with his elderly aunt, June Gallier—or, Tante Ju. He no longer worked, was barely self-sufficient, and relied on the state for most of his needs: something Charles Jackson would have abhorred, but on which Crazy

Chookie depended. Lord only knew what would happen to him when Tante Ju finally succumbed to the chronic cough that had plagued her after forty-five years of smoking Chesterfields. Chookie would maintain his government subsidy, but not her meager, fixed income. More importantly, he'd have no one to take care of even the most basic of life's needs like cooking, something all Creole kids did with great aptitude by the time they reached eight years of age. He would still be entitled to food stamps, but he would not be able to shop for groceries by himself and would not have enough cash left over to cover the monthly bills. Medicaid would help, but it wouldn't take care of all his ongoing medical expenses. Despite Theo's overwhelming desire to do so, when the time came, he wouldn't be able to help Chookie in any meaningful way. In the meantime, he kept his eye on him and helped however he could.

Chookie was a prime example of how this country's so-called *safety net* often let otherwise deserving people slide right through its gaping and ever-widening holes. From the outside, except for a few prominent scars on his head and face, Chookie looked strong and healthy, and time after time, case workers denied him the benefits to which he was entitled, benefits that would allow him to stay in a facility that could properly care for him: a man able in body, but feeble in mind.

Theo's role as Chookie's self-appointed protector gave just a hint of purpose to his otherwise upside-down life. He felt that, in some way, he was helping the childlike giant, who had once helped so many young boys who otherwise would have found themselves dead in the streets, in juvie, or worse: a permanent resident of New Orleans' notorious Orleans Parish Prison. The prison was just a few short blocks away from the *hood*, and the mean streets never failed to ensure that the inn was full, all cells occupied, and that the famous *tent city* received its daily complement of new campers. It was a merry-go-round of misery and the second home of too many of these mostly young black men whose futures were destroyed by guns, violence, drugs, and a lack of the most basic education needed to fill out a simple job application. This was the result of a corrupt, broken government that dangled its promises of better schools, job training, and social programs overhead like carrots for the price of votes.

Theo was concerned for Chookie's well-being and checked in on him from time to time to ensure he and Tante Ju were getting by. That wasn't Theo's concern today, though. His eye was blackened, his upper lip swollen, and the adrenaline from the fight was long gone. A great soreness had taken over him physically and mentally, and it was not likely to leave any time soon. Hopefully, he would be able to hide it from his mother, but that was unlikely, too. Covering bruises on the torso was no big deal. A shiner, however, was not as easily hidden.

# Chapter 4

## The Cypress

Theodore didn't remember much from his early childhood. Prudence foresaw, very accurately, that he would not have it easy in life. He had always been different from the others, but rather than being considered beautiful like Prudence, his fair skin, light eyes, and wavy hair meant a lifetime of bigotry and intolerance. It was Reverend Drummond who suggested that Prudence take the baby and move away from New Orleans to get a fresh start. After all, she was still a teenager at the time, and despite a deep desire to do so, Mamaw was in no position to assist in carting a toddler back and forth to *Château des Enfants,* the local school for early childhood development. It was not a sustainable situation, and Mamaw needed a break.

After several private discussions with Mamaw, Reverend Drummond did some digging and learned that Prudence had a distant cousin at the Cypress, an old plantation area about an hour from New Orleans. He suggested that the Cypress was the perfect place for them: close enough to the city that she could easily get to Theo's pediatrician and her GED classes, yet far enough that people from the old neighborhood weren't likely to run into her and dredge up the past.

Reverend Drummond set about finding the cousin to gauge whether she would be willing to assist. He enlisted the help of the right Reverend Dr. Cleophus James Hill V (aka Reverend CJ) of the historic Antioch Apostolic Church of the Blessed Redeemer, more commonly known as the Redeemer. In the event that the cousin was not willing to lend a hand, which was very unlikely given the reputation the community had as one that helped those in need, he knew Reverend CJ and his congregation would ensure that Prudence and Theo had proper housing, transportation, and a safe place for Theo to play and go to school. Given the character of Reverend CJ and the generosity of the community, Reverend Drummond knew they would be well cared for.

The search didn't take long. Reverend CJ found cousin Abbigail (Abby) Harrison, a local hairdresser in her mid-thirties with a young child of her own, who was roughly Theo's age. Fortunately, Abby agreed to accept them with open arms. Things were in place and it was time for Reverend Drummond to sit down with Prudence to discuss her next steps. It was a conversation Mamaw felt was best to have with a father figure. She also did not want to give the impression that she was kicking them out of her home, and Reverend Drummond had a way of putting people at ease.

Prudence's initial reaction was one of stubborn pride. She thought, whatever the circumstances, she could make her own way and wouldn't need help. However, she knew in her heart of hearts that she would need a great deal of help. After a few days of reflection, she agreed to meet with Reverend Drummond again and graciously, as well as gratefully, agreed to the arrangement. She spent the next couple of weeks getting things in order. Prudence wanted to make sure that Mamaw would be fine on her own, and spent as much time with her best friend Evie as she could. Evie was her lifeline to sanity, and being away from her would be the most difficult part of this new chapter.

It wasn't long before Prudence, with Abby's help, made the rounds to get her bearings. She found out quickly that the reputation of the people from the Cypress was well deserved. She was overcome with joy at the outpouring of support from the locals who loved having someone new to the area, someone from the *big city* with a connection with them—albeit a distant one. The community jumped right in and took up a special collection to help Abby with her added expenses, while Reverend CJ found Prudence a gently used car. She'd never had expenses such as gas and car insurance before, and she had no real skills, so the community solved that problem, too, by giving her odd jobs like light housework and babysitting. They did whatever they could to ensure the young family wanted for nothing and felt like part of the community.

It didn't take too long before she found a little apartment in a fourplex just down the road from Abby. The owner charged no rent on the condition that Prudence acted as a de facto manager, made minor repairs, and otherwise kept the place up.

Cousin Abby's people had lived in the area for hundreds of years toiling at the grounds of the old Cypress plantation home, a place that was clean, immaculately landscaped, and visited mostly by busloads of school children and tourists Tuesday through Sunday, eight a.m. to five p.m. It was closed on Mondays and holidays.

It was a sad irony that the employees, who were mostly nearby residents, were required to wear *period* clothes and give guided tours, telling the stories of the gentlemen planters and their families. The tours commenced with a forty-five-minute showing of the *main house* with its *parlor, music room,* and *east-facing bedrooms* of the children,

43

complete with their toys, which were made on the grounds with great care and craftsmanship with the finest wood, cotton, and paints. Toys for the slaves' children, however, were mostly crude dolls made of hay from the horse stalls and burlap from the sacks that once held their food. The royalty of the house could not let the slaves' children get the crazy notion that they were on the same level as their own.

The tour continued with a walk through the other buildings on the grounds, most of which were original to the property and were probably once inhabited by the ancestors of those who had to tell the ill-behaved kids and camera-wearing tourists not to touch the furniture or use flash photography. It was the highest of insults to have to spend more than an hour walking through each room of the house describing a glossed history of a glorified era, only to have to walk quickly through the sparsely furnished slave quarters and speak for a scant five minutes about their lives there. Straw-filled mattresses and hand tools were displayed, as were hand, feet, and neck shackles. The tour ended at the outside kitchen, a building larger than a block of slave quarters, and where the women toiled in the grueling Louisiana heat to prepare great feasts for the planter's guests. Even with this *historic* cruelty on display, the workers were required to convey a pristine picture that life back then wasn't *so bad,* because the slaves were well cared for and had plenty of food and shelter.

The true, unvarnished story of the Cypress and the cruelty that lived there for more than two hundred years remained untold and was long-forgotten, just like the stories of all the remaining plantations in the Deep South—places where, for the price of a ticket, one would never see the misery of the times, but rather the riches, excesses, and debauchery that defined the antebellum era. On the walls hung beautiful, commissioned portraits over brass plaques engraved with fanciful and nostalgic biographies of those who profited from the backs of their people, their *property*. White-columned homes and oak-lined roads raised generations of planters' pampered princes and princesses—children who didn't know any better and thought it was normal to *own* someone, to treat people who looked different from them as lower-class, to tell someone older than them what to do and expect it be done promptly or else immediate consequences would flow. "But they are part of the family," the lady of the house would say. Families, however, didn't stick their own out on the *back forty* in cramped living conditions that weren't much better than those of the plough horses. Families celebrated birthdays, attended weddings, funerals, and seasonal gatherings—all of which were permitted, though subtly discouraged at plantations such as the Cypress. Families had empathy and understood the plight of those who did not come to this land by choice, and were not indifferent to all of the indignities suffered. Families ensured their children grew and developed, were educated, and participated in society on an equal footing with others and without regard to one's color or station in life.

In reality, *family* during the antebellum era was another word for *owned*. Sure, there was the occasional mischievous prince who was sent out to the fields to sweat and cut the cane and pick the cotton with the other *members of the family,* who, in their southern royal minds, were beneath them. It was demeaning for his highness to be seen with *them*, and the work was meant to be a punishment for unsavory actions, not to enrich daddy and his friends, as was the mission of the day. Besides, he was back in the big house at sundown when he'd finished his penance, with a black mammy waiting to bandage his soft, blistered, pink hands and feed him his supper before sending him off to bed, tired, defeated, and having learnt his lesson—at least temporarily.

Why, indeed, would the immaculately heeled lady of the house bother taking care of her *own* son? That was the job of the mammies, who should have just been thankful that they were not out in the sun digging the muck out of horses' shoes, feeding them, and cleaning out their fetid stalls.

Quite the contrary, a southern lady's job was to organize lawn parties, teas, and balls, and to ensure men's smoke-filled parlors were ready for their clandestine card games with bourbon and branch water, woolen coasters, and crystal Irish tumblers just within reach of their yellowed, nicotine-stained fingers.

Even in today's *modern era*, the main source of employment at the Cypress was the very same cane fields, which made one question whether anything had *really* changed since the end of the Civil War—or, as the old sons of the south called it, the War of Northern Aggression. Life was tough and grounded in time at the Cypress, and an attitude of oppression still permeated the fabric of the area. In a sense, the people had yet to taste the freedom that was given to them by their ancestors almost one hundred fifty years ago. Even as a small child, Theo could feel the history that enveloped the area, and he saw the impact in the eyes of the descendants: a subtle vacuousness that was perceived rather than seen.

# Chapter 5

## Back to the Easy

Time quickly passed and Prudence learned much about simpler life outside the city lights during her ten years at the Cypress. Despite the unwavering support of Abby and nearby friends, she knew a return to the city was inevitable. Mamaw was the one who needed support and Prudence was duty-bound to do for Mamaw what Mamaw did for her and Theo. Besides, ten years was a long time, and while the Cypress was peaceful and bucolic, it was not her home. Moving back would be yet another chapter in her history. Prudence's only trepidation was about how the move would impact Theo; the Cypress was the only home he knew.

After careful and deliberate thought, they made the move back into Mamaw's house. Prudence quickly got a job as a hotel maid downtown, and Theo enrolled at nearby Bragg Middle School—named after Braxton Bragg, a U.S. Army officer before the war, advisor to Jefferson Davis, and a Louisiana sugar cane planter. In other words, a slave owner.

It seemed that whether it was at the Cypress or at school, Theo could not escape the specter of slavery. What was doubly disconcerting was that he probably had blood from the ancestors of slave owners coursing through his veins. It was a dichotomous struggle he lived with daily.

Prudence would usually get home around 5:30 in the evening to help Theo with homework, grab a quick bite to eat, then run off at about seven most nights to help at the Antioch for evening services. She was normally home by ten to ensure Theo was in bed. She was a hard worker and a woman of deep faith, a faith that had been tested time and again and that she would come to need more than ever to weather a storm of unimaginable torrent that would land in the coming months.

Even in a house filled with people, Theo felt alone. He didn't fit in at Bragg, a school that, although the majority of its students were black, still housed confederate sympathies inherited by those spoiled princes descended from their monstrous ancestors, whose arrogance and disdain for the black man roamed the halls of the school named after the famed general. It was hard enough entering a new school when friendships had already been forged and groups established. Looking different from everyone else didn't make matters any easier.

Soon after the move, Prudence found herself cleaning hotel rooms and lobby toilets in the morning, then waitressing in the Quarter from lunch to close at a relatively new, fancy French restaurant on Bourbon Street called La Bonne Cuisine, where the *bon vivants* ate and acted as window dressing for passersby. They sat at tables with limitless self-importance and indulgence, and usually drenched themselves in Sazeracs no matter the time of day. They were the true epitome of those stuck in a bygone era in the city that time forgot. Still, it was a good fit for Prudence since the haughty clientele tipped well, and Mamaw could be there for Theo until she got home. Those were the good times, the end of which began with Mamaw's passing.

# Chapter 6

## Oscar and Opportunity

"And the judge peered down from the bench sliding his glasses to the end of his nose and said, 'PAROLE?! Son, there ain't gonna be no parole for a long time 'cause your parole officer ain't even been born yet!' He almost broke his damn gavel! 'Case closed!'" laughed Oscar Brimley, the managing partner of the venerable law firm of LeRoux, Godchaux, Bouligny & Tooley. Oscar was in his element as the ringmaster, holding court, telling old war stories loud enough that all within earshot would have the privilege of hearing his larger-than-life ramblings.

Standing at a fit six foot two with an immaculately coiffed head of mostly salt-and-pepper hair that once was jet-black, Oscar still cut quite the figure and had a definite air about him. His icy blue eyes could cut through diamonds, and his sun-kissed tan, courtesy of holidays spent on the sugar sand beaches of the Florida Panhandle, gave him a youthful appearance that he used to his advantage. He would often say, "Old age and treachery would always trump youth and enthusiasm."

His almost youthful stature was replete with his stereotypical striped, blue seersucker suit over a heavy starched white Perlis shirt adorned with the iconic embroidered crawfish with French sleeves held together with *fleur-de-lis* cufflinks, all wrapped up by a canary yellow tie with nautical flags. White suede bucks with pink rubber bottoms topped off the look, and a booming, authoritative voice seasoned by thirty years of Scotch whisky ensured that people would have no choice but to take notice when Oscar Brimley walked into a room. It was a decidedly goofy look to those outside the Deep South, but the debonair Oscar could pull it off with ease wherever he went, and with a Gatsby-esque *savoir faire* that Redford himself would envy.

Prudence approached the table. "Y'all doing okay today? Want a top-off of y'all's tea?" she said with a mile-wide smile that lit up the room.

"Prudence, you know me too well," said Oscar. "Just a little more'll do, thank ya."

She curtsied, saying with a purposeful drawl, "My distinct pleasure, suh." She giggled playfully while pouring the sweetened brown water beverage that was a staple of lunchtime in the Deep South.

Oscar was on his customary Thursday lunch-and-learn with the rank and file, which usually lasted from noon to night. He felt comfortable around Prudence, probably because of her lighter skin color and that incredible smile she wore all day, every day. Members of the firm talked around her as if they didn't mind her seeing their self-righteous smirks or hearing their vapid conversations. Men like Oscar were so entrenched in centuries-old bigotry that they didn't even realize it. It was *de rigueur*, and they acted as judge, jury, and executioner of comity in their isolated world. They were the deciders of what was and wasn't acceptable in their genteel society, which was nothing like the rest of the country or, indeed, the civilized world.

For hundreds of years, the Oscars of the world had quietly ruled New Orleans—a slow-boiling Creole gumbo left simmering in a black iron pot for days, bubbling, but never burning. It was a French-founded, Spanish-influenced, slave-riddled, beautiful yet decadent, southern port city, which at one point was the country's gateway of commerce: the all-powerful Queen of the South. It was truly a living irony and a vestige of a time from which the country could never quite escape, and for which it couldn't atone.

Prudence marveled at the laid-back nature of these lawyers, their seeming ease with frittering away a day, and by the lunch tabs they ran up, she knew theirs was a lucrative business. She also knew that, by and large, most lawyers really helped people; otherwise, the profession wouldn't have been so successful and respected for so long. She occasionally eavesdropped, and behind all the bluster, she learned about some of the good being done by at least the younger attorneys, who awkwardly forced laughs at Oscar's patter from the past, when the practice was more of a profession and less of a business.

Until she started working at the restaurant, Prudence had never heard the term *pro bono,* but she researched it and learned that it meant, essentially, helping the poor who could not afford a lawyer: the isolated elderly, those out of work, those who were alone, those who just felt helpless and didn't know where else to turn.

Prudence enjoyed helping people, but each evening at the Antioch seemed just like the one before and she wanted something different. The thought of working in the legal profession intrigued her. She knew that, in addition to helping people, she could undoubtedly make more money at a law firm than she ever could serving morning coffee, beignets, lunchtime roast beef po' boys with au jus mixed with mayonnaise running down one's forearm, and cups of turtle soup topped with a tablespoon of dry sherry. More importantly, perhaps, was that she'd get benefits, particularly health insurance. She and Theo had been very lucky that they'd enjoyed good health, but at any given point, disaster could strike.

At that moment, she had a crazy idea. Working at a respectable law firm, making more money, and helping people seemed like a good turning point for her life after Mamaw's passing, and perhaps she would make enough money to where she and Theo eventually could get their own place. It would be good for her self-confidence, and it was a good time for Theo to be exposed to better opportunities and expand his horizons.

As she was headed back to the kitchen, Prudence abruptly spun back around and approached the table, interrupting Oscar mid-sentence. "Hey, Mr. Brimley, what do you think about me becoming a legal assistant or paralegal or something like that? I'd like to eventually leave this fine dining establishment and serve people in a different way, do some good for people who really need help. I think I'd be able to do that by working in a law firm like yours. I've been serving y'all almost a year and I know lawyering is not all just about the fancy talk and complaining about judges that y'all do. With your resources, you make a difference, especially in your pro bono program, which I've heard y'all talk about." Prudence hoped the use of the legal term would give her more credibility, but also knew that stroking Oscar's overinflated ego in front of a crowd of young lawyers was a good way to plant the seed and get her in his good graces. Then again, she considered that putting him on the spot could have the opposite effect. Still, Prudence thought it was a risk worth taking. "You think I'd have a shot at joining your firm one day?" she boldly asked.

Oscar responded in an almost condescending tone, knowing there was no chance in hell the firm would agree to take someone *like her*. "Why, of course, Pru, you'd make a fine addition to the firm. Just let me know when you finish those paralegal courses, ya here?" Pausing a moment, he looked around the table at the young faces and quickly realized that she would, indeed, make a fine addition. He could tic off several diversity boxes by hiring her—woman, minority, single mother—plus she was a hard worker. It didn't hurt that she was beautiful and good with people. Yes, this would be a great way to endear himself to the millennial dandies— young lawyers that were more *enlightened* and more inclined to have a five o'clock run through Audubon Park than to drink a good Pimm's Cup at Napoleon House.

The dandies loathed dinosaurs like Oscar Brimley and saw his ilk as the kind of lawyers that gave the profession a bad name. Oscar knew of their disdain for him, but he thought that by bringing someone like Prudence on board, he'd be looked at in a new light. No one would be able to say that LeRoux, Godchaux, Bouligny & Tooley was beneath adding a little diversity to its ranks. The firm had a high profile in the city and did not need negative press. Its cotton-white dynasty was quickly fading due to several recent retirements and increased calls from the bar for more *diversity* and *political correctness*. Oscar thought that this political correctness crap was killing the soul of the country and dramatically changed the culture of the firm over the last five years. *Good gravy, they even put a half-breed in the White House. What's next, a woman?*

It wouldn't be long though before he could leave it all behind, so Oscar decided to head the calls for diversity off at the pass and give no reason for anyone to call the firm anything other than *progressive*. After all, they were the leading firm of the city, and with Prudence they could safely get ahead of the diversity curve and force the other firms to follow suit. Besides, she was a safe bet. They knew her, her temperament, and that she was smart. Perhaps more importantly, she'd be a good girl and do as she was told since she had something to lose; she had responsibilities and couldn't afford uncertainty. They knew she'd do anything it took to hold onto that job once it came her way.

Prudence's simple question, he thought, was the catalyst he needed to escape unwanted scrutiny and focus on his real mission. Yes, hiring Prudence Jean-Batiste as the first black woman to hold a job at the flagship office other than secretary or receptionist was what the firm needed at this turning point in its history. Unintended consequences and collateral damage often followed quick and selfish decisions, and Oscar would, as he always did, go in big and quickly. He was used to making decisions much larger than this on a daily basis, and this was too good of an opportunity to let slip away. He didn't want to give Prudence a chance to think twice. He wanted to be looked at as being magnanimous, a forward-thinking trailblazer. The dandies would un-doubtedly be awed by his largess.

"Tell ya what, Pru," Oscar said while holding her stare. "On second thought, why wait for that paralegal certificate? I want you to start at the firm right away, first thing Monday morning if that suits you. I'll talk to your boss, so don't worry about your duties here. The firm and our clients make up a great portion of his business, so I'm sure he'll be happy to accommodate us, and if you don't like working at the firm, I'll see to it that he gladly takes you back." Oscar, with a drink still in hand, continued in a softer, yet authoritative tone that injected a slight seriousness into the conversation. "We're going to hire you first as a legal assistant in our pro bono section. From what you just said, it sounds like a logical place to start, and something that would be of interest to you. For the next six months, though, half your job will be getting you through a good paralegal program. You will be doing work that can have an immediate impact on folks in the inner city, Prudence." Looking around the table, he gestured to one of the younger lawyers. "You'll be paired with Jimmy O'Leary here, our as-sociate from Boston who joined the firm a few months ago." He put his free arm around Jimmy's shoulder. "Don't worry about the tuition and books, either. We'll cover that. I assume you graduated high school or at least have your GED?"

Prudence nodded in the affirmative with her attention now rapt and focused, a glazed look in her eyes while a million thoughts ran through her head. *Who knew such an impulsive question could lead to a life-changing job offer?*

Then came the deal sealer. "Prudence, you're like family, but even better." The sycophants at the table nervously chuckled at Oscar's behavior, but he quickly changed back into his pompous self as kingmaker, seemingly making a mockery of the situation. He continued while pushing slightly back from the table, "Prudence, it would be *our* distinct pleasure to have you join our firm and stand as a grand example that someone like you, a single mother with a child still in school, can make it. Someone who works as hard as you do can make it."

Prudence's head was spinning, "Why, Mr. Brimley, I, I…"

Oscar bristled for effect. "C'mon now, Pru, this is a no-brainer, a chance of a lifetime. Whether you know it or not, my dear, your ship has come in like the powerful Natchez steamboat paddling down the current with ease through the muddy mouth of the Mississippi River on toward the clear, aqua blue waters of the Gulf of Mexico," he said while making a wide sweeping motion with his arm toward the river. "I need your answer now before the Sazeracs wear off." He chuckled as he surveyed his audience, who were all eyes and ears at this point with the sudden realization as to why Oscar Brimley was so successful. He could still sense some hesitancy on her part, though, so he made a slight course correction. "Think of it this way; you also will make new friends and broaden your social base. Above all, you'll have more time to spend with Theo."

"Well, I…" Prudence stammered.

"Tick tock, Prudence." Oscar feigned playful impatience and made a clicking noise while wagging his finger like a metronome—a power move for certain.

"Okay, why not? Nothing ventured, nothing gained, right?" she said with a shrug of her shoulders and an even greater smile than before.

"It's settled, then," said Oscar, raising his hand over the table and giving it a light tap as if he had a gavel in hand and was rendering a verdict in a high-stakes case. "See you tomorrow morning at eight sharp. We're on the seventeenth floor of Oil Centré Tower, right over there." Oscar pointed in the direction of the shiny building towering over the city's skyline. "Tell the receptionist you are coming to see me. She'll be expecting you."

"I don't know what to say other than thank you," she said. "Thank you. Thank you for this wonderful opportunity. I... I'm speechless!"

"You are most welcome. We look forward to working with you," said Oscar with a quick glance at the dandies, then back at Prudence. "Wear a nice dress, too. If your wardrobe is limited, we'll take care of that. You'll be representing the firm in front of clients and at the school, so you'll need to look the part. Prudence, this is your new life and I am happy to be the one to give it to you. Welcome aboard."

Oscar was positively giddy at the prospect of parading Prudence around the office, proudly showing off his girl and cementing his place in the firm's history as the dinosaur that continued breaking the color barrier and shattering the glass ceiling. In his grandiose mind, he would be seen as a true pioneer for diversity, not only within the firm, but for the legal profession as a whole. This move, he convinced himself, meant that he would ride off into the sunset high on the saddle when he retired—something he hoped was only a year or so away if everything went as planned.

He laid it on thick and with an arrogance that befit the man. He almost laid it on too thick and with a subtle, yet biting condescension that would otherwise have caused Prudence to pass on the opportunity to work with this old guard Dixiecrat. Remembering that Oscar and his minions often publicly displayed their arrogance and political incorrectness, she realized that while this truly was a fantastic opportunity on its face, she'd have to swallow her pride every day and withstand the stares and whispers throughout the halls. Still, the upside was that she would be making a better life for her and Theo, while helping some folks along the way. Mamaw always told her, "You have to take the good with the bad and make the most of the opportunities the Lord presents to you."

At a minimum, she would learn a new skill and never have to serve fried oysters and crawfish étouffée again; *she'd* be the one ordering those New Orleans staples. It wasn't that she *needed* a new career, because she was otherwise happy with her life and its simplicity. However, she couldn't help but think that this would be a good move on several levels. She would also be able to spend more time with Theo, so for that she was genuinely thankful. *And away we go!* she thought to herself, ready for yet another new beginning.

While it all sounded so good, Oscar's *like family* quip stung a little and quickly brought thoughts of the Cypress to the fore. How many times over the centuries had that phrase been spewed by the plantation kings and queens? It was then, as it was in this case, a phrase oft used when trying to convince someone, whether property or employee, that whatever notion was being peddled was a good thing—something that, in reality, couldn't be passed up lest severe consequences flow.

# Chapter 7

## Evie

Thoughts of hurt pride quickly dissipated and gave way to bewilderment. This was all too much for Prudence to process, and she needed help putting it all into perspective. The best person for the job was obvious: Evie. Prudence had kept up with Evie over the years, albeit sparingly since both were busy with their lives and heading in different directions. The last she'd heard, Evie worked downtown at Élysées, off Canal Street: the Saks 5th Avenue of New Orleans. She decided to give it a try, hoping she'd be there that evening. As luck would have it, Prudence found Evie in the shoe department and walked up behind her.

In a disguised tone of voice she said, "Ahem, excuse me, miss, but is anyone going to help me? I've been here five whole minutes!"

Evie immediately jerked her head around. "Prudence! Oh my God! I'd know that beautiful voice anywhere. Look at you. You haven't changed a bit."

They embraced and held each other tightly. Prudence immediately felt at ease; Evie was her rock.

"Evie, I'm so glad I found you. I have a very big decision to make and I'm not sure what to do," said Prudence with a sort of blankness to her voice.

Evie replied, "Well, you've come to the right place. Let's move over by the Jimmy Choos and I'll pretend like I'm selling them to you. Tell me, Ms. J.B., what's going on that's got you so flustered?"

"Since I've been working at La Bonne Cuisine, some of my regular, very generous customers, are hotshot lawyers." Prudence paused for effect.

"Okay, so…?" Evie impatiently asked.

Prudence replied, "Well, you'll *never* guess what happened to me today, so I'll just tell you! On a lark, almost kidding really, I asked the head guy if he thought I should go back to school. Maybe be a paralegal. *Then*, I went all in. I asked him if he thought I'd have a shot of joining a firm like his. I don't even know why I asked him. I just did."

"Yes, yes, and what'd he say?!" replied an excited Evie.

Prudence gathered herself and said, "Evie, he offered me a job on the spot. He wants me to start tomorrow morning. I'll work in their pro bono clinic half-days until I get my paralegal certificate. They'll pay me a salary, cover my tuition and books, and—get this—they offered to buy me some clothes if I needed them. I don't know what to do. This is so huge. The building is even huge: Oil Centré Tower. Tell me, Evie, tell me what I should do!"

Evie just stared at her in disbelief, and after what seemed like minutes finally responded. "Really?! You don't know what to do? You… don't…know…what to do? Girl, I should pinch you. Is there even a decision to make here?"

Prudence gave her a puzzled look and said, "Well, what if they aren't doing this for the right reasons? What if I don't like it? Mr. Brimley told me that wouldn't be a problem, that he'd make sure I got my wait-ressing job back if I wanted. He said—"

"Oscar Brimley?!" Evie abruptly interrupted. "*The* Oscar Brimley? Over at LeRoux Godchaux?"

Prudence wondered how she might know of the firm, but then it dawned on her that the lawyers and their wives probably spent a ton of money at Élysées, and they probably said a ton of things they shouldn't while trying on shoes that could cost as much as Prudence made in a week.

"His assistant, Bernadette, comes in here all the time. 'Oscar needs this, Oscar needs that, where's that dress Oscar ordered?' Probably spends all that money on his mistresses." Evie said that last part slight-ly under her breath, but Prudence still gaped as if she'd shouted. "Oh, c'mon, Prudence the prude! You know these rich guys have girlfriends everywhere, so don't look so surprised." Evie continued, "Look, it sounds legit to me, and I know the firm. Real good people there—well, most of them. Bernadette is a saint, especially for putting up with what she puts up with. It sounds to me like Oscar sees in you someone he likes, and, like everyone else who knows you, knows you don't belong waiting tables. You said pro bono, right? Well, he probably also sees you as someone relatable. Pru, this is good. No, it's way better than good. It's absolutely amazing! You really don't have a choice here, do you? Just think of the opportunities you could give Theo that you aren't able to right now!"

Prudence exhaled. "As always, you're right, but I don't have a thing to wear and I'm still working two jobs. I really don't have time to shop."

Evie chirped while spreading her arms in a wide, sweeping gesture, "Well, you've obviously come to the right place."

Prudence, now nervous again, looked around and replied, "Evie, I can't afford this place."

"You can use my employee discount. We'll start with some shoes over on the clearance rack. Do you have a dress? You're still all church-going, right? You're bound to have at least one dress. I'm going to buy you a scarf as a present. This is all so exciting! I'm so happy for you! Pretty soon you'll be the one spending all that money, pumping up my commission," she said with a grin.

# Chapter 8

## The Venerable Law Firm of LeRoux, Godchaux, Bouligny & Tooley

Since the early 1820s, LeRoux, Godchaux, Bouligny & Tooley served the legal needs of its clients throughout the south in matters large and small. In addition to the New Orleans flagship, the firm had satellite offices in Baton Rouge, Houston, Biloxi, and more recently, Denver: a move made in the aftermath of Hurricane Katrina. It was the *go-to* firm, because of its storied and noble history. They'd seen it all: slavery, wars, emancipation, reconstruction, financial crises, oil booms and busts, as well as hurricanes, floods, rig explosions, oil spills, and any other major happenings throughout the Gulf South.

Though they would have had everyone believe otherwise, their clients were not ordinary people who really needed help. They were banks, insurance companies, industrial behemoths like Big Oil, Pharma, and Agra: really, anyone who could swing a big stick with determined force, and, when required, wreak havoc and mayhem upon the *little guy*.

Every company these days needed a mission statement to ensure that its employees were *engaged* and that a cohesive *corporate culture* was established. The firm was not immune to these societal demands, and the managing partners hated this type of politically correct, touchy-feely crap. So, a few years ago, they came up with a clever mission statement with a powerful double entendre. *We make a difference.*

And they made a difference, alright—the kind of difference the *little guy* feared and was powerless to defend against.

The partners in this law firm were no dummies, not by any stretch of the imagination. They had enough self-awareness and were shrewd enough to know that they'd have to be dragged into the diversity-ridden twenty-first century kicking and screaming. Begrudgingly, they acknowledged the need to bring in more people who were an anathema to their very existence: more women, minorities, and young lawyers who sincerely wanted to make a difference rather than a fortune. The firm, however, was well-established, and with proper structuring, the flagship could easily navigate those most unpleasant waters. Houston and Denver could take it on the chin and hire the right number of diverse employees needed for the firm as a whole to *look* the part. The New Orleans office chipped in a few, with Prudence being the newest. The sad truth, however, was that the pro bono section, even though it was managed by the paralegals with oversight from associates, operated as a shadow firm that defeated the whole purpose of highlighting the firm's diversity efforts and, by extension, the profession as a whole. It was on a different floor, far away from the firm's main clients. Even the wall one saw when stepping off the elevator was void of the firm's name or logo, and there were no nameplates on the office doors. Yes, the firm was certainly getting with the times.

# Chapter 9

## A New Day

The streetcar slowed, screeched, and mildly jolted to a hard stop in front of Oil Centré Tower. The logo of its anchor tenant, GATZE Oil & Gas, Inc., was emblazoned on the side of the building and still illuminated. The logo was omnipresent throughout the Gulf South and stood as a symbol of the power that the oil and gas industry still wielded. Prudence's knees were shaky, and she wobbled off-balance while making her way down the sunken aisles with old wood and brass-hinged slide-back benches on either side of her. She almost dropped her purse and the worn leather valise portfolio she found at Mamaw's. She didn't know why she brought the darned thing, probably as a comfort item so she could feel more professional and hide her trembling hands. She was, after all, embarking on a new journey, one that would forever change her life and the lives of those she loved.

The sky was clear and the air was brisk that transformative morning. A good sign, she thought. She walked on the cracked, uneven sidewalk toward the building, still not used to the expensive pumps she'd bought at Élysées from Evie last night. She'd spent too much money and absolutely hated to buy on credit, but she knew she couldn't wear her old, flower print church dress with scuffed restaurant flats. She had to make a good first impression and it was easier to find shoes than it was a proper dress in the limited time she'd had. *How do women wear these things all the time?* she asked herself.

Today's journey down the famed St. Charles streetcar line was really no different than the hundreds like it she'd taken before. She normally started her commute early in the morning, before Theo woke, at the bus stop in front of a convenience store on Airline Highway across from Mamaw's house. The trip normally took about an hour and a half due to the two bus routes needed to get to the foot of Carrollton Avenue, where she boarded the streetcar for the long ride downtown. Although there were many stops along the way, it was a beautiful ride that passed by some of the city's local landmarks like Camellia Grill, Tulane, Loyola, and Mr. Oscar Brimley's beautiful three-story Victorian mansion on Rosa Park Place, just down from Audubon Park.

The park was beautifully groomed and adorned with majestic moss-filled live oaks, colorful azalea bushes, and quiet, root beer brown ponds full of bright green lily pads. The regal white egrets seemed to ignore the calls from the zoo animals on the other side of the park. In the springtime, the park bustled with Loyola and Tulane college coeds lying on their blankets in the morning sun, getting mentally ready for classes or shaking off the prior night's revelry. A gaze upward might find a few students sitting in the trees reading a good book, hiding in plain sight.

Prudence felt as if she was making the commute for the first time. As she made her way to the tower, a chilly, yet refreshing gust of wind pierced the thin, flowery dress she usually wore to services on Sunday. Though decked in her finest dress and new shoes, she felt woefully out of place. Before long, she noticed eyes were upon her and that the small smiles on people's faces were directed at her dress. Just as quickly as she was filled with confidence, the tables turned, and a dull sense of inferiority consumed her.

Clouds rolled in, bringing with them a cold snap of blustery wind that wove and swept through the downtown buildings, creating a vortex. Coupled with Louisiana's infamous humidity, the cyclonic wind sent a bone-chilling shiver through her despite the outside temperature being a relatively balmy eighty-two degrees. She felt completely out of place and knew she ultimately would put aside her pride and take Mr. Brimley up on his kind offer to update her wardrobe.

Today, however, was not the day for brooding or shopping. She needed to get settled and meet her new coworkers. Though she was surrounded by hundreds of people bustling through downtown, she'd never in her life felt so alone and out of place. For a second, she thought that perhaps she'd made a mistake, but quickly pushed that notion out of her mind, steeled herself, and gave a slight tug on her dress to straighten it a little. She walked along the marble floor of the lobby toward the elevator bank. Though her confidence was fully restored, she was still a little wobbly on her feet and prayed she wouldn't cause an unwanted scene by slipping on the impeccably waxed floor.

Prudence quickly checked her hair in the elevator's mirrored walls as the doors opened up to the seventeenth floor. She exited, and, like a bride on her wedding night, took her first step over the elevator's threshold toward her new life. *No turning back now*. She was a little queasy and somewhat intimidated by the office's opulence. Its dark, oak walls and the marble floor, which had the firm's logo prominently etched into it, gave way to carpeted hallways adorned with fine artwork. Just one piece of that art was probably worth more than Mamaw's house. Prudence had never in her life seen anything this fancy, and it definitely would take some getting used to. She wondered how a place like this could possibly know the struggles of the folks Prudence was hoping she could help in the pro bono section. Maybe the people in the clinic were warmer and the surroundings more pedestrian. Yes, this definitely would take some getting used to.

"I'm here to see Mr. Oscar Brimley," Prudence cheerfully said to the receptionist who was young, beautiful, dressed immaculately, and probably sat down for eight hours a day making four times what Prudence made waitressing on her feet for twelve.

"Please take a seat over there," said the smiling receptionist, somehow still adopting the same snooty air Oscar often had about him in the restaurant. She nodded toward a large couch situated next to pitchers of water infused with lemon, melon, and cucumber. Steadier now, Prudence ambled instead toward a leather cordovan-colored Victorian chair—the type of which one could easily slip off if one was not careful.

*Geez, whatever happened to plain ol' Kentwood water coolers with their welcoming glug glugs?*

Before sitting, Prudence picked up a magazine from a frosted glass, antique table from the Napoleon era; it was probably bought on Royal Street at a ridiculous price, at least twice what the stores on Magazine Street would charge. Standing over it, she thumbed through a magazine unlike any she had ever seen. The Condé Nast publication was thick and had glossy, elegant pages filled with ads for luxury items of which she'd never even heard: Gucci, Louis Vuitton, Burberry, and BottegaVeneta, just to name a few. In it, she found fascinating stories of the jet set and cruisers who *vacationed* in places like the Caymans, the Amalfi coast, or the islands of Split and Phuket, about which she'd only heard because of the tsunami that dominated the world's headlines for months. The pictures of Lake Como were stunning, bordering on otherworldly.

Sinking into the grand chair, Prudence was enchanted and intimidated at the same time. She never had *vacationed*, unless a day trip to the beach in Gulfport, Mississippi, counted. With the magazine in hand, she swept her dress under her legs and situated herself on the wingback chair, and, as if on cue, awkwardly slid forward a little. She quickly caught herself before anyone could see, or so she hoped.

Just as soon as she sat down, a well-dressed, but dowdy, plump sort of woman with chained librarian glasses positioned on the end of her nose appeared. She surveyed the reception area and called for Prudence, just as a nurse would call for a patient from the waiting room. She had an air of authority about her, and Prudence quickly surmised that she had to have been none other than Bernadette, Oscar Brimley's secretary. In reality, she probably controlled Oscar instead of the other way around. Because of their mutual connection to Evie, Prudence knew she had to make a great first impression. She smiled, stood up from the chair very carefully so as not to slip off, and walked over to the lady with her hand outstretched awkwardly and perhaps a bit too soon.

"Bernadette Forrester. Nice to meet you," said the woman as she firmly shook Prudence's ice-cold hands.

"Hello, Ms. Forrester, it's a pleasure to meet you," Prudence nervously replied as the somewhat dour lady sized up her dress. "I'm Prudence Jean-Batiste." In an effort to establish an immediate rapport, Prudence added, "I think we know someone in common. Evelyn Cormier?"

Bernadette broke into a warm smile. "Evelyn, at Élysées? I absolutely adore that girl. She is so stylish and something of a mind reader. She always gets the right look, usually on the first try. Please, call me Bern, dear. Oscar has told me so much about you. It's as if you are his *other* other woman."

Just as Evie had surmised, Bernadette had just confirmed that Oscar had at least one mistress, which was not unusual for powerful men of his stature. Prudence blushed a little and didn't know quite how to respond. One thing she did know, however, was that she and Bernadette would get along famously.

The pair walked down the hall, past the busy bullpen of secretaries feverishly typing up the documents that would eventually be looked at by judges and explained to juries in the historic courtrooms of Louisiana. The bullpen was in the middle of the room, near the associates and their windowed offices. The area was brightly lit, warm, and the action was fast-paced, much like the lunch crowd at the restaurant, which put Prudence a little more at ease. Bernadette held open the door to an interior room on the outer rim of the bullpen.

"Your office is right in here, dear. Oscar will come by to talk to you around nine, after his conference call."

That meant Prudence would have to cool her heels for at least an hour before she would see Oscar. How she wished she had kept that travel magazine, for she felt somewhat silly sitting in a chair at a desk, waiting and with nothing to do. A story about Bermuda certainly would have helped pass the time, not to mention she felt like she was in a treacherous triangle.

Suddenly, she noticed a few raised brows and knowing glances among those in the bullpen that seemed to say, "So, that's her." Ensuing nods among them indicated to Prudence that they felt she would do just fine, and that deer-in-the-headlights look would soon go away.

After sitting in the oversized office for a little more than an hour, a smiling Oscar bounced over to her doorway with a personality unlike she had ever seen on him. *This must be the Oscar the rest of the world sees.* Impeccably pressed navy suit, shiny shoes, radiant, bright white shirt starched so that it could probably stand on its own, and not a hair out of place on his well-coiffed, salt-and-pepper head of hair: Oscar was an affable whirling dervish of energy, quite the opposite of his lunch persona, which was a little more rumpled and a lot more arrogant. All eyes in the bullpen were on him, as if he were a general walking into the room, totally in command and ready for the morning's inspection.

"Goood morning, Pruuudence!" said Oscar.

"Good morning, Mr. Brimley," Prudence replied, looking around at all those eyes now squarely on her, gauging her reaction. They probably thought Prudence was either a diversity token or a new protégé, but probably the latter. They quickly resumed their duties as they tried to avoid eye contact with the general.

"Oh, come now, Prudence, call me Oscar. Everyone here does," he said, looking around the bullpen with a grin. The ladies smiled back, though some appeared more forced than others.

"Oh, I, I don't think I cou—"

"Suit yourself," he cheerfully said.

After years of addressing him as Mr. Brimley, Prudence was at somewhat of a loss and thought this, too, was probably part of his act. Like Jekyll and Hyde, Oscar would turn from affable to arrogant, depending on his audience.

Oscar quickly turned and started walking away, as if he was uncomfortable in this part of the office. "Let's go, follow me."

They walked quickly down a long hallway, passing the young associates in windowed offices that were much smaller than hers. They were reading and looking at law books, and some stared at their computers. Next, she caught a glimpse of the partners' offices; most of the partners were on their phones and gazing out the windows, where they could watch the tugboats glide along the Mississippi River near Algiers Point.

The last stop was the corner office. *Wow!* thought Prudence as she gazed around Oscar's office, which was more like a museum with tiled floors, bookcases, and statues, as well as a telescope near the window. Beautiful plants, fresh flowers, and fancy paintings surrounded a separate sitting area with small couches. In the corner was the *pièce de résistance*, the thing that was the envy of the office: a private restroom with a shower near a small closet containing spare shirts, jackets, and ties just in case Oscar had to attend a last-minute dinner or make a quick trip to the courthouse. Never mind that he hadn't been there in years.

"Please, have a seat," said Oscar, motioning to the chairs in front of his desk. They were purposely shorter than *normal* chairs to give Oscar a lording presence over anyone fortunate enough to sit in front of his majesty's throne. She suddenly felt like a child in the principal's office. "Prudence," said Oscar, suddenly serious, leaning forward with his hands clasped on the oversized marble desk. "Welcome, and thanks for coming. I'm very glad you decided to join us. I hope your experience will not be uncomfortable. Yours will be a different mission than that of many others here. As I'm sure you've noticed by now, there is a hierarchy. There are bullpens and interior file rooms at the bottom rung, and little ol' me all by my lonesome at the top." Prudence suddenly realized that her office was a converted file room, which was why it was larger than the associates' and had no windows. "I put you near the bullpen on purpose; the ladies there are very sweet, and while you are not a secretary, you're not quite a paralegal, either. We had to put you somewhere and I hope you don't think that we're trying to call attention to you. Quite the contrary," said Oscar as he pointed downward. "The paralegals are on a different floor and I told them that you were here by my invitation, that you would be working the first half of the day in a cubbyhole in the pro bono section as a legal assistant. They know you will spend your afternoons on the upper floor in your office and they won't disturb you—at least, they shouldn't. The firm uses paralegals for most of the pro bono work because, frankly, they're cheaper, but just as good as the newer associates. They'll behave, I promise. And if someone gets out of line, you just let me know and I'll run their arse out of here. We're all team players here, Prudence. Can't afford to have office drama or any weak links."

What he didn't tell her was that the paralegals feared Oscar and looked to the associates for guidance and protection. Oscar was notorious for *running peoples' arses off* at the drop of a hat if he felt that someone wasn't a team player. Translation: everyone had to do what Oscar told them to do, immediately and with smiles on their faces. He was in control of this firm, although Bernadette came through every now and then to put everyone at ease. Oscar might have been the boss, but he wasn't always there, and it was Bernadette who ran the place then. If you were a paralegal at LeRoux, Godchaux, Bouligny & Tooley, you did not look Oscar Brimley directly in the eye and you spent half your time trying to keep him blissfully unaware of your existence. That was a fruitless effort, though, because Oscar knew everything about his firm: everything about *everyone.*

"Now, Prudence, after your lunch hour I want you in your office, five days a week for the next six months doing your homework and studying your course assignments. You can stay late at night or even come in on the weekends if you need to, but I know you have your son to look after. Just know that everyone here is willing to help you out if you ever have any questions. We already have you registered, and your books should arrive Wednesday or Thursday. Classes start next Monday. Bern!" Oscar yelled at the door, slightly startling Prudence. It was his idea of an intercom. "Bern, please come here when you get a chance. Prudence needs to be escorted back to her office, so she doesn't get lost," he added with a little laugh and a wink as he fell back to his Dr. Jekyll persona.

Bernadette walked in and motioned for Prudence to follow her. She could see that Prudence now looked nervous and ill at ease, so she offered some comfort once Oscar's door closed. "You'll do just fine here; don't you worry. When we get to your office, you'll see some paperwork from human resources. You'll also find some books about the firm's history and the things we've done over the years, as well as some legal pads, pens, and other office supplies. Think of any questions you might have and write them down on the pad. We'll go over them tomorrow. Remember, there are no stupid questions, so err on the side of inclusion and ask anything that comes to mind. There's a lot to learn about working in a law office; it's much different than the rest of the world. Sit tight for the rest of the day and I'll come get you later and we'll do some shopping at Élysées!" she said excitedly, feeling like a fairy godmother dressing Cinderella for the ball. "Evelyn Cormier is my favorite salesperson and she'll take good care of us."

Another reality set in, though, as Prudence felt curious eyes follow her and then flit away as she passed their offices. She thought she would be able to fly under the radar, but it looked like she already had a reputation there.

*Great. The paralegals will hate me when they find out the firm is paying me like a paralegal, covering my tuition, and buying my clothes. They will find out through the grapevine and Lord only knows what the story will be by the time it spreads to the rest of the office. They'll probably think the firm is going to buy me a car, too. I guess this is what the big time feels like. Stay strong, Prudence. Have faith. Deep breaths—it'll be alright.*

The shopping excursion threw a wrench in her evening plans, but how could she refuse? She couldn't. At least her schedule was being disrupted by another night spent playing dress-up with Evie. The downside—as if she didn't have enough to worry about—was that

Theo would be home alone a little longer than normal and there was no way she could attend evening services. *Reverend Drummond will understand,* she thought to herself.

# Chapter 10

## Breaking It Gently

"Bus must've broken down, boy," Theo said to Japonica, who was well rested after a day of sleeping. The dog smiled and wagged his tail playfully back and forth, knowing he'd be fed soon. "She's usually here by now. Guess we'll need to make our own supper tonight. Rice and beans? Maybe a little sautéed ground beef with some Tony Chachere's on top? Or maybe we should just stick with Purina for you. That okay?"

It was going on nine o'clock before Prudence finally got home, exhausted and laden with fancy shopping bags and what appeared to be a shoebox with the name and logo of some designer that she would only know after spending a few hours in one of New Orleans' finest stores. She plopped down on the couch, which was uncharacteristic of her. Upon getting home, she usually just greeted Theo and Japonica and started supper in the kitchen.

"Wow, what's with all this, Mom? Why are you wearing your church dress?"

Prudence had not seen Theo since the previous night. She wanted to see how the first day went before telling him about her new job. No sense getting him all worked up if she wasn't going to go through with it.

"Sit beside me, Theodore. I need to talk to you."

That worried Theo since she only called him that when he was in trouble or something serious was going on. However, before she could find the right words to explain what was going on, Prudence caught sight of his black eye and swollen lip and exclaimed, "Theo! What happened? Did those boys do this to you again?"

"It's nothing, Mom, really. Now, what's going on? What's with all this stuff? You got me nervous now," Theo said, quickly pivoting back to the subject at hand.

"We're going to talk about this black eye, but there's something else I need to tell you now. Theo, things are changing for us. Good changes," she said as she pulled him down to sit next to her. Taking his hand in hers, she paused as she noticed his raw knuckles. "Theo, I'm no longer working at the restaurant. Remember that big shot lawyer I've told you about?"

"You mean the clown," Theo replied.

Prudence didn't think she gave him that impression about Oscar, but kids were smarter than anyone gave them credit for, and, looking back, she could see how he might put two and two together with her description of his seersucker suits and martini lunches.

"Yes, the clown," she chuckled, settling down and breathing a little easier now that the ice was broken. Japonica joined the conversation by looking up from his spot, his tongue and tail gleefully wagging. He knew something was going on. "His name is Oscar Brimley and he runs one of the biggest, most successful law firms in the city. Well, yesterday he gave me the opportunity of a lifetime. Theo, I took a job at his firm and I'll be studying to be a paralegal. This is a good thing; it means I should be able to spend more time at home now."

"You *what*?" Theo exclaimed.

Prudence didn't expect that reaction. However, she understood that any big change could be unsettling to a teenager. She continued, "I can't fully explain it. Heck, I can't even process all of this myself because it happened so suddenly, but something told me to make this change, Theo. Something inside said that I needed to grab this opportunity and run with it. Believe me, I've thought this thing through, and if I'm going make a better life for us, I need the resources to do it. I need something more than what the hotel and the restaurant can give me, and you need a change of pace since you're obviously having trouble at school. I know it's not all your fault, but the fact is that there is an issue and we need to address it." She paused and looked around the sparsely furnished room. "You know, we've really never had a house of our own. This is Mamaw's house, and we've been blessed to be able to stay here with so many beautiful memories. But, we need a place that is all ours. Maybe somewhere near one of those private Catholic schools where the students are a little more accepting and the teachers have the luxury of smaller classes and more one-on-one time with their students. It's not going to happen overnight, but I needed to start somewhere and that somewhere was today. It may seem like a lifetime away to you, but you'll be finishing school soon and starting a life of your own."

If there was one thing about Theo, it was that he had complete faith in his mother's decisions. She was his idol, his rock. Theo thought about all of this for a minute and said, "Okay, Mom, I trust you. I'm good with this."

Prudence stood up and kissed Theo gently on the head before whispering in his ear, "We're going to talk about that black eye after supper."

79

Theo recoiled as tears welled up in his eyes. "Well, let's talk about it now. Let's just get it all out there, Mom."

Prudence was startled by his reaction. Theo looked at his mom, took a deep breath, and as stoically as possible told her what happened. How he pounded the kid after he and his cronies insulted Prudence. How the bullies taunted him for looking different, roughed him up, and made his life a living hell on an almost daily basis. How he never told his mother any of this, because she had it rough enough and he didn't want to burden her with his problems lest it remind her of the day she was viciously attacked and had her innocence stolen.

Now it was Prudence's eyes that were swimming with tears as she cradled her son's head in her hands. "Oh, Theo. I'm so sorry, baby. Why haven't you told me any of this? We need to talk about these things. There's nothing we can't get through as long as we're open with each other."

"You mean like when you turn our world upside down by going to work with those clowns? Open like that?" Theo replied with biting sarcasm.

It would have been easy for Prudence to chastise Theo for his blatant disrespect, but she knew he was right. She easily could have sat down with him Thursday night and talked about it. It wouldn't have changed anything, except that at least Theo would have felt like he was part of the decision-making process. He also was mature and smart enough that he might have even given her some good advice—like wearing something other than the flower dress her first day.

"Open and honest from now on?" she asked.

"Yes, Mama, open and honest from now on," Theo replied. They embraced, as if sealing the deal.

One thing was certain, and that was that Theo was hurting and needed some help, or at least a positive change. Prudence decided to speak with Reverend Drummond and ask if Theo could spend time at the Antioch after school. Perhaps he could help with after-school activities, do his homework there, or read to the little ones in daycare who were waiting for their parents to get off work. Maybe Japonica could tag along. He loved people and was normally a calm dog, an old soul toward which people generally gravitated. Maybe Theo would pick up some domestic skills and could help Chookie more and exercise his mind a little. Yes, getting Theo more involved at the church would be good for him, would give him somewhere he could feel like he was making a positive contribution to society. They'd both start making a difference on Sunday by going to the Antioch to see Reverend Drummond.

# Chapter 11

## Settling In

Monday morning. New day. New dress. New purpose. New life. With a tag still hanging off the back of her new dress, Prudence arrived at the office early and immediately searched for Bernadette. She still did not know a soul at the firm and was hoping Bernadette would walk her around and introduce her to some people later. Her paralegal class wouldn't start until the next week, so she was anxious to start learning about the firm's pro bono section. Prudence told Bernadette that she felt completely inadequate since she knew nothing about the law. After gently snipping the tag from Prudence's dress, Bernadette told her not to worry about that.

"Stop that kind of talk. You may not know the *law,* but I have a sense that you know people and you know the kinds of problems they encounter. Problems like past due child support, overdue rent payments, child custody fights, and battered women. Defining the problem is half the battle right there, because you can't solve a problem if you truly don't understand it. I can tell that you care about people and you don't view them as just an opportunity for the firm to tick its pro bono box. You certainly know more about those things than these pinhead baby lawyers. Hell, I've learned so much over the years, I'd wipe the courtroom floor with them if I ever went up against them in a real trial. Give yourself some credit, girl. Start out strong with these people and they'll respect you rather than run you over."

Prudence needed that confidence boost, and she knew Bernadette would become a true friend. She was good for Bernadette, too. It was about time the firm brought in more women who didn't look at their reflection in the mirror all day and worry about which designer outfit to wear to whatever party was on the firm's social calendar.

Every section of the firm had a name; secretaries were in the Bullpen, associates in the Hall, and the partners' hallway on the other side of the building was known as the Coast, because those guys and gals were just coasting on the backs of the associates, counting down the days to retirement. They topped out in their careers and knew they'd never be managing partner, but they would never leave as long as the firm continued to churn money. Oscar had his own small hall in the corner of the floor that was known as Valhalla, a little play on words and a little psychological seed to the associates in the Hall to keep them hoping they could someday reach Valhalla. On the floor below, the work areas for the paralegals and their support staff was known as the Tank; on the other side of the floor, walled off behind a blank door, was the nameless, faceless Clinic, where the pro bono work was carried out.

First stop: Jimmy O'Leary's office at the beginning of the Hall, just opposite Prudence's office and across from the Bullpen. Jimmy came in early most days, and that morning Bernadette could see that he was busy balancing pro bono with revenue-generating files; yellow meant pro bono, and green, naturally, meant revenue. Jimmy seemed to have more yellow files these days, and if he was going to meet his numbers for the year he'd have to work extra hard and learn to delegate.

Bernadette lightly tapped Jimmy's open door, startling him from a deep thought. He almost spilled his coffee mug and knocked a file off his desk. Bernadette chuckled a little and said, "Morning, Jimmy. If you have a moment I'd like to introduce you to Prudence Jean-Batiste, who is joining your pro bono group." Bernadette didn't realize that Jimmy already knew Prudence from the restaurant.

"Yes, yes, Prudence, great to see you again. I hope Bernadette is taking good care of you; she's the best. Later today, I would like to bring you down to the paralegal's floor, which we call the Tank, and introduce you to the rest of the team, as well as the folks in the Clinic. I just know you'll make a great addition to the team."

Jimmy was excited to have someone at the firm who was newer than him. Prudence would not be as cynical as the others who had worked there for years without much promise of further career advancement. He felt he'd have someone he could mentor and mold.

James "Jimmy" O'Leary graduated from Boston College Law School a few years ago and decided to get an LLM in admiralty law at Tulane University School of Law. Growing up in Boston, he'd always loved the sea and was drawn to the Gulf South with its warm breezes, sun-kissed coastline, bountiful fisheries, sugar sand beaches, and historic shipping ports. After studying in New Orleans, he decided that he would make his home there, where, from a lifestyle perspective, the pace was a little slower than it was in the northeastern part of the country. From a professional perspective, New Orleans was the seat of the famed United States Court of Appeals for the Fifth Circuit: the foremost authority on maritime issues.

Jimmy's childhood was not easy. He grew up in a single-parent household in South Boston, which was known for its blue-collar workers and lower middle class. In high school, Jimmy ran with some rough crowds, but he worked hard for every grade and made it his mission to one day leave Beantown and chart his own course. The hard work paid off and he landed an academic scholarship to Boston College. Four years and a 4.0 GPA later, he was offered a scholarship to Boston College Law School. He again excelled, making moot court and law review all three years. He narrowed down his interests and was accepted to Tulane, where he earned his LLM. This, he thought, was the quickest way to get into a top law firm; Tulane's alumni pipeline was strong and wove throughout the city, as well as the Gulf South.

LeRoux, Godchaux, Bouligny & Tooley accepted him after the first interview, and he started his career there a little more than a year ago. As a native Southie shaped by his Irish Catholic working-class roots, when he learned the firm was expanding its pro bono program, he jumped at the chance and volunteered to manage it. Oscar liked Jimmy very much and saw him as a protégé, unlike the other dandies who, for the most part, merely churned hours like tugs pushing barges through the swirling waters at the mouth of the Mississippi River.

However, Oscar wasn't quite ready to let Jimmy into the inner sanctum. Not yet. He would have to prove himself, and Oscar had been thinking of just the right test. That would come later. First, Oscar wanted to test Jimmy's people skills by integrating the firm's new darling into the stale stable of cynics.

# Chapter 12

## The Real Work Starts

"How's it coming along, Prudence?" asked Jimmy.

It was the beginning of week two, and in addition to getting settled, Prudence had read the will of a recently deceased husband of an elderly woman who was too upset to start the probate process and couldn't afford an attorney. Another file revealed a landlord-tenant dispute over a security deposit the landlord was refusing to release. The landlord claimed damage to the property, which could be proven to have been preexisting before the tenant moved in. The verbiage in the lease was very complex and so full of legalese that the client could not interpret it. Prudence didn't know how to interpret it from a legal perspective, either. After a reading, though, she couldn't believe that landlords would require tenants to sign such draconian documents. It was a Hobson's choice, though, and the wording of the lease was very clear; sign here or you can't lease the property.

"Well, Jimmy, I'd like to say everything is just fine, but to tell you the truth, I'm feeling a bit overwhelmed at the moment. I never knew so many people needed help with what seems like simple problems, which in actuality can be quite complicated. I'm afraid of making a mistake that winds up getting someone hurt."

"Prudence, don't worry about that," said Jimmy. "It's my butt and my license that is ultimately on the line, which is why I read everything before it goes out—hence the big yellow pile on my desk. You know more than you realize. Try not to overthink things and just keep your eye on the obvious and logical, because that's where you usually find most of the answers to—as you put it—these complicated problems."

"Thanks, Jimmy," Prudence replied. "Thanks for that vote of confidence. I really appreciate it."

"No problem. Have a great night, and I'll see you bright and early tomorrow morning," Jimmy said with a wave as he walked away.

*It's only Monday, but I think I'll stop at Winn-Dixie, splurge on a bottle of merlot, and then take a long, hot bath with a lavender bath bomb,* she thought. Prudence wasn't much of a drinker. In fact, she couldn't remember the last time she'd taken any alcohol, and she was normally tipsy after half a glass. She had a better understanding about how the pressures of dealing with the problems of others could get to lawyers, who too often internalized them as their own.

A lawyer's life was like a pendulum; there were highs when a case was won or a contract signed, and lows when a child was taken and sent into foster care, or when an elderly parent was abused by members of their own family. The phrase "that could drive someone to drink" made a little more sense now. It was especially true of those working in the Clinic, because they dealt with real people and real problems, not just businessmen or insurance companies who could afford to part with money or move on after losing a case. Those who couldn't afford a lawyer to take their case certainly couldn't afford the aftermath of an adverse judgment.

And it wasn't just money they could lose; if someone found themselves on the wrong end of a lawsuit they could lose their home, their children, or in some cases, their freedom. Not even those who were in fact innocent of the crime for which they were wrongfully convicted could rest easy until the case was closed. The law was far from what one saw on TV or billboards, and the real heroes were the ones helping regular people with sometimes significant problems—unsung heroes who balanced the law with equity, hoping a judge or jury would be persuaded to rule in their clients' favor.

# Chapter 13

### Theo's Purpose

"Hi, Mom," Theo said as he walked past where she was sprawled out on the couch, exhausted. He had a definite spring in his step and Japonica was in tow, tongue and tail wagging, excited to see where Theo was taking him this crisp evening.

"Well, hello yourself, young man," Prudence replied. "Where are you going?"

"Japo and I are going to volunteer to help Reverend Drummond get ready for bingo night at the Antioch. He agreed to pay me."

"Now, Theo, we've gone over this. It is not *volunteering* if you get paid. I'll have a word with Reverend Drummond about your so-called volunteering. We might be able to find a happy medium here."

"Well, what if he is really paying Japo for making an appearance? Everyone there loves that dog. In fact, I'm a little concerned he won't want to come home with me one day," Theo said, grinning and looking down at Japo, who looked up at him with even more excitement.

After a playful stare-down, she blinked, and they laughed together. It had been a long time since they had done something like that, and things seemed to be headed in the right direction. Theo's grades picked up since he was spending more time at the Antioch and studying, as opposed to getting beat up at school. Prudence's new life at the firm was well underway, and the restaurant was becoming a distant, but fond memory of simpler days. That night, they came to the happy realization that they were settled. They were *finally* at home. It took way longer than either would have imagined, but their weekly mom-son check-ins seemed to keep their relationship on a solid foundation. The weekdays were too busy for serious conversations, but they quickly got back on track as soon as they could.

For the moment, the attacks on Theo seemed to have stopped, and he was hopeful that they would become a thing of the past. Spending more time at the Antioch helping Reverend Drummond was exactly what he needed to help him build his self-confidence. Above all, it gave him real purpose, more than just caring for Japonica. Of the two, though, Japo was his favorite. Who wouldn't love that ole cayoodle?

# Chapter 14

## The Redeemer, A Storied Past

The right Reverend Dr. Cleophus James Hill V of the Antioch Apostolic Church of the Blessed Redeemer was a portly, fire and brimstone preacher in the traditional sense, whose heart was as tender as that of a teddy bear. The *Redeemer*—as it was oft called—was the first of the few Antioch churches in southeast Louisiana, and was founded by Reverend CJ's great-great-grandfather, who did so with the permission of the Cypress's owner at the time.

In order to get permission to build the church, which was desperately needed for the souls at the Cypress, Hill—as he was called by his owner due to his name and to an ill-fated attempt at escape that resulted in him tripping over a furrow in a cane field and then tumbling as if he was rolling down a hill—had to appeal to his owner's sense of greed. He did this by an act of betrayal of sorts; the justification was that the church would lift the spirits of the slaves of the Cypress, making them more productive and thereby generating more profits for the massa and missus of the house. Anything that would generate revenue and didn't cost massa anything was appealing; all that was needed was some wood and a few days of hard labor by his stable of bucks. Hill was given forty days to build the church. On day thirty-nine, a giant wooden cross was raised and set atop the pine steeple, and the oak doors of the Redeemer were opened to anyone in search of a spiritual respite.

The church grew as the years passed, and the Redeemer was emblematic of the holy place from which its name originated and stood tall as a symbol of strength in the community of those who were wrongfully oppressed by the Cypress for generations. Reverend CJ usually stood sentry at the doors of the Redeemer, waving at the diesel-spewing tour buses as they sped onto the next stop on their itinerary. The doors were original to the building, overlooking the main house as they seemed to keep the devil at bay, protecting those worshipping inside who hoped and prayed for freedom.

Reverend CJ, like his father, grandfather, and the many generations of Hills before them, tended to his flock's every need, whether it was counseling a troubled youth headed down the wrong path, advising a young athlete agonizing over which football or basketball scholarship he should choose, or providing for single, unwed mothers who were cast aside by conventional society because of their *loose morals,* never mind the callous cowards who left them to raise the baby they'd created.

Since the late 1850s, the Redeemer was a peaceful place where one could seek and find community, redemption, or a fresh start down a new path. One could learn to harness the power of newfound freedom and to lean on each other as they sought to catch up with the rest of the country. And it was as beautiful as it was peaceful, with carefully crafted stained glass windows that rivaled those found in the towering cathedrals in Europe and ornate woodworking throughout: from those massive front doors to the glorious cross that seemingly touched the heavens.

The pecky cypress ceiling and pews contrasting with the parquet pine floors was a marvel to behold. In fact, it was Reverend CJ's great-great-grandfather who, befittingly, carved the pulpit from the trunk of a beautiful, felled live oak to make way for the southwest quarters that would be reserved for the cane workers.

Truth be known, if someone wanted to learn about the real living history of the area, the Redeemer—with its sturdy, but squeaky original floors that allowed daylight to shine through—should have been the real destination on the tourist route, not the Cypress's main house, which was merely a museum trapped in time.

In addition to field labor, the Cypress was known for its resident Senegalese artisans, whose work survived antebellum burnings and could still be seen from the French Quarter to Virginia courthouses. Unlike Sherman, most Yanks were more interested in destroying the economy of the planters than they were burning churches. Indeed, most of the church burnings would come later in history, during the Jim Crow days of terror.

While cane was king, glassblowing, metalsmithing, and carpentry were specialties of the Cypress with a low cost of capital. It was the toil of the artisans that further enriched the plantation owners and industrialists who profited during the Civil War. In a cruel twist of irony, it was the artisan slaves who made the bullets, rifled the long barrels, carved the stocks, and forged the wheels for the big guns and cannons that were later aimed at their liberators. Another unfortunate irony was that it was Prudence's great-great-grandmother who sewed the beautiful, sturdy, rebel gray uniforms that stood up to the climate and wore well through battles, as well as the Louisiana bramble and swamp thickets. They offered a stark contrast to the dainty quilts sewn for southern belles who waited for their Johnnies to either come marching home or return in a casket carriage.

# Chapter 15

## Officially (Para)Legal

It was the busiest and quickest six months of her life, but Prudence Jean-Batiste finally found herself the proud holder of her paralegal certificate, and it was time for her to permanently move to the Tank, where the paralegals darted about swiftly like fish bobbing back and forth from their cubbyholes to the stairs, the library, the mailroom, and running down the city sidewalks to the halls of justice. Her timing was perfect, too, because a cubbyhole had just opened due to Oscar running someone off who thought they were above the team. Some of them thought he was just looking for an excuse so he could turn around and give the space to Prudence, thereby avoiding the need to build out more space or embarrassing someone by moving them to a less desirable station. All eyes were still on her. *Stay strong, Prudence. Have faith.*

There was a present waiting on Prudence's desk. It was the first official file that she was expected to work from start to finish. An elderly woman was having trouble organizing and paying for prescription drugs through the labyrinth that is Medicare. The free clinic in Algiers lost some paperwork, and the nine-to-five bureaucrats with mind-numbing, dead-end jobs were in no hurry to help find it.

Waiting was not an option, though, because this lady suffered from high cholesterol, diabetes, and hypertension due to decades of indulging in the staples of the New Orleans diet: creamy, buttery, fried, fatty foods, and lots of it. It seemed to Prudence that this situation would be more appropriately put into the hands of local charities like United Way, but since Katrina, the local philanthropic organizations throughout the greater New Orleans area, and indeed, the entire Gulf South, had been strained beyond capacity, and were slow to rebuild to their prior state of readiness.

The Clinic, however, would not let this woman fend for herself and was ready and able to help. Besides, issues with government departments *were* legal issues. Citizens had certain rights, and there were forums for bringing claims and obtaining administrative remedies, making these matters legal at their very heart. Not everyone was equipped to protect themselves, but the firm handled several of these cases annually. Prudence was teamed with Jane Champagne, who had been with the firm for more than thirty years and saw these sorts of cases all the time. She was the Bernadette of the paralegals, and part of her job was to train Prudence. This would prove to be a big challenge for Prudence, because Jane suffered no fools and expected a short learning curve, especially since Miss Priss just waltzed into the firm and had *everything handed to her*. Jane's philosophy was to throw the chicks out of the coup as soon as possible, and Prudence was no exception.

"Prudence, the client is here," said one of the secretaries from the Tank's bullpen, which was considerably smaller than the one for the lawyers. It was the B-Team, so to speak.

"Client," Prudence proudly said to herself. She liked the sound of that much more than *miss* or *waitress*. Still, she was nervous and frantically looking for Jane, who was nowhere to be found.

Prudence had some general client relations training, and speaking with people came naturally to her due to her years of waitressing. Life in a law firm was quite different from the real (or restaurant) world, though, and she was taught to greet the client warmly and guide the conversation. Some clients could drone on and on, spouting information that, while interesting and compelling, had no probative value. Telling their story was cathartic, because they were finally able to speak with someone they knew could help, or was at least empathetic enough to try. Prudence needed only the relevant facts, so her job was to deftly cut to the chase and frame the legal question. In order to do that, she had to be in charge of the conversation. This was unfamiliar territory for her, at least as far as complex problems were concerned. Fussing at cooks for undercooked Snapper Pontchartrain or burnt beignets was one thing, but being the last line of defense for vulnerable persons of no means with sometimes life-changing problems was quite another.

"Good morning. I'm Prudence Jean-Batiste and I will be working with you. Now, how can we help you today?" She purposefully started with the phrase "working with you" to plant the seed that the client needed to be an active participant in the process. Sometimes a bad client could ruin a good case, so she needed them to be thoroughly engaged. She used the word "we" to project strength and convey the notion that it was the horsepower of the firm that was behind her and would see to it that the problem would be handled appropriately.

The frail woman extended a slightly trembling hand, saying, "Good morning, Ms. Jean-Batiste. My name is Effie Johnson and I need a little help with my medications. The medical clinic don't help none, and I can't get no one on the phone at the Medicare. Just automatic recordings telling me to press this number and that one, and no one ever on the other end. Calls are dropped for no reason. It's like you can't talk to people no more. It's all just so frustrating and I'm just about outta my medicine."

Prudence replied, "Please, Miss Effie, call me Prudence. Don't you worry your heart none, because we're going to help you with this, ya hear?"

A colloquial touch usually personalized tough situations, and it didn't disappoint this time, either. A small tear welled up in Miss Effie's eye as she breathed a sigh of relief, like she just knew she would finally get the help she needed. Prudence, however, was a bundle of nerves that she hid well behind her stoic persona. This was her first time dealing with Medicare; she didn't have a clue what to do and Jane was nowhere to be found.

*Think Prudence, think.* What was it that she learned in her courses? Gather the facts and frame the issue. In another deft move, Prudence got up from the table and walked around it. She sat right beside Miss Effie, took her hand, looked her in the eye, and calmly asked a series of questions. Over the course of the next half hour, Miss Effie opened up, gave thorough and thoughtful answers, and was completely engaged. Prudence began to put the pieces together and learned a very valuable lesson right then that usually took others months to master; while the paralegal merely navigated the waters, it was the client who piloted the boat.

Jane had been watching from afar and was duly impressed. Her opinion of Prudence was immediately changed. It was a stroke of genius to sit next to the old lady and hold her by the hand. That would be encouraged among the team from now on. It obviously put Miss Effie at ease and allowed Prudence to be seen more as her friend, thereby making it far easier to elicit needed information. Genius. Thus began the formal legal career of Prudence Jean-Batiste, and she couldn't have been happier.

# Chapter 16

## Impressing Rachel

"So, is she as good as everyone says?" asked Rachel DeRouen, a senior associate who was on the fast track to making partner.

"What she lacks in legal acumen and experience, she makes up for with her people skills and desire to work and learn. So, yes, in a way, she is as good as everyone says," Jimmy said, praising Prudence's contribution to the pro bono section. "I'll give you a great example. A few weeks ago, she met a young man who was having trouble paying the rent on his house off Carrollton, near the old library with the lions in front. The manager of the property was some hard-ass who worked for some uptown landlord—a doctor, I think—who was threatening to evict him.

"The associate with the file wanted nothing to do with it and she couldn't find a paralegal who was interested or who had the bandwidth to run with it. It was a dog; the hours involved would be disproportionate to the time it *should* take to resolve that type of matter, and she was running behind on her monthly average billings.

Besides, the client probably couldn't have paid anyway, so she kicked the file over to the Clinic.

"So, Prudence sits down with the young man, took *all* his information, which was overkill for the situation, but that's not the point; besides, it's better for her to have too much information and not need it than to need it and not have enough. Anyway, she asked him what amount he would be able to pay on a monthly basis. She also asked whether he was willing or able to work at one of the landlord's other properties to pay off the back rent. They could take that opportunity to establish a reduced rent for a longer period and more generous payment terms with a thirty-day grace period instead of ten days, if the landlord agreed. Apparently, he's been doing carpentry work since Katrina and has fallen on some tough times, but he has some capacity now because, even though the rebuilding efforts are not fully complete, projects are getting harder and harder to come by. He's very skilled and normally takes large, specialized projects, especially on the uptown Victorians with their intricate woodwork on doors and cabinets, bannisters on spiral staircases, and refurbishment of those old, flooded wood floors, making them look brand-new—or at least maintaining a consistent look. Working on trade would also be a way for him to keep his skills sharp, and if he does a good job maybe he'll get references from this rich doctor and his yacht club friends, with their boats and beach houses on the Gulf Coast.

"But I digress. She offered to call the manager on his behalf and propose the terms, and the client agreed. Prudence called, said she was a representative from the firm—I need to talk with her about that later—and made the pitch. The manager offered to get back with her and called not fifteen minutes later to agree to the terms. Now, was this a *legal* problem, per se? Probably, because it dealt with leases and breaches, but in a practical sense this was really a business deal, and she handled it masterfully. I think it comes from her innate intelligence, problem-solving skills, and pure desire to help people."

"Wow," Rachel said. She rubbed her chin with a pensive, yet playful grin. "I'm going to have to steal her and bring her into the real estate section. Before too long, Oscar is going to want to send her to law school."

"Oscar's going to do what?" said the man himself as he ran through the hall like a whirling dervish, whistling as he spun by.

"Oh, nothing," Rachel replied. "It's just that our Miss Prudence helped a young man with a lease on a property owned by some rich uptown doctor who wanted to evict him."

"Where's the property, do you know?" Oscar asked.

Jimmy chimed in first. "I think it's one of those small houses over by the library with the lions."

"Must be one of Doc Hertz's places. Dr. Richard Hertz, the urologist. Ol' Dick Hertz!" Oscar said with a laugh as he skirted on the edges of an HR incident.

Not to be outdone, Rachel added, "I'm just glad he's not a female gynecologist from a James Bond movie."

Oscar chuckled and breathed a quick sigh of relief. He didn't know Rachel that well and therefore didn't know whether she was *one of the guys*, but he had no filter either way. Although she didn't seem to mind, he resolved to mind his Ps and Qs from then on. The office was quickly filling with a new generation of snowflakes and buttercups that would call him out on his boorish jokes in the future.

"Back on track, guys," Jimmy said as he turned to Oscar. "This was a good thing for Prudence. She sat down with this young man, learned about him, framed his problem, developed a potential solution, and proposed that solution to the other side. She solved his problem. That's what we do. It didn't hurt that she invoked the name of the firm, but as

I noted to Rachel, that's something we need to address. In fact, maybe we can do a lunch-and-learn in the office and talk about when and if someone should tell opposing parties or counsel that they are a *representative* of the firm. We can't have paralegals giving the impression that they are lawyers."

Jimmy was proud of that on-the-spot idea. He was, after all, merely a junior associate and relatively new to the firm, looking for ways to earn his spurs and outshine the other associates.

Rachel just rolled her eyes. She felt he was too eager, and if Oscar felt the same way it wouldn't bode well for Jimmy when it came time for promotions. No one liked a kiss-ass.

"Great idea, Jimmeroo." Oscar nodded at him. "Ask Bernadette to set it up. Lunch comes out of your budget."

He was serious, too. Right then and there Jimmy realized he was *paying his dues*, and it wasn't all pennywhistles, moon pies, and RC Colas around here. This was, after all, a serious business, a big business where partners earned millions by minding the store and ensuring the minions were spending wisely. In the final analysis, this would be viewed by Jimmy as a good expense, but he'd be sure to get prior approval next time before making a commitment like that: approval and access to someone else's budget.

Oscar spun away on his heels and Rachel resumed her conversation with Jimmy. "I was half-kidding about stealing her, but with the way you laid out her qualities for Oscar, I'm sure I'll snatch her away at some point. Seriously, though, maybe I could give her a couple of small real estate files to see how she does? BB wants me to work on some permitting for a client who wants to tear down some historic building. Does she have her own Westlaw account yet?"

*Well, that's just great. My budget will get pounded, I'll get pounded, and I'll likely lose my high-profile protégé within the year. Great job, James!* Jimmy lamented.

Noticing the disappointed look on Jimmy's face, Rachel smiled and said, "Welcome to the big time, ol' Jimmeroo. It's easy to fall into one of Oscar's traps."

"Send her the files," Jimmy said, somewhat deflated as he turned and walked away without looking at her.

# Chapter 17

## The Jamboree

"Sieg…HEIL! Sieg…HEIL! SIEG…HEIL!" The crowd, in an almost hypnotic trance, chanted with synchronized fists rocketing into the endless black night. Adorned with stereotypical hoods and satin clown suits, with some on horseback as a nod to their heroes of the good ol' days, they surrounded a giant blazing cross that lit the clear sky over Lake Pontchartrain. They were eager to get on with the night's business, which was nothing more than contrived pageantry designed by the Leadership to forge loyalty. Fueled by their drinks of choice—whether that be beer, bourbon and branch, or homemade shine—the Troops erupted in a fury. Each chant was louder and more powerful than the last, booming like a barrage of Confederate cannon fire echoing through the piney Northshore woods.

It had been a few months since they held a jamboree this size, and the reason for that night's gathering was the shooting of a tourist couple from Houston in town for the Saints/Texans preseason game. It was the tenth French Quarter killing of the year, and the reconstituted United Aryan Knights, a well-organized and powerful group comprised of ragtag KKK, neo-Nazi wannabes, were all beside themselves with pent-up anger over the killing of another white man and white woman caught in the crossfire of yet another senseless gangland shooting.

The couple was headed back to their hotel after an enjoyable night of raucous revelry, eager to catch a few hours of sleep in preparation for the game. Then, without warning, bullets filled the thick air and indiscriminately rifled through the crowd, hitting anyone and anything in their way. The crowd of tourists filling the street scattered like ants, and screams of horror could be heard blocks away. The Texans were ambling down Bourbon Street at 3:30 in the morning with Pat O's Hurricanes in hand when they were shot. The legendary bar's motto was etched across the lower part of the crumpled box containing the shattered and bloodied souvenir glass. *Have Fun!* Indeed.

The gangs had spun completely out of control recently, and the UAK had to regroup and *reeducate* them. If they didn't, the whole enterprise would be in danger of collapse, or worse, brought into the light of day. These types of high-profile killings averaged more than one a month, and the trend had to stop. For the time being, the UAK was fortunate enough to remain under the radar of both the FBI and the ATF. In spite of these senseless disruptions, the Leadership maintained its focus on the mission. Money continued to pour in like Louisiana rain, and the flood of cash held the police and politicians at bay. It was business as usual, albeit on a fragile foundation. The Leadership couldn't afford any further missteps, and swift action was needed. Priorities had to be adjusted, and order restored. Examples had to be made. Lessons would be learned—hard lessons.

While jamborees were normally opportunities for the Troops to muster for a group therapy session—the Leadership's idea of a corporate retreat—this gathering was driven by a specific purpose. The Leadership was incensed, and not because some overweight, gaudy, T-shirt-wearing tourist couple was killed. To the contrary, the Leadership's source of consternation was the fear that the killings would have a chilling effect on tourism throughout the entire college and pro football seasons, putting yet another crimp in their cash pipeline, which was fed at the top end by the Mexican cartels who expected prompt payment in cash, blood, or both.

The street gangs—the worker bees of the enterprise—would need to put their petty differences aside, lay low, and keep their noses clean until the city was safe again: a laughable notion despite the fact that Nagin fancied himself to be a law-and-order mayor in the post-Katrina world. What sweet irony that the UAK Troops used the inner-city gangs as moneymakers in the same manner as the plantation owners used their slaves to reap their fortunes. Some things never changed.

The Leadership had legitimate economic concerns over this French Quarter fiasco, but the Troops were oblivious to the direct impact it would likely have on the UAK's ability to maintain momentum. The Troops, as always, maintained a shortsighted focus on the incident itself and how it served to galvanize those loyal to their *cause*: white power. To the Leadership, the Troops were merely a means to an end to further *their* cause, the color of which was neither white nor black, but green: the color of money.

# Chapter 18

## The UAK

The UAK was founded in the mid-1950s as a radical, ideological hate group. Its main purpose was quite simple: the suppression and subjugation of the negro, the white race's domination of the country, and exploitation of the resultant spoils. Its actions were delivered effectively by boorish men, whose cowardice was ironically made evident by their anonymity. Members came from every level of society, from longshoremen working the docks off Tchoupitoulas Street to bankers, doctors, politicians, and lawyers. The group was effective, feared, and a force to be reckoned with. Over the last few decades, however, the UAK increasingly lost its panache and became viewed by would-be members as stale and outdated, almost comical. It lacked focus and strength, and it was rapidly dying on the vine.

Increased involvement and invasion by the feds resulted in the New Orleans mob takedown of the early '80s. When that mission was complete, the feds, as was always the case, remained and set their sights on a new target: hate groups, with the biggest target being the UAK. Through the introduction of anti-hate crime legislation in the '90s, the feds possessed the tools needed to chip away at the organization, as well as endless taxpayer funds. More prosecutions at the lower levels led to a substantial decline in membership, rendering the group a mere shadow of its former self.

Until a few years ago, the general public's perception of the UAK was that of just another aging, feckless white supremacist group hanging on to bygone days and the belief that it could still further its cause—an almost laughable notion in the Clintonian age of political correctness. In order to modernize and project a cleaner image, the group changed its tactics from overt aggression to the subtler message of maintaining the purity of the white race and defending its rights. However, like any other group, the UAK could not deliver its message without money and tactical assets.

Before the Leadership assumed control, the UAK obtained its funding in disorganized, clumsy, and sometimes high-profile ways. Money came in sporadically and mainly through the sale of drugs and trinkets at gun shows, which sometimes resulted in felony arrests. Competition from other groups and the inner-city gangs were roadblocks as strong as ramparts.

The UAK had all the basics of a well-run criminal organization: a common message, loyal followers, access to drugs, and the ability to dispassionately dispense violence. Despite having the basics, the UAK had never reached its full potential. It was a great moneymaking opportunity for anyone who had a modicum of leadership skills and financial acumen. Whether because of natural attrition or just disdain for the direction in which younger members seemed to be steering the organization, key members of the old guard were leaving in droves. It didn't help that incidents involving younger members were becoming more frequent, ferocious, and public in high-profile places. The Leadership had taken notice of some of the incidents for quite some time; its interest was piqued.

# Chapter 19

## The Leadership

The Leadership was calculating when it came to determining the quickest route to the capital needed to accomplish its main goal: Project Azalea. It employed a typical four-phase business plan: capital, employees, product sales, and enterprise growth. The UAK seemed to be the right group at the right time; it was a feeble group galvanized by a message rooted in its forefathers' prejudices, but flaccid in its ability to further its ideals. It was ripe for a takeover, and the Leadership seized the opportunity to move it in a new direction—its direction.

The takeover began a few short years ago. The Leadership's front-line officers slowly infiltrated the group, and with the help of strong personalities and a well-crafted playbook, the first phase was underway: the stockpiling of cash. Typical mob tactics reminiscent of the city's fabled Storyville era were used. Bread-and-butter marijuana sales, French Quarter massage parlors, high-stakes private poker games, and a cyber-based escort circuit got the mission off to a solid start. The initial cash grab was the easy part, and it came together quickly, much to the astonishment of the members.

With cash in hand, phase two kicked off and recruitment efforts began in earnest. New blood was desperately needed, and the Leadership developed a yearlong manning strategy to recruit specific types of miscreants and wanderers, which would come to be known as Troops. The targets were young white men who were easily influenced and looking for quick cash, as well as a place to call home. Titles, roles, and responsibilities were key to any business, and the UAK was no exception. The Leadership was astute and knew that mission statements were necessary for focus and discipline. It was a simple prospect for the Leadership; grab as much money as possible in the shortest amount of time and execute the plan while hiding in plain sight.

For the UAK, the message propagated by the Leadership was even simpler; maintain focus on its founding mission of preserving white pride and white power. The founders had no choice but to fall in line. Those who did not wish to do so were forcibly "retired" and were given generous packages for their silence. Recalcitrant resisters and agitators would quickly "disappear," never to be seen again. The Leadership did not resort to concrete shoes embedded in the bottom of New York Harbor. Swamp gators were more efficient, and, like the pig farms in New Jersey, left no evidence behind.

The new direction of the group did not sit well with its remaining founders, who were too tired and too powerless to stop it. Most were resigned to their fate and eventually stepped aside to embrace their new roles as the group's elders. As was the case in any business takeover, a smooth integration of old and new was crucial, and the elders were incentivized to cooperate. They possessed the tribal knowledge needed to maintain the ideals upon which the UAK was founded, as well as the influence over those whose membership predated the Leadership's takeover.

The strategy was masterful and immediately yielded results. What was planned as a yearslong effort was completed in three months. Through a twisted propaganda campaign using a different view of the world, young men in their early twenties—untethered by the societal shackles of marriage, careers, mortgages, and kids—were bombarded with a simple message. *They* were the ones being oppressed and *their* rights were under attack, not those of the blacks, illegal aliens, or the LGBT community. The package was easy to package, too; the white man's dominance in the country was systematically being diminished by the agendas of the progressives and the globalists.

The campaign was executed through a simple three-pronged attack. First, demonstrate how endless calls for diversity in the workplace increasingly resulted in jobs going to less qualified workers. Second, identify the progressives' emasculation of white men running rampant in mainstream media through commercials and movies, depicting white men as stupid, hen-pecked husbands or inferior coworkers. Third, highlight the proliferation and parading of homosexual and interracial couples on primetime TV shows.

The largest targets were unemployed, uneducated, blue-collar laborers who worked or had worked the peaks and valleys of the Gulf South's oil and gas industry. Smaller targets were similar types of misfits: military washouts with no immediate prospects for gainful employment. Collectively, they were the dregs, the outcasts of the industry and society in general. Those who could find work were usually the first to go when layoffs started, which seemed to happen too frequently, and with heartless callousness. White workers on ships and offshore drilling rigs carried much more overhead than did Filipino and Vietnamese deckhands, or roustabouts who rarely complained about spending months at a time on the salt. The UAK would be the logical place for such men to gravitate toward: a place full of like-minded brothers looking for purpose.

Well-funded and infused with new blood, the Leadership kicked off phase three. The street gangs needed to be brought in line and converted to a sales and distribution organization. Timing was everything, and the fates smiled on the UAK; many of the gangs' old stomping grounds had been razed, and bungled attempts to reach their pre-Katrina strength resulted in too many of their members being caught and jailed. Public fights amongst themselves over women, money, and territory impeded progress as well. The Leadership would exploit these weaknesses and redirect their energies. Consistency, a heavy hand, and structure were needed to establish a new order. It could be done through the carrot or the whip; the choice was theirs.

New Orleans' gangs were shortsighted, poorly organized, and filled with uneducated amateurs. Katrina had scattered them to the winds, to places like Baton Rouge, Atlanta, Memphis, and Houston. Unable to gain traction in their adopted homes, they eventually dribbled back to New Orleans, but never rebounded in any meaningful way.

The UAK amassed a small tactical team to conduct a few quick roundups, make a few examples, and bring the gangs in line. The message was simple; the UAK gaveth by providing organization and generous payments to drug dealers, and the UAK could taketh away by unleashing a reign of terror that would bring even the toughest of gangs to heel. It didn't take long for the gangs to heed the message.

The first three phases of the Leadership's takeover of the UAK were largely complete when phase four kicked off. An oft-used business principle was then put into practice; create a sales plan and bring proven products into markets at a price point that would keep current customers, as well as attract new ones. The UAK's strengths were abundant with cash, a robust and growing membership, and total control of the distribution network at the street level. Attentions then turned to increased profitability through a new focus on premium products like cocaine, heroin, and the cheapest product with the largest margin: meth.

With any product-based enterprise, the supply chain was the Achilles heel, and the UAK was no different than any other. The Mexican cartels were the only game in town, and they controlled *all* of the products. A joint venture would benefit both parties. The cartels would guarantee a steady supply, and the UAK would ensure that it was safely and efficiently imported and distributed through its side businesses and network of street gangs. It was a simple business proposition; if you can't beat 'em, join 'em.

# Chapter 20

## Consequences

Unlike the loud days of old, when it was a badge of honor for the UAK to have a street level rally hit the evening news, the Leadership preferred discretion and dissuaded the Troops from a belief that one could succeed and grow by causing a public spectacle. There was no need to show up at black pride rallies in costume, holding Confederate flags and chanting, "WHITE POWER!" Success, the Leadership would teach, comes internally and organically from the grassroots level. The jamborees were established as an outlet to channel inner strength. Trudging through the woods with brothers in arms in the dead of night forged the *esprit de corps* needed to keep the Troops focused, compliant, and under the radar.

Except for the UAK's official historian, cameras, smartphones, as well as video and audio equipment, were strictly verboten at jamborees. All such items were turned in at the main road, switched off, and placed in a lockbox before costumes were donned and torches lit, lest some knucklehead post something to Snapchat or allow his position to be known by a Facebook check-in. This was a zero tolerance policy, and anyone running afoul of it would be dealt with on the spot and in a most unpleasant manner.

Punishment was simple and effective: bullwhip to the back. The newest Troop would administer the lashes harshly while the offender was tied to a tree. If the newbie pulled back on the blows, hoping to spare a brother pain, said newbie would receive a punishment equal to that of the offender, plus one lash. The biggest cruelty, however, is that it was the offender who picked the tree to which he'd be tied and the number of lashes he was to receive—too few, and the amount chosen would be doubled by the ranking member on site. The punishment was psychologically effective, too, because the offender was treated just as runaway slaves were: tied to a post, exposed to a crowd, and mercilessly whipped to serve as an example.

For the Leadership, these types of policies were extremely important in maintaining order. A low profile was necessary to accomplish its goals with the most impact. The policy was adhered to religiously, and there had been only one instance of a sentence having been carried out. In that case, the offender hadn't taken any pictures or posted anything. He simply forgot to take his phone out of his pocket. When his *Dukes of Hazard* ringtone went off, the ranking member had him grabbed immediately. The offender picked a nearby thin, longleaf pine with sharp bark and was aggressively strapped to it. The idiot gave himself a sentence of fifteen lashes, which was promptly doubled by the ranking member. The truth was that the number chosen was going to be doubled anyway, just to emphasize the seriousness of the policy.

# Chapter 21

## Project Azalea Blooms

Like most major capital projects, the first phase of Project Azalea began with developing a budget and securing cash, followed by smaller activities that acted as guideposts for larger portions. The bulk of phase one was on autopilot. With the UAK faithfully and effectively playing its part as the money pot, the Leadership kicked off the second phase: the purchase of prime real estate in strategic areas, beginning on the outskirts of the French Quarter and the Faubourg Marigny, which was the city's second suburb and a place of growing popularity.

Money was laundered through Indian casinos located on the tribal lands of the Chitimacha, Coushatta, Choctaw, and Tunica-Biloxi. Expansion would be quick, aggressive, and spread through the Warehouse District and Claiborne Avenue, thereby encircling the area where the remaining housing projects stood. The endgame was exploitation of these areas by taking prime corner properties, buying old teardowns for parking lots, refurbishing some historically significant areas, and razing undesirable ones. This would result in creating open-air ecosystems established in key areas, much like Houston's CityCentre: the perfect model for the Leadership to emulate.

If those rhinestone cowboys could do it, why couldn't the Leadership replicate the model on a smaller scale, albeit with a spicy Creole flair? New Orleans already had one of the best tourist infrastructures in the world, and was a destination for major sporting events and concerts at the Superdome and the New Orleans Arena. The arts scene, while small, boasted the Louisiana Philharmonic Orchestra and was host to quality musicals, plays, and seasonal off-Broadway shows at the historical Saenger Theatre on Canal Street. For those seeking more excitement, a world-class casino sat at the end of Canal Street, just a block from the French Quarter and a street hop away from the mighty Mississippi River. And for the very wild at heart, the entire city shut down once a year for the world's largest street party: Mardi Gras, the economic lifeblood of the city, and indeed, the entire state of Louisiana. The city's bread and butter, though, was tourism and conventions. The busy convention season began in spring, with clean, crisp air and beautiful azaleas bursting with color and taking center stage in many of the Victorian gardens flanking the famed St. Charles streetcar line.

The function and charm of New Orleans far outshone Houston: a concrete megalopolis and the largest city in the south. While strip malls and apartment complexes littered Houston, a town with traditionally little regard for its history, the famed French Quarter was a marvel to behold, a glimpse into the past, and an architectural and religious irony. Streets with French names were lined with Spanish buildings, adorned with ornate wrought iron balconies, all within walking distance of the country's oldest operating cathedral—the majestic St. Louis Cathedral, which was an island of reverence surrounded by a sea of decadence. It was the heart of the city and full of contrasts, with fine dining near bawdy bars, cheap T-shirt shops just a stone's throw from famous antique stores, and the wandering homeless walking the same streets as the landed gentry. Buggy rides, artists, street musicians, and fortune-tellers provided pleasant diversions and completed the scene.

The Leadership's project would build on the Quarter's infrastructure and enhance it through upscale shopping areas, smaller convention sites, parking lots, luxury urban condos, boutique hotels, and more fine dining. The dilapidated docks of the Warehouse District, a hub of commerce during the city's glory days, would be upgraded and expanded to include weekend farmers' markets, sound stages, recording studios, production lots for indie films, and incubators for artists, musicians, and small startups with an emphasis on the film, tech, hospitality, and food industries. Plans had been drawn for a new streetcar line that would follow Tchoupitoulas Street to the bend in the river near Audubon Zoo. Bed-and-breakfast cottages would be sprinkled throughout the Garden District and Uptown neighborhoods near the current streetcar line, providing a landing spot for the traveling upper crust—local flare as opposed to the typical Bourbon Street tourist trap. All of this would attract a more genteel crowd, whose appetite was fed by single malts, Malbec, and *entrecôte avec haricots verts* in an ambience like The Columns hotel. In other words, people who would stand in stark contrast to drunk college kids and out-of-town businessmen satiated by beer, booze, and hot dogs eaten on the hoof while ambling along Bourbon Street in the wee hours of the morning, just before the break of dawn.

# Chapter 22

## Lawyers, Guns, and Money

Since the dawn of time, currency in one form or another was required to accomplish anything. This was certainly the case in Louisiana, where there was a rich, bordering on proud, political history of greed and graft. The Leadership knew local and state politicians would have to be procured to grease the skids for the purchase of properties and historic buildings. New zoning laws would streamline city permits, and tax concessions would attract small businesses. A bought-and-paid-for police force would dust off the playbook used by the Irish cops in New York during the western European emigration at the turn of the twentieth century. The NOPD was charged with maintaining order by knocking heads, but at a more rapid pace and with much more violence than would otherwise be necessary to keep the peace. Gangs were corralled to manageable areas and violent crime was being pushed out of the city into Metairie and the West Bank in order to avoid public incidents, such as the recent tourist slayings.

The time was ripe for a renaissance of this once majestic power-house of commerce. Government housing and poor neighborhoods, a drain on culture and resources for decades, would be systematically replaced by gentrification that would be the envy of all major cities. It would begin with quick land grabs, followed by a naturally expanding economy fueled by skyrocketing real estate prices, the impact of which would result in a more desirable place to raise a family. Profitable businesses would attract the money that for decades had fled New Orleans and landed nearby in Metairie, Kenner, and the Northshore. Those *white-flight* societies had become stale and were spread too thin due to the brain drain of the late 1980s and the decimation brought on by Hurricane Katrina. An entire generation of Louisiana's best and brightest were scattered across the country, looking for the life they never could have in the Crescent City.

The Leadership hoped that newer generations would flock back to the state in droves, wanting to be a part of something new, something vibrant. They would bring with them their young families and buying power, which would increase tax revenue needed to update the city's crumbling municipal services base, but that was the government's concern. The Leadership would just sit back and reap the benefits.

Banks were needed to launder money, and, most importantly, the Leadership needed the backing of a respected law firm large enough to support real estate transactions and legitimize the underlying business structure to limit liability and withstand government scrutiny. It was a stereotypical *lawyers, guns, and money* operation that had been replicated throughout human history. The ruse would be fronted by respectable businesses, and the rules were simple; create demand, control the supply, minimize costs, insure against risks, and maximize profits. Business was business, and the products could be anything, whether it was industrial oilfield equipment, peanut butter, diapers, or meth. Structure, discipline, and compartmentalization were all things the Leadership did with great aplomb, thanks to its members' corporate and professional backgrounds. It would be all too easy to use the UAK's *cause* to galvanize loyalty and gin the money to fund the project.

# Chapter 23

## A Mule for the Cause

As far as the rank and file members of the firm were concerned, William Thomas Falke and Lawrence Robertsen were the owners of Knight Trucking & Logistics Company—just another client of the firm whose business had shifted from the volatile oil and gas industry to a more *recession-proof* business. The Leadership could have gone with almost any relatively stable industry, such as food or medical, but specifically chose logistics for two reasons: to traffic drugs from Mexico, and to mobilize the heavy equipment contractors needed for the construction and/or restoration of the buildings located on their newly acquired properties. The business was self-funded and totally outside the ambit of the UAK.

Knight Trucking had three revenue streams: direct payments from the UAK, third parties who shipped their goods along with the drugs, and the contractors who were required by the Leadership to use their *preferred vendor* to mobilize heavy equipment. It was an elegant front, and not an amateur operation by any stretch of the imagination. If need-ed, it could operate on a totally legitimate basis. In typical oil patch fashion, operations were clean and efficient. A fleet of shiny black and gold trucks adorned with the ubiquitous *fleur de lis* surrounded by the company's name was complemented by uniformed drivers who were mostly veterans—a requirement of Robertsen. All vehicles were equipped with the latest high-tech equipment that tracked time and mileage, which the Counselor deemed necessary to ensure compliance with government regulations. Everyone at Knight Trucking knew that *any* legal or compliance questions were to be immediately referred to the Counselor's law firm.

The company itself owned nothing, leased everything, and carried all types of cargo. With the exception of transports for third parties, it was all contrived, a paper tiger created to keep the appearance of a bona fide business. To help maintain the façade, the Counselor required that Knight Trucking conduct actual operations, maintain downtown office space, and keep accurate books, invoices, leases, bills of lading, and export licenses, along with everything else a legitimate import/export business would need to withstand the scrutiny of quarterly fi-nancial audits, which were approved by accountants from the largest accounting firms. Accountants were never allowed site visits, and be-cause everything ran so smoothly, they didn't question the underlying operations. They cared only about the numbers, which were always perfect. The Leadership wanted to ensure that Knight Trucking & Logistics Company would be considered the easiest client with whom the accounting firms did business, and that the audits were clean and conducted quickly and quietly.

Project kickoff meetings were held in the opulent Knight Trucking conference rooms in Oil Centré Tower, which impressed the ju-nior auditors. The audits were conducted in the finest suites in the luxurious Louis XIV Hotel, which was influenced by the opulence of Versailles and connected by a skyway to Oil Centré Tower, so weather was never an issue. Breakfast, lunch, and dinner prepared by the city's finest chefs from marquis restaurants would be served in breakout conference rooms located throughout the hotel to keep groups segregated. Junior suites were made available to any auditor who traveled, or any local ones that wanted to spend the night. The philosophy was simple; keep them busy, well-fed, and comfortable so they could complete their work quickly and run back to their offices to tell their colleagues how auditing Knight Trucking was the most amazing business experience they'd ever had.

Knight Trucking's office space had a receptionist and a small staff whose only job was to process the paperwork and take marching orders from an office manager who relied heavily on the associates in the law firm when compliance and HR issues arose. Whenever there was an issue or question, the drones had a standing order—clear it with legal.

Robertsen learned from his many years in corporate America that those drones who worked in office buildings simply worked with paper and computers and had no idea if what they were doing was legitimate or not. They always deferred to the lawyers whenever documents needed to be reviewed or signed.

The drones came in for the nine-to-five daily grind and created invoices, took sales orders, issued purchase orders, handled government compliance, and processed the leases for the distribution fleet and operations centers. Other corporate office staples, such as blue jean Friday, office birthday parties, and team-building trips to bowling alleys or exclusive showings at nearby movie theaters, occurred regularly. Employee-of-the-month certificates were awarded in ceremonious fashion, and there was a brag wall of framed fake certificates from the American Trucking Association indicating that Knight Trucking

& Logistics Company had received gold-level Safety and Efficiency Certification for three years in a row.

To further the charade, Robertsen had created a few silver- and bronze-level certificates for past years, which gave everyone an incentive to focus and maintain the gold-level. Everyone had to pull their carts in the same direction, and there was a concerted effort to maintain a positive corporate culture in line with its mission statement. *People matter.* It was crafted to keep everyone focused on their jobs, which were legitimate as far as they were concerned.

Employees were not allowed to visit operations sites. However, it was human nature to want to see things in person to better understand how their small role impacted the company overall. Knowing this, Robertsen went the extra mile and adorned the offices with pictures of the fleet and die-cast model trucks in the lobby to show an evolution of the trucks the company had used over the years. He was extremely careful not to display pictures of the outsides of offices, lest people recognize one from their hometown and stop by for a visit the next time they took their standard two-week vacation to visit "Grandma" in Beaumont or Ocean Springs.

To further lessen the mystery, during spring break a truck or two would visit Oil Centré Tower and take up space on the downtown street. To avoid scrutiny, KTL obtained a rubber-stamped permit from city hall. Employees would sit in the cabs and pretend they were big rig truckers. Kids milled about, climbing under the flatbed and tooting the horn when it was their turn to sit in the cab. To limit injuries and add a sense of awe, official safety briefings were held in conference rooms and catered by top New Orleans chefs. KTL wanted to both impress the families and ensure there were no workers' compensation or insurance claims.

Except for the third-party transports, it was all fake, and very Enron-esque. The drones had no idea they were part of a criminal enterprise and just followed orders: in at eight, forty-five minutes for lunch, out at five, weekends off. Rinse, wash, repeat. Keep them well paid, incentivized, interested, and above all, in the dark. If Robertsen knew one thing about corporations it was that placating the masses and keeping them content meant fewer questions, and therefore, fewer problems. Stroke their egos rather than their pocketbooks. Certificates cost only five bucks, but coupled with a reserved spot for the *employee of the month,* was worth more to many than a paltry five percent raise. That would just be a blip in the check and ultimately absorbed by their lifestyle. A certificate, however, would hang on the wall forever announcing to the world that they were *the best*—at least for a month.

# Chapter 24

## Under Radar

As far as most partners and associates of the firm knew, the goods traded and transported by KTL were ordinary—vegetables, manufactured goods, leather, and textiles. The associates in the firm found it a little odd that such a successful business did not advertise and essentially flew below the radar. In the final analysis, they really didn't care as long as they could bill hours, which they did happily and heartily.

The firm ran everything that was not part of Knight Trucking's day-to-day operations. To make it difficult to track the ownership of the company, the firm established a web of subsidiaries, all of which were Delaware corporations; it was a very common jurisdiction due to its ease in administration and settled corporate law. To avoid suspicion among the firm's members, its offices in New Orleans, Houston, and Mobile administered the subsidiaries. Unaware of the real role they were playing, associates liaised with the banks to ensure the money was properly accounted for and the books were kept clean. They had no idea they were driving an elaborate money laundering operation.

The Denver office was used mostly for the Leadership's mineral interests in the Niobrara shale play and as a stopover at Oscar's ski chalet in Aspen, which was needed to entertain Knight Trucking's managers and the firm's other major clients. Oscar's main challenge was two-fold; keep the politicians in line, and ensure no one in the firm could put the pieces together. They had to be kept in the dark. Otherwise, the whole operation would be uncovered.

Oscar handpicked the senior partner managing the real estate section, Brian "BB" Brady, to handle all property purchases and permitting associated with Project Azalea. BB was none the wiser since the work was given to him piecemeal, as if it were related to different clients. He couldn't possibly put two and two together, and if he did, Oscar had enough dirt on his private life to ensure his loyalty. Oscar's private investigators often reported that BB frequented underground bars with young men half his age. BB was a smart lawyer, but he wasn't very bright.

# Chapter 25

## The Swamp

Growth and branding were the measures of success for all enterprises, criminal or otherwise, and the UAK was no exception. To maintain mystique, a rebranding was needed for two reasons: to distinguish the old UAK from its newest incarnation, and to use that distinction as a recruiting tool to attract those not easily swayed by ideology. One had to be very careful when rebranding, otherwise old regime loyalists would be alienated. Hard lessons were learned in the oil patch. For every successful ExxonMobil merger, there was one that never truly established its own identity. Sometimes the simplest solution was best, so rather than erase its culture entirely, the UAK would be referred to informally as the Swamp.

There was another reason for cultivating a strong brand and corporate culture, a very forward-thinking one—expansion. In business, expansion often came through different avenues, such as organic growth or acquisition. Given the UAK's main source product came from

Mexico, the Leadership foresaw an opportunity to expand and create efficiency in the distribution channel throughout the I-10 corridor. Just as business leaders established 30-60-90-day business plans, so, too, did the Leadership. Because the New Orleans market was at maximum buying capacity, growth would come through acquisition from west to east. The UAK, with its newfound economic power and fundamental culture of preserving whites' rights—a view shared by hundreds of groups around the country—would slowly enter the territories starting in Texas and moving on through to the Atlantic Ocean.

Branding would facilitate the move to join forces. Each new group would include the same management structure and would be referred to as an enclave with its own name. Texas groups would form the Cowboy enclave, those in Mississippi would form the Coast, and Florida would be named Emerald, a nod to the emerald waters of the Redneck Riviera off the Florida Panhandle. Alabama would act as a natural barrier to establish some distance from the Coast and Emerald. It was a great plan, albeit a plan for another day. Maintenance of the Swamp was the primary focus.

# Chapter 26

## Rulers of the Mean Streets

In the Swamp, the most reckless and violent gang was Calliope. The gang's nexus was the French Quarter, and its members wore bright yellow bandanas. Contrasting with the chaos of Calliope was the subtlety of the Drakes of Desire, whose members wore purple, the color of royalty and ubiquity throughout the region, thanks to the prominence of the LSU tigers. The Drakes were more disciplined in the way they dispensed violence, and, on the whole, caused the least amount of trouble. The two gangs often fought in popular public areas heavily frequented by tourists—much to the dismay of the UAK. The normal clichés and principles of warring factions applied just as much to a well-run criminal enterprise as they did to world politics, where checks and balances of power were necessary to maintain peace and prosperity. Mutually assured destruction was an age-old strategy, and the UAK made sure that adequate resources and a propaganda machine maintained such an environment. Without question, the UAK always fell on the side of prosperity and did its utmost to keep the gangs apart.

Peace, however, was a fanciful notion maintained by the most comfortable of peoples. The ecosystem from which the gangs originated was neither peaceful nor prosperous. Conflict and greed were the norm, and the UAK employed a containment strategy to keep everyone in line. While the gangs were usually kept in line by the Alpha division Master, a title purposefully created for oppressive effect. It was the specter of the UAK as a whole that loomed large and acted as the ultimate incentive for enclave divisions and gangs to behave appropriately. It would take only a few hours for the Swamp to round up enough Troops to keep rogue gangs or scofflaws in line through overwhelming force—the use of which the UAK was most adept.

General Herman Krieger headed the Swamp, the epicenter of the UAK. At more than six feet tall and weighing about 195 pounds, Krieger maintained a trimmed, taut physique. With a high and tight haircut that carved his graying blonde hair, dark blue eyes, and adequate biceps augmented by polos and tight T-shirts gave him an authoritarian aura of which der Führer himself would approve.

The Alpha branch distribution network was efficient; Troops supplied the drugs to the gangs, who peddled product throughout their territories. Weekly *tributes* were paid via drop box brigades from locations determined by the division Master thirty minutes before pickup—always in plain sight of security cameras to prevent any repeats of an incident that happened a few years ago when some Calliope members thought they'd be cute and attacked an Alpha branch drop box brigade in the French Quarter, killing two and seriously injuring three of the Swamp's finest.

The UAK was patient and orchestrated payback the following year that still sent a cold chill down the back of any gangbanger who dared even think about stepping out of line. The blitzkrieg was referred to as *Schwarze Nacht*, which in German meant "black night," and was an ode to General Krieger. It was quick, comprehensive, efficiently executed, and very effective. A small group of Troops were sent deep into the projects on reconnaissance shortly after dark one evening. When they were confident of the whereabouts of the gang's leader, the rest swooped in during the middle of the night and took out large numbers of the Calliopes. A few Drakes were roughed up in their territory to send home the message that if one stepped out of line, all would pay the price. The skirmish itself took less than ten minutes and was made to look like a gang war, so the cops and the media thought that was indeed what happened.

Because of the attack on Alpha branch, General Krieger began the practice of simultaneously sending drop box brigades to collect the tributes while scatter Troops hid in plain sight to quickly quell any attack. Such an operation really wasn't necessary for Beta (prostitution) and Gamma (gambling), but consistency was key, so pickups utilizing the same plan were executed. More Troops, however, meant more overhead and a greater chance of having the operation blown wide open, but it was a necessary nuisance—just another cost of doing business.

Although Masters and Sergeants were fairly levelheaded, ordinary Troops typically were not—nor were they very smart. Most were recovering meth-heads, recreational drug users, or heavy drinkers. None, however, liked the prospect of joining the ranks of the citizenry of Orleans Parish Prison, so most were content to just follow orders and collect a check. In addition to safety concerns, consistent operations helped to combat the real risk of Troops getting caught up in a deal gone bad. The UAK, and in turn the Leadership, could ill afford having its members getting arrested and then seeking immunity, flipping for the prosecution, and going into the witness protection program. Lessons from the mob takedown were heeded; there were plenty of former mobsters working at hardware stores in podunk towns in Idaho and Kansas. A miserable existence to be sure, but better than being dismembered by the UAK citizenry, who lived in OPP and were serving long sentences and acting as the UAK's eyes and ears.

When necessary, it was easy to orchestrate a gang war and have thugs kill one another. Just spread some misinformation and disinformation about their mamas and their bitches, let them stew in their juices for a while, and ensure they met during a weekly drop box pickup with a beautiful shootout ensuing almost immediately. Wait for the cops to come and arrest the surviving gang members, and the UAK's bought-and-paid for assistant district attorney would ensure that prison terms were long enough that the UAK's prison gang could mop up. Problems would come into play, however, if the gangs took it upon themselves to shoot up Bourbon Street. It was one thing to have battles in the projects, and quite another to have one on one of the most famous streets in the world.

# Chapter 27

## Krieger's World

In theory and in practice, things ran smoothly. The money flowed like water through the mouth of the Mississippi River. However, because of the latest tourist killing, the police would likely be required to conduct another roundup, which would undoubtedly snag some of the big money dealers already on their radar. The danger was twofold; product wouldn't move as quickly, and weekly payments to the cartel were still expected to be made in full and in a timely fashion. The UAK risked being ratted out in exchange for lighter sentences, not to mention the money it would take to keep cops from going overboard, which was always an invitation for lawsuits, as well as the very real prospect of the Department of Justice bringing in a monitor. This would all but destroy the well-oiled, greasy-palmed monster that was the New Orleans Police Department.

There were natural checks and balances, though. It was widely known that, whether from the outside world or inside OPP, the UAK always made certain there'd be no flipping or plea bargains. All it took was a few instances of bench presses gone wrong in the gym or an inmate accidentally falling on a shiv in the chow line and usually the problem would take care of itself. The UAK was omniscient, omnipresent, and took care of problems swiftly, efficiently, and violently. No willing witnesses, no loose ends.

Reining in the cops had become more of a challenge, because a good show of force was needed more often to make the citizens *feel safe*. In reality, the city was no safer than it had been for the last forty years. Nosy action reporters didn't help, and the new mayor and police chief hadn't quite gotten with the program yet. The Leadership temporarily allowed the fantasy that the elected leaders were the ones running the city, but could not stomach the damn ideological do-gooders and their "time to take back our streets" mantra.

The Leadership faced quite a challenge and the time was right for a reeducation of the elected officials to help get them in line and explain how the city really worked—at least in theory. Robertsen made a mental note to work on this with the Counselor soon.

As expected, the police roundup occurred, but the net was cast wider than previously estimated. The UAK's cash crunch would be greater than originally feared, and would occur much sooner than expected.

"Put Robertsen on notice," Krieger barked to Mario Cerata, Master of the Swamp's Alpha division. "He needs to tell the Counselor to get his lawyers ready with some cash to put up bail and contribute to the DA's reelection campaign so we can get these gangbangers back in business and moving product! And you need to find out which one of those stupid assholes pulled the trigger first, so I can make an example of him." Krieger's face was beet red, and purple veins swelled and pulsated on the sides of his head as he screamed the order. "Raid his shithole of an apartment at 02:30 hours. Take him to Natchez and string that bastard up from the highest damn pine tree you can find! On your way out, pick up a couple from the other gangs and scare the everliving shit out of them. Let them see it, show them what happens when you play around in the Swamp. Handcuff 'em! Put hoods over their nappy heads! Throw them in the back of the pickup with that monster of a fighting pit bull you have. Don't hesitate to give a little break tap or take a sharp corner on your way there to teach them about the laws of centrifugal force! When it's over and he's swingin' in the breeze, let 'em all think they're next up on the limb. Shave the head of one of them and drop him off in enemy territory."

Krieger became angrier with each passing moment out of the fear that he'd miss his profit targets for the month, or worse, that Robertsen would pull him out of the Swamp. He turned away from Cerata and thought aloud, "This macho thug crap has got to stop. It's bad for business. If these attacks keep happening in high-profile places like the Quarter, the tourists will go elsewhere, and those college kids will stop spending Daddy's money and their loan checks. Our football season and Mardi Gras customer base will drop twenty-five to thirty percent overnight. Robertsen is on some kind of capital campaign, so we're in the spotlight and we have to deliver. Same thing goes for Beta and Gamma—turn up the heat. Tell 'em their 'insurance premiums' will increase starting tomorrow!"

After settling down a little, Krieger turned back to Cerata and continued in a quieter tone and developed a more business-like solution. "When you get back from Natchez, step on your product by half, raise the price by fifteen percent in the first week, then twenty percent the next week, and twenty-five percent the week after. Get three more girls for Beta and increase the hourly prices by five percent, and the à la carte services by fifteen percent. Raise the ante for the games in Gamma and steer more customers to the ponies and the dogs. Alpha's customers might balk a little, but they have nowhere else to go and they'll need their fix, so they'll come around to the new reality, albeit begrudgingly. Double the frequency of the drop box pickups to two per week. Oh, increase the vig, too. The high prices might cause some of them to have to finance their monsters. The reality is they have nowhere else to go." Krieger continued, "Natchez should settle things down for a while, but make sure the Troops keep a ready eye on the others. I could give a flip if they shoot each other in the projects, but keep them out of sight of the street corners, hotel lobbies, and ATM cameras in the Quarter, especially on Bourbon and Royal.

"Lastly, when your boys get back from Natchez, I don't want any details as to how it's all carried out. The last time your skags bragged to me about what they did to that big boy they left for dead near the Quarter a few years ago, it put me in a bad spot because I had too much information. The bigger mistake was not making sure he was dead, but that's a different matter. I don't know where he is, but I heard he's living outside the city with his aunt and is basically a retard, so there's no need to finish him off; it's not worth the risk. If I know too much, I won't be able to pass a lie detector test. Just take care of it. I have a feeling I'll know real quick-like when it's done. Dismissed!"

Cerata knew Krieger was serious and got a major pit in his stomach, because what he was asking was just pure evil, and he knew he had to carry it out exactly as Krieger laid it out or he'd be the next one swinging from a pine tree. The mob did some bad things in its day, but it seemed like child's play compared with what was about to happen. This was much more than tuning a guy up by smashing his hand with a hammer, or even taking a guy out from time to time and stealing his cannoli. Although he couldn't employ an argument of moral equivalence here, Krieger's was a scorched-earth policy like none Cerata had ever seen. He knew Krieger was crazy, but he also knew this plan would work.

Cerata composed himself in an effort to hide his nervousness from Krieger. He knew what to do and he was going to use his normal brigade, minus the dumbass who started the Charles Jackson incident. "Yes, sir. I'm on it!" Cerata said with a half-Nazi salute as he spun on his boot heels to walk out the door.

"Cut that shit out!" Krieger said. "I'm not a godamn Nazi. I'm a businessman."

"Keep telling yourself that," Cerata said under his breath.

# Chapter 28

## Cerata

Master Mario Cerata began his career as a mob heavy when he was very young. Despite his loyalty and acumen, he was never a *made* man, probably because of his light brown, wavy, wiry hair, and the bright hazel eyes that belied his true Italian-German heritage. The fact that he was not *made*, however, was probably what saved him and allowed him to slip under the feds' radar. After the mob takedowns in the late '80s, he had to earn a living and his skillset was unique and very specialized. Choices were few, and everywhere he looked he was surrounded by amateurs and wannabes. Nothing could match the mob in terms of its power, strength, and cohesiveness through the various families, which had their own specialties, ranging from whores, horses, dogs, chickens, cards, and cocaine. Then, Kuwait was invaded, so Cerata enlisted in the Army and spent five years in the desert, only to return to an uncertain future of journeyman jobs. He drifted from town to town, and while he was not homeless, per se, he wasn't settled, either.

As a returning vet, Cerata didn't exactly have the warmest of receptions. When he came home from Desert Storm—despite the "support the vets" crap broadcast all over TV, yellow ribbons tied to trees and utility poles, and welcome committees at airports and bus stations—he soon found himself alone and estranged from society the minute he collected his luggage from baggage claim. That national *support* lasted all of fifteen minutes in the country's Zeit Geist before the media eventually moved on to other news cycles, from terrorist attacks to panytless Hollywood starlets titillating the paparazzi with wardrobe malfunctions while stepping out of their Porsches and limos.

The military world quickly gave way to the real one; housing was unaffordable for many, jobs were scarce, and family relationships were often strained due to the ever-present fog of war. Incidents of domestic violence increased, as did the rate of suicides. Despite the various laws dating back to 1865 designed to help vets assimilate back into society, jobs still were few and far between. Employers didn't want to hire the new generation of returning soldiers for fear that some vet with PTSD would *go postal* and shoot up a store full of customers. Unfortunately, some things never changed, and the real national shame was, sadly, that local military facilities were ill-equipped to handle the mental needs of returning warriors who sacrificed so much, yet received so little in return. Cerata was no exception.

Eventually, he was recruited by Robertsen and found a home in the UAK. Cerata came in as a mid-level Sergeant and quickly rose to Master. At the time, the UAK was in the midst of its change in leadership. It was very disorganized and undisciplined, so any improvement at all would be noticed, and it didn't take long for Cerata to become a rising star. He saw an opportunity and quickly formed several platoons within Alpha division, each with distinct missions that were unknown to the others. Compartmentalizing them into smaller groups made them easier to manage and provided a sense of mystery. It was Cerata who came up with the idea of the drop box brigades after a few collections went wrong, the Charles Jackson incident being the biggest fiasco.

He brought the confidence, organization, and discipline that the military had drilled into him during his Army days. The intimidation skills he learned while busting knees for the mob on the wharfs off Tchoupitoulas Street was second nature to him. This Natchez thing, though, was a few steps above concrete shoes and broken legs, and exceeded the violence he'd observed during his mob days by tenfold. It was also far beyond the pale of anything he ever saw while getting shot at in the desert.

The divisions operated just as the mob families did. It was simple business planning and the same structure was used. The methods and unifying message instilled within the rank and file, however, was quite different. Instead of tough guys in shiny suits with cheesy gold chains and diamond-studded watches driving Lincolns and Caddys listening to Sinatra, he dealt with greasy, tattooed rednecks wearing wifebeaters and driving old Chevy S-10 pickups with Confederate flag bumper stickers. Beer cans in the bed and a little Hank blaring out the windows topped off the stereotype. Cerata looked beyond the appearances, something he learned to do in the Army. The Swamp's Troops all had the same tactical training, a discipline that the mob lacked. Consistency was the key to mitigating risk and avoiding errors. Cerata's focus was on one's abilities, and with a little field training in the piney woods, complete with makeshift urban street settings mirroring those of the French Quarter, the Troops quickly learned to act as a cohesive unit while on drop box runs. One would be a fool to think that these guys weren't every bit as dangerous as a mob man. In fact, they were more dangerous, because it wasn't just money and power that fueled the base of the UAK. It was an ideology, something that, while not shared by

Robertsen, Krieger, and Cerata, was encouraged as a means to maintain focus.

After David Duke's failed gubernatorial run in 1991, which was supported by several white pride groups in the eastern part of Louisiana and even some of the surrounding states, the timing was right for someone to take up the mantle that had slipped through Duke's fingers. While he could rally thousands for his cause, his defeat resulted in groups scattering to the four corners with no clear leader. Cerata recognized that ideology could be more powerful than simply peddling drugs and extorting money, and he saw why the Leadership chose the UAK; its historical convictions, tired membership, proximity to the city, and logistical ease would allow for rapid expansion throughout the I-10 corridor.

Rallying the right people around the right *cause* made the UAK an unstoppable force. Skilled players were also needed, and Robertsen's new recruits would need to assimilate quickly. The risk was two-fold: one, becoming tainted with the white supremacist movement and falling out of favor with genteel society, and two, going native and buying into the sick ideology.

Personally, Cerata could deal with the societal aspect and knew that he'd never get a real job again. He also was strong enough to maintain his own principles that, while questionable, were not based on the color of one's skin. His military experience would serve him well in this regard. Everyone had worn the same green, bled the same red, and saluted the same flag. He'd have no reason to hate, which made it much easier for him to put on a show and convince the others that he was one of them.

# Chapter 29

### Rachel Borrows Prudence

"Jimmy, do you think I could borrow Prudence for a new file?" asked Rachel. "This one requires some explanation, so I'll need her for a couple of hours initially. I can't just drop this one on her desk."

"Do I really have a choice?" asked Jimmy with a clenched jaw and a smirk. His head was slightly turned to evoke a hint of equal parts sarcasm and frustration.

"No, you really don't," replied Rachel, who immediately realized how bitchy she came across. "Sorry, I didn't mean to sound like *that*. Oscar just dropped this on BB, who just dropped it on me, and he wants me to use paralegals to do the grunt work. I don't even know what this is about, other than it being a real estate matter. I haven't read the files and I know BB hasn't, because he told me they are with Bernadette. All the paralegals are tied up, and I think this is a great opportunity for Prudence to build on her recent real estate experience. Besides, this one involves municipal bureaucracy and permits. She's proven herself to be good with people and can navigate those waters better than asshole associates—present company excepted, of course—and grizzled, cynical paralegals."

"Okay," relented Jimmy. "I'll send her over first thing tomorrow morning."

Rachel began to walk away and paused to say, "Thanks, Jimmy. I owe you one."

"You bet your sweet ass you owe me one," Jimmy said under his breath, but within earshot of Rachel.

She indeed heard Jimmy and made a slight stutter step, but then continued down the hall with the makings of a wry smile on her face.

With that stutter step, Jimmy immediately knew Rachel had heard him. Even though he had a secret schoolboy crush on the slightly older woman, Jimmy immediately regretted what he'd done. *The cat's out of the bag now, ol' Jimmeroo. I guess we'll see whether she'll ever fess up to hearing it.*

Just when he was finding a groove with Prudence in the pro bono section, Rachel threw him off track. He felt this temporary derailment would escalate and not be temporary at all when all was said and done. Once Rachel got her talons into something, she never let go. This was why she was so successful. Jimmy was merely a junior associate, after all, and he knew Rachel would likely pull Prudence into her group before too long.

First thing the next morning, Rachel gave Prudence a summary of the matter and told her the files were in Oscar's office. Prudence walked somewhat timidly down the Hall, realizing that this would be a high-profile assignment. She didn't know why, but she felt a little intimidated. Bernadette was on the phone, but gave Prudence a quick nod and a smile, then motioned for her to go into Oscar's office. Prudence walked in and didn't see Oscar, so she assumed he had not yet arrived at the office. She walked over to his immaculate desk and picked up the stack of files.

As she exited Valhalla, she waved to Bernadette, who was still on the phone. Seeing Bernadette's reassuring smile gave Prudence a quick boost and a new sense of self-importance. She beamed as she walked through the Coast and smiled at the partners as she passed their offices. A few returned the smile, but most were glued to their computer screens, as if in a trance. At the same time, she was a little overwhelmed, because she would have to go through the stack, copy the files, and organize them to be able to make sense of her task.

It was the little things that worried her. Would she remember to put the papers back in the exact order after copying them? Would she remember to look at the front and back of each page? Would she remember to input the right client case number into the copier so the billing would be accurate? At $.20 per page, she thought it was a little extravagant, and perhaps an unfair charge, but when she thought about her task, she realized that it was a reasonable charge given that she could not highlight pages or make margin notes on original file documents.

Prudence was quickly learning that there was a lot about law firms and their billing practices that appeared to be nickel-and-diming clients, and charging for copies was one of them. Paper and toner weren't cheap, and files often filled several boxes or even filing cabinets. A major arbitration could take up an entire floor. Billing for copies not only recovered a hard cost, but also ensured that expenses were allocated to associates and partners proportionately, therefore minimizing waste. It was also a great way to identify abusers.

Many clients, however, bristled at these types of *internal* costs and considered them part of the cost of doing business, as was the case in their own companies. A contractor wouldn't charge a customer for copies made during the course of a project, so why should a law firm be any different? Clients also disliked that the partners used their files as training exercises and charged associates' time when they were essentially just suits in a room observing the partners in action. Most clients thought training was just another cost of doing business. The optics in using paralegals was more palatable, however, because the firm could be viewed as minimizing costs by using employees that came with cheaper hourly rates. The reality, however, was that paralegals often billed far more hours than the associates, thereby costing clients more money, not less.

Optics were everything in the corporate world, and law firms could play the game just as well as any Fortune 500 monster. Most offensive, however, was the use of internal meetings as a means to pound the file. For instance, if a partner in the real estate section had a specific question on an environmental matter, it was expected that he or she would briefly consult for a half hour or so with the partner or an associate that was a subject matter expert. Clients thought such a brief consultation was merely transferring the firm's tribal knowledge, and therefore something that should be included in the partners' $700 hourly rate, which was the inherent benefit of using a large firm rather than a boutique firm of lawyers who all had a similar practice. For matters requiring a substantial amount of time, however, clients accepted that partners would consult with each other on a regular basis, provided the client was informed in advance.

This heads-up was crucial for in-house counsel who not only decided which firm handled a particular matter, but also held to budget estimates so that the finance department could set the proper reserve in order for monthly cash flow estimates to meet Wall Street's expectations. Optics. Fuzzy math. Without in-house counsel's insight and knowledge of the business, and more importantly its strategy, a firm easily could go down a rabbit hole that had nothing to do with the real issue, thereby making the exercise take longer, be more expensive, and needlessly frustrate the business operations.

# Chapter 30

## The Renaissance

Once she was settled back in the Bullpen, it wasn't long before Prudence realized that there were different colored files in the stack she took from Oscar's office. She wondered why, then quickly made sense of them. The normal pale green folders were labeled and numbered, so they were obviously part of the firm's filing system. The light blue folders were void of labels and carried a prominent stamp: **"PERSONAL AND CONFIDENTIAL—OSCAR BRIMLEY."**

Prudence copied the files and quickly returned the stack to Oscar's office in the hopes that he wouldn't notice they were even gone. She hastily reconstructed the series of events in her mind. Bernadette was distracted by a phone call and waved her in, thinking Oscar would give her the files. Oscar wasn't there, so she picked up the only stack on his desk, assuming it was for her. Quite simple: cut and dry.

What Prudence did not see, however, was that, unbeknownst to Bernadette, Oscar was in his private bathroom at the time Prudence walked in. Oscar didn't see Bernadette combine the files into a single stack earlier that morning, and he didn't know Prudence went into his office and removed the files. When Oscar exited the bathroom with a fresh, bright white shirt and yellow paisley power tie, he strolled swiftly through his office, grabbed his briefcase, and passed Bernadette, still on her call. He gave her a quick head nod and smile as he walked down the Coast. Oscar was in a hurry for a client meeting with Robertsen and Falke, and thought he'd put the files in his briefcase. He didn't notice the stack was no longer on his desk when he left.

While Prudence had once beamed with pride and bounced down the Hall on her way from Oscar's office down to the copy room, she now had a pit in her stomach the size of a Creole tomato. She crept her way back to Valhalla, hoping no one would notice her. Fortunately, Oscar was still in his client meeting and Bernadette was at lunch, so Prudence carefully returned the stack of files to its original place.

It was a strategy meeting. The U.S. Department of Interior was withholding its approval for the destruction of a historic building that was due to be razed and replaced with a small multiuse hotel meeting center ironically named Renaissance d'Orleans. It was to be the cornerstone of Project Azalea. Oscar and Robertsen knew what had to happen, however, they were unsure as to what they needed in order to accomplish the task. It was one thing to buy crooked state and local politicians, but Oscar's self-imposed rule was that the feds were off-limits. Robertsen agreed with and respected this rule, so it was decided that Oscar would use a city councilman as a proxy to convince the feds that the historical significance of this particular property, located in the Faubourg Marigny and far away from the slave trading houses, would not be erased from history.

The property originally acted as a holding pen for slaves, most of whom were sick from the voyage from Africa. The newly arrived chattel needed to be medically evaluated and quarantined, lest they infect everyone at the auctions or in their new *homes* in one of the many plantations in the Deep South. Thirty years ago, it would have been unheard of to destroy such a building, but in the early 2000s, there was a burgeoning movement to erase signs of the Confederacy. This gradual eradication movement entailed renaming schools and streets named after slave owners and reducing the number of *offensive* buildings throughout the city. However, the historically significant buildings in the Quarter were allowed to remain as tourist sites.

The irony, however, was that places like the holding pens that were sprinkled throughout the city were good tools for the professional race-baiters to keep the coals hot and ready for the next Rodney King beating. Police brutality often served as an easy billow to fan those flames.

These signs of the past also helped provide the proper amount of *schadenfreude* that the politically correct establishment wished to propagate throughout the city, lest people forget its dark history.

It was a dynamic used throughout the country. Progressives came to the aid of the *oppressed,* who could be a criminal refusing to comply with legitimate orders. Pick a target (the police), freeze and isolate the issue (gin up emotions in a neighborhood or downtown business center), personalize it (the innocent teenager being beaten by the police), and polarize people (march through the streets, break a few windows, steal a few TVs, and throw rocks at the police for the national cameras). The race-baiters sat back and gleefully watched the carnage while they waited for those federal dollars to roll in: Department of Justice investigations of police department protocols and sensitivity training. The *coup de grâce* would be putting cops on trial for doing their jobs. Some had to leave the force or move from the state after their inevitable acquittal.

The sad truth was that the families of the fallen, the rioters, march-ers, and those with the bullhorns, were merely cogs in a sick process to which they were blind. Wash, rinse, repeat for the next news cycle: a few weeks on the East Coast, months of silence, then another upris-ing, maybe next time in the Midwest. The reality, however, was that the same sixteen-year-old punk in the projects who stole a purse con-taining a few credit cards and a couple of hundred bucks would get a good beatdown by New Orleans' finest and an unusually long pris-on sentence, while an *upstanding* government official who redirected millions to his cronies would not only escape prison, but most likely would be reelected and hailed a civic hero.

Methods employed by the national race hucksters were one thing. In Louisiana, politics, not race-fueled civil disobedience, was the game and the black vote was a necessary *bloc vote* for the Democrats, who used the vote to keep their own in office and keep state funds flowing into specific areas in the name of education and programs intended to help the disenfranchised get their *fair share*. Huey Long-style social-ism had been in place in one form or another since the 1920s, long be-fore it became chic with the Ivy League intelligentsia. "A car in every garage and a chicken in every pot" was the message, and who wouldn't want that? It was a message and a method Republicans never figured out. Their mantra of "lower taxes and smaller government" fell on the deaf ears of those who were too poor to pay taxes and who needed the government to help them with the basics in life, such as education, food, and housing.

In more recent times, the occasional governor of the great state of Louisiana, Edwin Edwards, furthered that cause until his unceremoni-ous fall from grace. The more the vestiges of the past disappeared, the less disenfranchised and oppressed the local blocs would feel, and be-fore long, they would splinter. The race hucksters would lose credibility since the desired answer to their message of oppression would be that race relations were actually improving. The prospects of jobs based on merit would supplant the message of entitlement, which was at the crux of their agenda. The unintended consequence of this political movement, coupled with increasing gentrification, would splinter the bloc even further, rendering it impotent and thereby calling to a halt decades of government intrusion and dependence.

It was, indeed, the right time to speed up the execution of Project Azalea. The pendulum was swinging ever so slowly; upscale businesses were moving in and hundreds of menial jobs were being created and filled by those who, ironically, were pushed out of their homes because of rising property value. More tax dollars meant more money for the real crooks: the new breed of politicians who were eager to spend government dollars for their own purposes. Yet another irony was that, where once poor people lived in the city and lapped up entitlement programs that encouraged many to sit at home rather than work, those same people were being pushed out, only to have to come back into the city for their dead-end nine-to-fives.

# Chapter 31

## Permitting

When Oscar returned to his office after the meeting with Robertsen, he saw the stack of files on his desk and wondered how he could have missed it on his way out. He attributed this oversight to old age, coupled with anxiety over the issues at hand. It would take a few thousand dollars and perhaps a hunting trip, but the anxiety would eventually disappear. The challenge, however, was determining whose pockets to fill.

For Oscar, the permitting for the Renaissance d'Orleans was the most crucial part of Project Azalea. This particular property offered easy ingress and egress from an accessible two-way street, which fed directly onto I-10—perfect for travelers who wanted to get to their beds quickly, whether from a long day of travel or because they were fleeing from the land time forgot in time to catch that last flight out of Louis Armstrong Airport. The split was fair. Robertsen and Falke would take the hotel, retail, and lobby bar revenue, while Oscar would have the restaurant and outrageously priced parking proceeds, all of which would flow through different shell corporations that Oscar's firm would set up.

None of this would happen, however, unless the permit was granted in time for the beginning of construction, which had to be substantially completed by the beginning of the next fall's tourist season, with the remainder being ready to host springtime conventions. Permitting fell under BB's real estate section, and since his bonus was pegged against the success of the opening, he was highly incentivized to ensure things went smoothly. BB was kept in the dark and oblivious to the backstory. All he knew was that the justification summary for the permit needed to be as tight as possible, which was why he put his best gal, Rachel, on the file. Rachel, in turn, drafted Prudence, who, at about that time, was feeling quite overwhelmed.

Prudence possessed information she probably shouldn't have, but she didn't know if BB or even Rachel knew what was in Oscar's personal files. She had to operate on the assumption that they didn't know, and the hope that Oscar didn't notice anything out of place after he returned from his meeting with Falke. She was petrified, and would need to proceed cautiously until she could determine who she could trust. In the meantime, the file copies would be stowed at home under lock and key.

# Chapter 32

## Updating the Antioch

"C'mon, boy," Theo called out to Japonica. "We're going to be late and Reverend Drummond is counting on us. I have to paint some walls and you need to look pretty and be a distraction for the after-school crowd."

Japonica picked up the pace with more panting and faster tail-wagging, his old bones heeding the call of duty. He loved these days when he was the center of attention. It sure beat staying cooped up all day waiting for Theo to come home. He felt a new sense of purpose, as did Theo, who was impressing Reverend Drummond daily with his handyman skills and commitment to serve the community.

The Antioch had shown its age for quite some time; peeling paint covered the walls, and an old squeaky air conditioner was limping along through another hot spring and would soon face the ferocity of the brutal Louisiana summer. The water heater provided only tepid water at intermittent pressure, and a gas stovetop in the community center was seemingly haunted and often turned itself off and on with no cook in the kitchen. Serendipity came in the form of a strong boy helping an ol' preacher man fix up a tired church while a dog-turned-babysitter captivated the attention of the little ones, whose stomachs often growled and whose souls needed uplifting.

Reverend Drummond saw Theo and Japonica coming down the sidewalk. "Theo, thanks for coming by. How are you doing today?"

"Mildewing, reverend! Get it, mildeeewwing?"

"That's a good one, Theo. I needed a little humor today! Speaking of mildew, please make sure when you prep the walls for painting that you wipe them down real good. That one over there is gonna need a second coat. Also, be sure to scrape more of that old paint off first. Otherwise, the new paint won't stick like it's supposed to."

Theo didn't have much experience as a painter, but what he lacked in experience was overshadowed by his enthusiasm and coupled with the fact that he was a quick study. "Okay, reverend, consider it done."

The extra step meant that Theo would fall short of his goal of painting the last two walls. He would've rather gotten it done right than quickly, and even though he would fall short of one goal, he was proud of the work he did. A painter never knew when to stop, though, so the end of the day was usually signaled by Japonica, who would saunter over with a stiffer gait and a little lick that told Theo that it was time to go home for his evening feeding. Playing with the kids was great, but some were a little too rough for his old bones. Dogs craved routine, and Japonica was no exception; dinner was at six o'clock.

When they got home, Theo looked around and thought that Mamaw's house could use some fixin' up, too, but that would have to wait. Keeping his commitment to Reverend Drummond was more important than throwing a fresh coat of paint on the porch walls. He would need to fix that screen door soon, because with his new purpose, Japonica was used to exercise and he was going through that hole in the screen with increased frequency. He usually headed down to Chookie's house for a pat on the head and a scratch behind the ears. He never left the neighborhood, but often stayed out later than Theo liked. Besides, Prudence didn't want Theo on the streets looking for him after dark. The rule was: when the streetlights came on, it was time to go home. Not only was it safer, but Theo often had to stay up later these days to study and complete homework, something he used to slough off—hence the historically bad grades.

Working at the Antioch turned that tide. His grades improved. There were fewer beatings by bigots, and Reverend Drummond was now a positive male figure in his life, just as he was in his mother's. Theo felt like a new man and finally knew what happiness felt like. Prudence was filled with both relief and pride, because the goal of every mother was to ensure that home was a happy and safe place. She also was anxious that her new job seemed to be taking away too much time from Theo.

"Hi, Mom," Theo said with a smile while bouncing into the kitchen just off the porch, Japonica in tow by his side. "How was your day?"

"Just fine, sweetie." But Theo could tell that something was on her mind. Prudence sensed this, so she gathered herself. "I got a new file today. A client wants to tear down a building and replace it with a newer one. I'm excited, because I get to learn a little more about how real people, not politicians, make the government work."

"Yippee," said Theo twirling his finger in the air with an eye roll punctuating a feigned, sarcastic happiness. "How exciting."

"Well, I'll have you know, mister, that getting a permit isn't just filling out a form and bringing a check to city hall. You must build a case justifying *why* you want the permit, and then you have to show *how* you will use the property. I'm not doing that just yet, but I'm reading some older files to get a sense of how to write these things. This new file will be my first," Prudence said with a forced smile.

"Wow, that is kinda cool, Mom," Theo said with all hints of sarcasm now gone.

"So, sweetie, tell me about your day," replied Prudence in a happier tone.

"Well, Japonica got to play with a new kid today. The kid was *special needs*. He had Down syndrome, or something like that. Some of the kids teased him, but most just ignored him. Japonica moseyed over and sat down right beside him. The kid started petting him and his face lit up like a Christmas tree. I also learned that sometimes you have to paint a wall twice in order to get the right color. We're changing the color in the church office from that off-color royal blue to a more—what was that color? Oh, yeah, eggshell white or something like that. Some of the office ladies said *earth tones* were more pleasing to the eye, and as one put it, 'created a better ambience in which to work.' I actually had to look that one up, ambience."

"And school? How'd that go? Things better on that front?" Prudence asked as if she hadn't spoken to her boy in ages, which wasn't far from the truth.

"Yes, ma'am. I thought I was in trouble because my science teacher held me after class. He told me that I must be studying harder, because I turned my C into a B+. Now the other kids hate me," Theo said with a slight drop in his voice.

"Oh, sweetie, they don't hate you. They're just jealous. Some of those kids don't have the benefits you do, and when they see you having some success it reminds them of that. It should act as an incentive for them to do better themselves, but it's easier to be jealous than to study more."

Theo thought his mom was probably right, so he finished his homework and went straight on to bed. Tomorrow would be a busy day, beginning with a morning math test and ending with the last coat of paint drying on those last two walls in the office at the Antioch. Japonica took his cue from Theo, retreated to his space, and curled up on his favorite blanket between Mamaw's chair and the couch. Soon, the only sounds in the house were those of the crickets and cicadas outside conducting their evening symphony, accented by an alley cat singing on top of a fence somewhere in the neighborhood. Theo loved this quiet little neighborhood, and with all of the upheaval in his early childhood, Mamaw's house really felt like home. Sleep came quickly that night, and the next school day flew. Before he knew it, Theo had a scraper back in his hand, chipping old paint away.

# Chapter 33

## Eye for an Eye

"That's the one," Tyler Elgin Loomis assured his cousin, Earl Patrick Tyler. "That high-yeller bastard who knocked my front tooth out and busted my eye. And see that? Over there? That's his soon-to-be scalded-ass mutt."

Earl peered through his binoculars from across Airline Highway from a corner gas station. As a rising star in the UAK, Earl was usually first in line to get the latest military grade equipment. Surveilling Theo was good target practice. "Him?!" said Earl, chuckling. "That scrawny little bastard whipped your big, doughy white ass?!"

"C'mon, ET, you know as good as anyone that if you're caught off guard and knocked off-balance, and the guy you're fightin' is madder 'n hell, he can get you in one of them MMA holds and just wail on you 'til his hands break. And it didn't help none that those useless, sumbitch, so-called *friends* of mine just stood there and didn't kick Mr. High-yeller's ass, or at least drag him off me."

"MMA hold? Wailing 'til his hands break? That scrawny half-breed probably can't even spell MMA, much less put someone in a tag-out hold. And how could he bust his hand punching you? His fist would just disappear. Like punching a marshmallow!" Earl howled with laughter.

"Cut it out, ET," said Tyler with a trace of embarrassed anger.

Earl, sensing he might have pushed it a little too far, toned it down. "How many live in the house?" His focus turned back toward the house. "We want to make sure we eliminate all targets," he continued, thinking military lingo would impress his little cousin.

"I think it's just him and his mothah. I know it's his grandma's house, and I think she died sometime last year," replied Tyler. "The irony is I think his mom is the one that they talk about passin' around about sixteen years ago during some gang initiation ceremony. Matter of fact, I think it was in that new neighborhood right over there. Is that true, Earl? Ha! Ya think they knocked her up and young Theo come from that night?" Tyler laughed, slapping him on the back.

Earl kept his gaze on the target and ignored his cousin. He pulled back from the binoculars and turned toward Tyler. With a wry grin that exposed his Copenhagen-brown teeth he said, "Well, little cuz, they're not going to know what hit them when we start, and we ain't gonna finish until the dirty deed is done. Word has it that Krieger is gettin' ready to take a bunch of gangbangers over to Natchez and is gonna hang one of them, old school. That last tourist shootin' has got everyone madder 'n hell so, as Krieger puts it, an example must be made. Boy, I'd love to be part of that one."

But that was just ET spouting off. In reality, Earl would be scared to death if he were asked to saddle up for a job like that. He just liked to talk tough. He wasn't against getting some experience in the name of training and retribution for his little cousin, though. This would be easy, he thought. No gangbangers would come looking for him. No one would even see him. Swoop in an hour before daybreak, torch the house, and head back to the Northshore in time to meet the others before sunlight when they would receive the order of the day. None would be the wiser. The perfect plan! Perfect plans, however, often were betrayed by inexperience, poor execution, and frayed loose ends.

# Chapter 34

## Miss St. Louis

"Now ya know I can't do that Oscar. She's a fed," said Councilman Clayton Hébert. "She was just transferred from St. Louis and doesn't know a damn thing about how things work around here."

"Well, then," Oscar said slowly, with his jaw set for emphasis and giving Clayton a slight jab in the chest with his index finger. "I guess you'll just have to teach her now, won't you? You still have that girl in your office? Lauryl?"

"You mean Lorna? Yes, Lorna's still with us," said Clayton.

"If you want to make sure Mrs. Hébert doesn't find out how *with* you Lorna still is, you better find a way to get this done!" Oscar said, pulling out all the stops.

"Goddamnit, Oscar! That's bush league. Pure chicken shit. I wouldn't think even you would go *that* low," Clayton said nervously.

"Relax," said Oscar, "I just wanted to impress upon you how serious this is. The firm will increase its donation to your campaign fund, and you see to it that Miss St. Louis is dazzled. Convince her that razing this eyesore is good for the city, good for the country. It's in your district, right? Get your Loyola history buddies to craft some type of credible story that maybe taking a door or a wall from the building, along with some artifacts, and putting them on display in the Cabildo gives it an even greater historical significance. More people would see it that way, than if it's kept in its original site. We'll incorporate the story in our justification summation so it's part of the public record. We'll put a plaque of recognition on the wall with your name. Everybody wins." Oscar continued, his voice rising in desperation. "Tell her we can take pieces of it and hang them on the wall in the restaurant or over the bar. We could display some smaller items in glass cases throughout the lobby. Tell her we'll name the goddamn restaurant after the building or whatever she wants it to be called. Tell her whatever the hell you want, just tell her to approve the damn permit and approve it fast!"

Oscar prided himself on being a fast thinker who could come up with grand schemes on the spot. He decided to raise the stakes.

"Tell you what, Clay," he said in a more collected way. "In addition to taking care of the *welcome to New Orleans* expenses through campaign contributions, I'll float an idea to my client. I think you could blow Miss St. Louis away by telling her that there's a move afoot to establish a new black history museum in the city within walking distance of the property. We could call it the slavery museum, or some other crap. I think I could get my clients to prime the pump with a $1 million initial donation, and they would match private donations up to another two million payable over the next five years. That's five million dollars, Clay. It would all be done on an anonymous basis, because trust me, you wouldn't want your fingerprints on the funding aspect. Then, you can tell Miss St. Louis that she should apply for federal dollars through some kind of grant. Feds love throwing money around and she'd be seen as a hero, especially for such a *progressive* cause.

"You could make as much noise about this as you want to and get out in front of it. This could set you up for a senate run. When's Charbonnet's term up? Three years? You run for your council seat next year, see this project through until construction is complete, and a few months after the dedication ceremony we can get the opening of the museum to coincide with your announcement of the senate run. Make a big splash. Construction of the hotel will be complete, so you can make the announcement at your campaign kickoff party at the Renaissance d'Orleans, and everyone wins. Miss St. Louis comes roaring into town with new goodies waiting for her, you move up the political ladder, the Renaissance will get some free press and some of its money back, and I'll get my very own senator, so I won't have to build museums next time I need something done on the federal level. It's perfect for you, Clay, because you don't even have to resign from your council seat in the unlikely event that you lose." Then, in a power move that only Oscar Brimley could make, he held Clayton's gaze for what seemed like an eternity, leaned over his shoulder, and whispered in the politician's ear. "If you help me, I'll see to it that you become the most powerful politician this state has ever seen. If you don't, you'll never hold public office again. In fact, the only thing you'd be able to do is to sit in your six by eight cell for fifteen years and think back on this very day and what might have been."

Councilman Hébert pulled back suddenly in horror and disbelief and looked at Oscar as if he were the devil himself, but with icy blue eyes that cut like a dagger instead of horns and a pitchfork. He stammered, "You wouldn't dare—"

Oscar cut him off and in an eerily calm manner stated, "Oh, wouldn't I, Clayton? Not only do you know that I would, you know that I can. And if you didn't know by now that I would or could do something like this, then you are as naïve as you look. And as you go through your feeble-minded thought process, there's something else that you should know about me if you hadn't already figured it out. I...do...not...bluff."

Clayton's knees were about to buckle, and his head was spinning much like Prudence's did when Oscar brought her into the firm.

"Those were some damn good ideas, Clay. I suggest you give me your answer right now before I look around for another councilman, because there are plenty of you worthless peckerheads to choose from."

"Hold on now. You're right, Oscar. Those are some great ideas, and I could probably go in with that and might not even have to put any hard money in her pocket. Her name is Diane Rosenberg. I think she's one of those liberal Ivy League altruists. Maybe a few political dinners at Galatoire's or Commander's Palace, introduce her to a few celebrities or athletes, go to a few campaign events at the Saenger. I can get her on the Historic District Landmarks Commission. She probably doesn't make a lot of money, so if we can't give her cash, we could give her a good lifestyle, make her look good at work, tug on the heartstrings a little. Find her a new boyfriend or girlfriend. I know she's not married, but I don't know what team she plays for. Yes, I can work with that," Clayton said, head down, scratching his chin, wheels still spinning.

Oscar had the authority and knew Falke would be good for the three million if it meant getting this project back on track. Spread out over a few years, it wouldn't even be a drop in the bucket.

# Chapter 35

## A Celebration Premature

Oscar had assured Robertsen that the permitting for the Renaissance would take less than a month. To hit the ground running, Oscar's commercial transactions team had already prepared and issued RFQs from the state's leading contractors. Rachel and Prudence did a magnificent job on the permit application, and Oscar was just giddy. With some hard work by Prudence and his schmoozing of some fine folks down at New Orleans City Hall, the permit was approved in record time and with the strong recommendation from Diane Rosenberg (aka Miss St. Louis). She was moved by the historical preservation story Oscar's Loyola team created. BB's team did a masterful job of crafting the rationale for tearing down an eyesore and replacing it with new construction for a business, which translated into jobs. She was also quite pleased that its history would be prominently showcased and preserved at both at the construction site and the Cabildo, the site of the transfer of the Louisiana Purchase in 1803. Prudence was proud,

Rachel beamed, BB saw a superstar in the making, and Oscar was ec-static. And, except for the esteemed Councilman Clayton Hébert, no one knew this was Oscar's baby from stem to stern. The glory was all Mr. Hébert's, and Oscar maintained his mantle as kingmaker.

Oscar called the team into Valhalla. "Okay, guys and girls, get your finest ready for tomorrow night and join me for a project kick-off dinner at Bene Cucina and mandatory nightcaps at the Carousel Bar in The Monteleone. BB's made all the arrangements and the chef has a special French/Italian wine pairing menu for us straight out of her new cookbook; a signed copy will be at your seat. Only one guest each since we have limited space. For those of you who hav-en't been, Cucina's is the latest Gulf Coast/Italian fusion restaurant and it is fantastic. This may seem like we're getting a little ahead of ourselves, and I'd normally wait and have this type of celebration *after* the project has concluded, but this is extremely important for one of our biggest clients, so I thought it best that we get together and get this project started on the right foot."

Oscar was giddy because he knew the fix was in, and the granting of the permit was just the start. After all, it was his project, too, and his unsuspecting team was making his retirement dreams become a closer reality.

The office was abuzz, and all eyes would be on Prudence for the foreseeable future. Prudence, however, did not feel comfortable with the unwanted scrutiny that would follow her around, especially in the wake of her having found Oscar's files.

She was amazed at how quickly fortunes turned. One day she was filling tea glasses, and almost the next she was invited to dine at one of New Orleans' finest restaurants with tuxedoed servers waiting on *her* hand and foot, filling *her* glass with tea. While her wardrobe had improved a bit, her social life had not, and she couldn't think of anyone to bring to the dinner. Jimmy would probably not be comfortable since he wasn't in the real estate or commercial transactions sections. In fact, Jimmy was still finding his way in the firm and had recently been sort of a free agent floating in and out of different groups for smaller projects and managing the pro bono section. He wasn't pigeonholed into a certain group and he enjoyed the variety, but he was afraid he wouldn't be able to get traction and get into a department where there would be relative security. Associates like Jimmy needed the backing of a department in order to get more files and be part of a *special* bonus pool, one in which free agents never get to swim.

A work dinner wasn't the kind of event she could invite Reverend Drummond to, either. Besides, he probably wouldn't accept the invitation. And, it just wasn't the right place for Theo, who had homework anyway, not to mention the fact that he was a minor and there would no doubt be copious libations served with a side of colorful language. Prudence didn't approve of that, either, but rather tolerated it in the interest of her new career.

She decided to go alone, show up right after cocktails and stay through dessert. For comfort, she'd make sure to try to sit next to Rachel or Bernadette. As fate would have it, there was an empty seat next to Bernadette near the end of the table, whereas Rachel was sitting at the head. Rachel was dressed to the nines in a beautiful, very low-cut, cobalt blue cocktail dress, adorned with a ruby bracelet, pearl earrings, and a modest gold necklace with an emerald teardrop pendant that fell softly just above her cleavage. She wasn't as well-endowed as some of the surgically enhanced guests at the table, but she was stunning, and all eyes were on her. It cut against the grain of fashion to wear rubies, pearls, and emeralds in the same ensemble, but Rachel had her own style and pulled the look off with ease.

BB felt somewhat slighted over not being asked to sit at the other end of the table, but he knew Rachel deserved her day in the sun. His ego was somewhat soothed, because he and wifey number two were seated next to Oscar and a thoroughly bored Mrs. Brimley.

Bernadette didn't bring a guest either. So, she and Prudence chatted throughout the evening and learned more about each other. They were developing a closer relationship, more of a friendship, which was sometimes not the wisest thing to do in the workplace—especially with someone like Bernadette, who wielded a lot of power and influence. Still, they had a lot in common. Like Prudence, Bernadette was a single mother who started bussing tables through college and eventually worked her way up to a legal secretary position. Her kids were long gone and had their own families, so work was all Bernadette had at the moment. She had worked with Oscar for more than fifteen years and couldn't see herself anywhere else. She knew Oscar was nearing retirement, albeit an early one for an attorney his age, and pondered her next move in life. Gerard J. Talbot III, Esq., was the heir apparent to Oscar, and he had his own staff that he would likely keep with him. When the time came, Bernadette said she would prefer to hang on to her office through the transition, but she wouldn't be in a position to retire for several years—long after Oscar left. Oscar made it known that Bernadette would always have a job at the firm, but she didn't want to work for the other partners. Not only did she not like them, but working at that level might be viewed by some as a demotion, even though she would be the highest paid secretary in the firm.

Normally, when lawyers moved through the ranks within the firm, they were required to use the support staff of the lawyer that preceded them. This made sense to some degree, because it ensured continuity for some of the case files the attorney would be inheriting. However, it could often be disruptive. Just like any other company, a law firm could be destroyed by office politics, so everyone did their best to keep the peace out of fear that Oscar would run someone off for not being a team player.

Every legal secretary wanted to support the most senior lawyer, and because Gerard made it known that he was going to bring his secretary with him, it didn't look like there would be available office space for Bernadette after the transition, unless another senior-level secretary spot opened up. She pondered approaching Jimmy about supporting the pro bono section and convinced herself that this would not be viewed as a move down, just a different move altogether—a good move. She would be the top dog of the section and she already had the respect of most within the Clinic. It would be a nice change of pace, getting to learn about real people and their problems. Also, the thought of working closer to Prudence was quite attractive.

She thought about discussing this with Prudence during dinner. However, she then thought better of it. Instead, she unwittingly dropped a bomb that shook Prudence to her core. The wine flowed freely, and Bernadette, whose tongue was loosened after three glasses of Pinot Noir that probably cost two days' pay, confided that since the time Prudence took the stack of files from Oscar's desk to copy, Oscar had been giving her some funny looks—as if she'd done something wrong. He hid it well, because his actions and demeanor stayed the same and he didn't actually *say* anything, but Bernadette knew it might come up soon since Oscar had asked her to set some time aside in the morning.

Bernadette leaned in and said, "Remember when you took the Renaissance files to copy? Well, Oscar called me into his office by phone this morning, which he rarely does, because his normal summons is to just yell my name through the door. I knew immediately that something was going on since he made a single comment in a very serious, yet polite tone. He said, 'Bernadette, did someone take a stack of files off my desk a few weeks ago?' I replied that, yes, you needed to copy them so you could get up to speed in order to help Rachel and that you needed copies so you could highlight sections and make margin notes without damaging the original copies. I found it curious that he asked about it after all this time, but I assumed you saw him when you took the stack from his desk. Was he not there when you walked into his office?"

Prudence replied a little defensively, her eyes as wide as saucers, "Well, he wasn't at his desk and I assumed he was in the bathroom, so I went ahead and took the files. I didn't think it would be very professional to talk through the door, and instead of just waiting for him to come out, I thought it was more appropriate to just take the files and leave. I figured he knew someone was coming to take the files. I didn't think it was a big deal."

Bernadette said in a calm, reassuring voice, "No, no, you didn't do anything wrong. I think Oscar just noted that the files were out of order. I have no idea why this came up today. Perhaps it's because that part of the project is over. You didn't do anything wrong, but next time, let's make sure he actually is in the office before you go in and take something off his desk. This was totally my fault. I shouldn't have just waved you in while I was yammering on the phone. If anything, I was the one who was unprofessional. Don't worry. Like I said, he's not *acting* any differently, but I've known him long enough to be able to see when his wheels are spinning. It's his way of telling me to not let it happen again, and I can assure you that I won't put you in that situation again."

But Prudence *did* worry. She thought that not only would Oscar be watching her every move, but he would also assume that Rachel saw the files, which could spell trouble for her. She worried herself to the point that she suddenly excused herself to go to the ladies' room to collect herself.

When she returned, Bernadette asked with some degree of concern, "Are you okay, dear? Was it something I said? I told you it was no big deal."

"No, that's not it, Bernadette. It must've been a bad oyster *en brochette* or something. I've never had them before. All this rich food probably gave me a little indigestion. I'm really sorry, but I'm not feeling well. I think I should go now. Please thank Oscar for inviting me. I don't want to disturb him. He seems to be in the middle of one of his famous war stories. I think I heard all of them when I was working at the restaurant."

Prudence gave a slight smile as she rose from her chair, thinking a little levity on the way out would convince Bernadette that things were okay on the office front and that it really was indigestion that was bothering her. Bernadette started to ask her if she would like her dessert boxed up and taken to the office so she could eat it later, but Prudence left too quickly for her to get all of the words out.

When Prudence finally got home, she felt as if she was going to be sick. Theo was still up doing homework. He looked up and asked, "Mom, you okay? You look like you're not feeling well. You look a little queasy."

"Yes, honey, I'm fine. Just a little tummyache. Even though I've worked in them, I'm not used to the rich food in those fancy restaurants. It's late, so finish up your homework and get on to bed."

Prudence knew there'd be no sleep that night, so when she assured herself that Theo was in his room for the night, she took out the light blue files and started to read through them. She had gone through only a few of them, partly because she was so busy with the green files and the permit filing, but mostly since she didn't want to know what was in them. She stayed up all night trying to make sense of it all. She already was intimately familiar with the green files, which were all fairly straightforward and seemed normal. They contained copies of partially completed permits, legal memos supporting the client's position, and, most fascinating of all, a letter from a professor at Loyola detailing how this project would enhance the historical significance of the site, not diminish it. Some files contained drawings, blueprints, and pictures of renderings; others were filled with historical data that probably supported the professor's letter. Prudence didn't recognize the address for the Renaissance and had never actually thought about going there to see the site for herself. She jotted it down on a yellow sticky note, put it in her purse, and made a mental note to go to the property to see what all the fuss was about.

The light blue files, however, were very complicated, as if they were written in code. Lots of numbers, spreadsheets, and some of the same conceptual drawings and blueprints as contained in the green files. Page after page was filled with made-up words and odd numberings that made no sense at all. There were dates next to numbers, each with a letter or two at the end, which she deduced stood for street names, which were easily recognizable. One even matched the address of the site where the Renaissance would be built.

Her curiosity was piqued, and she wanted to get to the bottom of it all, but she knew that would take a long time. The hours passed quickly, and the dark of night gave way to the light of dawn. Prudence, almost in a stupor, realized she needed to make Theo's breakfast and get herself ready for work. She'd dive into this another day, when she was fresh and had a chance to digest it all, so to speak.

At 6:30, the bird clock on the kitchen wall greeted her with a warbler's song. While she loved the sounds of singing birds, on that particular morning she could have done without. It was Mamaw's clock, however, and after she passed, Prudence decided to keep it as a constant reminder of Mamaw's days in the kitchen and their time together over morning cups of Community Coffee and biscuits. She especially liked it when the cardinal chirped at ten every night, which was the time Theo was normally in bed and the two of them would talk about their days. Mamaw fondly brought to life tales of bygone days, even the days of strife in the Deep South where the lives of black folk were considerably darker than they were in the present. Their cause and marches led locally by Revs. Drummond and Hill, and nationally by the good Reverend Dr. King, were all noble in their purpose, and while she looked upon those days with pride, Mamaw also lamented the current generation, its cynicism and cultural vulgarity, fostered by fatherless children and the glorification of a so-called *thug* lifestyle. Kids these days could drink from whatever water fountain they wished and sit on any open seat on the bus. They had no idea what real oppression was and probably couldn't care less.

# Chapter 36

## Prudence Earns Her Stripes

Rachel gave a light knuckle-tap on Prudence's office door at 7:45 that morning. The office was empty, and no lights were on. Although the meeting was set for eight o'clock, as far as Rachel was concerned, if you weren't at least fifteen minutes early to a meeting, you were late. Prudence knew this and hurriedly rounded the corner, meeting Rachel in the doorway with her arms full of files from the Clinic, which was a definite no-no since Jimmy was the only one who was permitted to take files from the Clinic.

"So, the early bird arrives. Nice of you to drop by," Rachel said in a slightly sarcastic tone that Prudence believed was Rachel's way of letting her know that she was annoyed with her for not being *on time*. However, Rachel let the moment quickly pass. She couldn't wait to drop off a new file containing three, three-ring binders and several bankers boxes, all filled to capacity.

Some of the documents were dated two months ago and contained what appeared to be construction contract documents. The binders comprised a bid package and corresponding draft quote from a construction company for the building of a three-story parking garage a couple of blocks away from the Renaissance, another present bestowed upon Oscar by Falke.

Prudence had never seen so many drawings and plans and different types of documents, all of which were completely foreign to her. She thought it was rather brazen for the customer to have already solicited bids before the permit was approved, especially since preparing and delivering these packages to contractors could be very expensive for both parties. Often, tens of thousands of dollars were spent in the form of engineering man hours, the procurement of project insurance policies, and potentially the hiring of pricey specialty engineers and consultants who were usually brought in on a project-by-project basis and not part of a company's normal stable of engineers and project managers as well.

Customers sometimes had more than one construction company working in parallel, preparing conceptual drawings, placing orders for long-lead equipment and materials, and pulling together project teams, all with the knowledge that only one company would be awarded the project. The loser was sometimes paid for their efforts, often on a cost basis with a slight profit margin around five percent. The cost of the bid for the winner, however, was normally rolled into the project.

As if the task wasn't daunting enough already, Rachel asked Prudence to write a summary memo on the parking garage construction project files. Rachel gave her a piece of paper and said, "Now, Prudence, I know you've never done this, so here is a little cheat sheet for you and a file from another construction project to use as a go by. What I need you to do is read through the entire contract to make sure all sections correspond to the table of contents and index, make a note of which clauses are missing or contain incorrect section headings, and highlight any clauses that are in the contract, but not on the cheat sheet, and vice versa. Then, check all cross-references in both the body of the contract and the scope of work—which is contained in an exhibit to the main contract—look for inconsistencies between the change order protocol and change order form, and make sure there is a reference to builder's risk coverage in the insurance exhibits. Lastly, verify all exhibits are complete and labeled properly.

"The nomenclature must match throughout all documents. For example, if 'Company' is used in an exhibit, but 'Customer' is used in the main contract, it could cause confusion, so it should be consistent throughout. Just identify it by highlighting the appropriate word and sticking a red flag on the page. I can fix it on the native document during my review. Also, you don't need to be a math genius to do this, but add up all numbers in the quote sheet to make sure all of the totals match. Everything should be in order because we had some very experienced paralegals put the bid package together. It's all there for you, and many people have gone through these files already, so this exercise is more of a last look—a sanity check, if you will—as well as a good training exercise for you. I'll have someone from risk management on hot standby to answer any questions on the insurance coverage.

"Prudence, I hope you realize this as an opportunity for you to shine again, so please for your sake and mine, make the best of it. Remember these four rules and you'll be fine. One, there are no stupid questions. Two, be comfortable with, but verify the things you know. Three, ask for help and be uncomfortable with the things you don't know. And four, above all, be proud of your work. I estimate this task will take you about six hours in total, and I am rarely wrong."

Making Prudence drink water from a fire hose was purposeful. Rachel wanted to gauge her attitude and aptitude. She counted on Prudence reaching out to other members of the firm, and she wanted to see how

Prudence would respond to a task that was almost impossible for even a seasoned paralegal. She would soon be part of Rachel's group, and Rachel demanded no less than perfection. It was a risk she was willing to take, as Prudence was the darling of the firm, a champion of the poor and the girl who could get things done at city hall. Good press for Prudence meant good press for Rachel, but as self-serving a notion as that may have been, Rachel truly wanted her to flourish and grow and maybe one day go to law school herself. She respected Prudence and was proud of what she'd accomplished in life. In a way, Rachel felt like a big sister.

Prudence was overwhelmed at the scope of the project and the fast pace at which everything happened in the office. She was working on some files for Jimmy, too, and it didn't help that she was bleary-eyed and exhausted from lack of sleep due to her examination of the light blue files, but she knew she had to rise to the occasion.

Rachel could sense that Prudence was a little flummoxed and didn't know where to start. She moved toward her a half step closer and said in a softer, more reassuring tone, "Prudence, this will be a piece of king cake. Everything is in order. Just follow the rules, use your cheat sheet, and refer to the go by memo, which, by the way, is from the early '80s, just prior to the 1984 World's Fair, which was an unmitigated disaster and an embarrassment to the city. I went to a Flock of Seagulls concert there as a grade-schooler—way before your time—but that's a story for another day. Or maybe it was The Fixx. Whatever. The point is that at that time, the World's Fair committee had to apply for the same types of permits before they tore down some historical sites and rundown houses, so the subject matter is similar to what we are dealing with now for the parking garage. You don't need to read and understand the contract clauses or exhibits. Just ensure all is in order from a structural point of view and make sure that your memo, yellow stickies, and flags capture everything you notice so I can go straight to those sections and make revisions. Sometimes we live with these files too long and overlook some of the changes made throughout the drafting process, especially the cross-references. The wrong cross-reference could have disastrous consequences in a lawsuit over a bad project.

"If possible, I'd like to have this completed by noon tomorrow, because I need to incorporate your work into that of the other team members. I'm the one that pulls it all together, and BB will need the completed file by noon so he and I can review it together in time for the client meeting, which starts at 2:30."

Prudence's head was spinning. She said to Rachel in a panicked tone, "Team? Pull it all together? I...I didn't realize this project was so big. I thought it was just a simple construction project for a plain parking garage. You know, move some dirt, make it flat, and put some blacktop on the surface. Oh, Rachel, I hope my work won't stick out like a sore thumb as compared to the other paralegals and associates. This is only my second major file. Not that the pro bono clients are any less important, but this is high-profile within the firm and I've never dealt with a construction project. What if I miss something? What if the numbers don't add up?"

Rachel moved even closer and gently put her arm around Prudence's shoulder as she said, "Prudence, dear Prudence, I will be the only one looking at *your* work. I know you're new at this, so don't worry. Remember, I'm the one that pulls it all together. BB will see *my* work, which will include yours, as well as that of everyone else on the team. I will be brilliant, and you will bask in the glory. Clear? Just stick to the script. If you do that, it won't take me much time to pull everything together, assuming the others pull their weight, which, sadly, does not always happen—at least to my satisfaction. This ain't my first rodeo, so track me down if you have any questions. I'll be in the office all day and you can always reach me any time on my mobile."

# Chapter 37

## Overwhelmed

Prudence was exhausted after a sleepless night of reviewing Oscar's files and because of the pressure of the new project, but she dug in and spent the first part of the morning familiarizing herself with the material in the binders. On the one hand, all of this stuff was completely boring, and the pages all looked alike. On the other hand, she saw it as a puzzle where everything was interconnected; clauses cross-referenced each other on different documents, as well as within the main one, physical exhibits matched the verbal descriptions, and the scope of work corresponded to the sections in the pricing sheets set out in the binders.

Around 9:30, Jimmy walked into her office, which was strange, because it was usually the other way around. "Prudence, we need to get down to the pro bono section right away." Jimmy continued while they walked down the Hall. "Miss Effie fell this morning and the hospital is giving her nephew, Lamont Wilson, a hard time about her Medicare coverage. I need you to look into this immediately. I'm swamped with work on a case where some vessels collided in Lake Pontchartrain a few years ago. Apparently, some rich cardiac surgeon Oscar knows was drunk on the high seas. While he was showing off his seamanship to some of his doctor buddies and Big Pharma executives, he rammed his million-dollar toy into the port side of an oyster barge owned by Gordo Evanovich—also known infamously as 'the crazy Croatian king of the oyster beds.' Evanovich was piloting home after a long day of harvesting the beds in the Rigolets off the coast of Lake Borgne. He was nearing the Lake Pontchartrain Causeway and the wake from the yacht caused his barge to slam into the northbound span, putting it out of commission for two months and adding thirty minutes to the already hours-long commute downtown for thousands of people.

"Not only that, but because of a political fight with the state over permitting and approvals for bridge design, the delays and repairs cost the Lake Pontchartrain Causeway Commission even more money due to more expensive construction and lost revenue thanks to an increase in carpooling and the blooming of a boutique bus service with express routes to Metairie and downtown. It's a nice new business for the area, but there will be fewer commuters and the Commission is unlikely to recoup its lost revenue. The wreck resulted in three deaths and serious injuries to some of the survivors. The yacht was totaled, and Evanovich's brand-new oyster barge was severely damaged, mortgaged, and uninsured. We represent the doctor who is being sued not only by Evanovich and those injured, but also by the family of one of the deceased—a woman who was a passenger on the yacht. The firm gets paid from the insurance company, so win or lose we'll amass a small fortune since it will take years to wind this through the courts. What a racket! Plaintiff lawyers are gamblers hoping for a big payday, and the defense lawyers are like the house; they always win even if they lose.

"I wish we were representing the oyster fisherman, though. His livelihood will be interrupted for at least two years. Poor guy has a big hill to climb in proving his damages because his business is mostly on a cash basis, which means no receipts. He's managed to evade the Louisiana Tax Commission and the IRS for decades. Now his chickens have come home to roost and he is under audit. He'll likely lose it all, and will probably go to jail. He would have been much better off playing it straight and paying his taxes, but since he's part of the Croatian oyster mafia, I don't have too much sympathy for him. No one really knows, but from what I understand, they pool all of their money to buy politicians to make sure the Vietnamese can't get fishing permits and infiltrate their territory. At the same time, they manipulate the price of seafood for the whole Gulf Coast, all from a few little seafood wholesale storefronts in Chalmette. This has been their way of life for at least three, maybe four generations. It's like the Italian mafia with all of the families, but without the violence, shiny Lincolns, and gold chains.

"So, Evanovich is trying to get money from the good doctor, but doesn't have receipts and can't prove his monetary damages beyond the physical damage to the boat, which, as I noted, is mortgaged and uninsured. And, because he's evaded taxes for so long, his tax skeletons have come out of the grave like lost souls escaping through the gates of St. Louis Cemetery. He can't afford a tax defense lawyer or a criminal lawyer, and his greedy plaintiff lawyer, known as the Gator, didn't find out about the tax issue until midway through discovery. You've seen the Gator on TV with his cheesy commercials where he yells that he 'chomps and chomps and chomps until the insurance company does the right thing.' The Gator can't drop the case now since he's in too deep. He also doesn't want to put forth his best effort, but he must straddle the line between effective representation and malpractice. He has what's called a dog of a case and is really pissed because his friends are now mercilessly teasing him. He'll probably lose at least one hundred grand before it's all over, and due to an arcane contingency fee arrangement, the plaintiff lawyer essentially makes a bet and assumes all of the costs. If he wins, he normally wins big and gets to recover his costs *plus* more than thirty percent of the amount of the judgment—more if he wins on appeal.

"Now, to add insult to injury, the oyster mafia has disavowed Evanovich since they don't want to be caught in the tax investigations. The light's starting to shine on them now, and they want a little cloud cover so they can maintain their low profile. Evanovich won't turn on them since the oyster mafia, while not usually violent, will make him and his family disappear in the oyster beds. They know the Gator won't turn on them either, since he's already been left a few subtle messages. The day after he agreed to take Evanovich's case, his Mercedes was keyed and the tires were slashed right in his driveway. For all of his TV bluster, the Gator is really a wimp and scared shitless now. He knows stories about the oyster mafias are true and not just urban myth."

"Yes, I heard about the damage to the Causeway," Prudence said. "One of the girls in the Bull Pen told me the rest of the story. One of the Big Pharma guys on the yacht was from Indiana and was in town for a tradeshow boondoggle. And one of the women, who was not his wife, was thrown overboard and died. She wasn't wearing a life vest because she was topless. The poor girl drowned when the barge ran over her. The wife divorced him, and he lost his cushy job. I heard he now works at some imaging center in Lafayette, Indiana, making less than half of what he was before the accident."

Jimmy smiled like the cat who ate the canary, "Prudence, that's not the *rest of the story*, as Mr. Harvey would say. What the gossip queens in the Bull Pen don't know, and what you will keep secret, is that Mr. Pharma made regular trips to New Orleans and the topless woman was his mistress. And, get this, to top it all off…she was pregnant!

"Okay, sidebar's now over. Let's get back to helping Miss Effie. I'll save war stories for another time. I don't have all of the facts yet, but Miss Effie slipped on a wet floor in one of those big box stores like Target or Walmart. She broke her hip and is in and out of lucidity because of the morphine they gave her. As you know, she weighs all of eighty-five pounds, so those drugs do quite a number on her."

As fanciful as Jimmy's stories were, dealing with Miss Effie was personal and sobered Prudence right up. If she hadn't been before, she was *really* overwhelmed then. While she had some dealings with the Medicare offices, it was only for Miss Effie's medicine. She hadn't dealt with hospitals, most of which were private institutions, and she was frightened that she would do something that would put Miss Effie's finances, or worse, her health in jeopardy.

Jimmy saw the panic in her face. "Don't worry," he said. "My old friend, Denise, works at the same hospital. I'll ask her to guide you through this instead of the person giving Miss Effie's nephew a hard time. I've asked you to jump into this since you already have a relationship with Miss Effie, so she'll trust you. I'll call Denise in a few minutes."

This gave Prudence a little comfort, but between the magnitude of the situation, the complexity of the construction bid, and the fumes she was running on due to lack of sleep, she was seriously questioning her new career choice. Waiting tables was one thing; this job was much more stressful. It did pay well, though, which gave her and Theo some financial breathing room. Theo didn't worry anymore about her having to get a second job to help make ends meet, and he was free to resume being a kid. He had turned a corner in the last few months and spent most of his time after school studying and helping at the Antioch. It was too late to disrupt the family again by going back to the restaurant, so she would just have to push through this as best she could.

Prudence was surprised at how smoothly things went at the hospital. Denise was a tremendous help and Miss Effie's affairs were straightened out, giving Lamont a great deal of relief, at least on the financial front. The next challenge would be Miss Effie's physical rehabilitation and home care. Lamont agreed to move in with her, but he had a full-time job as a driver for a furniture company and no training in how to deal with her needs. Besides, Miss Effie was too independent to be put in a nursing home and the stress of being away from her home would have been more detrimental than beneficial. Lamont would just be a warm body in the house, but he'd help as much as he was able.

Prudence had a feeling that she would get dragged into the matter in more than a legal capacity. Once someone was given a pro bono file, they were usually linked to that client forever, if not longer. This was good on two fronts: continuity and career development for the support staff. Seeing matters through to resolution resulted in happy clients and a sense of accomplishment and self-confidence, which was the basis for advancement in the firm.

Prudence spent the rest of the morning on the phone with the hospital, finalizing details and arranging Miss Effie's transport home. Before she knew it, five o'clock rolled around. Prudence realized she'd missed lunch, so she went down to the food court on the second floor for a quick bite. She picked up a foot-long roast beef po' boy, a bag of Zapp's jalapeño chips, and an orange Fanta soda with a rather long flex straw. She knew she'd have to stay late into the night to get at least halfway through the bid documents, and she'd have to come in early in the morning to complete the task before the deadline. She finished her meal at her desk so she could continue reading, hoping that she'd get through the majority of the bid package.

Shortly after she finished eating, Prudence nodded off at her desk. She shook it off and plowed back into the task headfirst. The hours flew by, and when she came up for air, it was seven o'clock. She decided it was time to go home so she could hopefully see Theo before he went to sleep.

Except for the dull light from gray skies coming through the ornate skylight during her brief stop in the food court, she hadn't seen the sun, or her own son, all day and would likely not see either the next morning before heading back to work. Her goal was to finish early and impress Rachel. She did not want to disappoint her, as she was still riding a high wave in the wake of her success in getting the permit for the Renaissance approved. At the same time, she didn't want to run the risk of Jimmy or anyone else putting another task on her plate before she completed this one. She had a newfound respect for her colleagues and marveled at how they were able to work on so many different matters at once while keeping them all running smoothly, like a well-oiled machine with its many parts working in harmony.

# Chapter 38

## A Different Kind of Cocktail

Upon arriving home, Prudence walked through the house, scratched a sleeping Japonica behind the ears, gave Theo a good night kiss, and collapsed on her bed. In her exhaustion, Prudence left the door off the porch slightly ajar. Theo hadn't patched the screen door yet, so in the still of the night, as he did every night to ensure his masters were safe in their beds, Japonica walked through the house and noticed a thin light from the streetlamp peeking through the open door. Japonica nudged the door open and crawled quietly through the hole in the screen door, then took the opportunity to take a midnight stroll through the quiet of the neighborhood.

Around 3:30 in the morning, he helped himself to some leftover macaroni and cheese casserole and *daube au jus*, topped off with a torn piece of stale, buttered French bread—all courtesy of Chookie's garbage can, which already had been knocked over by some pesky opossum.

"That's the one. See where that mangy-ass mutt is?" said Tyler Loomis, pointing toward the house.

"You sure? I thought it was that one over there," said Earl Patrick Tyler as he nodded in the direction of another house while peering through his new pocket night vision scope.

"No, you're looking at the right one. That's his mangy-ass mutt digging in the garbage."

They crept closer, keeping quiet so as not to alert Japonica. When they were within throwing distance, Earl heaved the Molotov cocktail, filled with the finest UAK moonshine west of the Mississippi. It sailed through the air as if in slow motion, dripping flames along the way like tracers ahead of patriot missiles headed toward the center of Baghdad. It breached the thin kitchen window and landed on the floor, immediately spreading flames throughout the room.

By the time Chookie awoke, the thick, black smoke had already consumed Tante Ju, who lay on the floor with her lifeless hands stretched toward her bedroom door. With his room now ablaze, Chookie just stood in the middle of his room, crying, coughing uncontrollably, and utterly confused. Japonica rushed into the house barking as loudly as he could in the hopes that Chookie would hear him. Chookie heard Japonica through the roar of the inferno and followed the barking. He made his way toward the front of the house and escaped through a side door. Japonica followed him, but got trapped by a flaming support beam when it fell. Barking gave way to helpless yelping, and except for the sounds of the fire, the yelping quickly gave way to silence. He burned to death in a most horrific manner. If all dogs went to heaven, ol' Japo was up there, curled at the feet of St. Pete.

"What's that big boi doing in the yard?!" Earl yelled nervously. "I thought only high-yeller and his mother lived there."

Tyler replied, "Well, I saw the dog and thought—"

"You *thought*? You *thought*?!" Ear screamed, thoroughly enraged at his cousin. "You *stupid* asshole, we firebombed the wrong house?! We need to get out of here *NOW*!"

"Earl, those houses all look the same and I...I..."

"Shut the hell up! We need to get our gear and get out of here." While Earl was putting the night vision scope back into his pocket, something dropped to the ground—a shiny bronze coin he got after his initiation into the UAK. On one side, *SWAMP* was written as a bottom rocker under a pecky cypress tree. The other side featured the words *UAK* and *Troop* (indicating Earl's rank) acting as a top rocker around the UAK's infamous logo, which consisted of two water moccasins vaguely resembling the Nazi's SS logo inside a white circle surrounded by vermillion and onyx Confederate stars and bars outlined in a pure white border—naturally.

The coin was part of a recently established custom within the UAK started by Krieger, similar to the one in the military meant to instill brotherhood and camaraderie. Each UAK member was required to carry a challenge coin at all times. If a member barked "coin" to another, and he couldn't slam it down immediately, he would have to pay a fine. That could be anything from buying the next round of drinks on the spot to bringing a few whores to the next house party.

As one rose within the ranks, coins would be retired and displayed in a trophy case, neatly arranged within the same type of plastic cubes or shadowboxes used for autographed baseballs, football helmets, basketball shoes, or other memorabilia. The display was good for morale and gave one a sense of accomplishment and motivation to move up to the next level. Robertsen learned years ago in one of his business psychology classes that it was the little things that kept employees focused, happy, and productive. Robertsen learned that if one observed carefully, one could better understand what made a person tick and exploit it to get the most productivity out of someone, or tailor a reward geared toward their tendencies. Sometimes, a company hat and T-shirt or an office party could make someone's day and keep them focused. Dissatisfaction and a lack of focus, however, could poison an organization, and the UAK could ill-afford to lose members simply because they were not challenged or rewarded for their efforts. Threats of bodily harm or even death sometimes were not enough to keep someone quiet if ever they were inclined to have a moment of conscience and leave. One person could bring the whole enterprise down, so the Leadership did its utmost to create a culture of family; one would never want to leave *home*.

Earl and Tyler fled the scene undetected, and, except for the coin, left no trace. They hoped no one would ever associate them with this heinous act and vowed never to speak of it again. That coin.

# Chapter 39

## The Antioch Reels

The fire rocked the sleepy little neighborhood, and Theo's worst fear came true when he learned that Japonica's burned body was found beneath some smoldering beams with his chain collar and name tag scorched, but still intact. He was beyond consolation and instinctively knew that this was likely retribution from the boy he'd beaten so badly at the end of the last school year. He couldn't tell anyone, not yet. He was already ostracized at school, and he didn't want to be the scourge of the neighborhood or of the Antioch's congregation, too.

Everyone focused on Chookie, who was taken over to the Antioch's newly painted community center to be looked after by some of the ladies who, when they weren't in attendance at services, doctors' appointments, or funeral homes, spent most of their days at the Antioch, knitting and bragging about their grandchildren. The faithful of the Antioch were an integral part of the community, and they were needed more than ever. Chookie was sad, frightened, confused, and needed care and comfort from those who were of his aunt's generation, whom he knew well. Chookie was in a very fragile state and had not yet been told about his aunt or Japonica, so the congregants did their best to divert his attention for a while longer.

Theo decided to skip school to help out until he was satisfied that Chookie was being properly looked after. The whole scene was surreal, like a horrific nightmare. His heart ached, and he was completely despondent, but Theo turned his thoughts to his self-imposed sense of duty to Chookie.

Prudence was torn between staying behind to console her community and going to the office to finish Rachel's project. In reality, there was no choice but to report to work. She felt guilty for having to do so, yet justified it by coming to the correct conclusion that she could get more accomplished at the office than at the Antioch. She knew that she could probably find some resources through the pro bono clinic. This wasn't a legal manner, per se, but Prudence had recently dealt with several government agencies and charitable organizations, and she knew that with the right help from the right people, she could help find a suitable place for Chookie, at least in the short term.

In the meantime, the congregants turned to their leader, who was a great shepherd and had led his flock through tough times before, but none tougher than this. Reverend Drummond gathered everyone.

"Okay, y'all listen up, time to develop a plan. Let's go in the chapel." Reverend Drummond looked over the haggard group staring at him with blank faces and defeated countenances. "C'mon now, just like Sunday service." The group began to file into the pews. "That's it, everyone take your seats."

With his usual calm manner, he again looked out at the group of weeping and weary, and walked toward one of the ladies seated at the end of a pew in the middle of the church. He bent over and in a soft, reassuring voice asked her to take Chookie to the office in the community center and to stay with him, which she gladly agreed to do. He wondered why Chookie was led into the chapel in the first place, but quickly dismissed the thought and attributed it to the shock of the circumstances.

Reverend Drummond walked back to the front of the room, and in a casual manner meant to convey more of a sense of community as opposed to a Sunday sermon, sat on the steps in front of the first row. He looked at the floor, took in a deep breath, looked up, and spoke. "We've been through a lot over the years, and we'll get through this, too. Now, here's what we need to do."

Theo assumed the role of taking fastidious notes while the right Reverend Dr. Honoré Drummond spent the next hour ticking off the tasks and assigning responsibility—coordinate with the fire and police departments to understand how the investigation was going to be conducted, contact the utility companies to ensure electricity, gas, water, and cable TV accounts were taken care of, and above all, look after Chookie for a few days until a proper facility could be found. While Reverend Drummond would take interim responsibility for Chookie's care and well-being, he looked to a man who had recently retired from the postal system to see to his immediate needs like food and clothing during his stay at the community center.

Satisfied that all major tasks were identified and properly assigned, Reverend Drummond paused, looked around proudly, and addressed the flock. "Folks, it's often said that the Lord works in mysterious ways, and while this tragedy may seem senseless, and hurts us so very deeply to the core, there is a reason for all of this. God has a plan. Have faith. Now, let us bow our heads in prayer. Dear Lord, please guide us through these dark days. Be with us as we work through this tragic chapter in our community. We pray for the well-being of our neighbors and loved ones. We pray for Chookie, and that you keep your loving arms wrapped around him. We pray for the repose of the soul of a beautiful woman who served you and all of us so faithfully through her great many years on this earth. We thank you for the many blessings you've bestowed on us, and pray that you take care of those who can't help themselves. We also pray for those who committed this deadly act, and that they may come to know you and repent for this act of pure evil. Above all, Lord, we pray that soon we will come to understand your purpose for this tragedy, and that all involved will be brought to justice. In Christ Jesus's name we pray."

In unison, the crowd responded with one voice. "Amen!"

When Prudence arrived at work, she immediately went to Jimmy's office and told him about the house fire. She asked him if she could devote some time to helping get Chookie sorted with temporary care. Not only did Jimmy approve her request, he decided to spend some of his own time tracking down friends of his who were social workers or lawyers who dealt with family affairs and could work on the legalities that people tended not to take into consideration during these types of emotional situations: medical powers of attorney, guardianships, authority to work with government agencies, etc. It was one thing to *do* all of the necessary things, but quite another to get them done formally and officially.

After several calls, it was decided that the Crescent City Shelter for Women and Children was the best place for the short term. Chookie was kind, childlike, not violent, played well with children, and readily accepted help. After leaving their dangerous spouses and boyfriends, the women at these types of shelters wanted to help—even if only to take their minds off their particular situations. Yes, this would be the perfect temporary home for Chookie and would give Reverend Drummond and Prudence the time they needed to find a suitable place—like an assisted living community—that could meet Chookie's needs. Long-term care, however, would require hundreds of thousands of dollars, and the little Antioch community simply wasn't deep enough to carry that type of load.

Everyone in the community loved Tante Ju and wanted her to have a proper Christian burial. She had no life insurance or burial policy, and her meager savings was not enough to cover immediate funeral expenses. Even though there weren't many assets, it would take months to probate her estate and sell the property. Of his own accord, Reverend Drummond took up a special collection at the next day's service to cover some of the funeral costs. One of the congregants worked for a florist who graciously donated arrangements for tables and a beautiful spray, complete with Tante Ju's favorite flowers: Mardi Gras purple hortensias. Another owned a funeral home and agreed to donate the preparation of the body and help pick out a peaceful burial site. Unfortunately, due to high crime and murder rates, the funeral business was one of the city's most lucrative industries. The work would take a few days longer than it would under normal circumstances, and he was happy to help, but paying clients came first.

Jimmy was ready to tap into his network of friends in government agencies. Hopefully, they could help navigate the bureaucratic spider web and find a place for Chookie as quickly as possible. Even with friends in high places, the process would likely take two, maybe three months, and there was only so much a shelter could do for him until then. It would be quite disruptive for Chookie to be shuttled around to different places during the interim, but it would also be too big a burden for a single shelter to assume.

Reverend Drummond and his congregation pitched in through donations and volunteers to lighten the load of the shelter, and some of the wealthier lawyers at LeRoux, Godchaux could take advantage of a wonderful opportunity for a tax write-off. As the latter would likely be a one-time donation, Jimmy struck while the iron was hot and the incident was still front and center in the current news cycle. Prudence took a step back and drew from her experiences with Katrina; the disaster that ensued after the storm was due to the dysfunction of FEMA, local officials, and charitable organizations who operated independently and wound up duplicating efforts in some areas and leaving glaring deficiencies in others. Prudence thought it was the right time to introduce Jimmy to Reverend Drummond with the hope that by doing so, they could pool resources and develop a cohesive plan for Chookie's future.

# Chapter 40

## Reality Sets In

Prudence completed her project and submitted it to Rachel by ten that morning. She was so tired, she felt as if she had a hangover. She had never actually had a hangover, but she guessed the feeling was probably similar to what she was experiencing then. The remainder of the day was a blur and she decided to leave the office a little early, thinking Rachel and Jimmy wouldn't mind or even notice her absence.

When she arrived home, she plopped down on the couch and immediately fell asleep in a house that hadn't been quiet in a long while. Theo made it an early day at the Antioch and came home at about 5:30, saw his mom lying on the couch, and grew very anxious, not knowing whether something was wrong or she was fired from her job. It was not like his mom to be home in the middle of the day. He walked over to the couch and gently nudged her shoulder, trying to wake her without scaring her.

"Mom? Mom, are you okay?" he asked.

Prudence awoke from her hard sleep, a little uncertain at first as to where she was. "Oh, Theo, what are you doing home so late?" she said.

Theo replied, "Mom, it's only 5:30. What's wrong? I'm worried about you. You worked all night and left early this morning."

"Thank you, son. Thank you for looking out for me, but nothing is wrong. I'm just exhausted. It's because of what's going on with some projects I had to complete for work, and this thing with Chookie has put everyone on an emotional roller coaster. You know how on those lawyer shows on TV, everyone in the office works super hard all the time? Well, art imitates life, as they say. It's real, and I'm just not used to putting in those kinds of hours and maintaining that fast pace. In fact, I've thought about going back to waitressing, but there's no sense in doing that now. I may be tired, but there are so many people who are worse off than we are, and I'm in a position to help them now, so my woes pale in comparison. Now, don't worry about me," she said while playfully pinching his cheek like Mamaw used to do. "Just be sure your homework is finished and you feed Japoni—" Prudence choked back tears and pulled Theo close, holding him tightly. "I guess I loved that cayoodle more than I realized."

They both broke down and wept with the sudden realization that there would be one less heartbeat in their home.

Later, Theo walked through the house and looked at what remained of Japonica's things: toys, blankets, medicine, and the spot where he used to sleep, between the couch and Mamaw's rocker. He then re-tired to his room for the night; he wasn't completely convinced his mother had told him the whole story, but he was satisfied that she was okay and that all those hours at the firm had probably been well spent. Besides, he had his own responsibilities to tend to between homework and helping out at the Antioch, which would seem emp-tier with Japonica's absence. Theo was amazed at the impact his four-legged friend had on the community, and he was proud he died a hero and not the victim of a careless car accident or long illness. The community would be in a state of shock for quite some time. Theo had it in his mind to ask Reverend Drummond, when the time was right, whether the Antioch could honor Japo in some way, like putting his picture on the wall in the office or designating the kids' playroom as the Japonica Room or Japonica's Playhouse—something befitting such a heroic friend to the community.

# Chapter 41

## Connecting the Dots

Fresh from her power nap and satisfied that Theo was in his room for the night, Prudence went to her room, closed the door, resumed her study of the light blue files, and sketched out some notes. All the while, she thought, *What could be so important that Oscar would have so many files for one little permit? And why would there be so much early activity surrounding the contracting bids for a simple parking lot?*

She could feel in her bones that something didn't quite add up. And then she remembered that the name of the construction company that submitted the bid, KTL Construction, Inc., was very similar to the name of the firm's export/import client, Knight Trucking & Logistics. The two had to somehow be connected.

She looked hurriedly thumbed through the pages in front of her. There it was, a simple word contained in a simple sentence buried in a meaningless paragraph: road. Sometimes, it was the simplest of things that became catalysts for major events. Those four little letters provided Prudence with the little spark she needed to continue her investigation of the light blue files.

*Road* permits were needed for KTL to transport its equipment. The word *road*, however, could stand for many things: the name of a street, dirt roads, gravel roads, the road less traveled, and the obvious meaning, a highway. KTL was the contractor. Logistics companies mobilized heavy construction equipment using roads, and this she knew because of the many permits she saw bearing the name of the company that allowed it to move big equipment on highways and through city streets. And, what pulled it together for her was the name itself. KTL undoubtedly stood for Knight Trucking. KTL road permits. It all started making sense.

Prudence hurriedly fired up her laptop, logged on to the firm's network using a VPN, and began a search for "KTL." She saw files, and not just for the permitting for the construction project on which she'd been tirelessly working, but also in conjunction with many other projects where permits were required—building permits, fire marshal permits, liquor permits—just not the type of permits needed to tear down a historical building. Hotels, parking lots, meeting centers, parks, strip malls: it was all there.

Then, she spotted it. A folder labeled "KTL Construction, Inc." Prudence double-clicked her mouse and saw several subfolders and files. Some pertained to different types of official documents, such as an EIN number from the IRS or a listing of executive management personnel on the certificate of insurance for key man coverage. One subfolder looked particularly interesting: "Delaware Department of State." In it, she found many files, one of which was entitled "Articles of Incorporation." Scrolling through that file, she saw the name of the ninety percent shareholder, Knight Trucking & Logistics Company, and the ten percent shareholder: O.B. Enterprises, LLC, a limited liability company based in the Cayman Islands.

Prudence slammed her laptop closed, and with a deep breath, said aloud, "Oscar Brimley." She had a pit in her stomach the size of Dallas, beads of cold sweat dotted her forehead, and she felt the sudden urge to vomit. It would be another long, sleepless night.

After a few hours of fitful sleep, she woke up, fixed Theo breakfast, and saw him out the door. Her thoughts were muddled, and she couldn't think straight. Between her exhaustion and her racing thoughts, she knew there would be no way she could go to work without calling attention to herself. She'd already left early the day before and had never called in sick. Not knowing how to handle the situation, she called Bernadette.

In a hoarse voice that was well rehearsed, she said, "Bernadette, this is Prudence. How are you this morning?"

Bernadette replied in a cheery voice, "Prudence! I'm fine, dear. How are you?" Without waiting for a reply, she continued, "Hey, look, girl, you are the talk of the town right now. Rachel is talking you up big time and I see the makings of a political campaign to pull you into her group. No doubt Jimmy will be pissed, but there's no way he can stand in the way of someone's advancement, especially a newbie like you who also is brand-new to this field and who has excelled in it so quickly. Not to get ahead of myself, but I'm so happy for you! Now, what can I do for you?"

After a pregnant pause, Prudence composed herself and responded, "Oh, Bernadette, I'm so flattered, but I don't think I'm ready for that kind of move right now. I'm quite happy in the Clinic. I really enjoy helping people."

"Prudence, my dear, I hate to tell you this, but I think it's already done. Oscar and Rachel were here when I arrived early this morning and they're still huddled up. I heard bits and pieces of their conversation and your name was mentioned quite a few times. Oscar would interject little phrases like, 'We need to ensure Jimmy comes out smelling like a rose, because this will be a big blow to him and he'll need some cover, some positive press, and to save some face in front of his colleagues and in the eyes of the firm at-large.' And then Rachel would say something like, 'Don't worry, he'll be seen as the best mentor in the firm and the folks in the Clinic will want to work with him more than ever. They'll see him as a kingmaker—or, in this case, a queenmaker.'"

Prudence paused again and then said, "That's all great, but the reason I called was to tell you that I'm not feeling well and will not be coming into work today. I didn't know who else to call, since I've never called in sick before, and I hate the thought that I might put someone in a pickle today. I hope it won't cause any problems."

Without hesitation, Bernadette cheerfully responded, "Girl, whether you know it or not, you're on top of the world right now. You deserve a little break considering the wringer you've just been through with that major project and the fire in your neighborhood—not to mention what lies ahead with Rachel's high-octane group. Don't worry. I'll cover for you. I'll tell Jimmy you're having *women's issues*. Men get all embarrassed and queasy if you say that and never ask questions. They usually close their eyes and stick their fingers in their ears! It's hysterical."

"Thank you, Bernadette. I promise I'll be there tomorrow."

"No problem," she replied. "I hope you feel better."

Once she was covered at work, Prudence had the whole day to herself. She was confident that folks at the Antioch were doing what they could to help Chookie, and there really wasn't much she could do there anyway. She decided today presented the perfect opportunity to visit the historical site that was the subject of the permit. See what all the fuss was about.

It was one of the most beautiful days she had seen in a while. In fact, she noticed that she had never seen St. Charles Avenue in such a way. Even with her exhaustion and anxiety over the whole KTL situation and the burning of Tante Ju's house, she noticed the flowers had exploded into full bloom along the avenue, highlighting the beautiful Victorian homes that symbolized the pinnacle of success in the Crescent City. The air was crisper than normal, and the morning sunlight was surreal and iridescent, almost as if she were starring in a movie filmed with a special filter. Very prophetically, the flowers around Oscar's house seemed especially colorful and bright, particularly the mauve crepe myrtles and yellow azaleas.

Unlike most mornings, the streetcar came to a smooth stop at Washington Street, very softly and without the normal screeching and jerking—almost as if it were riding on a cloud. The walk down Washington Street to Tchoupitoulas took much longer than she'd estimated, but Prudence took in the fresh air and the beautiful trees, pondering the mysteries behind the walls of Lafayette Cemetery No. 1 at the foot of Conery Street. She was reminded of one of Theo's favorite jokes. *Why do they put walls around the cemeteries? Because people are just dying to get in and the neighbors are really quiet.* An old, corny joke, but one that never failed to give Theo a contagious chuckle.

She arrived at her destination and was amazed by what she saw. There was so much new construction underway in the area: strip malls in their final stages of completion, a small meeting hall for conferences, a little green space with skinny saplings, and young hedges presumably intended to be some sort of park. An overgrown lot on Jackson Avenue was littered with beer cans, cigarette butts, and the rotting shell of the historical building that was to be torn down. The lot was just down the street from the site of the Renaissance d'Orleans, and often caught the attention of the media due to the historical significance of the building and the publicity surrounding the permitting process once news of the museum spread throughout town. It was all anyone could talk about. On the green space on a lot between Jackson Avenue and Josephine

Street, she noticed the sign. *Space for Lease—Will Build to Suit—The Azalea Group, LLC.* Prudence made a mental note to look up the company during her next clandestine search through the firm's files.

# Chapter 42

## A Signature Symbol

He saw it in the field, glinting as if beckoning to him. Theo walked over, bent down, and picked up the shiny, bronze coin that reminded him of a doubloon; one side had *SWAMP* stamped onto it, and the other had *UAK*. Probably some type of logo for a fancy Mardi Gras krewe, he thought. The coin was slightly smaller than a silver dollar, yet larger than a fifty-cent piece. It had a nice heft to it. He put it in his pocket and decided that he would show it to Reverend Drummond the next time he went to the Antioch.

When Theo arrived at the Antioch, all hell had broken loose. Chookie was not doing well and the shelter was at its wits' end, unable to continue to care for him. Reverend Drummond took it upon himself to call a meeting of congregants in the hopes of finding Chookie another temporary place to stay, but the only place available was all the way across town and charged $25 per night—a price cheaper than kenneling a dog, yet too steep for the Antioch to assume and still provide services to the rest of the congregation. Everyone knew the Antioch was not a long-term solution, but the immediate need had to be addressed. Sadly, Chookie was to be released from the shelter in two days. Reverend Drummond decided to halt the renovations and break into the church's rainy day fund, take up an additional daily collection, lean on nearby churches for support, and continue to look for adequate, affordable housing for Chookie. The last thing anyone wanted was for Chookie to become entangled in a government web of bureaucracy, or worse, homeless and walking the streets. The real fear, however, was that pressure would be applied to members of the church to take Chookie in, and while everyone wished him the best and wanted to help, none wanted or were equipped to assume the responsibility.

Toward the end of the day, when the commotion settled and Reverend Drummond was enjoying a quiet moment, Theo took the opportunity to privately show him the coin. Theo asked, "Reverend Drummond, what do you make of this coin?"

Taking the coin from Theo's hand, the right reverend smiled, looked it over, and then froze. The three little letters shook him to the core and he immediately put two and two together: UAK. He hurriedly pocketed the coin, leaned in close to Theo, and whispered in a soft, yet serious tone, "Theo, where did you find this coin? You're not to tell anyone else about this, okay?"

Theo grew nervous and did not question the fact that Reverend Drummond pocketed the coin. He was concerned by the change in his demeanor and felt compelled to reply in an equally soft tone, "Over near that vacant lot across the street from the neighborhood."

"Thanks, Theo. I know it's a little early, but you go on home now and I'll see you tomorrow. If you don't mind, I'd like to keep this for a while so I can see that it gets to its rightful owner. After a while, if no one claims it, you can have it back. Sound good?"

Theo smiled, shook Reverend Drummond's hand, and said, "That's a deal!"

As if he didn't have enough on his plate with the renovations and getting Chookie sorted, now Reverend Drummond had the UAK to deal with. It was as if his life had come full circle. It had been decades since he'd had any direct confrontations with the hate group. After Dr. King's assassination, an emboldened UAK sought to tamp down the civil rights movement in New Orleans through a systematic campaign of domestic terrorism unlike any seen in recent history. The UAK was the reason he moved on from his public involvement in the civil rights movement and dedicated himself fulltime to growing and nurturing the Antioch.

But for some unknown reason, it appeared that the UAK had reared its ugly head and was back in the picture. He was certain the firebombing was their handiwork. Why else would a coin with their logo show up in such close proximity to the burned house of a poor old black woman? Were they trying to send a message?

Reverend CJ was always a good resource Reverend Drummond could turn to in times of crisis, and he was a lifesaver when he rallied the troops at the Redeemer, just as he did when Prudence and Theo needed to get out of the city. When he called the next day, however, Reverend Drummond detected a little distance in CJ's voice. A little hesitancy.

"Yes, CJ, I'm certain it's them. Theo found their coin in an empty lot near Tante Ju's." Reverend Drummond paused and listened to his long-time friend try and reason through the situation on the other end of the line. "No, I don't know why, and that's what's most troubling about all of this. I really don't expect you to *do* anything, I'm just letting you know what's going on so you can keep your eyes and ears open."

Theo stopped at the Antioch on his way home and walked into the office just as Reverend Drummond hung up the phone. "Everything okay, reverend? You sounded a little out of sorts just now. Can I help?"

Reverend Drummond replied, "Oh, hi, Theo. I didn't see you standing there. No, nothing for you to worry about, my boy. I was just talking
through some issues with a friend. This job can get a little overwhelming sometimes, and this is just another one of those times, what with
trying to juggle this thing with Chookie, finalizing the renovations, and
the normal day-to-day duties of an old preacher man... But that's my
job, and not your cross to bear."

"Okay, just let me know if there is something I can do. I guess I
didn't realize that things could get so busy and complicated here, and
it never occurred to me that you have a real *job*. I just think of you as
a reverend."

Seeing the setting as a prime teaching moment, Reverend Drummond
slowly rose from his chair and put his arm around the young lad's shoulders. "You know, Theo, being a reverend isn't just preaching in the
church and running bingo games and after-school bible studies. It's serious business. Facilities need to be managed to make sure they don't fall
into disrepair, which is why we're doing this renovation. Then, there is
the daycare, which needs volunteers like you so we have enough people
every day, and activities to keep the little ones busy, many of whom
don't get regular meals at home or a safe place to play after school. And
let's not forget those in crisis like Chookie, those who need a shoulder
to cry on after they have suffered heartbreak, those celebrating the birth
of a newborn baby, or burying a cherished relative. So, you see, being a
reverend means you are many things to many people: preacher, handyman, social worker, psychologist, a friend to those in need, and above
all, a preacher of God's word. It really is a big job. Ever thought about
being a man of the cloth? We need all the help we can get."

"Wow," said Theo. "You make all of that stuff seem so effortless.
You just let me know if there is something more I can do to help out,
because it seems like we're at an standstill with the renovations, at

least until Chookie's sorted. I'm not too sure I could be as good a reverend as you, in all honesty. I'll certainly add it to my potential list of future jobs, though."

Reverend Drummond responded, "Thank you, Theo, but I really don't think there's much you can do right now. Wait—on second thought, maybe you can read to the children or play a little basketball with them? Everyone's still down about losing Japonica. He really had a positive impact on this place and was every bit a member of the staff here as anyone else. He will be missed for some time to come."

"You got it. Glad to do it. I, more than most, know kids just need to know there's someone around who cares about them." Theo thought for a moment and seized the perfect opportunity to ask, "Say, do you think we can do something to honor Japonica when the renovations are over? I was thinking maybe we could name the playroom after him, maybe put his picture on the wall over there. Maybe we can paint the door white, and I could get the kids to draw pictures of Japonica and their favorite memories of him, then cover the door with them. I heard that sometimes it's tough for kids to verbalize their emotions, and drawing pictures is a good outlet and coping mechanism."

"Theo, you're an amazing kid, you know that? Always thinking of others, putting their needs above your own, helping your mom, keeping an eye on Chookie, rescuing Japonica, helping an old man throw some paint on the walls, doing some handyman work, and all while keeping your grades up. You're really something special. I think honoring Japonica is commendable, and it's a very fitting tribute. Done! We'll find an appropriate way to honor him. Now, go along and find a book to read to the kids. You can go home after that."

# Chapter 43

## Reverend CJ's Getting Nervous

Oscar stared out of his seventeenth-floor window, looking down at a towboat pushing a cargo barge as it made the sweep turn up the Mississippi River. It was a sight he'd miss dearly. "Calm down, CJ. What do you mean by *coin*? What kind of *coin*?"

Reverend CJ's breath was labored, and he dabbed the sweat off his brow with a satin handkerchief with a beautiful paisley design. "The UAK. Honoré just called me a minute ago. The Jean-Batiste boy found some coin in a vacant lot near where that house fire was. Honoré said the boys in the satin hoods carry these coins as a tradition or some stupid shit like that. He's certain it's the UAK, but neither of us can figure out why, after so many years of leaving us alone, they'd be back at it. Them boys are running the gangs hard trying to squeeze every dollar they can, but they're all business these days and aren't into burning houses."

Oscar replied, "Well, I don't know much about what Robertsen and those miscreants do. All I know is what they tell me from the business side. I'll let him know. I have a feeling this won't be welcome news. Thanks for telling me, CJ. I'll take it from here."

"I hope they don't do nothin' crazy again, like how they tore up that boy in Natchez. Even though he was a gangbanger and drug pusher, he had a good heart. Just wound up with the wrong crowd. He would've been better off if I'd kept him here. Oscar, I've got a really bad feeling about this."

Oscar didn't wait to reply and immediately hung up the phone. He picked it up again and immediately dialed Lawrence Robertsen. "Larry, I think you've got a big problem."

# Chapter 44

## The Quail is Flushed

"COIN!!" barked the Sergeant with a sadistic smile on his face, hoping that he'd flush out the numbnut who dropped his coin in the field across from Tante Ju's. Four hands immediately rocketed into the front pockets of dirty blue jeans, fumbling through car keys, cigarette lighters, pocketknives, and loose change. Three coins emerged, slamming onto the weathered bar of the little juke joint in Madisonville.

Earl took an empty hand out of his pocket and yelled, "Shit! Shit, shit, shit!" A sinking feeling overtook him, and he immediately realized what had happened. Hoping panic wasn't written across his face, Earl steeled himself, and, with a copper taste on the back of his cotton-dry tongue, cleared his throat. There was a slight nervousness to his voice and a wry, almost forced grin on his face that belied his recognition of the seriousness of the situation as Earl replied, "Well, I guess this is my time in the barrel. What's it gonna be, fellas?"

A millisecond's pause, as well as the slight twitch on the face of Earl Patrick Tyler, was enough for the Sergeant to rest easy. He'd found his man.

The man closest to Earl put his arm around him, looked around at the others, and spoke. "Well, guys, whatta ya think? A round of Dixie Beer?"

The Sergeant's booming voice bellowed, "Nope! That horse piss isn't good enough for my crew tonight." Except for "Ace of Spades" by Motörhead blaring through the quarter-fed jukebox, a deafening quiet was suddenly cast about the room. The Sergeant stood from his bar-stool, speaking to no one in particular as he locked eyes with Earl and then said in a particularly authoritarian voice, "That lightweight piss water ain't gonna cut it, boys. We're goin' top shelf. Tonight, we'll have flamin' Dr. Pepper shots. Barkeep, line 'em up and keep 'em coming."

The flaming jiggers of Bacardi 151 stood sentry next to frosted mugs filled with Abita Purple Haze awaiting the fiery plunge. Earl would have the honors. One of the Troops draped his arm around him and recalled the famous wartime quote, "Once more unto the breach, dear friends!" The Troops then encircled Earl and chanted in raptured syncopation.

*"Heeere's to brother Eaaarl, brother Eaaarl, brother Eaaarl. Here's to brother Eaaarl who's with us tonight. He's happy, he's jolly, he's FUCKED UP BY GOLLY, here's to brother Eaaarl who's with us tonight. So DRINK TO YOUR FATHER, DRINK TO YOUR MOTHER, DRINK TO YOUR BROTHERS, DRINK!!"*

Committing an unforgivable breach of decorum that further differentiated him from his brethren, a nervous Earl Patrick Tyler gave a quick blow and extinguished the flame *before* dropping the jigger into the black lake lager. He downed the libation in one gulp, and the burn of the rum slid quickly down his throat, punctuating a forthcoming punishment he knew was his destiny once it became known that he did not merely forget his coin, but lost it.

The Sergeant looked disapprovingly at Earl, and, still holding his gaze, barked to the rest, "Drop 'em in hot, boys. Remember to let the beer put out that flame. One gulp, or else you'll be the one buying the next round."

In unison, three Troops dropped the flaming liquid like a mortar round into the mug. With the firewater doused, they threw their heads back, quaffed the drink in one gulp, and continued with the night's entertainment by ordering round after round, far more than Earl could afford. He would pay dearly, in more ways than one.

# Chapter 45

### Paying the Piper

It was a bright, crisp morning on the north shore of Lake Pontchartrain. General Herman Krieger opened the door and motioned to the chair in front of his desk. "Mr. Tyler, please have a seat."

Earl Patrick Tyler wondered what all this was about. Was he getting a promotion? Probably not, because Cerata was usually the one who took care of that. Krieger was calm and a bit too formal, so Earl knew this couldn't be good.

Krieger sat in his chair and with his elbows propped on his desk as he stroked his goatee and stared at Earl. After an uncomfortable pause, he finally spoke. "Mr. Tyler, I understand you lost a coin challenge the other night?"

Earl didn't know whether or not he should respond, but after an uncomfortable pause, he realized Krieger wanted an answer. He replied with a nervous chuckle, "Yes, sir, I sure did. Cost me more than a hundred bucks in Dr. Pepper shots. Boy, I sure won't let that happen again."

Krieger knew the answer to his next question, and after a longer, even more awkward pause, he said, "May I see it, please? The coin? I'm sure you have it with you now." Earl's face turned pale white; he knew he was in real trouble. Krieger continued, "Don't bother answering, because I know you don't have it."

*How in the hell does he know that?* Earl asked himself, but immediately dismissed the thought as irrelevant.

Krieger continued with a more authoritative tone, "Mr. Tyler, now that we've established that you don't have your coin on your person, the next logical question is *where* is your coin currently? At this moment?" Herman Krieger deliberately slowed his cadence and deepened his voice. "Mr. Tyler, it is becoming increasingly obvious to me that you have no idea where your coin is. Am I correct?"

Krieger rose from his chair, walked around the chair of Earl Patrick Tyler, and put his head next to his ear. Through clenched, coffee-stained teeth—and with breath so rancid it would make three-day-old shrimp smell as sweet as a Magnolia bloom by comparison—he asked a dramatically different question. "Mr. Tyler, I won't ask you if you fire-bombed that house off Airline Highway, because I know you did. What I want to know is *why* you did it." Krieger straightened himself and walked in front of Earl, raising his voice even higher. "What possessed you to do such an idiotic thing? What was going through your tiny, little, shit-filled brain? You know we try to maintain a low profile around this place, yet you thought it was a good idea to burn a house down and kill an innocent person? Do you know what kind of heat is going to come down on us because of that damn coin? We don't kill people, Mr. Tyler—at least not without a good reason!"

Krieger slowly walked around Earl's chair again and sounded like a jury rendering a verdict before the closing arguments. He looked back at Earl and said, "Mr. Tyler, obviously you know your severe lapse in judgment cannot go unpunished. We have yet to decide the nature or severity of your punishment, so in the meantime, you are hereby stripped of your rank and confined to the grounds, where you will report to Master Cerata, who will see to it that your days are unbearably painful and your nights are filled with agonizing fear. You will be under constant surveillance, so don't even *think* about trying to leave the grounds." Ramping up the volume and intensity of his cadence, Krieger continued, "If Master Cerata says, clean the garbage cans, you WILL clean the garbage cans. If he says cut the grass, you WILL cut the grass. If he says peel a bag of potatoes, you WILL peel a bag of potatoes! Until I say otherwise, you will turn your phone in and you will not have contact with the outside world. You will not speak to your little dipshit cousin or your brothers here unless Master Cerata approves, and even then you will keep your conversations to a bare minimum. AND you're not gonna say jack shit about this meeting, or why you are doing what you are doing or not doing! Is that understood?!"

Earl replied, "Yes, Mr. Krieger, I, I underst—"

Krieger cut him off, "You address me as General, you miserable piece of shit. Mr. Tyler, as the head of the Swamp, I am responsible for everyone and every goddamn thing that goes on around here, and you have put me in an impossible position. You, Mr. Tyler, whether you know it or not, have started a series of events that will go who knows where. You, Mr. Tyler, through your carelessness and stupidity, have jeopardized our way of life and rendered our future uncertain. You are not to address me any further. Do you understand? In fact, don't you ever look at me again. Do you understand? Now, Mr. Tyler, get the hell out of my office! Master Cerata will see to it that your punishment is swift, severe, and final."

Shaking uncontrollably, and with tears welling in his eyes, Earl replied, "Yes, sir." He exited the office, knowing that whatever was about to happen to him would not be good.

Krieger picked up the phone and barked, "Mario! That piece of shit is headed your way. See to it that you work his ass to death. You have free reign to do to him whatever you and the boys want. Break his fingers and make him scrub the toilets with a toothbrush if you want. Have the boys hold him down and shove a goddamn coin up his ass. I don't care what you do to him, but by the end of the week, see to it that he never sees the light of day again!"

Krieger didn't wait for Mario to reply and slammed the phone down. He was just glad Reverend CJ called and gave him the heads-up so he could plan for some damage control. Ironically, out of all of the members of the UAK, Reverend CJ was his best soldier and constantly provided quality kids who could hit the streets and move product.

# Chapter 46

## Prudence Confesses

It was the end of the day, and, knowing that she was about to go to a point of no return, Prudence gave a determined knuckle-tap on the door. "Jimmy, do you have a moment? I need to speak with you about something."

Jimmy, sensing that something was troubling her, replied, "Sure, Prudence, I always have a moment for you. Is something wrong at the Clinic?"

Prudence replied with a meek, almost taciturn voice, "No, nothing like that. I don't want to talk here, though. Can we meet in Jackson Square in a half hour or so? Maybe at Café Du Monde?"

Jimmy could tell by her tone that something was bothering her. "You got it. I'll meet you there. Are you okay?"

"Café Du Monde, thirty minutes," was all Prudence said on her way out of his office. She evoked a darkness that Jimmy had never seen before. Something was not right.

The half hour flew and Prudence waited anxiously at one of the side tables next to a wall behind the café for as much privacy as she could hope to find in such a public place. She chose the famous café since it was very noisy, and two colleagues grabbing an afternoon cup of coffee and eating a few beignets smothered with powdered sugar was more plausible than if they were seen sitting side by side on a park bench in Jackson Square, engaged in serious discussion.

Jimmy approached the table with a worried look. "Okay, Prudence, what's this all about? What's got you so upset?"

"Is it that obvious?" asked Prudence somewhat rhetorically. "Jimmy, something is going on at the firm and I can't make heads or tails of it. I don't know much about the business side of law firms, so this may be something, or nothing at all, but Mamaw always told me that 'if something don't feel right, it probably ain't.'"

"I don't understand. What do you mean by *business side*? You got me worried now. C'mon, let's get it out on the table and we'll deal with it. I don't like seeing you like this." Then, Jimmy suddenly realized that what was about to be said would probably be a turning point in his relationship with Prudence and the firm. Jimmy leaned in a little closer toward her and lowered his voice. "Prudence, we haven't known each other very long, but I've known you long enough to know that you have a great heart and integrity, and you would never knowingly cast someone in a bad light. You must trust me. Whatever it is, whether proper or not, will not leave this table. I promise. If it's nothing at all, I'll say so and we'll take this as a learning opportunity to tell you a little about how and why business deals are structured." Then, as if to emphasize his support, Jimmy leaned even closer and held her gaze. "But, if what you have seen is truly wrong, I'll be there to support you. I wouldn't want to be associated with people who don't share my values."

Prudence leaned back in her chair and took stock of her surroundings—starlings fluttered about, the fans in the café spun slowly and slightly off-center, the majestic statue of Andrew Jackson, the savior of the Battle of New Orleans, as well as the Cabildo and Presbytère flanking either side of the St. Louis Cathedral, whose bells had peeled in times of both joy and crisis. At that moment, the bells chimed, announcing the two o'clock hour, and she suddenly felt an unexplained sense of peace.

With a deep breath of faith, she looked back to Jimmy and laid it all out. "Okay, a few weeks ago, while I was working on the permit for the Renaissance d'Orleans, Rachel asked me to copy a stack of files from Oscar's office. I was to copy them and then place the contents back in exactly the same order. I went to Bernadette's office to get the files. She was on the phone and motioned me into Oscar's office. Oscar was in his restroom, so I didn't see him and thought he wasn't there. Bernadette was still on the phone and waved goodbye as I was leaving. She told me later, at the celebration dinner at Bene Cucina, that she'd assumed Oscar gave the files to me directly. A pretty simple misunderstanding under normal circumstances."

Jimmy gently interrupted her. "Prudence, I don't see anything wrong with that, and neither do you. I can see you are stalling a little. You have to trust me and tell me what's going on—*everything.*"

Prudence straightened herself in her chair, cleared her throat a little, and continued. "I'm getting to that. As I was copying the files, in the stack among the green client folders were several light blue ones marked **"PERSONAL AND CONFIDENTIAL—OSCAR BRIMLEY."** I was on autopilot and didn't think anything of it while I was making the copies, but the files stood out as I was putting the stack back together. I quickly went down the hall to return the files, hoping and praying that no one was there. Thankfully, both Oscar and Bernadette were away from their desks, so I went into Oscar's office and put the stack back in the same spot. I was scared that if Bernadette or Oscar were there, they'd see the light blue files. I can't explain it, but I had a feeling that those light blue files weren't meant to be in that stack." She looked down at the table and continued. "I knew something was not right. I knew it was not the right thing to do, but I did it anyway."

Jimmy was getting anxious. "Did *what* Prudence? I know you are holding back."

Prudence looked Jimmy straight in the eye and said, "Jimmy, I made a second copy of the light blue files and kept them. I've never done anything like that before and it felt so wrong, but something compelled me to do it."

With a little more frustration in his voice, Jimmy commanded, "Okay, so it was wrong of you to take the files, but that's not why we're here, is it? What is going on?"

Prudence replied, "In the files, there were lots of code names, symbols, diagrams, as well as the names of some of the clients. I noticed KTL Construction, which is the company that's going to build the hotel. Then, I noticed a form document called a parent company guarantee— or something like that—indicating that the construction company was owned in part by Knight Trucking & Logistics, which is the firm's client, and which happens to have an office in this building. The other owner was O.B. Enterprises, LLC, which obviously stands for Oscar Brimley. I don't have all of the pieces, but don't you find it strange that a logistics company and a member of the firm own a company that is getting the contract for the construction of a new hotel? Remember how intense Oscar acted while we were preparing the permit to raze the historical building, and how giddy he got when he kicked off the project with that extravagant dinner? Those are the actions of a person who has a vested interest, not a lawyer happy for his client."

Jimmy paused a moment, then replied, "Well, nothing really

prohibits a member of a firm from being a part owner in a client's business as long as there is transparency, the bylaws of the firm are adhered to, and the canon of ethics is obeyed. There may be some ethical questions, but nothing illegal, per se. It's a little unseemly for my taste, but based on these limited facts, I don't think we need to bring this up. Let sleeping dogs lie, so to speak. Sometimes lawyers take an equity interest in a client's company as payment for their fees instead of money. Having said that, yes, I do find the types of companies involved here to be a little strange, but nothing stands out other than that it is a high-profile project. That's not the whole picture, though, is it? Who owns the property and the hotel?"

Prudence, feeling a little better since Jimmy had not overreacted, said, "That's the problem. I know that information is buried in the files somewhere, maybe even on the firm's computer servers. My gut tells me that there's a lot more to this, but I don't know what to do and I'm too tired to keep staying up all night to try to figure it out. I'm burnt out, but if Oscar truly is into something inappropriate, I need to know so I don't get caught up in it. I have a reputation and a family I need to protect. But, I need to keep going until I get to the bottom of this."

"Okay, I'm sold. I don't see anything glaring, but there is something strange going on and now you have me curious as hell. I'm going to help you dig into this. Hopefully, it is all coincidental and this is just a strange business deal, as opposed to something unethical or even illegal. Oscar is a smart guy, and this could be nothing more than a potentially lucrative setup for his retirement. However, if your gut is telling you this is all leaning toward something sinister, then I think you will need my help. This is definitely worth pursuing."

Prudence breathed a big sigh of relief and said, "Thank you, Jimmy. Thank you for trusting me and not just dismissing my concerns."

"Don't thank me yet. It will take some time to decode everything, and I'm sure there is more information that is not contained in the light blues." Jimmy stared out at the statue of General Jackson and continued. "We need to decode the information in the light blue folders and dig into the server to see if there are any more links between Knight Trucking & Logistics, KTL Construction, and O.B. Enterprises. I think going down that road will help us solve this thing. I need to get those light blue files though without raising suspicion. It would be unusual and gossip-worthy for me to go to your house or vice versa, and you cannot risk taking the files to the office, so we need to find a way for you to get those files to me."

"I got it! The Antioch! We'll do it at the Antioch," said Prudence, almost to herself.

"The Antioch? You mean *your* church? Prudence, I don't know about that. I think that might raise some eyebrows. Some would think it'd be strange for me to go back and forth to your church all the way across town. I don't think anyone would think something bad is going on, but it would be on peoples' minds. I mean, a white Catholic boy going to a black Baptist church?"

Prudence looked directly at Jimmy and said, "You're right. Even though people might think that it would be okay, it would appear strange and some questions might come up. People would probably be curious, and we'd be drawing more attention to ourselves, not less. How about this—let's hide in plain sight!"

"What do you mean, plain sight? The problem is that we need to stay under radar. That's the whole point. We need to be *out* of sight."

Prudence beamed with a *cat-that-ate-the-canary grin*. "Jimmy, what if we did pro bono work at the church? The firm would be bringing the help to the people who need it most instead of people seeking out the help at an intimidating downtown skyscraper that they probably couldn't get to anyway."

Jimmy, with an almost defeated voice, said, "I don't think that would work at all. I think everyone would think that it's great to help people, but that it'd be too expensive. Time is money to these people, and if I spent even a few days a week out of the office, two things would happen. One, thousands of dollars of billable hours and expenses would be spent on every visit. Two, the Bullpen would think you're on a boondoggle since you're brand-new to the firm, yet you'd get to spend time out of the office while they barely get an hour for lunch, which is usually taken at their desks. No, it's too risky."

"Okay, I see your point about the Bullpen, but why do you think it would cost thousands of dollars for each visit? Doesn't the firm write off those expenses and highlight the hours as pro bono? I'm doing the work anyway, and I'm sure you're just going to make a few trips out there, so what's the difference if I work here or there? Wouldn't that be a good thing?"

Jimmy replied, "It's a little more complicated than that. You would have to have a lawyer working by your side the whole time since you'd be out of the office. Even if they write the whole thing off, at $325 per hour for a junior associate like me, that's serious money. They still need to pay salaries. And, as Oscar always says, cash is king. Besides, it wouldn't be just salaries, Prudence. There are ancillary costs, too. We would be expected to submit an expense report for mileage at $0.54 cents per mile and a per diem of maybe $20 per day. Let's not forget the *boondoggle effect*, which would probably dampen morale at the office and create some jealousy, which would probably cause Oscar to fire someone just to make an example and hopefully steer the team back to happiness. He'd employ the old 'the beatings will continue until morale improves' method. So, think about it. What looks like a great idea on paper can be poisonous for an office, cost someone their job, or drive others away from the firm."

"Don't you think that's a little far-fetched? Don't you think the good would outweigh the bad here? If something sinister is going on, office morale and expense reports will be the least of our worries." Prudence pleaded her case like a seasoned attorney.

Jimmy replied, "Hey, I'm with you, but let's look at reality. Remember, the firm has been the most successful in the Gulf South for more than one hundred years, without having a pro bono clinic until recently. So, why would they spend a fortune just to better an already established brand? They're not going to dump even more money into some feel-good program to help a bunch of poor people. Sorry it sounds so crass, but it's the truth.

"Sure, we've been helping people, but that's a windfall, not the reason it was started. At its heart, the firm's not too big on altruistic ventures. Let's look at the numbers for me having to be out of the office just two days a week. Let's say an ordinary workweek is a laughable forty-five hours, which at my billable rate adds up to around $58,500 per month. Two days, or sixteen hours a week, would be spent at the clinic. That's $20,800 per month. Prudence, that's $249,600 on an annualized basis for my salary alone. Add you and it is a substantial amount of money in lost billable hours. Kick in mileage, a per diem for each of us, office expenses, extra phones, a copier, and IT equipment, and it's close to half a million dollars per year. And you know that with Oscar, everything would have to be top-of-the-line. Do you seriously think the firm's going to leave that kind of money on the table? That just won't work. We have to find another way."

Prudence would not let up. "I think you're too pessimistic. Oscar is big on diversity, and I know that's the *real* reason I was hired. I'm not as naïve as you think I am. Let's face it—hiring me was mutually beneficial. And what better way to make his big ego even bigger than to highlight his new wonder girl as a champion of the poor. He'd jump at this since it would further increase the stature of the firm and better his brand. Half a million bucks is a drop in the bucket for the firm, and he's got the power to spend the money. The firm will write it all off anyway. He would also get the sadistic pleasure of all of the other firms in the city being pressured into following his lead. I'm going for it, Jimmy. He wants to play *bourré* with the diversity card? That's a trump I have in my pocket. I got a whole church full of diversity. He likes me, and this will be done before you know it. We'll work on the files at the Antioch. I'll even make Oscar pay to install Wi-Fi at the church. Another magnanimous gesture from King Oscar. The irony is that he'd be funding his own investigation!"

Jimmy decided to end the conversation there. "Go for it, girl! Remember rule number one in negotiations; if you don't ask, you don't get. So, ask for it all and then some. Let me know how it goes after you speak to his *highness*. I hope your gut is more spot-on than my hesitation."

# Chapter 47

### The Bill Comes Due

"What do you mean, *federal investigation?*" exclaimed Robertsen.

"Settle down, they're not going to investigate *you*," Oscar replied. "You've got nothing to do with this. The investigation hasn't even started yet. I just got the heads-up from a friend of a friend in the U.S. attorney's office. It could be months before this gets off the ground, and we'll try to delay it as much as possible. It'll disappear with the next news cycle."

"What in the hell are you talking about?! Of course this'll come back to me! That miscreant burned down a poor black lady's house, killing her and leaving a brain-damaged man-child homeless. Someone will come forward and say something. You know they've had a file on the UAK for decades. It won't take too long for them to place me in the mix. That's what the feds do, Oscar. They dig and dig and dig. They always find out.

"First, they'll interview everyone in the neighborhood and eventually get to the preacher—Reverend Drummond, I believe. He won't want to talk, because he knows it will get back to the UAK and they'll burn another house or even his church. So, they'll squeeze him, and in exchange for some federal protection, he'll eventually give up the UAK. Next, they'll find every UAK member in OPP and squeeze those who might be up for parole soon, and they'll be convinced to enter witness protection in exchange for giving up whatever information they have. They will give up Krieger. Remember him? The one that strung up one of those gangbangers in Natchez, which, by the way, occurred across state lines and is a hate crime? Krieger will tell them everything because he's too much of a pussy. He also doesn't have an equity position in Azalea. He won't get a piece of the pie, so he'll squeal like a stuck feral hog. He'll know that it's over and won't want to go down with the ship, so in a last-ditch effort to save his own skin, he'll give me up.

"I'm going to play the long game while my lawyers tie up the investigation as much as they can. This will frustrate the feds even further, so they'll start to follow the money, which will lead them to the gangs, which will lead them to the drugs, which will lead them back to the money, which will then lead them to our friends in the police department, city council, and whoever you've been handing our money out to. It's over, Oscar. It might take a year or two, but this thing is eventually going down like the *Titanic*, and all because the little boy of your new paralegal got into a fight at school with some redneck, whose cousin was in the UAK and careless enough to lose a friggin' coin. Do you get the picture now? Speaking of your paralegal, they'll squeeze her, too, and eventually get to you if they haven't already done so. One way or the other, it's going down."

Oscar interrupted, "Don't you think you're being a little dramatic here? The UAK didn't do this."

252

Robertsen exploded, "What in the *hell* are you talking about?! Haven't you been listening to a goddamn thing I've been saying? It doesn't matter whether the UAK did it—one of their people did. You know, for a smart guy, you're pretty effin' stupid sometimes. They've got the coin, Oscar. Don't be so naïve! Remember? The coin? The one with *UAK* written on it? I just told you that's how they're going to get to the UAK. They're going to go after everyone associated with it. They're going to interview the grandkids of the grand poo-bah who started the group. They'll terrify the wives and girlfriends through midnight raids of their houses, take their computers and official-looking boxes of documents. They'll show up at their places of employment and lead them out in handcuffs in front of all their friends. The media will have a field day, because you know they'll sink their fangs in this. And don't think for a second the feds won't eventually get to Falke. If they do, we'll never be seen or heard from again.

"You've obviously never personally been the subject of a federal investigation, Oscar. Remember when we got caught up in that bribery scandal years ago, with that logistics company out of Brazil? They investigated nine companies and three of them still have *observers* in their offices, approving everything from business class tickets to Singapore, to staplers and pencils. And, it's the companies that pay for the *observers* and the outside law firms they report to. Imagine you've been found innocent and you have to live as if you're guilty just because of some greedy vendor who probably didn't even get a lot of money out of whatever it was he did. It's really never over, too, because you have to pay for all of it and you are forever after on the government's radar.

"We spent a fortune with your firm, as well as on that hotshot white-collar defense firm in DC, and they looked at *everything* so they'd be able to mount our defense. An army of government accountants looked at every invoice associated with that company. Investigators took my operations people for hours at a time, scaring the shit out of them. Each visit cost me at least eight hours of billable time for not only a lawyer or two from your firm, but two or more from the DC firm. Damn Yankees treated it like a vacation and were in no hurry to go back home. You better believe that it'll come back to us. You're pregnant with this, too, so I know you'll work your ass off to make sure we get out of this, right?" Robertson admonished.

"Okay, okay, you made your point. I'll see what I can do," Oscar conceded.

"I'm not paying for any of this, Oscar. You need to put your big boy britches on and saddle up."

Oscar replied, "Now hold on a minute, my people didn't torch that house. Yours did. If you want the firm involved, I can keep my time off the books, but I have to charge for everyone assigned to the file so the firm's books are clean. I may be a greedy son of a bitch, Larry, but there are some fine people in that firm and I don't want any more lives ruined. I'll make sure the team is as lean and efficient as it can be, I can give a deep discount on the final bill, and we can squeeze our vendors, but we'll have to run this just like every other project with monthly billing. Later, we can talk about how I might also contribute through my holdings in Azalea."

Robertsen was indignant as he said, "You cocky son of a bitch, you sound as if you are in a position to call the shots. I don't give a rat's ass about anyone in your firm. We might all be looking at decades in prison. Did you forget who you're talking to here, Brimley? We made you! Every nickel you have is due to our support over the years, and now you dare to tell me how it's going to be? If people at your firm get hurt, it's all on you. We didn't make you take the money, or the holdings, or the ownership interest in the construction company. And, lest you forget, you're the one that came up with the project in the first place.

Hell, you're the arrogant bastard who named it while staring at all your precious azaleas out the window of your mansion—a mansion, by the way, you could've never afforded in the first place if it weren't for the business I gave you for the past twenty plus years!"

A more contrite Oscar replied, "Okay, let's take a deep breath and a step back. Regardless of who eventually pays for all of this, whether it is my firm or not, you will have to hire a law firm and pay the bills just as you would in any other legal matter. That's all I'm talking about here. To avoid further suspicion, this must look like any other legal matter. And if you want to keep costs down, you've got no choice other than to use my firm. Any other firm will hose you down and take you to the cleaners. I have the history and I run the goddamn firm, so I can really help in that regard. I know this whole situation sucks, but you have to admit that we had nothing to do with this, and neither did you.

"We'll get some of the old-timers in the UAK to be the face of this since you obviously cannot be seen to be a part of it. Besides, they've always enjoyed their time in the spotlight, and they'll likely not be touched by any of this. It's bad enough that our firm has a history of representing some of those reprobates in the past, but we're strong enough to withstand the outcry over having to represent the reprehensible again in the interest of allowing our system of justice to work. I've got some friends in the ACLU who would love to get in on this. It would give them some good publicity and allow me to maintain a low profile."

Robertsen collected himself, faced the wall, and replied in a rather calm manner, "Oscar, you still don't get it. You're the biggest whore I know, and I know a lot of them. You just can't help yourself, can you? I don't give a shit how the firm comes out or what side of the fence you're on. I do see your point, however. While none of this is your firm's fault, you definitely are involved, and whatever happens to the firm is on you. We're going to have to throw a ton of money at this, and all the Mexicans care about is getting their money on time. So, you'll need to get creative."

# Chapter 48

## The Ends Are Justified

"Aw, c'mon Oscar. It'll be great." Prudence thought she could evade suspicion by getting as close to Oscar as she possibly could, even butter him up if need be. It was a strategic move made mostly out of fright and self-preservation. She continued, "Just think of the headlines Oscar. 'LeRoux, Godchaux brings help directly to the disenfranchised.' 'Champions of the Down-trodden.' Blah, blah, blah. The other firms would be so jealous that you were on the cutting edge in pro bono, community-based services to those in need. They'd have to follow suit, which makes you the leader. Besides, the more firms imitate our firm, the more people will be helped, so it truly is a win-win. This couldn't hurt politically, either. You'd have the mayor and city hall in the palm of your hand, and we'd never again have to move heaven and earth to get a permit approved."

Oscar scratched his chin and thought to himself, *Dear, dear Prudence. So naïve. It's not about the clients or the downtrodden: especially the downtrodden. If anything, the firm would prefer things like a longer permitting process. More time means more money from clients who are used to paying big bills.*

What sold Oscar, though, was the political angle. The firm would be tied up with the UAK mess, so this, along with the ACLU support, would definitely help. Little Miss Pru was on to something. This would be a huge differentiator that would help the firm's image, and with this looming federal investigation of the firebombing, he needed high friends in higher places. Thinking on it a little more, he thought that maybe if he had a presence in the place near the firebombing, it would throw the feds off the trail. Return to the scene of the crime and help with the cleanup like a murderer who begs to be on the jury in the trial of an innocent man framed for the murder *he* committed.

After a silence that was a little too uncomfortable for Prudence, Oscar finally spoke. "Done. You and Jimmy make it happen and charge everything to my budget. I'll tell Jimmy that he's going to run it. If the church doesn't already have it, make sure IT installs high-speed internet and make sure those from the firm who work there have secure VPNs installed on their laptops. If they don't have laptops, get them laptops. Give the church full access to the Wi-Fi. If there's not a room with a door and lock for a makeshift office, build out the size of a generous file room they can use when/if the clinic is closed or moved. Don't buy the furniture, rent it. Make sure the office and the area near it are painted, and install new flooring. A few grand here and there is a good investment to make the joint classy. It helps the firm maintain its reputation for excellence, and provides us with invaluable goodwill in the community. I'm going to write off some of the expenses as a donation to the church, but don't go overboard."

"Oh, Oscar, thank you so much! You won't regret this," replied Prudence, knowing full well that Oscar was financing his own investigation.

Prudence and Jimmy went straight to work. They used labor and bought materials from companies owned by congregants, one of whom hired Theo, who needed some pocket change. Everything had to be legit, so Prudence went the extra mile and made sure the contractor got the construction permit, which was granted in record time although the work would probably be done before final approval was given. No matter. This was going to happen one way or the other.

It took a week and a half, but the LeRoux, Godchaux, Bouligny & Tooley Legal Clinic: Antioch Division was open and ready for clients. There was always the good with the bad, though, and Prudence felt a little guilty that she and Jimmy couldn't devote all their time to the people who needed it most. They only took a few files to make it look legitimate and turned away almost everyone who visited the clinic, saying that they were busy. This gave them a very short window, because even though some would extol the virtues of the clinic, it wouldn't take long for others to figure out that not many people were being served.

# Chapter 49

## The End of Earl

"Sure, Mr. Cerata, I'll meet you there. I'll be sure to come alone, but why. What's this all about?" asked a nervous Earl Patrick Tyler.

"This is for the jamboree. Why am I even explaining myself to you? Are you questioning me?!" accused Cerata.

"No, not at all it's jus—"

Cerata cut him off. "Good. Get your ass down there, *tout suite!*"

Earl arrived at Aryan Cove, sacred ground for the UAK and the site for the group's jamborees. He took stock of his surroundings, which looked much different in the daylight. The bonfire pit in the clearing with black soot covering the cinder block borders. Cords of wood, chainsaws, axes off to one side next to cans of gas, diesel, a few lawn chairs, and empty beer cans spread all about. It was a setting fit for a nest of vipers of the redneck genus.

Suddenly, he realized that he was the only one there. A sick, empty feeling came over him as a copper taste spread across his tongue and throughout his mouth. He picked up a few beer cans, went to the wood-pile to burn off some nervous energy, and chopped a few small logs for kindling. After a while, he looked up and saw Master Mario Cerata drive up with a few UAK heavies with stoic faces and square jaws set like steel, all spoiling for a fight. Earl recognized them as part of the crew that went to Natchez. The blood drained from his face and he nearly passed out.

"Nice afternoon, Mr. Tyler, isn't it?" said Cerata.

"Ye-ye-yes, it is, Master Cerata. A beautiful day in paradise," stuttered ET, knowing that Cerata's formality didn't bode well for him.

"I see you've been chopping a little wood over there. Good. That'll make building the next bonfire that much easier. I like your initiative," Cerata said in a very calm manner as he and the crew crept forward. "Yes, yes, it will be a beautiful inferno. A fire that will make the devil himself both proud and jealous, don't you think, Mr. Tyler?"

Earl looked around and replied with a dry throat. "Yes, I, I suppose so. Are we having a jamboree tonight? I thought the next one wasn't for a couple of weeks."

"Indeed, you are correct, Mr. Tyler. The next jamboree is a couple of weeks out. Can never be too prepared, though, can we?"

"I suppose not," Earl replied, now fearing the worst, but resigned to his fate.

Cerata pointed toward a grouping of trees off in the distance, looked at Earl, and said, "Mr. Tyler, do you mind following these fine gentlemen to those trees over there? There are some good limbs I think will make some fine support beams for the bonfire. It looks like they'll need an extra hand to cut them down and strip the branches."

One of the heavies was holding an axe, tapping the blunt side of the head against one of his massive paws and grinning all the while. Earl followed the crew in silence, dreaming of an impossible escape. Running would be useless and would probably make matters worse.

The hope was that there would be a few lashes and maybe a gang-style beating resulting in a broken bone or two, cracked ribs, and maybe a black eye. That was wishful thinking. Small tears welled up and leaked from his eyes. The crew decided to walk him about fifty yards further than the outcrop Cerata had pointed to. These guys were pros and believed this would be a better spot to bury what would be left of the earthly remains of Earl Patrick Tyler.

"String him up," said one of the crew. "Let's get this over with. I have a date in a few hours."

The others chuckled at this while grabbing Earl by his arms. They secured a rope to each wrist and flung them over a tree branch, then hoisted him high enough so that his bare feet barely touched the ground.

The pain was unbearable. His wrists started to bleed and the lactic acid in the muscles in his narrow shoulders burned. Tears continued to stream down his face.

"Any last words, douchebag?" one of them said, chuckling as he gave the whip a few warm-up snaps.

"Screw you!" replied Earl, realizing at that moment that his last moments on earth would be at the hands of a gang of ignorant skinheads.

Each crewmember administered roughly twenty-five lashes with a frayed bullwhip, complete with frayed leather strands at the end. They continued until Earl passed out and then drug him back to the bonfire pit.

"Make sure he doesn't wake up and you get rid of all of it," ordered Cerata. "I don't want anything left of that piece of shit. Bones, ashes, all of it. Hell, use the chainsaw if you think it will speed things up. Chuck whatever is left into Lake Pontchartrain. The cops will probably use cadaver dogs, but the trail will run cold. Now, one of you numbnuts forgot the shovel and ice chest, so I have to go back into town, because apparently I can't trust any of you with even the simplest of tasks. I'll be back in about an hour, so don't screw this up, too."

# Chapter 50

### Lamb to the Slaughter

Rachel picked up her phone.

"Ms. DeRouen, would you please meet me in my private conference room adjacent to my office?"

The weight of recent developments weighed heavily on the brilliant mind of Oscar Brimley. BB was the only one in the firm that Oscar could trust, and he gave Rachel very high marks for her work with Prudence during the permitting of the Renaissance hotel. He would have to rely on BB's endorsement and make a leap of faith by bringing Rachel into the fold, if only to a limited extent—for now, anyway, and for a sinister purpose.

Rachel walked swiftly down the Hall and opened the door to an empty Valhalla conference room. She was concerned about Oscar's formality and racked her brain to think of anything she might have said or done to warrant a private meeting in his seldom used conference room. It was quite rare for an associate, even a senior one, to enter his conference room, much less have a meeting there. Her thoughts ran wild from the highest of highs to the lowest of lows.

*Am I being promoted to partner, made head of a section, or being moved from one section to another? Am I being fired? Is Jimmy or Prudence being fired? I haven't seen them much lately.*

The anxiety was written all over her face and in her body language.

A somewhat subdued Oscar gently opened the door to the stately room with mahogany walls, a long maple conference table, and eight high-back chairs upholstered in supple, jet-back Italian leather that was butter smooth. Topping it off was the AV system with two big screen TVs, microphones in front of each chair, built-in wall speakers, and a parabolic microphone hovering over the conference table. No one else in the firm had equipment as high-tech as this setup, and the irony was that it was seldom used, as far as anyone knew.

Oscar entered the conference room and mustered up his gregarious Dr. Jekyll persona. "Ah, Rachel, thanks for coming on such short notice." He noticed that Rachel looked anxious, if not dour, and forced a smile as he said, "Relax, this won't take long." He continued, holding Rachel's worrisome gaze. "Rachel, I've called you here to discuss a new project. Of course, this goes without saying that this is a confidential matter under the attorney-client privilege, and you are not to speak about this matter or this meeting with anyone except me—not even Bernadette, BB, or government investigators. You will answer only to me. Agreed?"

Rachel immediately straightened in her chair and, with eyes as wide as saucers, said, "Of course. I'll speak of this with no one, unless you instruct me to do otherwise." Her anxiety was replaced with a palpable fear.

"I know that you will, but I was duty bound to emphasize the point. I hope you understand that. Apologies for the cloak and dagger, I just had to get that out of the way so that you could honestly say that you were warned if ever you were asked."

Rachel's straightened up even more. *Warned? What the hell is Oscar dragging me into?* She collected herself and said in a clipped tone, "Fear not, I've been duly warned."

"Good." Satisfied that he'd scared the living daylights out of Rachel. He continued, "With that out of the way, let's get down to brass tacks. A friend at the U.S. attorney's office gave me a courtesy call since he has reason to believe that Knight Trucking & Logistics, my largest client, will soon be the subject of a federal investigation for tax evasion. I won't tell you the details yet since a grand jury has not been convened and he did not give me any specifics about the breadth or scope of the investigation. Nevertheless, I want to be as prepared as we can be to provide certain information that I know will be subpoenaed, and that's where you come in.

"At the start of any federal investigation, the feds look for obvious abnormalities. Mistakes in books and records violations can attract more jail time than the underlying crime itself. If the target is a company, they want to see the articles of incorporation, minutes of board meetings, subsidiaries, bank accounts, names of lobbyists, agents, or anyone they think might be able to provide evidence or valuable information. They take that information and indict smaller fish on minor charges to put pressure on them to turn so they can then go after the big fish. As you know, my client—no, the firm's client—is a big fish the feds would love to make an example of.

"Believe me, life as you know it is over if you are the target of a federal investigation. Family members are hassled, friends flee, business dries up, your money is sucked up and transferred to white-collar criminal lawyers, and even if you are found not guilty, you are exhausted, broke, empty inside, and all alone." Oscar looked away while saying this, as if he had already resigned himself to that fate. He continued, "Anyway, that's why the small fish are usually eager to make a plea bargain in exchange for little or no jail time, or entrance into the federal witness protection program. Remember that movie, *My Blue Heaven,* with Steve Martin? Probably before your time, but the point is that's what happens. Game over. They truly do *follow the money*, as the adage goes, and there is always a crime since the feds normally won't do or say anything without having all the proof they need first. That's why their conviction rate is ninety-nine percent. A *not guilty* verdict is rare, and usually saved for politicians or drug lords.

"Anyway, I need you to scrub all of the company's official documents, as well as those of its subsidiaries, affiliates, or joint venture partners. I need it all: minutes of meetings, filings, receipts for payment of fees, tax returns, names of shareholders, and anything else that you can find. I've already instructed BB that, effective immediately, you are to pass off your current files to others within the department and start on this project right away. Bernadette will give you the billing codes. Remember, neither knows anything, so you can speak with her only about billing codes and file numbers, and with BB only about the files you are passing off.

"I estimate this will take you at least a month. You will need to gather information from secretaries of state at the state level and their equivalents of foreign jurisdictions. I know the Cayman Islands is one of them and they are notoriously on *island time*, so start with them first and review whatever they give you *very* carefully. The feds will pay greater attention to those records coming from a foreign government, and, more importantly, whatever peckerheads get assigned this case will get a trip to the Caymans, courtesy of the taxpayers. Let me know straightaway if you think it will take you longer. Thanks, and sorry this is such a rush job. I know you are busy and would like to get back to your regular life as soon as possible."

Emphasizing the point that he was a benevolent dictator, Oscar couldn't help himself and had to put a spin on it, *Oscar style*. "Rachel, you will find that, at the end of this, you will come out smelling like a rose. If you work hard, you'll get easy hours out of this—a lot of hours. Best of all, I will inform BB that you will be promoted to junior partner and will be his official number two in the department. We've chatted about it in passing before since I wanted to plant the seed. He'll endorse the move. Best of all, I will determine your bonus this year, and I've already decided that you'll be brought into the partner bonus pool. The calculation will be based on your new salary and it will not be prorated; it will be retroactive to your most recent raise. I trust this is to your liking?"

Rachel could see beyond the pitch. This was a little over-the-top, even for Oscar. Whenever Oscar made a deal sound too good to be true, it usually was. The recent exception was when he hired Prudence. Still, there was an ulterior motive there, too. She'd have to tread very carefully.

"Oh, one more thing I haven't told you. Prudence will not be joining your group just yet. I had her and Jimmy open a pro bono clinic at her church. Some feel-good project that likely will put the firm in good stead with the city and the bar association."

It was too much for Rachel to process, and the only thing she could manage to say was, "No problem. You can count on me."

Oscar had a sinister reason for choosing Rachel, and had no problem using her as a means to an end. She was young, smart, and more importantly, she had no immediate family, and no large group of friends. He knew that by asking her to start the investigation in the Caymans, she would find out very quickly about his ownership of O.B. Enterprises, and he wanted her to know sooner rather than later so he could look out for any change in her behavior. If she got squeamish, he'd bring her deeper into Project Azalea and buy her off by giving her an offer she couldn't refuse—one quite different from the plumb that he just gave her. She would be set for life, but the information she had would weigh her down and eventually wear her out. He had her locked up under the attorney-client privilege, and she couldn't be called as a witness without risking her career and her reputation. This was most definitely the cheaper, preferable route. Either way, she was a lamb to the slaughter.

# Chapter 51

## Reality Check

Rachel froze. There it was, in writing: O.B. Enterprises, LLC. It was an exempt company, so there were neither shareholder nor director names listed in the public registry, and the corporate address was that of a local law firm in Grand Cayman. It didn't take Rachel long to figure out, however, that O.B. stood for none other than Oscar Brimley. She broke into a cold sweat and realized that Oscar had saddled her with this project by design. She knew Oscar would eventually be caught up in the federal investigation, and that she was being used to do all the yeoman's work. The word *warned* suddenly took on a different meaning, and all Rachel could think about was how to get out of this mess.

Until this moment, Rachel had never experienced real fear. Now she was experiencing it on two levels—personally, because she knew she could not betray ruthless people who could cause her great harm, and professionally, because there was no way she could break the attorney-client privilege and continue to work as a lawyer. She went home, and, after a long jog through Audubon Park, she decided which way she would go: business as usual. She would maintain a professional demeanor and keep personal interactions with Oscar at a minimum, communicating with him mostly via email and text while hoping that the paper trail could help exonerate her as an innocent cog were she to become a target of the investigation.

She would need to consciously control her behavior around colleagues in the office and hope her fear wouldn't show through. She had to have a story ready in case she was asked if anything was wrong. She decided on, "a family member was just diagnosed with inoperable cancer." She could not use a death in the family as an excuse since it would be too easy for some idiot who doubted her story to try to verify it by doing an obituary search. HIPPA laws would protect someone with cancer, though, so an investigation would run into a dead end very quickly. If pressed, she'd simply state that the family member requested that the matter be kept within the family, and that she would respect those wishes.

Rachel DeRouen was like a nutria caught helplessly in a trap, screaming in the swamp through the night until some trapper put him out of his misery. Rachel was definitely trapped, and only a miracle could free her. She prayed that life would continue as normally as possible, and more importantly, that neither she nor those for whom she cared would get hurt in the process. Rachel cried that night until it hurt. She knew this turn in her life was as unsettling as it was uncertain—an uncertainty she would likely endure alone.

# Chapter 52

## Mission Accomplished

The phone broke the silence, and he picked it up on the first ring. "Krieger."

Cerata replied, "Mission accomplished."

Krieger breathed a sigh of relief. "Good. I need a deep dive on that son of a bitch. I want to know who his family members are, where they live, where they work, where they go to school. I want to know what they had for dinner last night and what brand of toothpaste they use! I want to know it all. No detail is too trivial. Robertsen is on my ass and we need to make this whole problem go away. I'm counting on you to make it happen. You are to use any means necessary, clear? Use whoever you need to, but make sure you use only those who have the most to lose. The Counselor is on it and finding out whatever information he can, but he doesn't know shit about what happens in the field. If anything, he'll be a liability and we'll need to deal with him later. For now, we need to pump him for every last detail. I don't think I can stress enough the seriousness of the situation. At any moment, this whole thing can blow up on all of us, and I mean *all* of us."

"Understood." Cerata worried that this was the mob takedown all over again, and that at some point, it would be every man for himself.

# Chapter 53

### Reverend CJ Spins It

"Yes, hello. This is Reverend Honoré Drummond with the Antioch Faith Church in New Orleans. How are you today?"

"Oh, hi, reverend. I haven't heard your voice in a while. I'm just fine. How are you?" said the cheery receptionist on the other end of the line.

Reverend Drummond replied, "I'm fine, dear, thank you for asking. Is Reverend Hill around? I'd like to speak with him if he's not too busy."

"Oh, I don't think he is ever too busy to speak with you, reverend. He's around here somewhere, maybe out back reading scripture with the kids. May I ask what this is in reference to?"

Reverend Drummond took a deep breath and exhaled slowly. "It's about that firebombing in the neighborhood. You might have heard of it."

"Yes, over there at that poor woman's house. That was horrific. We're all saddened by that," she replied, the cheery mood having been replaced by empathy. "I'll track him down for you straightaway. Hold on just a minute, please."

It took longer than she hoped, but when she finally got his attention, she whispered the news in his ear. Reverend CJ was reading *The Giving Tree* by Shel Silverstein to the children, and almost dropped the book as he stood up.

He whispered to the receptionist, "Please continue and then start another book. I'll be back in a few moments."

Reverend CJ went straight to the office and hurriedly picked up the phone. "Drum, what's going on down there? Are they sure it wasn't just a house fire? How's Chookie? This is terrible, just terrible. Ju really was a pillar of the community." Then, knowing full well that the UAK was behind this, and scared after his conversation with Oscar, he tried to sow some doubt. "Are we really sure it's the UAK?"

"CJ, I already told you it was the UAK. I'm certain of it. Remember the coin Theo gave me?" Reverend Drummond replied.

"Now, let's not jump to conclusions. How can you possibly know for certain? That coin could have come from anywhere at any time. C'mon, Drum, they've been under radar for years. It's not like that anymore. I mean, they're still a repugnant bunch, but they've been sticking to drugs, gambling, and generally beating up gangbangers. They've left black folk outside the city alone for decades."

"CJ, we're all still scratching our heads. Like you said, they've left us alone for decades, and I can't think of a single thing that might have sparked this."

"Well, let me ask you this," replied CJ with a slight pause. "How do you know it was the UAK and not some other nutjob group? Aren't you jumping to conclusions?"

Reverend Drummond was getting frustrated. "How could it be anyone else, CJ? Their initials are on the coin, as is their flag. Are you doubting what I'm saying? Do you really think I'd attribute this to such a powerful group that could single-handedly destroy everything we've built over here without having clear evidence?! This is not like you, brother."

CJ replied, "You're right, I'm sorry. It's just that this is so out of character for them. I was just praying it could have been someone else. I heard that group mainly stays in their own world, and while they are noisy in the streets with that white power crap, it's just noise. Not this, though—not a burning, especially the house of such a sweet lady. I'm really heartbroken over this, Drum. Really heartbroken."

In as serious a tone as he'd ever had, Reverend Drummond spoke very deliberately and very slowly. "CJ, let's put this to bed *right* now so that there is no further doubt. A UAK coin was found in a field near Taunt Ju's, and some people say they saw a couple of white boys running away. If the coin wasn't there, I might have thought it was someone else or maybe even a house fire Chookie could have started accidentally. But, that coin is proof enough for me, CJ, and it should be proof enough for you. We need to see what we can dig up, but we have to be extremely careful, or else someone could get hurt. If that were to happen, let it happen to me or you, no one else. We already have one person dead and one who can't fend for himself. We have to find out what happened and stop this from escalating."

"Honoré, I hear you loud and clear, brother, and I'll turn over every stone until we get to the bottom of this." The magnitude of the situation lay heavily on CJ's heart. "I'll see what I can find out. All those boys I sent from the Cypress on those mission trips to the inner city to help the folks in the projects—good boys, boys who just wanted to get away from here and find a better life for themselves. For them to be exposed to this? For the UAK to be involved? Man, it's like the '50s and '60s all over again. You need to find my boys and hold them close, Drum. You need to make sure they don't go across that lake and try to right this horrible wrong on their own, or go asking questions around the gangs in the French Quarter. As good as those boys are, this generation is quick to act. They think they know what oppression is, and in their own minds, I can see how they would think such a thing. But they ain't been through what we been through. They haven't seen how evil destroys and peace eventually triumphs, although sometimes at too high a cost. Tell 'em that good things came because of us and Dr. King. They need to stay out of this and let the justice system work.

"I'm going to call a friend at the DA's office and see if she knows anything. Remember that young, pretty white gal who works downtown? She worked with the feds to help them investigate voter fraud? If we're lucky, she can help us and suggest to the feds that this be classed as a hate crime, and let them take it over. Lord only knows the NOPD won't be too interested, not for some ol' black lady's house that might have been an accident. If it's not happening on Bourbon Street, the mayor won't spend the resources. And the Jefferson Parish Sheriff's Department can only do so much, because I'm betting all of the real information is across the lake. The feds are the only ones that can centralize everything across parish lines. I'll let you know what I find out."

Reverend Drummond was surprised at CJ's new demeanor and scattered thought process, but he attributed it to the seriousness and unpredictability of the situation. "Thanks, CJ. I'll keep things tamped down over here as best I can. I'll look for those boys and keep them focused on helping out over here. I didn't realize you had so many working on inner-city missions. Did I tell you that fancy law firm Prudence works for is setting up a legal clinic here at the church? I tell you, CJ, that girl is an angel sent from heaven above and I can only think she was set on the right path by you and the good folks in the Cypress. She's always thinking of others. She could have stayed with waitressing and doing odd jobs and made a decent living, but she saw an opportunity to better herself and help others, and she took it at that law firm. And it has been great for Theo, too. Prudence works long hours, and since Theo got into that fight he's spent most of his time over here helping me with some painting and watching the little ones with that dog of his. He died in the fire, you know—the dog. I tell you, CJ, change is the only constant, and we have to stay the course and rely on the Lord to help us through troubling times like these. Stay in touch, okay?"

Reverend Drummond hung up the phone and wept silently. Even the strongest of men needed a good cry to clear the mind. He didn't know why this was happening, but he feared it was just the beginning.

# Chapter 54

## Mulling it Over

"See, Jimmy," said Prudence. "They're all connected. Knight Trucking, KTL, O.B. Enterprises, more shell companies in tax-friendly jurisdictions like Luxembourg, Bermuda, and Jersey Island off the coast of France—they really tried to hide their tracks."

"It's not so much hiding their tracks, which they definitely tried to do. It's more tax planning than anything," Jimmy replied. "These guys are very sophisticated businessmen, and no doubt they have a grand plan. With the size of this organization, it's gotta be a big one. But why? Why go through all this trouble? Why a logistics company *and* a construction company? Why all the property purchases? And why call it Project Azalea? Oscar, in all his vanity, probably looked out the grand window of his mansion and saw all the beautiful azaleas in bloom. However, it's more likely a clue. I mean, W.T. Falke and Lawrence friggin' Robertsen? Are you kidding me? Falke was at the very top of one of those midsize oil companies, and when I say midsize, I'm talking about a multibillion dollar company that is only *mid* in comparison to the supermajors.

"He was a great philanthropist, a patron of the arts, and set up endowments at the big colleges here: UNO, Loyola, Tulane, Xavier, and even Delgado. Mystery now solved as to where he went after his board kicked him out after the last bust. That rig fire off Galveston gave them plenty of cover to get rid of him. I know he owns Wild Iris Vineyard in Sonoma, and he is probably a majority shareholder in Knight Trucking. I guess he couldn't stay away from business and wanted something a little more *recession-proof*. I was still in law school at Tulane when the rig fire happened. It was all over the news, and our rather liberal professor was an environmental activist who used the accident as a platform to rail against the oil industry. It was as if Falke was the whipping boy and poster child for what's wrong with the industry. The professor just couldn't get it through his thick head that fossil fuels are the lifeblood of this state—something he needed to drive that 1970s Beemer he still tooled around town in, and to power the air conditioner of his fancy home that probably smelled like applewood pipe tobacco. If that pinhead really cared about saving the planet, he'd have ridden his bike to school, but I digress. Falke is the CEO schmoozer type, and Robertsen was his operations guy. They worked together at several companies. Falke would swoop in after a major acquisition and come in as CEO, get a handle on the business, and then transition his people in. Robertsen would then run the show until they could make the venture profitable enough to flip it.

"Okay, here's what we'll do. Since you've already done permit work for KTL, you go ahead and see what you can find in their operations records. I have no doubt that there's a lot of good stuff in the files due to all the permits they've applied for over the last couple of years. I'll look into Knight Trucking & Logistics. Except for the trucks you see on the highway, the company doesn't appear to have a big footprint in Louisiana. I'll have to dig real deep. I have a friend at the U.S. Department of Transportation who might be able to help me pull permits and export/import licenses for whatever it is they truck in and out of the country. If I find anything linking KTL to Falke, I'll follow that trail, too. His philanthropy appears to have vanished, so it's fairly obvious we're dealing with a guy who has a chip on his shoulder the size of the Atchafalaya Basin Bridge."

Looking a little overwhelmed, Prudence replied, "Okay, let's do it. I don't have a good feeling about all of this, Jimmy, but I know we have to see it through."

"Prudence, we're in too deep now. There might not be anything illegal here at all, but we've got to keep plugging away just to be sure. On the other hand, we might find this whole thing to be a basket of water moccasins. My hope is that this will be a wasted effort, but I'm sure there's a bigger story here. I know it will be tough to maintain composure in the office, which is why I'm glad we were able to set up this clinic. Trust me, it'll be tough for me, too, because I'll have to spend more time downtown than you will."

# Chapter 55

## Briefing Falke

W.T. Falke was the only person on the face of the earth who could have rattled the otherwise unflappable Oscar Brimley. Oscar thought he was on the same level as Robertsen, but when Falke said jump, Oscar jumped.

If Oscar's conference room was obnoxious, Falke's was downright obscene. Windows nine feet tall with automatic sunshades gave a panoramic view of the city, and a butler's pantry led to a full kitchen. In the corner of the room nearest the French doors was a full bar with a top made of Italian marble. Behind the bar stood Galway crystal tumblers, brandy snifters, and wine glasses—ready for afternoon cocktails. The floor was a luxurious mahogany, so shiny one could see one's reflection. The conference table was hewn from a giant redwood from an old growth forest. It was so large one could lie in the middle and do snow angels. The only pedestrian thing about the setup was that Falke loved to put on an apron and play bartender. It seemed the only time he smiled was when he had a cocktail shaker in his hand, shaking it in time to some ragtime tunes coming from the room's speakers.

"Please follow me, gentlemen," said Falke's senior administrative assistant. "Just take a seat. Mr. Falke will be right in."

Lawrence and Oscar entered the room like schoolboys caught cheating on a test, waiting for the principal. After an uncomfortable silence of about five minutes, a diminutive William Thomas Falke walked through the door.

He ignored Oscar and immediately turned to Robertsen saying in an eerily calm manner, "Let's have it, gentlemen, warts and all. I have to know what we're dealing with before we make any more moves. We've been through rig fires and investigations before. This can't be much different."

Robertsen glanced at Oscar, cleared his throat, and replied, "One of Krieger's guys set that house fire. He did it on his own, trying to play big shot with his cousin, who was beaten up after school by some half-breed schoolboy. The idiot dropped his UAK challenge coin while he was running away. CJ says his reverend friend wants to get the feds involved and get this classified as a hate crime because of that coin."

Falke glared at Robertsen. "Challenge coin? What the hell is that? Hate crime? Activists? Half-breed schoolboy? House fire? Who in the *hell* are CJ and his friend? What kind of organization are you running, Larry? Are you seriously telling me that the DOJ might get involved because some boy beat up the cousin of one of those miscreants, and he turned around and blew up a house as retribution—the wrong house, apparently—and then dropped a friggin' coin? And now it's probably coming back to the UAK, and us by extension? I allowed you to use that group of losers to make money so we could buy our property and build hotels and restaurants and change the face of this city. You've jeopardized all of this 'cause of a goddamn coin?" Falke looked down at his folded hands on the table to collect his thoughts. He stood up without looking at Robertsen and Oscar. As he walked out of the room, he said to Robertsen, "Get Ti Pop on it and shut this whole thing down. Make it quick."

Robertsen's face turned ashen. He looked at Oscar and, in a panic, said, "Oscar, what are we going to do?"

Ever the coward, Oscar replied, "*We*?! You have a mouse in your pocket? What do you mean, *we*? This is *your* mess—you clean it up."

A furious Robertsen replied, "You're in this deep as me, asshole, except you get to go to your fancy law firm every day, chase skirts, and wine and dine clients. I have to live in the filth with all of those warped ideologues! If they ever find out that they are just a cash cow and aren't going to get anything out of all of this except for their paltry pocket change, we're just as good as dead. Look, I'll get Ti Pop queued up and you can look at your resources and see what you come up with. Don't do anything before Ti Pop calls you."

# Chapter 56

## The Great Oz Warns

"Hello. Redeemer. It's a glorious day in the house of the Lord! How may I hep ya?" the cheery, rotund man said as he answered the phone.

"CJ, it's Oscar. We need to talk."

"Oz! *Mah* man, the wizard, the head brutha that be in charge, the number one KKK mother-Klukker hisself! What can I do ya fer, Mr. Brimley?"

Oscar hated being called *Oz* and *wizard* because of the obvious connotation. Besides, he viewed himself as high above any UAK, white-hooded, Klansman wannabe. Oscar didn't need to hide behind a satin hood; he preferred two thousand dollar suits.

"CJ, knock it off. I've got a problem, which means *you* have a problem. A big problem. My IT department tells me she's been snooping around the Project Azalea files—she and that liberal peckerhead, Jimmy. And to think, he was going to be my protégé! I don't think they've put it all together yet, but if they keep digging, they'll do so soon. We have to put a clamp on this, or else things are going to get out of control and out of my hands real quick-like. The UAK will get involved, and you know those crazy sons of bitches don't mess around. You of all people know they'll start lynching and dragging y'all down dirt roads—and burning churches. Is that personal enough for you? I don't need to tell you that those methods are tried and true, so consider this a fair warning. When the shit hits the fan, you know your people will want you to get the feds involved; if that happens, we're all going down for the count. And when I say *we*, that means *you*, too, padre. For all I know, the feds are already looking at us. So, if you can't or won't handle this, it *will* be handled, and you won't like the way in which it will be handled. Like I said, it will be out of my control. Hell, it might already be out of my control. I had a meeting with Robertsen and Falke. Falke was a little too calm for my comfort, and that usually means he's made his mind up, so I hope to get out in front of that. I need your help, and you need mine.

"I'm losing my faith in you, CJ, and that's not good for you. We've made you a very wealthy man and you've done a great job sending those boys to the gangs into the city while keeping Drummond focused on his little church. So, you better come through like you've never done before. Ya hear me?! Shut that bitch down, too. Do something to keep her busy and away from that clinic. You do *not* want the UAK involved, because the only favor I will be able to do for you is to tell you when the fire trucks and ambulances are going to arrive, and that's only if I hear about it first, which isn't a guarantee."

There was a pregnant pause on the line, and scratching his shiny, bald pate, CJ responded in a subservient and formal manner. "Don't worry, Mr. Brimley, I'll handle it. I always do."

*We'll see about that*, Oscar thought as he slammed the phone down, knowing full well CJ was in way over his head this time. Or, maybe

Oscar was projecting his own insecurities and *he* was the one in over *his* head. Regardless, he had to create a contingency plan, because if he could not restore normalcy, Falke would, and that simply could not happen. He would lose everything, and all his hard work would have been in vain. The likelihood was that he'd become the victim of an *accident*. Loose ends would be tied, and if there was one thing Falke hated, it was frayed threads and loose ends. If necessary, New Orleans would be left in flames, so to speak. After all, it was just business.

# Chapter 57

## The Second Comin' of Ti Pop

It was a beautiful morning on the salt.

"Slow down, podna, I can't hardly understand ya," said Octavé Poupard (aka Ti Pop). "What's a UAK, 'n who is Oscar Bumbly? I ain't heard shit from y'all for almost ten years 'n ya call me in a panic, sounding like a sixteen-year-old who just drove his daddy's Cadillac in a ditch at two in da morning. I need a lil background information here, otherwise I can't help ya, podna. So, take a deep breath 'n slow down. 'N dis bettah not be one of y'alls industrial *messes*, eithah, 'cause I'm retired from dat shit. Dat strike in Trinidad almos' done kilt me. Remembah one of dem heavies went rogue on me in Port o' Spain 'n threatened dat lil girl of one of the roustabouts? I draw da line at kids, podna, 'n 'cause of dat *couillon* we didn' get nowhere near as much as we wanted from da union, 'n I done barely got out der alive. I'm too ole for dat shit now. I might be crazy, but I ain't friggin' *stupid*."

Octavé Poupard was Falke's fix-it guy back in the oil patch days. You could say he was a Cajun version of the Wolf from *Pulp Fiction*: *le loup-garou*. He was a crazy, uneducated, yet incredibly smart coonass raised on Bayou Teche among the Cottonmouths in the shade of the willow trees. He went to work in the Gulf of Mexico in the late '80s as a young roustabout on one of Falke's drilling rigs. After a hard kick on a well off the coast of Louisiana, Octavé fell on the deck and injured his back. Rather than risk going to court in the U.S. District Court for the Eastern District of Louisiana, where juries gave out money like SnoBalls on a hot summer's day in City Park, Robertsen offered Octavé a significant cash settlement and a permanent desk job at the company.

Fortunately for Falke, Octavé accepted Robertsen's offer and proved to be an astute operations manager, extricating the company from all sorts of messes, like shipyard strikes in Belfast during The Troubles, collecting payment for overdue invoices in Venezuela, and the *dead Mexican in the trunk* situation in Poza Rica, Mexico—all fairly standard fare for the oil and gas industry.

Poupard was a loyal soldier and would do anything asked of him. Falke exploited this, and the favors escalated. In exchange for ridiculous amounts of money, Octavé would get his hands dirty, and, if need be, bloody. He'd track down plaintiffs' lawyers and ruin their Lincolns, Cadillacs, and Mercedes while they sat audaciously parked at fancy restaurants. He'd corner them on the street and threaten to expose their dalliances. He'd make witnesses *disappear,* mostly with payouts, but sometimes with *accidents*—the kind that happened in the swamps in the dead of night, where the screams of the damned were indistinguishable from the forlorn cries of the nutria rat, which had been eating up Louisiana's beautiful swamps for decades.

It was during those oil boom times when Octavé Poupard transformed into Ti Pop. The more *problems* he fixed, the more his bloodlust increased. He became insatiable, and in order to maintain a reasonable sense of sanity and functionality, he began to compartmentalize and disassociate the psychopathic Ti Pop from the fun-loving Octavé everyone knew and loved. It worked for him until the strike in Trinidad, where Ti Pop died and Octavé came back home.

Octavé was one of a kind and didn't blend well into crowds. He stood at five foot seven and weighed in at a sturdy, stocky two hundred ninety pounds. His cue ball pate was augmented by custom frost blue tinted, tortoise shell Ray-Ban Wayfarers, and a perfectly coiffed goatee framed his round, cherub face. He kept a half-smoked, unlit cigar in the right corner of his mouth and chewed on it all day, every day.

At any point in time, half the world was looking for him because of past deeds. To become a ghost, he lived on a nicely outfitted, thirty-four-foot Morgan sailboat, docked at the Bay Waveland Yacht Club off the Mississippi Gulf Coast—close enough to New Orleans and Biloxi to indulge in his vices, yet far enough from danger in case he had to make a quick sail away into the Gulf to escape the wrath of a jealous husband, a jilted bookie, or a pissed off woman.

He loved fishing with a few local drinking buddies almost as much as he loved going to Death Valley on Saturday nights to watch his beloved LSU Tigers. On normal days, he could often be seen topside wearing his standard uniform: a weathered Panama hat, Ray-Bans, deck shoes with decaying soles, frayed khaki cargo shorts, and a faded purple and gold fishing shirt with a few buttons missing. He could usually be found with a fishing pole in one hand and an ever present Miller Lite in the other, housed in a worn, black coozie with cracked white lettering that said *Piss Off* on one side and *What The Hell Are You Lookin' At?* on the other.

Robertsen cut to the chase. "Pop, I need you to take care of a problem—a big problem. Now, before you say *no*, hear me out."

"No," replied Octavé. "I'll listen, but I ain't agreein' to nuttin'."

"Pop—"

Octavé cut him short. "Podna, don't call me Pop no more! I done tole y'all before, I ain't like dat no more. I'm retired. I'm gonna hang up right now if dis is anothah Trinidad goat rope."

"Okay, okay, I'm sorry. This is nothing like Trinidad, I promise. I think you'll find this one interesting." Satisfied that he seemed to have Octavé's attention, Robertsen continued. "How would you like to own a parking lot in the French Quarter near a brand-new hotel?"

At this point, Robertsen had no compunction about giving away Oscar Brimley's parking lot, or anything else of his.

"Parkin' lot?! What da hell I'm gonna do wit a parkin' lot? Put it on mah boat 'n take it fishin'? I ain't movin' to Nawlins just ta run some goddamn parkin' lot! I already look over mah shoulder all day 'n sleep wit one eye open all night. Why in da *hell* would I move back when half da city is prob'ly lookin' for me at any given point in time? No, suh, count me out."

"No, no. All you'd do is collect checks. We have others to run everything. We can even set up an offshore company for you so your name wouldn't be on any paperwork."

"I'm listenin'," replied Octavé, now in rapt attention. Anyone who knew anything about New Orleans knew that owning a parking lot in the French Quarter was a license to print money.

It took about an hour for Robertsen to lay it all out in terms that Octavé would understand. Falke's fall from grace at the oil company, their involvement with the UAK, Oscar's development of Project Azalea, Tante Ju's house, and the hanged gangbanger in Natchez: Robertsen left nothing out. Octavé didn't say a word, which Robertsen took as a good sign.

After a pause, which became too long for Robertsen's comfort,

Octavé spoke. "Here's da deal, podna. I think I can get Ti Pop on it *if*—'n this is a big *effin' if*—in addition ta da parkin' lots, I get a million dollahs 'n a new boat. *Peggy Sue* has been gettin' a lil cramped 'n I've been tinkin' 'bout an upgrade. Now you listen close ta dis part, podna, 'cuz here's da rest of da deal. Before I lift one of mah stubby fingers, it's gonna be *two* parkin' lots, da boat, 'n five hunerd gran up front, nonrefundable. Da othah five hunerd grand at da tail en' when I'm done 'n gone, 'n you'll definitely know when I'm *done*. We're gonna scope out mah part, too, 'cuz if dis ting goes sideways, I ain't takin' da fall. If we're clear bout what I'm a gonna do, I'm a gonna do it."

"Whoa, whoa, that's crazy, Octavé," said Robertsen. "I can't get approval for that. Besides, I said *a* parking lot, as in one."

"I ain't deaf. I heard ya say *lot*. Did ya hear me say *lots*? Dat's plural, as in more dan one—in case ya forgot math. Podna, if ya got me a million dollahs for a questionable bad back 'n a few broken fingahs back in da '90s, ya can get me a new row boat, a coupla squares of blacktop in da Quarter, 'n a few dead presidents. We done did crazier shit dan dat, so don't give me dat *poor me* jitterbug. Ya got ten seconds to choose, otherwise I'm headed out ta wet a few lines. Dey say da redfish are bitin' off Cat Island today somethin' fierce."

"Octavé, I, I—"

Octavé cut him off. "Seven seconds..."

"Okay, okay, deal," said Robertsen. "But how am I going to give you a parking lot now? It's going to take a couple of weeks to get the paperwork, and maybe a month to set up offshore bank accounts."

Octavé replied, "I'll take ya word on da blacktop 'n give ya a few days to set up all dat shit, but I'm pickin' out da boat today. I've had mah eye on one for a while, 'n da dealah's a podna. He'd let me have it on mah good name with *Peggy Sue* as collateral. I might not even sell 'er. Maybe I'll lease 'er out as a charter, maybe give some of dem Stanislaus boys some spendin' money while dey make tourists seasick catchin' croakers out near Ship Island. Oh, in case I didn't say so, da five hunerd gran is cash, 'n ya gots 'til da end of tomorrah ta get it to me. Da other five hunerd gran is also cash, to be held in escrow in Sea Port Bank here in da Bay wit da condition dat it's released when mah job is done *or* one year from tahday. Eithah way, I'm gettin' it. Da escrow is to be set up by da end of tomorrah, 'n I need a receipt directly from da bank.

"The parkin' lots will be sold undah separate contracts, ta be signed tomorrah when ya bring me da five hunerd gran in dead presidents, which are, by da way, to be nonsequential 'n in various denominations—obviously. Let's see how creative ya are; make sure da dates on da dollahs span da terms of at least four presidents. Da lots gotta be backed by title insurance 'n two, one million dollah lettahs of credit: one from Sea Port Bank 'n da othah from Hancock Bank. Half of each will be cancelable upon receipt of title after da lots are built, 'n da other half a year after dat. I also want a builder's all risk insurance policy on da construction, lettahs of completion from da contractors, 'n lien-free certificates from all subcontractors—all of which are ta be notarized.

"Da lots gotta be finished 'n ready ta accept cars. Da blacktop will be top quality 'n well striped, wit spots large enough for me to open mah Cougar 'n get mah fat ass out da car without hittin' da car parked next ta me. We might make it park-'n-pay, but if we decide ta man it, I want da attendant's shack ta be air conditioned, nicely outfitted, 'n a lil biggah dan da biggest one in da city. I want da attendants ta wear uniforms 'n I want *ya* to supply 'em. I ain't spendin' a penny on da operations. Oh, 'n no illegals. All dem poor bastards have ta be bonafide citizens of dese here United States. I want ya ta be able ta attract da best people, 'cuz I can't afford ta be dragged into anythin' five years from now if dey gotta problem at da lot or get deported by da feds. Speakin' of which, ya also need to get me separate liability insurance policies for each lot from different insurance companies, with a two million dollah umbrella from a third one. You can put dose into effect on handover 'n set 'em up ta auto-renew with da premiums linked to *ya* accounts—obviously. Ya want Ti Pop, podna, dat's da price. Oh, in case ya wonderin', dis ain't no negotiation," said Octavé, chomping on his trademark cigar with a grin as wide as the Lake Pontchartrain Causeway.

After what seemed like an eternity, Robertsen smiled and finally spoke. "Look at you! How'd you get so smart? I should've had you cutting deals with oil companies instead of busting nuts and breaking arms."

"Don't let mah good looks 'n lack of edumacation fool ya. I done tole ya," said Ti Pop. "I paid close attention to what ya ass-clowns was doin' when y'all was pokin' holes in da seabed lookin' for dinosaur juice. I learnt me a thing or two 'bout bidness. A few years aftah Trinidad, I was sailin' off da coast of Vanuatu 'n met a fella lookin' ta go into bidness. We met for drinks every now 'n den at da yacht club, swappin' lies 'n talkin' 'bout women 'n such. Anyway, he was sharp as a tack, 'n after I had him checked out 'n assured myself he'd be a trustworthy partner, we set up a few companies togethah: charter fishin' 'n divin', a seafood distributorship with exclusive deals at all of da big resorts in da area 'n Fiji, shit like dat. All of it is offshore 'n nobody stateside knows nuttin' 'bout it. Nor will dey, savvy? As far as everyone here is concerned, old Octavé is jus a fun-lovin', crazy coonass livin' his golden years on a boat in Bay St. Louis, drinkin' beer, flippin' cards, playin' the ponies, 'n chasin' loose women."

"Damn!" exclaimed Robertsen "Why the steep price then? It looks like you're set. You could live like a king over there and do whatever you want."

"Bidness, podna, jus' bidness. Now, let me ax *you* a question. When has *enough* evah been *enough* for ya 'n Falke, huh? Why do athletes come back for dat last season wit a ridiculous contract, riskin' a broken rib or a ripped knee? You pricks played wit fortunes like it was penny ante Texas Hold'em. Me, I plan on keepin' mah vast fortune. I wanna see how big I can make it 'n pass a good time doin' it. *Laissez les bons temps rouler* 'n all dat shit, right?

"Podna, *enough* ain't nevah *enough*, is it? When ya get ta be as rich as me it becomes a game, 'n if ya want Ti Pop ta get rid of dat lil problem of yahs, it's gonna cost ya—big time. If ya want me ta play da game, ya gotta ante up! 'N don't knock mah kingdom here. I got everythin' I want 'n den some. Besides, da Tigers don't play in friggin' Fiji! Aaiieee!" Octavé was laughing so hard inside he was about to burst. Ti Pop continued, "Now, den, be a good boy 'n get dis pahty started. Ya can *staht* by bringin' mah money tomorrah. 'N I want *ya* ta bring it, personally, ya hear? I don't want none of ya lackeys out here pokin' round mah paradise. Dey'd prob'ly kill me out of jealousy. Until I say so, no one else knows bout dis—just ya 'n W.T.F."

Ti Pop thought he'd make Robertsen squirm and work hard for this. He was interested in seeing whether he could get Falke to go along with all of this without Robertsen saying too much. He was giddy and could just hear Robertsen say, "Trust me, W.T., I got this."

He didn't wait for a reply and hung up the phone, then said aloud, to no one in particular, "Well, *Peggy Sue*, thanks for the memories." He disembarked, jumped in his copper brown and cream ragtop '74 Cougar coupe, and drove off to the boat dealer in Gulfport.

# Chapter 58

## Expanding the Team

"Prudence, come see this," said Jimmy.

"What is it?"

"Look at this. It appears that the firm made a large donation to Councilman Hébert's reelection campaign, and there are a ton of receipts scanned into the file with the initials D.R. Suite passes to the New Orleans Arena, box seats at the Saenger, spa visits to the Windsor Court: this is just more than a fancy dinner every couple of months. This is some big-time luxury being spread around. It seems that the councilman is being bribed, or is bribing someone by proxy, and Oscar is keeping the receipts as blackmail ammo. It can't be a girlfriend, because everything is too public—except the spa visits.

"Wait a minute! I remember reading about a woman from the Department of the Interior who is championing the building of that new slavery museum. I think her name is Diane Rosenberg. Didn't all that come about as part of that permit you were working on for the Renaissance?

Hébert wasn't being bribed, *she* was! *He* was bribing *her*! Poor thing probably didn't even realize it. On the other hand, maybe she did and was just going along with it. Who knows? Safer for us to not jump to any conclusions. What I do know is that if this gets out, she won't be able to escape it if she wanted to. One way or the other, she's stuck."

"I think you're right, Jimmy. This thing is like a big bowl of jambalaya where you can't even tell what's in it: W.T. Falke, Lawrence Robertsen, Oscar Brimley, offshore accounts, trucking companies, construction companies, fast-tracked permits, the Azalea Group. What are we going to do? I'm worried. I've never dealt with anything like this."

"Me neither. This is new territory for me, too," replied Jimmy. "I've had some very interesting cases, but nothing like this. Let's think about it. We need someone else inside the firm to help us. I don't see any other way, and there's only one person I can think of."

"Rachel?" Prudence guessed.

"Rachel. But, I don't know whether I can trust her with this kind of information. If I bring her into this, she might become fearful and report me to Oscar—or worse, to the bar association. I could lose my job *and* my license. I know she's been spending a lot of time with Oscar lately and has not been seen in her section for some time. She's been a little standoffish, too, and I thought maybe she's been sleeping with him, but she's not his type. Oscar likes them young and demure. While Rachel is a young woman, she isn't his type of *young*, and she's certainly no wallflower, so I doubt there's anything there. Of course, it also could be that Oscar has her wrapped up in this and she's just as confused as we are. We probably know more, though, because I'm sure she hasn't gone into the files to the degree we have. I don't see any other way, Prudence. I don't want to insult your intelligence by saying I don't think you are up to this, but I'm fairly sure you haven't come across anything this twisted before. I haven't either, but I can work within the firm a little easier than you. No offense."

"Oh, no offense taken, Jimmy. You're absolutely right. This looks really, really twisted, and I agree we need all the help we can get."

Jimmy replied, "Well, as my old Irish grandmother used to say, in for a penny, in for a pound. I will jump in tomorrow morning, ask her to dinner, and just lay all the cards on the table. She's assertive, and most definitely an opportunist, but I think something is bugging her and the worst thing she could do is to tell Oscar, which she won't do. I think we have a little leverage."

# Chapter 59

### "You Want Me to WHAT?!"

"You want me ta *WHAT*?!" exclaimed Ti Pop.

Robertsen saw a slight chink in the armor. "You got your boat, your money, and your parking lots. You accepted payment, so this is the game you have to play, podna. A card laid is a card played, my friend. Maybe you should've asked more about *your* scope before taking *our* money?"

"Don't ya start dat cocky ass shit wit me, Robertsen, or ya'll wake up dead. Don't forget who ya dealin' wit here. I'll cut ya nuts off 'n shove 'em down ya throat, ya lil piece a shit." Ti Pop paused for effect and continued, "'N ya know I'm a man of mah word, too, so back off."

*That* was the Ti Pop Robertsen had been waiting for. Ready, fire, aim! "I know you're an honorable man, and I know that you don't bluff, but this is not completely out of the realm of other jobs you've done for us, so don't play the moral equivalence card on me. Remember, we made you a very rich man, and you wouldn't have been able to set up your little redneck paradise here and in Vanuatu if not for that money. You're pregnant with this now, Pop. There's no turning back." *Advantage, Robertsen.*

"I'm outta practice for dis level of shit, podna," replied Ti Pop with a little nervousness showing through.

"Oh, we just need your brain and organizational skills, Pop. Krieger and his band of merry men will do the heavy lifting."

"How well ya know dis Krieger character? How ya know he can be trusted?" asked Ti Pop.

"Don't worry about Krieger. He's tied up in this, too, and he's a good soldier. Besides, he knows the consequences of crossing us. Natchez was his idea. He knows that if he turns on us, that'll look like a day feeding seagulls at Biloxi Beach compared to what we'll do to him. Cerata is a former mob guy, so he won't say a thing to anyone. He'll do what he's told. Don't worry, it will be clear that you are in charge."

"Awright," said Ti Pop. "I can make dis go away, but ya ain't gonna like how it goes down."

"Pop, I don't give a shit what you do. Just get it done. If Krieger can string up a gangbanger from a tree and cook one of his own, he's up to it. He's a sadistic son of a bitch. He loves this shit."

"Whoa, whatcha mean, *cook one of his own?*" asked Ti Pop.

Robertsen replied, "Oh, I guess I didn't tell you everything. There's so much to this sordid tale that I suppose it's easy to leave out a few things. This whole thing started coming apart because some shit-for-brains tweaker left a challenge coin—or some stupid shit like that—in an empty lot after torching some old black woman's house. This asshole was so incompetent, he burned the *wrong* house. An innocent woman died, and a special needs man is now displaced. I'm pretty damn certain the feds are already here, so we wanted to get ahead of that. Krieger made the problem go away in his own way; he tortured the idiot, cut him up into little pieces, and then burned him to ash."

Octavé stroked his goatee a bit and looked out over the sun setting on the horizon of the beautiful Mississippi Gulf Coast as if it was the last time he'd see it. He turned to Robertsen. "Okay, Pop's in. Where I'm gonna find dese guys?"

Robertsen replied, "Sail *Peggy Sue* or whatever dinghy you are in now down to the marina near the Rigolets, near Slidell. Krieger and Cerata will meet you there in the late afternoon. I'd like for you to take them on the water for some early evening fishing. I want to ensure they're not being followed or surveilled. I'm not being paranoid— more cautious than anything."

"Awright, podna! Let's do dis! Ti Pop's back for one more glorious ride into da sunset. 'N he ain't nevah lookin' back! Aaaiieee!"

# Chapter 60

### Jimmy Drafts Rachel

"Galatoire's—how fancy, how unexpected. Is this a date, Mr. O'Leary? Because you know, I'm not much for younger men." Rachel teased and batted her eyelashes. Truth be told, she needed a break from all the recent stress, and Galatoire's was the perfect fix. She was curious, though, as to why Jimmy all of a sudden asked her to dinner. Did it have something to do with Prudence? Was Jimmy taking her place in BB's section due to all the time she'd been spending with Oscar? Her curiosity grew.

Jimmy replied, "Well, it's not really a date, per se. I just want a little break and I think you do, too. Not to pry, but you seem preoccupied lately. I've been burning the candle at both ends, and we both have Prudence in common. So, no, not a *date* date. Think of it more as a misery loves company situation."

"You're too cute," said Rachel. "What the heck? Let's go. I'll meet you there at eight."

Rachel thought Galatoire's was safe enough to keep the office grapevine in check: a New Orleans icon and historic mainstay of the French Quarter. It was usually loud, and always full of drunken lawyers and judges. Nice, yet not overly romantic. Yes, it was the perfect place from which to escape if Mr. O'Leary had ideas for dessert that weren't on the menu.

Jimmy drove straight from the Antioch clinic and arrived at the restaurant at 7:30. He got a table against the mirrored wall, about midway down, and ordered some liquid courage: a double Maker's Mark Old Fashioned with extra maraschino cherry juice, raw cane sugar muddled with a blood red orange wedge, and a fresh mint leaf to give it a unique Big Easy flair. It was going to be either a really short or very long dinner, and he'd rehearsed how he would broach the subject. He decided that he'd get right to it and throw it all down on the table. At this point, he had nothing to lose and everything to gain.

Rachel arrived at eight sharp and looked as if she had walked out of the pages of *Vogue* in a formfitting, forest green, low-cut dress. Her hair was down and slightly curled, and she wore Jimmy Choo pumps. She was accented by a Burberry clutch and a Bvlgari drop pendant that could have easily cost $5,000. If she wasn't treating this as a date, she could have fooled Jimmy, because he had never seen her look more stunning.

He sat, mouth agape as she approached the table. With a big, flirtatious smile, she said, "Well, hello, Mr. O'Leary. Mind if I join you?" The waiter approached, pulled her chair out, and asked if she cared for a drink. As she was sitting down, she turned to him and said, "I'll have whatever he's having."

"Yes, ma'am, of course."

"Well, hello yourself, and please forgive me if you think I'm being too forward in saying how beautiful you look," said Jimmy, a little stunned at the words that had just escaped his mouth.

Rachel replied, "Why, that's not forward at all, Mr. O'Leary. Thank you for the compliment. I don't get out much and I must wear this every once in a while, before it goes out of style. Not bad, huh?"

*Not bad at all*, thought Jimmy to himself. He didn't know what to read into it, but he had a good feeling that Rachel was very comfortable with him. At a minimum, it was definitely a sign that she wanted to talk about something.

The waiter returned promptly with Rachel's drink and a replacement for Jimmy topped with a wink and a wry grin. There was no need for menus. As was the custom, if you were a regular at Galatoire's, your waiter would suggest restaurant favorites, along with the day's special dishes or, *poisson du jour*. No need to agonize over a busy menu. Before they could speak, another waiter appeared with hot mini loaves of French bread, ramekins of soft butter, puffed potatoes, and fried eggplant sticks topped with powdered sugar—on the house.

They each took a few bites of the food and swilled their drinks. Jimmy spoke first. "Rachel, I suppose you're wondering why I asked you to dinner?"

Expecting a question along those lines, she replied, "Well, I figured you thought I was hungry and needed something to eat."

She held his gaze and leaned in a little as Jimmy dropped the bomb. "Rachel, I think Oscar is involved in some illegal activity. At a minimum, it is likely unethical."

Rachel almost spit her drink out, composed herself, and waited a few seconds before responding. "Thank God! I knew something was up. I'm glad I'm not the only one thinking there's something fishy going on at the firm, but how can you be so sure it's illegal?"

"I'm not certain just yet, but we really don't like what we're seeing."

"*We?*" replied Rachel. "Who's *we?*"

"Prudence ca—"

Suddenly angry, Rachel interrupted him. "Prudence? You dragged that sweet girl into this? What's she got to do with it? You've got no business involving her, James."

"No, no, you don't understand. Rachel, this whole thing started with Prudence. She's the one who approached *me*. I don't know where we are right now with this whole thing or where it'll take us, but she's stumbled onto something that's way outside her comfort zone and *she* came to *me*," Jimmy said. "We started digging and are finding more and more information. We definitely do *not* like what we are finding. In fact, it was Prudence who suggested we start the legal clinic at her church so we could have an off-campus place to do our research and exchange information. She knows I'm here, speaking with you. Rachel, we need your help. We can't do this alone."

Staring out the window, taking in the unique French Quarter scenery and muffled street jazz like it was the last time she would see the eccentricities of the city in a normal way, she turned and said, "A few weeks ago, Oscar pulled me in on a project to get information ready for a potential federal tax investigation of Knight Trucking. That's what's kept me preoccupied recently. He singled me out and wanted to tie me up in the attorney-client privilege because of all the permitting work I've done. Based on what you're telling me, though, I can see that he might be setting me up. He knows I'll find everything and won't be able to say a damn thing. Damn him!"

"So, I suppose you know the link with KTL Construction?" Jimmy asked.

"Yep, and I suppose *you* know about O.B. Enterprises and this Azalea Group, whatever the hell that is?"

"Rachel, I know it all. Probably more than you do by now."

The two sat and looked at each other for a moment until Rachel finally broke the silence. "What are we going to do? We can't just go to the police or the bar association. He probably owns the cops, and the bar would never believe us over Oscar. I most certainly cannot let on that I suspect anything, because he might not be doing anything illegal. Or, if he is doing something illegal and thinks I'm on to him, I could be in actual danger. I'm really worried."

"Me, too," replied Jimmy. "I know we have to do something, but what? We can't get Prudence much more involved because she's not savvy enough to navigate through this, and we can't get her son involved by extension. What else can we do at this point?"

"Well, at this point, we're not going to talk about it anymore tonight. We'll finish off our lovely grilled pompano topped with crabmeat and a chardonnay beurre blanc sauce. Then, we'll have a caramelized crème brûlée with a fiery Café Brûlot. Then, you'll walk me home."

"Home? I don't even know where you live."

"I live over in the warehouse district just down from the Windsor Court. It'll be a little hike, but we can talk more along the way and clear our heads a little."

After one of the best dinners they've had in a long time, they walked down Bourbon Street toward Canal and Harrah's Casino, Louisiana's only sanctioned land-based casino, the Coushatta, Choctaw, Tunica-Biloxi, and Chitimacha Native American nations notwithstanding. While they did not walk hand in hand, they walked close enough that their fingertips brushed a time or two. Neither was ready to admit it, but there was a mutual attraction that became a little more heightened in light of current events. The Old Fashioneds and Café Brûlot didn't hurt, either.

They stepped into the lobby of the apartment building, and, as if he couldn't get out of there fast enough, Jimmy stammered, "Well, you're home, safe and sound. I really enjoyed dinner. See you around the office."

"Not yet, mister. Remember, you're walking me *home*. I'm not quite there yet," Rachel said, and not too subtly. "I've got a brand-new bottle of Bulleit Rye, so we're going to make a couple Vieux Carrés, talk a little more, and… Well, we'll see what happens."

A familiar waft of Café du Monde coffee and chicory woke him, and he was greeted by a morning sun that filled the room with a radiant white light. Jimmy shook off the cobwebs and fumbled around for his clothes.

"How do you take your coffee?" Rachel asked from the other room.

# Chapter 61

### Intel

The soft orange sun started to set and the water gently lapped at the hull of the twenty-five-foot Boston Whaler, Ti Pop's bayrunner that was big enough for a few pals to fish from, yet small enough to tow behind the Cougar.

"Okay, we'll go over dis once again. Tell me everytin' ya know 'bout dis Earl Tyler charactah. I wanna hear it all." Ti Pop was getting frustrated with Krieger and Cerata. Neither was apparently willing to accept the authority of their new master. They moored the boat and walked into the back room of the marina that was owned by one of Octavé's friends.

Krieger repeated, "Like I said, Tyler was a military washout, but a very good tactician, a good shot, and excellent at hand-to-hand. He was up-and-coming, and then, out of the blue, he burned down an old lady's house. He didn't tell anyone he was going to do it, so he definitely was not showing off for our sakes. We'd never have known about it, either, if not for that coin he dropped. That goddamn coin."

"Yeah, yeah, da coin. Ya already said dat. What else? He had a fam'ly? A job? Was he a druggie? Was it personal? Come on, boys, ya gotta do bettah dan dis."

Cerata replied, "Well, he did odd jobs here and there, but he wasn't a druggie—as far as we could tell, anyway. He was more of an adrenaline junkie and thought very highly of himself. Liked to brag a lot."

"Okay," said Ti Pop, sensing some momentum. "Now we gettin' somewhere. What else? Other dan his UAK pogues, who he spent his time wit?"

"He mentioned that he had no siblings and his parents were killed in a car crash when he was in his late teens. His aunt and uncle wouldn't take him in, so he bounced around foster homes until he was old enough to join the Army. He talked a lot about his little cousin and how he wanted to bring him into the UAK as a legacy after he finished high school, but that was about it."

"Where da cousin goes ta school?" Ti Pop asked.

"He goes to Bragg. It's actually within walking distance of the burned house," Krieger answered.

Ti Pop scratched his bald pate and said to no one in particular, "Let's keep our eye on da cousin. I'm willin' ta bet he's prob'ly da key ta dis whole ting." Ti Pop had a hunch, and his hunches were normally spot-on. Ti Pop continued, "So, if I got dis straight, we know 'bout da coin, 'cause who was it? Reverend CJ? Reverend CJ called da Counselah 'n tole him dat his reverend friend—Drummond is it? His friend Reverend Drummond at da local church was given da coin by some mulattah kid from school. Dat means da kid knows Drummond 'n prob'ly spends time at da church, right? We need ta find out more 'bout Drummond, his relation ta CJ, their relation ta da boy, 'n everythin' we can find on da boy: parents, siblings, family, friends. Basically, we need ta know everythin' 'bout the whole goddamn neighborhood. Get me some intel on dat, 'n we'll plan our next move."

"Okay, boss," said Krieger, resigned to the fact that Ti Pop was calling the shots and comforted by his apparent command of the situation. "Mario and I will dig into it over the next couple of days and get back to you."

"Tomarrah," replied Ti Pop.

"Excuse me?" said Krieger.

"Did I stuttah, podna?! Get me da shit tomorrah."

"Tomorrow? Don't you think that's pushing it?" asked Krieger.

"I'll give you da benefit of da doubt 'n jus' pretend dat ya didn't hear me da firse time *or* da second time. I want ta know everythin' by tomarrah evenin'. Look, fellas, we ain't got a lotta time ta mess round wit dis. Dis is ya numbah one priority. Drop what ya doin'. I don't know whethah ya dumbasses can appreciate Mr. Robertsen's level of anxiety at da moment, but I've worked wit da man for decades, 'n if he thought enough of dis situation ta get mah fat ass off da couch, den ya can bet ya ass dis is pretty damn important." Ti Pop continued raising his voice a little for effect. "Gentlemen, we gotta get ta da bottom of dis *tout suite*. Like ASAP, 'cause I can't make anothah move without havin' as much information as possible. So, get ya heads out of ya asses 'n get me some goddamn intel! Be resourceful, 'cause if ya can't get dis job done, I'll get some othah asswipes from ya shit pile of idiots ta do it! Is dat clear enough for ya assholes? Y'all ain't gonna talk ta Larry directly unless he speaks to ya, 'n don't worry 'bout dat happnin', 'cause he's done wit y'all! Y'all are all mine now. Get it?"

Krieger and Cerata looked as if they'd just snapped out of a coma and were hearing all of this for the first time. An anguished recognition washed over them and they looked at each other while walking briskly out of the room. Ti Pop stood still and stared at the worn wood floor.

A little smirk came across his face and he stroked his immaculately groomed goatee. *Pop, we gonna have us some fun fo sure. We're gonna ride out into da sunset in a blaze of glory.*

# Chapter 62

### Trio for the Cause

"Jimmy, where have you been? I've been calling all morning—your apartment, your mobile. You had me worried."

"Sorry, Prudence. It was a late night. I must have turned my mobile on silent to get a few hours of uninterrupted sleep. I'll be sure I can be reached from now on. On another note, she's on board." Jimmy was not above telling a little white lie now and then to avoid judgment or impugning Rachel's reputation.

"Who? Rachel? So, I guess dinner went well?" she asked.

Jimmy dodged the question. "She'd already found some of the same stuff we did, all on her own and all right in front of Oscar because he asked her to do it! She doesn't have as much information as we do, but she found enough to make her nervous. She's running scared at the moment since he's got her wrapped up in this and she knows she's expendable. However, she's relieved now that she's not alone and will work from the inside. We'll continue with our work on the outside here at the clinic. We just need to figure out how we can meet with her and compare notes without raising suspicion. Dinner wasn't a problem since it's not unusual for colleagues to occasionally meet up for drinks and dinner, especially at Galatoire's. You are a common denominator in the firm, so it makes sense that she and I would have something work-related to talk about. I think that was a one-time event, though, so we have to think."

"A burner phone," Prudence said.

"A what?" asked Jimmy.

"You know, a prepaid cell phone. Drug dealers use them all the time. At least that's what I understand from TV. We can all get one and she can call us on her breaks and after work. She can go to Kinko's and copy or scan documents to us. We can create some new email address-es and then use the Antioch's Wi-Fi so it's not routed through the firm's servers. If Oscar has her working on something secret, it would make sense that she'd be out of the office and use a place like that instead of doing it at the firm," explained Prudence.

"I love you, Prudence Jean-Batiste! You're a genius!"

# Chapter 63

### Evie's on Board

"Whoa, slow down girl," said Evie. "What in the café au lait are you talking about? Oscar's dirty? You don't think Bernadette is mixed up in this, do you? I sure hope not; I really like her. I think I'm a good judge of character, too, and I've known her a long time, so it would crush me to think she was doing something that wasn't on the up-and-up."

"No, Bernadette knows nothing about this. I'm sure of it. She might know bits and pieces that Oscar might have fed to her, but she's oblivious. I think she's clean."

"Okay, then," said Evie. "What's the play?"

"Oh no. No way, Evie. I'm not dragging you into this," Prudence insisted.

"You've got no choice. From what you've told me about them, I'm sure Jimmy and Rachel are good people. Do you think they can be trusted when the beignet hits the fan and spreads powdered sugar everywhere? I'm sorry, but you're stuck with me until the end."

"Evie, I'm serious, I can't let you do this."

"Prudence Jean-Batiste! When have you *ever* known me to back down from trouble? Don't worry about me, girl. Look, I'm not married, I have no kids; all I've got is a boyfriend who is more like a *friend with benefits* that I could drop today and neither of us would shed a tear. Out of everyone involved with this, you have the most to lose, and I have the least. I can't let you go it alone, not this time. I was saddened that I wasn't able to be with you when we were kids and you were raising Theo. We're going to hit this thing head-on, girl, and we're going to see it through to its bitter end."

Prudence knew she would never be able to deter Evie from anything once her mind was set. "Okay, Evie, but I'm not giving you many details—only enough so you can help me strategize. Oooh, bright idea here! Rachel and I can pass files and information back and forth through you at Élysées. We'd never be there at the same time, and everyone at the firm knows you. This will be a change of pace for us, so there might be questions surrounding the increased interest in shopping we'll have. If Bernadette or anyone tries to pump you for information, you can say that Rachel has been very busy lately and is engaging in a little shopping therapy ordered by Dr. Evie. I haven't bought anything since I've joined the firm, and I'm spending my time outside the office at the clinic. I have to represent the firm and dress well, so it wouldn't look too out of the ordinary if I came here more often."

"Now you're talking. Wait, what clinic?" asked Evie.

"Oh, forgot to tell you. I convinced Oscar to let me open a pro bono clinic at the Antioch. Jimmy is the supervising attorney, so he comes in two days a week. We've been doing our research there. Oscar doesn't have a clue he's actually funding his own investigation. It is the perfect cover since I don't have to bill any files, so no one really knows what I'm doing with my time. It really bothers me, though, because the people I'm supposed to be helping aren't getting the help they need. I see it as a short-term sacrifice. When this is all over, I'm going to do my best to make up for lost time. There are a lot of people out there who are a lot less fortunate than us and can't afford an attorney. I'm not just talking criminal defense, either. I've learned that our government's bureaucratic systems are burdened by regulations impossible to wade through, especially those who are poorly educated. Battered women, children who float through the foster care system in households that are just in it for the money, as well as elderly people who need help with burials and probation of estates: the law touches everyone in almost every aspect of their lives and most don't realize it until it is too late."

Evie took a step back to absorb everything she'd just heard. "Here's why you need me. I love you for your desire to save the world. You have a heart as big as the whole Gulf of Mexico, but you need to stay laser-focused. I don't know if you can see this, dear Prudence, but you're on the wrong side of some very powerful people who are not beyond doing unspeakable things. What would Theo do without you?"

"Without me?! Evie, do you know something I don't? You're making me nervous," exclaimed Prudence.

"No, I don't know anything specific. What I do know is the power some of these firms yield in this city and beyond. I hear things all the time from the people who know best: the women in the firms. I'm like the bartender the drunk tells his woes to when he loses his job, his wife leaves him, or the hairdresser who gets all the juicy gossip about who is boinking who in the office. It's a two-way street, though. An employee discount used here and there, an expired coupon getting an override through the system, or accepting an exchange beyond the thirty day policy. The stuff you see on the TV shows is real, Prudence. Art really does imitate life. The women who come here do so not only to shop, but also to vent. Some are scared to death by what they know, and I've heard it all: uncooperative witnesses being blackmailed into cooperating, plaintiffs being *persuaded* to drop a case against a major corporation, secretaries forced to forge documents or sign affidavits, bad cops who don't show for trials they promised to attend, a crooked judge who knows how he's going to decide before the first witness is called. What scares me the most is the sudden and *accidental* suicide. It's really a shame, though, because that one percent of bad apples tarnishes the whole profession, which really is honorable despite the cheesy billboards and cop shows on TV. Why do you think I like working the floor? I don't want an office job. It's exciting right here. I get to live vicariously through people and without having to worry about sleeping with one eye open. It's really a guilty pleasure."

"Oh, Evie, I should've come to work with you years ago. I have another question for you. Not that I would expect you to know anything, but do you think Bernadette knows anything?"

"Well, my number one rule is to not disclose stories or sources. I do not want to cut the grapevine," Evie said. "Having said that, I can tell you that Bernadette has never indicated that she's involved with or even knows about anything untoward at the firm. You can form your own conclusions, but as far as I'm concerned, with Bernadette, what you see is what you get. *I* certainly trust her."

"Thanks for the reassurance. That's exactly how I think of Bernadette, but I couldn't possibly bring her into this."

"I don't think you need to. In fact, I won't let you, because she's a sweet lady and doesn't need any more drama in her life. Besides, she brings me lots of business," said Evie with a smile.

"We need to keep the circle tight and limit communication. You have all you need with Jimmy, Rachel, and me. Let's be careful with Rachel, though."

"Rachel?" replied Prudence. "What's wrong with Rachel? Don't you think we can trust her?"

Evie replied, "I'm pretty sure we can trust her, but while I know her, I don't know what she's capable of. She's a strong woman, and when push comes to shove, self-preservation kicks in. I wouldn't be surprised if she would turn if it meant her safety or her livelihood. Prudence, from what you're telling me, it looks like Rachel has been purposefully dragged into this. She was so happy about her advancement through the firm and getting you brought over to her group, but if this thing goes sideways, I think she'll shut down and go her own way."

"Wait, you knew about that? Has she already confided in you?" asked Prudence almost indignantly.

Evie cocked an eyebrow and put her hand on her hip. "Girlfriend, that's old news. She's been in here a time or two and bragged about this new girl who was working with her, and she said she was conflicted about stealing her from another group. Who could that be other than you, Miss Pru?"

"Evelyn Cormier, I'm shocked. Why didn't you tell me?"

"Settle down. I didn't know firsthand since she never told me any names. Even if I knew, though, I wouldn't have told you because of my rule. Now, before you lose faith in me, just know that I'd break that rule in a second if I ever heard anything that might hurt you or Theo, even if it was just a rumor. As far as what Rachel may or may not have told me, though, I'll stick to my rule. I think you're smart enough to pull that information out of her when you sit her down and propose your idea. It is because of Rachel's involvement that I even considered joining your information underground railroad. Until I hear from you, I'll be on hot standby. We have a sale coming in the next few days, so that'll be a good time to get this train rolling."

# Chapter 64

## The Plan

"So, lemme get dis straight. Take it back ta da top." Ti Pop was getting a clearer picture. "Earl Tyler's cousin, Tyler Loomis, was beat half ta death by some scrawny high-yellah. Loomis complained ta big Cousin Earl, who wanted ta help Loomis get revenge. Cousin Earl was some cocky membah of ya F-Troop who liked ta show off 'n wanted to impress lil cuz. Da cousins wanted revenge and burnt down da house dat high-yellah 'n his momma lived in, 'cept it was da wrong house. *Someone*, ya say prob'ly High-yellah, found Cousin Earl's challenge coin, whatever da hell dat is, in a field near da burnt house. Assumin' he's da one who found it, High-yellah gives da coin to one Reverend Drummond. Said reverend calls his friend, one Reverend CJ."

Cerata interrupted Ti Pop. "His name is—get this—Reverend Dr. Cleophus James Hill V. He's a pastor at some church down there called Antioch the Redeemer, about an hour outside the city. It was established by the slaves of the Cypress plantation in the mid-1800s. Hang enough money in front of someone and they'll do just about anything, present company included, apparently. CJ sends young bucks from the plantation into the city, and the UAK places them in gangs to push the drugs. CJ gets a kickback. Effin' genius!"

Ti Pop shot up and almost spilled his beer. "Ya shittin' me? Dey got deir own preachah man ta give up his own people? Dhat's hysterical! Some tings nevah change. Dat's how dey all got here ta begin wit, ya know. White devils huntin' in da jungles, givin' trinkets to da first chief who would sell his rival tribe out. Dat's da history of da slave trade dat no one talks 'bout, 'n obviously nothin' has changed. Dey still sellin' out dere own kind. Da gang warfare of dose days, though, makes da thugs of today look like lil children. I'll pay da reverend a visit real soon. Send him a message he'll understand loud 'n clear. Coincidentally, Reverend CJ is prob'ly in cahoots with da Counselor, who is really da managin' podna at High-yellah's momma's fancy-pants firm. Da Counselor helps da Leadership fund biddnesses, which means he's connected ta ya two ladies. High-yellah's momma prob'ly got dirt on da fancy-pants firm 'n is doin' some diggin' on said Counselor from her firm's poor peoples' clinic. Does dat sum it up?"

"Yes, sir," said Cerata. "That's what we found."

"Are ya absotively posilutely sure? 'Cuz dat's all a lil too neat, dontcha tink?" Ti Pop knew the pieces fit, though, because Robertsen had already told him most of it, especially the part about Prudence investigating the Counselor (aka Oscar Brimley).

"Yes, sir, I'm pretty sure," confirmed Cerata.

"Goddamnit! *Pretty sure* doesn't feed da bobcat, Super Mario. I cain't make a move 'til da facts are verified."

Cerata paused a moment, then said, "Yes, sir, your summary represents the facts as we know them today. Verified."

Ti Pop put his chin in his hand, stroked his immaculately coiffed goatee, and, while looking down at the shiny deck of the newly christened *Betty Lou*, responded, "Okay. So, it looks like da common link between High-yellah, his momma, da law firm, 'n Drummond is dat church."

"Yes, sir," replied Cerata.

Ti Pop scratched his neck where a mosquito had recently made a withdrawal from his blood bank filled with Miller Lite, and slowly looked up at Cerata. "Let's go ole school. Light up a cross in front da church tonight 'n nail a note ta da front door dat says simply 'n clearly, *Consider this your first and last warning*. Don't handwrite nuttin' else, neithah. Make a collage from magazines 'n newspapers, ransom style, like ya see in da movies. Make 'em big, too: da cross 'n da note. We need maximum effect."

"Are you sure, Pop? That will likely bring the feds in." Cerata knew this would happen from his mob experience.

"Mario, mah boy, I'm countin' on it."

# Chapter 65

## The Burning Cross

Flames dwarfed the little church, and the thick, acrid smoke stretched to the heavens. The heat could be felt from across the parking lot, and the sleepy congregation looked on in horror as three ladder trucks came screaming onto the scene to douse the inferno. It was amazing how much heat and smoke a makeshift cross made from a telephone pole could generate, especially when covered in creosote and diesel—the UAK's own special recipe.

Although the front lawn was destroyed, the buildings were spared. Whoever did this wanted to instill fear and dread that the old ways were back. The congregants were shaken and could only wonder why this was happening. Reverend Drummond could only speculate that it had something to do with the coin Theo found. Someone was sending a message, but what were they saying? Perhaps more importantly, who were they sending it to, and why?

# Chapter 66

## CJ's Help

It was daybreak, and Reverend Drummond's voice quivered as he spoke into the phone. "CJ, I…I don't know what's happening. First Tante Ju's, and now this cross with that cryptic note. What warning? Warning about what? What do we do? Something is going on, and I'm afraid it will only escalate."

After a long silence, CJ replied, "Listen, Honoré, I don't know what's going on down there, either, but here's what you are going to do. Effective immediately, you need to suspend all church services and activities: the center, the clinic, everything except for whatever's necessary to continue with the renovations. This will keep your people safe and buy some time while we poke around to see if we come up with anything. Plus, by having people on the property, you will have the appearance of conducting business as usual, thereby showing everyone that you will not be intimidated. We have to remove that burnt cross and repair the front lawn ASAP. I have a guy here with a small front loader and a flatbed. He can get some sod, tear up the yard, and lay the new sod down. I'll send him by this afternoon, and by day's end it'll look like nothing happened."

"I can't thank you enough, brother. Thank you so much for your support," said Drummond.

CJ knew that Drummond's thanks was misplaced, and definitely not deserved. It was not out of duty, but guilt that he was offering whatever help he could. The good Reverend Dr. Cleophus James Hill V was having a crisis of conscience and vowed to get to the bottom of this, come hell or high water.

# Chapter 67

## CJ Gets His

Bernadette was in an especially good mood and cheerily answered the phone with, "Good morning. Oscar Brimley's office, how may I help you?"

"Yes, ma'am, is Mr. Brimley available to speak?"

Bernadette's standard answer was that he wasn't *available*, but she could tell that the man on the other end of the line needed to speak with him urgently. "I'm sorry, sir, he's not available at the moment. If you give me your name, number, and the nature of your call, I'll make sure he gets the message straightaway."

"Thank you very much, but this is a very serious matter, and I would really appreciate it if you could slip a quick note in front of him. You can say that Reverend CJ Hill at the Antioch clinic needs to speak with him urgently about a very serious matter. I'll hold as long as it takes." CJ knew that invoking the name of the clinic might persuade Bernadette to encourage Oscar to take the call.

Bernadette put CJ on hold and yelled through the open door of Valhalla, "Oscar! Some Reverend Hill from the Antioch clinic says he needs to speak with you about something urgent!"

"Thanks, Bernadette! I'll take the call! Please come close my door," Oscar yelled back. He held the receiver to his ear, connected the call, and spoke with a somber tone. "Good morning, CJ. I'm truly sorry about what happened. I had no idea they would do something like that."

"*They*?! Oscar, you know damn good and well who *they* are. *They* burned a goddamn cross! A cross, Oscar. That's 1950s bush league shit!" yelled CJ.

"CJ, calm down—"

"I will not! I will not...calm...down. This is wrong, Oscar, and you know it. You've got old people and children scared over at that church!! Those children need a safe place to go after school, and now their parents won't let them get ten feet near it. No, this is definitely *not* a time to be calm."

"CJ, I've always been a straight shooter, and I have never lied to you. I swear I had nothing to do with this, and I had no idea anything like this would happen," Oscar replied. "I told you that unless you fixed this, it would be out of my hands. Well, it is now obviously out of my hands. In fact, I've placed a few urgent calls to Robertsen to see what's going on, and he's not returned my calls. I'm truly sorry, CJ, but this is on you." Oscar doubled down and took a more authoritarian tone. "And I'll tell you why that is on you, CJ. I was hoping you were up to the task. I was praying you'd be up to the task, but in the back of my mind I really didn't think you were, or that you'd take me seriously enough. Want to know why, CJ? It's because you're lazy. You always have been. And you're greedy in a selfish way, too. I admit, I'm a pretty greedy son of a bitch, but I also look out for my own. I treat my people fair, CJ. If I come into some money as a result of something untoward I might have done, I give a chunk of it away as a bonus to those who helped me. It helps clear my conscience. You, on the other hand, don't appear to have a conscience, because you keep it all to yourself. Think about it. Who is the only one with a new car down there? Who struts around in new suits and wears fancy watches that no one in your neck of the woods could ever afford? Not only do you keep it for yourself, CJ, you actually sell your own boys to those gangs so they can make money for the UAK miscreants who, in turn, kick some of it back to you. True enough that I benefit, too, but I'm not the one selling my boys out. Now that I think about it, you're more of a son of a bitch than I am. Actually, what you're doing and what you've done is, in its very essence, evil. I didn't fully realize it until this very moment, but you really are an evil person.

"After our initial conversation, I went to Robertsen and told him that I thought we'd need a contingency plan in case you couldn't deliver. I thought maybe he would use some of his boys to fire a few shots across the bow and scare the shit out of Drummond so he'd forget about investigating that coin. But this quickly escalated into something neither of us is prepared for. This looks like something Robertsen's fixer, Ti Pop, would do. I don't know anything concrete other than he's been seen in the Rigolets a few times, fishing. Rumor is he's got a new sailboat. If you had tamped this down when it started, we wouldn't be having this conversation."

"Oscar, you gotta help me on this. Can't you get your folks to give me a little room? I need some time," CJ pleaded.

"First of all, they're not *my* folks. Let's start from the beginning so it's clear to you why your time has run out. First, Prudence wound up with some of my files. I know this because some time back, I couldn't find them for a meeting. I was momentarily confused, but then I remembered they were on my desk, which means someone else had them. I pulled the activities log from the copy machine. To use it, you need a code. It copies and time stamps everything that runs through it. Prudence made copies around the same time, and the number of pages approximates the size of some files she copied for another case she was working on. She didn't change the code, though, when she started copying my files—a novice mistake on her part. Then, she started going through the firm's database at night. This is when I approached you, remember? You could have stopped this then, but you didn't. You didn't take me seriously."

"Oscar, I took you very seriously and already had the ball rolling. I—"

"I'm going to say this once. Shut up until I give you the floor. Do you hear me? Do you understand the seriousness of this situation?"

After a long pause, a contrite Reverend Dr. Cleophus James Hill V responded, "I'm sorry, Oscar. I didn't mean to interrupt. Please continue."

"Good. Where was I? After she started poking around, she brought Jimmy O'Leary, one of my finest young lawyers, into this and they thought they'd be cute by getting me to set up that clinic so they could chase rabbits through the firm's files. A very smart move on her part. That's why I hired her in the first place, CJ. She was off to a great start at the firm and had great things ahead of her. Then she came into possession of something she shouldn't have and got curious. And you know what curiosity did...

"Now, Jimmy's been seen at Galatoire's having dinner with Rachel, so I'm sure he roped her in, albeit a little earlier than I thought he would. You don't know her, but Prudence has worked with her very closely, so Rachel's a pivotal person in this. I don't know yet how they'll try to hide their tracks, but I'll find out sooner rather than later. Why was the dinner at Galatoire's suspicious, you might ask? Rachel is a man-eater who is focused on her career, and for a while, she's been a *friends with benefits* kind of girl, and not attached to anyone. I don't like man-eaters, so I don't feel bad about having brought her into this. I don't know what will ultimately happen to her, and frankly, at this point, I don't care. Jimmy is a little boy scout—not Rachel's type—so the two of them spotted together getting cozy at an expensive restaurant raised a few eyebrows. I would have expected them to pick a place with a younger crowd like Lucy's near her apartment, or Les Bon Temps on Magazine Street. Jimmy is a novice, very smart, but socially liberal, and I think he's running scared and wants to protect Prudence. I don't care what happens to him, either.

"CJ, I had to set up one of my own people, who is a real cash cow for the firm. Rachel was up-and-coming in the real estate section—the firm's most profitable—and now she's working with Prudence and Jimmy. Poor thing is scared to death, but I need to keep her close so I can see what she and the others are putting together. I can promise you that none of this is going to come back on me." Oscar became a little more animated as he said, "CJ, I know everything about my firm—everything! I know who is inflating bills, who the superstars are, which partners are trying to split off to start their own little fiefdom while looking me straight in the eye and telling me how happy they are here. I know the paralegals in the salt mines who are second-guessing their dead-end career choices and looking for new jobs while making up excuses like doctor's appointments or dead uncles' funerals to take half-days to go to their interviews. I know which associates are trying to make a name for themselves by stabbing their colleagues in the back, and I know which ones are sleeping with which secretaries. I know EVERYTHING!" Oscar paused and took the tone down a notch. "CJ, your task was simple—get Drummond to redirect his efforts away from that coin—and you failed. You failed in spectacular fashion, which has the following consequences: one, the UAK is going to close ranks, and two, so am I. Neither of these eventualities is good for you, my friend."

In a confident and cocky manner designed to suppress the fear rising within him, CJ said, "Oscar, why are you telling me all of this? You know I can bring you down with this information."

Oscar chuckled at the notion and asked in an eerily calm manner, "Is that a threat, CJ? That's not going to happen, and you know it. I'm just trying to emphasize how deep in the shit you got yourself by just sitting over there at your plantation with your thumb up your ass. The shame of it is that I really like Prudence and I fear for the safety of her family."

"Don't you dare harm that girl or her family! I raised her and her son, and I'll do whatever I can to protect them. I promise you I'll—"

Oscar cut him off with a nervous chuckle. "Don't be a white knight on this, because it will backfire. If you value your little kingdom over there, you'll just sit back and wait for all of this to go down. I will help you all I can since I like you—I really do—but don't try anything cute. This is way beyond your capabilities, and you know it. If I had any control, I'd find a way to get Prudence out of the firm and back to waiting tables, but I can't approach those guys, not now. I can't intervene, and I can't let on that I know too much. The dogs are off the leash, CJ, and there's nothing I can do except give you a heads-up when I come across information that can help you. At this point, that's not likely to happen. Believe it or not, they are keeping a tight leash on that fixer guy, at least in the short term. Probably because the incompetent fools in the UAK would screw it up somehow. From what I know about him, if it were up to him, he'd have burned more than a cross. He'd have burned the whole place down. A scorched-earth approach is simple and allows him to get back to his life with a few more dollars in his pocket. I'm told that once he's given a task, he answers to no one and doesn't care about collateral damage left in the wake of his destruction. When the Leadership is satisfied that he can work with the UAK degenerates, they'll likely take him completely off that leash. I can only imagine that Robertsen is doing everything he can to keep him in check. The dangerous part is that I understand he's a sadistic son of a bitch and enjoys chaos. I really want to help you, CJ, but like I told you before, the only thing I can do is tell you when the fire trucks will arrive—maybe not even that. I'm truly sorry."

Oscar hung up the phone without saying another word. CJ put his head on the table and wept as if he was in the Garden of Gethsemane, awaiting his judgment day.

# Chapter 68

## Evie Gets to Work

It was lunchtime. Evie took the package from Rachel who quickly walked away with a bag containing a pair of Balenciaga's latest pumps. This was her first foray into the world of espionage, and she couldn't wait until closing time, when she could pass the information on to Prudence.

Prudence realized that she hadn't fully thought through the handing over of the information, so she was careful not to be seen downtown. She spent most of her time these days at the Antioch clinic, and it would have been suspicious for her to suddenly show up near the office again in the middle of the afternoon.

She and Evie decided to meet for happy hour drinks at the Victorian Lounge at The Columns hotel in the Garden District, down St. Charles Avenue. It was the site of the filming of the Brooke Shields movie, *Pretty Baby*: a scandalous film, even by modern standards. Evie ordered a St. Charles Breeze and Prudence went with her standard Pellegrino and lime. Prudence had grown accustomed to social events at the firm, and although most of the firm's associates drank like sailors on leave, she still rarely drank. She knew that it would be suspicious if she didn't have a glass in her hand, so Pellegrino and a lime wedge in a tumbler with a little umbrella could easily pass for a gin and tonic.

They grabbed their drinks from the majestic mahogany bar, made their way to the back of the dimly lit room, and spied some empty seats. Prudence sat in a Victorian wingback, much like the one in the lobby of the firm, and Evie sat right next to her on a well-worn cordovan leather sofa.

"Prudence, this is so exciting. I feel like Nancy Drew deep in a mystery."

Prudence leaned in and was almost inaudible through the din of the crowd. She was on the verge of tears. "Did you hear about that cross burning? That was at the Antioch, Evie. In *our* neighborhood! I can't do this. I'm calling a stop to this whole thing, because I'm sure somebody knows what we're up to. I'm scared, Evie."

Evie looked away and took in the scenery. Tourists were gathered at the end of the bar, locals sat, drank Sazeracs, and ate shrimp cocktails. She drained her drink, signaled the bartender for another, took Prudence by the hand, and looked directly into her eyes. "This is exactly why I was brought into this. You need to be strong and have faith, girl. You are the strongest person I have *ever* known and have been more of a rock for me than you'll ever know, so I'm going to tell you this once and *only* once. It may feel like the walls are closing in—and they very well might be—but these people need to be stopped and you need to be the one to stop them. I can't think of anyone else with the courage and the ability to think quickly on their feet and bring the necessary resources to bear. You proved that by setting up the clinic. I'm not going to sit here and tell you it's going to be easy, because it's not.

I can't tell you that this isn't risky, because it is. And I can't tell you that people won't be hurt, because as sure as I'm sitting here, someone *will* get hurt and lives will be changed forever. But those are the cards we've been dealt, my dear Prudence, and backing down now is not going to change anything. In fact, it will probably make matters worse. I think we have an opportunity to get out ahead of this, but we must be strong, we must be creative, we must be thorough, and we must see this to its end—whatever that might be. I'm with you, girl, and we're going to regroup, reload, and take these people down."

"Evelyn Aimée Cormier, I love you. You are absolutely right. The easy thing to do would be to cut and run. We've got to see this through, whatever the cost. Like you said, it is not safe either way. Staying close to it might help us prepare a little better. Thank you, Evie. You're my rock."

"Always have been, dear. Now, time to focus. We need to get with Jimmy and Rachel and bring Reverend Drummond up to speed. He's been targeted, or at least the church has. He deserves to know. He might be able to help in his own way."

# Chapter 69

### CJ in the Crosshairs

"We had a nice little chat with the Counselor, and he gave him up within five minutes," replied Robertsen.

"Gave up who?" asked Ti Pop.

"The preacher we talked about. Reverend CJ. Pop, you better not kill anyone."

"I make no promises, podna. I get results. Dat's what y'all payin' for, right?" Ti Pop put his feet back on his new deck chair, thinking about his next move.

# Chapter 70

## Time to Talk

The day was unseasonably warm, and the bright blue sky was tinged with a purple iridescent glow and void of clouds. The air was silent and arid—unusual for New Orleans, which usually enjoyed a moist, slight breeze off Lake Pontchartrain. The grass was a vivid green, contrasted by a few white ducks waddling their way to the pond in City Park, where the water was a deep, dark, cottonmouth black. The setting was surreal, and it truly felt like the calm before a storm.

Reverend Drummond had picked the place. City Park was not near downtown and far enough from the Antioch to allow him to catch his breath and clear his mind. He surveyed his surroundings, looking at each person at the picnic table in turn, staring in utter disbelief. "How do you know all of this, Prudence? How can you be so sure it is people at your firm behind all of this? Jimmy, help me out here."

"Please, let me explain. I don't know for certain that the firm is behind the fires at Tante Ju's or at the Antioch, but I do know some people there might be involved with the people who are."

Reverend Drummond responded, "Okay, but how can you be so sure of that? This is not making sense to me. If people at the firm aren't behind it, yet they know the people who are, then they *are* behind it, Prudence. Ultimately, they are just as responsible."

"That's a fair point. Let's put it this way. I don't think the people at the firm are involved in making the decisions to set the fires. Let me back up and start from the beginning. I came into possession of some files belonging to the firm's managing partner, Oscar Brimley. I became suspicious that he might be involved in some illicit dealings, so I started digging into the firm's files. What I found was a trail of activity involving one of the firm's biggest clients, Knight Trucking & Logistics. I'm sure you've seen their trucks on the highway."

"Yes, but what does a trucking company have to do with the UAK?" asked Drummond.

"Reverend, please let me finish. This is all beyond me, so I want to be accurate. So, I followed the trail and looked at the corporate structure and the ownership. When I saw O.B. Enterprises was a shareholder, I knew Oscar Brimley was involved somehow. I panicked, and that's when I went to Jimmy. When I showed him the information I had, he confirmed that this was something worth digging into a little deeper. We couldn't continue our investigation at the firm since there was just too much information to go through and we couldn't risk getting caught, so I convinced Oscar to open up the clinic at the Antioch. Jimmy and I needed a place to continue our work."

"Prudence, I really can't believe what I'm hearing. You were on the trail of some evil people, and you brought your investigation to our church?" Drummond asked disapprovingly.

"Reverend, I'm so sorry. I thought—"

"That's the problem, dear. You *didn't* think. Listen to me now. I know you had the best intentions, but you did not think about the unintended consequences. You do realize that your decision put yourself and all of us in grave danger, don't you?"

Prudence looked at Reverend Drummond directly and said, "I know that now." She then turned toward Evie and continued, "That's why we are here. We must work with the hand we were dealt, the hand *I* dealt to all of you. What's done is done and now we must help and support each other. It's as simple as that. Anyway, we couldn't find anything in the files that would lead us to believe that the people involved are violent. In fact, W.T. Falke is an owner and a respected businessman in the community."

Reverend Drummond interjected, "Wait a minute. W.T. Falke is an owner of Knight Trucking? It's starting to make a little sense now. Prudence, I'm now willing to believe that W.T. Falke is involved with the UAK. I suppose that's what 'Knight' stands for? You said your research has led you to believe that Knight Trucking's books and records looked a little too clean, and, because of this, there is something funny going on?"

"The UAK? What makes you think that? I've come across nothing in the files that would make me take that leap. I'm sorry, Reverend Drummond, I didn't mean to be rude, but it seems like a stretch to me that someone like W.T. Falke would associate himself with a hate group," Prudence said, seemingly confused by this outlandish connection.

"Well, I wouldn't have made the connection either, were it not for the coin Theo showed me," said Reverend Drummond.

Prudence became very animated at the mention of her son. "Theo?! What about Theo? Is he mixed up in all of this, too?"

Reverend Drummond replied, "Prudence, please calm down. All Theo did was show me a coin he found shortly after the fire in the field near Tante Ju's. I immediately recognized it as a UAK coin because of their logo, but I didn't tell Theo anything. As far as I know, he knows nothing. I attributed Tante Ju's fire to the group because of that coin. I called Reverend CJ since he and I had some bad experiences with the UAK back in the day. They've kept to themselves for decades and have been dealing drugs with the street gangs, then all of a sudden they burn a house down? That part still doesn't make sense."

"Let's say, for argument's sake, that Knight Trucking is linked to the UAK," Jimmy chimed in. "Why? Even if you think the UAK was involved in the fire at Tante Ju's, what makes you think they're responsible for the burning cross at the Antioch?"

Reverend Drummond replied, "It's the United Aryan Knights, Jimmy. The size of the cross, the fact that it created an inordinate amount of smoke, the way that it was upside down: those are all their trademarks. The coin turning up in the field so close to Tante Ju's is another link. It had *UAK* written on it with the group's logo. They're definitely behind all of this, Jimmy, but again I ask, why? And, why now?"

The members of the group stared at each other for what seemed like an eternity. Rachel broke the silence. "Okay, since Oscar has me pulling files, I'll see what I can find on him and Falke, as well as if there's a link with the UAK. I agree with you, Reverend Drummond. I can't see how a businessman like Falke could be linked with that group, but at this point I'm willing to believe almost anything."

"That's simple," said Jimmy. "Isn't it obvious?" He looked around the table at blank faces staring back. "Money. Falke would do anything for money and I'm sure Oscar would, too. Don't you see? It all makes sense. Prudence found the link between Knight Trucking, KTL Construction, and O.B. Enterprises. Those companies, along with others, are involved with the Azalea Group, which is a real estate development group that has been building small commercial centers like crazy—with the latest and biggest being the Renaissance d'Orleans. Let's assume that Knight Trucking is laundering money due to its clean books. It looks legit since they operate trucks and should have some legitimate cargo, right? If that's the case, then we have to believe they also have illegitimate cargo, right? I understand their revenue is off the chart. Solution: clean the books, falsify manifests, etc. But, where does the money come from? Those projects cost millions." He looked around the table again. "The UAK! They're drug dealers, right?"

Rachel broke the ensuing silence. "Okay, I can go with that and I can see how they might think you and Prudence are on their trail through your investigation at the clinic. The cross was a definite message, but why burn an old lady's house down?"

Prudence suddenly gasped. "Oh no! What if it was the *wrong* house?"

# Chapter 71

## You're Fired!

"Larry, listen to me. We can get a handle on this." Oscar Brimley, the unshakeable man who could move mountains, was begging.

Robertsen replied, "Falke wants you out and there's nothing I can do about that. My instructions are very clear. Effective immediately, you and the firm are to cease all activities related to the businesses. You will continue to work on current litigation, but only to the extent necessary to get extensions and protect default judgments. You also will continue to work on real estate matters limited to activities absolutely necessary to protect permits and other deadlines associated with the Azalea Group. You have one week to provide a spreadsheet with aged payables and prepare billing invoices for ordinary activities conducted by the firm on our behalf up through today. You will not be compensated beyond today, so you'd better make the most of the time you have left. When we receive the invoices, we will transfer the money immediately. We don't want this hanging over our heads any longer than is necessary. Over the next month, you will prepare all active files for transfer to a law firm to be named later. Falke is holding a beauty contest now, and it might be one from Baton Rouge, Lafayette, or Shreveport just to get a little distance from this cesspool of a city."

"Goddamnit, Larry, you can't do that!" Oscar yelled into the phone. "We've got a deal and investments. We have commitments, we—"

"Oscar, there's no longer a *we*. Don't you get it? It was *your* people who decided to go digging around. It's because of *you* that Falke had to spend a fortune to get Ti Pop out of retirement, and I can't imagine what that crazy son of a bitch is going to do before this is all over."

"I can make this right. Just give me some time and we can get back on track. There's got to be a way," Oscar pleaded.

"There are too many variables at play here. Your people in the firm, not one, but *two* pastors, innocent people. For Chrissakes, Oscar, there are children involved. You may be a good lawyer with connections to the right judges and politicians, but you've got shit for brains and no street smarts. Not only that, your damn ego can't even fit inside the Superdome. Don't bother contacting me or anyone else in the Leadership. It's over, Oscar. You are on your own, and I have no idea what your future holds. If you get any foolish ideas about linking me or any of the Leadership to any of this, I don't think I have to tell you the likely outcome. You know a world of hurt will come to you and everyone you know and love. In fact, you'd likely be the only one to survive, and then you'd have the rest of your miserable life to think about your utter, abject failure. Goodbye, Oscar."

# Chapter 72

## Confronting Theo

For Prudence, the distant waning crescent moon was an omen, and the coal black of the night surrounding its halo brought on an unfamiliar loneliness. The absence of any other meaningful light punctuated that loneliness and her utter inability to find direction.

When she arrived home, still shaken from the day's activities, Theo greeted her in the kitchen.

"Hi, Mom. How's it going? I went by the Antioch today to help out a bit, but Reverend Drummond wasn't there, so I came home. I finished my homework, too. How about that?"

In a tone that matched her somber mood, Prudence looked at her beautiful boy and said, "Theo, honey, I've got to ask you something."

"Okay, is everything alright? You look sad."

"I was with Reverend Drummond this afternoon. We went to the park with some friends. Theo, why didn't you tell me about the coin?"

Theo thought for a moment, trying to recall anything about a coin that would make his mom look so upset. "You mean the Mardi Gras doubloon? Oh, that's just a coin I found in that empty lot near Tante Ju's. I gave it to Reverend Drummond and didn't think anything else of it. He asked me not to say anything to anyone, which I thought was a little weird, but I did what he asked and didn't say a word. Why, is it important?"

Prudence looked at her precious boy and said, "Well, it might very well be, honey. That *doubloon* is actually a coin that belongs to a group of very bad men."

"I *knew* it wasn't a regular doubloon. It felt too heavy and it had strange wording on it. What kind of group? Like a biker gang or something?"

"Theo, it is one of those hate groups. Reverend Drummond recognized the letters and design on the coin, and he confirmed it with Reverend CJ. Baby, do you know anything about this?"

Theo, growing a little concerned, replied, "No, ma'am. I just found the coin the day after the fire and gave it to Reverend Drummond. That's it. Do you think it has anything to do with Tante Ju's house? Or that time Chookie got beat up in the Quarter? I know those groups can hold grudges for years."

"Maybe so, Theo, but it could also have been just random, or even the wrong house. I don't know. None of it makes sense."

Theo froze and broke out in a cold sweat. He recalled that the boy he had beaten so badly had been giving him Cheshire Cat smiles in the days after the fire. He'd also heard rumors that he had a cousin in a biker gang. He'd had no idea why the kid was smiling, but it wouldn't be a stretch to think that the kid's cousin wasn't with a biker gang at all, but that he was really with a hate group.

"Theo, what's wrong? You look like you've seen a ghost."

"Mom, I think this might all be my fault," said Theo slowly.

"What are you talking about? How can any of this be *your* fault?" a visibly shaken Prudence asked.

"Remember when I got into that fight? Well, shortly after the fire, Tyler Loomis, the kid I beat up, was looking at me a little funny and I heard rumors that his cousin was in a biker gang. Maybe it wasn't a biker gang. What if he's really in that hate group and the fire was meant for *me*?" asked Theo, now very concerned.

"Don't go thinking crazy things like that, young man. You had *nothing* to do with this. It might very well be that Reverend Drummond knows for a fact that a hate group is behind the burning of Tante Ju's as well as that cross, but none of this was aimed at or done because of you."

Undeterred, Theo pressed, "But Mom, what if it's not a coincidence? What if that kid's cousin was just out for revenge and intended for that fire to be the end of it? That part *was* aimed at me. No one would ever have known that the group was involved had I not shown Reverend Drummond that coin. *That* part is on me. Tante Ju, Chookie, Japo: all *that's* on me, too."

Consumed with grief and self-loathing, Theo ran to his room and locked his door.

# Chapter 73

## Connecting Reverend Hill

The next day, Prudence took Theo with her to a follow-up meeting with Reverend Drummond at the Antioch. The fog of the morning set against the gun metal gray, cloud-filled sky provided a stark contrast to the meeting in the park.

Reverend Drummond spoke first. "Prudence, there may be something to this. As crazy as its members are, the UAK is a thorough group that runs a tight ship. The arson section of the NOPD said that the fire at Tante Ju's was likely started by a Molotov cocktail thrown through a window. That's a real amateur move. The UAK would never do something so sloppy. Let's assume, for argument's sake, that Theo's theory is correct. First, Theo gets in a fight at school with a boy who is rumored to have a cousin in a biker gang, which we now think could be the UAK. Later, Tante Ju's house is firebombed, but the fire was really meant for your house. Next, Theo finds a coin in a field soon after the fire and thinks it's from a Mardi Gras krewe, except that the coin is heavier than the aluminum ones thrown from the floats. Theo gives me the coin and I tell Reverend CJ about it."

Prudence gasped. "Please tell me Reverend CJ is not involved, too."

Reverend Drummond looked at Prudence with his mouth agape. "Prudence Jean-Batiste, how could you even think of such a thing?"

"Well, what if he *is*? You gave Theo room for crazy conspiracy theories. Hear me out," pleaded Prudence.

Reverend Drummond said with indignant disbelief, "Prudence, Reverend CJ and I raised you and Theo. He's the one who suggested we establish the Antioch here as a way to tone down the fires of the civil rights movement in the '60s. He takes young men from the Cypress and sends them to the city to better themselves. He's a good man."

Prudence paused a moment and held his gaze. "Reverend, if there's one thing I've learned while working at the firm, it's that life isn't always as it seems. It's only when you apply the facts against a theory of the case that the truth eventually comes out. Another thing I've learned is that sometimes, one has to be cynical and take a leap from logic before anything starts to make sense. As far as you know, Reverend CJ is where the coin's trail stops, right?"

"I suppose so. I haven't followed up with him since the cross burning, and I have told no one else. I'm sure Theo hasn't either," said Reverend Drummond, looking at Theo.

"No, sir, I've told no one else."

"You're not going to like this, but hear me out," Prudence continued. "Please bear with me, because I have to think out loud here."

Reverend Drummond, with furrowed brow and folded arms, nodded his head slightly. "Go on, but if you're headed down the path I think you are, you are correct. I'm not going to like this at all."

Prudence laid out her theory with the objectivity of a surgeon. "Let's go back to the beginning. When Theo and I arrived at the Cypress, I got a lot of help from the congregation: rent, groceries, a place to live, a car, daycare for Theo. It was more support than I could have ever hoped for, and it seemed to give Reverend CJ a lot of joy to be able to help me out. The Cypress is a poor community, though, and even if everyone had worked together, the congregation probably couldn't have sustained that level of support for all those years. Most of the funds given to me were from Reverend CJ directly, not from individual people. He probably even bought my car with cash. It might not have been a donation, as he led me to believe. And here's something you probably didn't know. Every two years, like clockwork, Reverend Drummond would buy a new Oldsmobile. He's had a light blue Cutlass, a navy Olds Delta 88, a burgundy Olds 98 Regency, and recently, a white Cadillac. All those cars were top-of-the-line. Where did he get that money? Again, the community could not support that lifestyle *and* help me at the same time." Reverend Drummond looked at her with rapt attention as Prudence continued. "What about the boys he sends to the city? Do you know who they are and where they wound up? Have any of them ever sought you out for guidance? I'd be willing to bet that Reverend CJ doesn't keep you in the loop, and as far as you know, he was setting them on a righteous path. I'd also be willing to bet that many of those boys wound up with the street gangs."

"Now, hold on a minute. That's taking it a little too far," argued Reverend Drummond.

Prudence paused, then looked at Theo and back at Reverend Drummond. "Is it? In our investigation we discovered that the UAK has been funding another group through dummy corporations that have been buying up property all over the city: downtown, the Garden District, the warehouse district, uptown. And there were some notes about plans in Mid-City. We found all this through the firm's files, which means that people in the firm are involved. I'm not going to give you names yet since we're not through investigating. However, there are some names you would recognize. Now, I'll bet the UAK has organized the street gang activity, keeping them out of each other's territories and giving them kickbacks. We know the UAK is in the drug trade. Everyone knows that. The only market is New Orleans, because their base is too far away from Baton Rouge or Mississippi. Who controls the streets? Who else but the gangs? If the UAK controls the market, and the gangs control the streets, doesn't it make sense that these unlikely groups are actually working together? Maybe they're not working at all. Maybe the UAK controls them through coercion. They have more money, are better organized, and don't fight amongst themselves. Otherwise, we'd see them on TV as much as we see these gangs. Maybe the UAK provides focus and organization, and has distribution channels through groups like Knight Trucking. The UAK maintains a low profile and hasn't been seen in the city in any significant way for decades, and the economy of the Northshore couldn't sustain the spending level maintained by this project. It's not as crazy as it sounds, is it?" Theo sat still with tears welling in his eyes. Prudence turned to him. "What's wrong, sweetie? I know this whole thing sounds kind of far-fetched and that you'd hate to think Reverend CJ is mixed up with this."

"He used to give me pocket money. Not much, but some," said Theo.

Prudence put her arm around him. "Baby, he was a kind man. He *is* a kind man, but he could also have his demons."

Tears ran down Theo's face and his body quivered slightly. Trying to maintain a strong countenance, he spoke with an almost unintelligible voice. "It's not just that, Mom. I told you, this is all because I got in a fight and I found the coin, isn't it? This is all on me. Tante Ju and Japonica are dead *because* of me. Chookie is homeless *because* of me. The Antioch almost burned *because* of me. The children have no place to play and the old folks have nowhere to spend their afternoons all *because* of me."

Reverend Drummond, convinced of the plausibility of Prudence's theory, took Theo by the hand, and gently said in a soft and reassuring voice, "Theo, if all of that is true, then it is *because* of you that we are now able to stop all of this. The Holy Spirit moves in mysterious ways. Good men do bad things, bad men do good things, and bad things happen to good people. We wake every morning not knowing what kind of day the Lord will give us. This situation is just another example of God's providence. Getting in that fight was the wrong thing to do, sure, but you did it to defend your mother's honor, which is very noble. Tante Ju's passing was violent, and no way for a proud, beautiful woman to die. Chookie's situation is very tragic. It is tough to see a once strong and exuberant man now so dependent on others. He was the protector and big brother to those kids in the projects, many of whom are now consumed by the streets because of people like Reverend CJ and groups like the UAK.

"Whether you can see it now or not, Theo, you have been and are now more important than you ever will know or admit to yourself. Japonica, a dog that would have been euthanized, was saved by *you*. He was a great help to the kids at the Antioch and died a hero by helping Chookie. He was as much a part of our family as any of us. The Antioch is still standing and is a place where your mother and Mr. O'Leary can finish their investigation. And *you*, my boy, *you* are the glue that holds all of us together and keeps us all focused. So, yes, in a way, this is all your *fault*, so to speak, but it is *because* of you that we now have this opportunity, an opportunity to right some egregious wrongs. So, fear not. With a little faith, and all of us working together, we are going to get through this."

# Chapter 74

### The Countdown Begins

The cool, white light of the full blue moon glistened on the sparkling Gulf waters between Pass Christian and the uninhabited Cat Island. *Betty Lou* was moored, and the water gently lapped against her hull. Court was in session, the honorable Octavé Poupard presiding.

Ti Pop set his Miller Lite down, took a deep drag from his uncharacteristically lit cigar, and blew the gray smoke toward the clear sky as he summarized his jury charge. "I'm gonna say dis only once, so y'all dumbasses bettah listen. Dis is goin' down simultaneously in exac'ly twenty-four hours from now. Mark ya watches. Kroger, tomorrah afternoon, ya take two trusted—whatcha call dem? Troops? You take two Troopahs down ta da Cypress 'n case da church. We want quick access in 'n out. Y'all gonna need ta keep a low profile, 'cause y'all be da only white boys out dere for a hunerd miles. Supah Mario, ya take two Troopahs ta case da church off Airline Highway where we burnt dat cross. Again, low profile. Dere'll prob'ly be feds patrollin' da area. I'm gonna take her, 'n I've already cased ha house. We ain't gonna screw wit da lawyers jus' yet. Dose greedy *couillons* will get what's coming ta dem soon enough. We need ta stay on course."

Ti Pop was in full-on mission mode. "Ya Troopahs will be sworn ta secrecy or else dey'll meet da same demise as Mr. Tyler, got it? Dis afternoon, y'all gonna get three Troopahs go shoppin' fah supplies. Each group will go ta different stores 'n buy enough materiel ta handle all three sites. Buy fertilizah bought at one place, 'n diesel at anothah, etc. Y'all get da point? Pay in cash 'n if any ordah is more dan ninety dollahs, ya go to anothah store—one in a nearby town, if necessary. We can't raise any red flags by havin' tattooed redneck skinheads all of a sudden showin' up at hardware stores 'n nurseries buyin' gas cans 'n fertilizah. Y'all don't look like da farmin' type. We'll meet in da woods at ya little Hitler hut tomorrah night, which is actually tonight in case ya numbnuts couldn't figure dat out. Herman, ya show at 19:45 hours, Mario at 20:30, 'n I'll get dere at 22:00 so we can put it all togethah. We get dere at different times ta ensure we ain't seen togethah or followed. Got it?"

Krieger and Cerata nodded simultaneously in agreement. Krieger asked, "Just so we're clear, we are to set them off at the same time?"

Ti Pop wanted to make a statement and reemphasize that he was in total control. He quickly jumped from his chair and grabbed the seated Krieger by his knees. With the ash from his cigar dropping onto Krieger's leg and spittle flying out of his mouth, he got in Krieger's face and yelled, "Did I stuttah, asshole?! What part didn't ya understand?! The part where I said I'm only gonna say dis once?! Whaddaya tink I meant when I said it was goin' down simultaneously in twenty-four hours? Why da hell else would I tell ya ta mark ya goddamn watches? Don't answer dat."

"Sorry, I was just making sure."

Still holding Krieger's knees, Ti Pop then turned toward Cerata.

"What about ya, Godfathah? Any questions?"

"No, sir," said Cerata, looking at Krieger with a wry grin. "I'll be there with my supplies at 20:30."

Ti Pop released Krieger's knees and went back to his seat. As he sat, he grabbed a couple of bottles of Abita Purple Haze instead of his standby Miller Lite, and tossed them to the other men. "Alrighty den, gentlemen, let's sit back, pop a top, wet a line, see if we can't catch a few croakahs before we get back. Today will be a busy, busy day."

# Chapter 75

## Ready to Roll

Prudence was getting worried. Jimmy was fifteen minutes late. He was normally very punctual. He finally arrived and went straight to the back of the clinic.

"Sorry I'm late. It's like people forget how to drive whenever there's a little rain on the road. Not only that, Oscar came to see me about some offshore pipeline claim I'm working on, which I found a little unusual. The section head is usually the one to ask me specific questions. Oscar rarely graces the Hall with his presence. He was also a little standoffish. I think he might have been trying to rattle me a little."

"He knows, Jimmy! He has to," said Prudence.

"I know, Prudence. That's why we've got to move fast. I think we have enough for me to get with my friend at the DOJ. She'll have enough information to satisfy the standard of probable cause to get a warrant, and I already emptied most of my stuff from my office last night. I left enough so it doesn't look completely empty, and I don't care about anything that's left, so I'll never need to step foot in that snake pit again. I think Rachel did the same thing."

"Shit!" said Prudence.

"Why, Miss Pru, I don't think I've ever heard you use that sort of language. My virgin ears are burning, and in a church, of all places!" Jimmy chuckled. "Don't worry, you can clean your office tonight."

"I know. I just didn't want to go downtown again. I guess I'll use it as an opportunity to bring Evie up to speed. I haven't been in the store lately, so it won't look suspicious if I'm seen there. Besides, my bonus check just cleared."

Jimmy's ears perked up and he asked, "Bonus?"

"Yes, this is the time of year when paralegals get their bonuses. You big shot lawyers probably didn't know that. It was a generous one, too."

"I guess the bonus I got last year will be my last one at the firm. I doubt there will be any money left once this all goes down. It's a shame, too, because there are a lot of good people there. When the feds bust in, everyone's a suspect until they're not, and their reputations will forever be tarnished—along with ours."

Prudence gave his arm a little love jab and, with her trademark smile, said, "Cheer up. It's all for a good cause, right?"

"I'm not very cheery right now. Do you understand what's about to happen? Do you remember the 2001 Enron case in Houston? It took down a Fortune 500 company, as well as one of the big eight accounting firms, all because a few at the top were greedy. Go search the YouTube videos. People were walking out of the building and were allowed only one box for their possessions. They were sitting on the sidewalks and crying while waiting for rides home. It was humiliating, and they had no idea what was happening or why." He looked her in the eye and spoke in a very somber tone. "That will happen to our friends and coworkers. All those good people are going to go through that embarrassment. Some will need to retain lawyers since they were working on matters pertaining to Project Azalea without even realizing it. Oscar did a masterful job of compartmentalizing everything and keeping everyone in the dark. Don't forget, you and Rachel worked on that permit for the Renaissance d'Orleans, and because she was Oscar's secretary, they'll likely keep Bernadette involved for months. She probably won't be able to get a job after this, at least not one in this profession or that pays as much. She'll be marked as a pariah. The same happened to many people during Enron. Rachel and I have licenses on the line, and I hope we can keep them. Prudence, we're not just dealing with greedy men who want as much money as they can get. We're dealing with pure evil here. These people have no regard for the lives of others. Everyone's disposable in their twisted fantasy world."

Prudence just stared in disbelief as she replied, "Oh, Jimmy, I guess I never thought of all that. I just thought it was all going to come down on Oscar and that would be that. You're right, though, everyone will be a suspect. I feel so horrible. Wait, do you think I'll need an attorney? You know I can't afford one."

"I don't think you'll have to worry about that. I'll work on getting as many immunity deals as I can for those I know had nothing to do with it—me, you, Rachel, Bernadette, maybe even BB, depending on how much he knows and how clean he is. He likes to talk a big game and loves the trappings of success, but he's basically harmless. Rachel knows him better than I do, but I think he's a good guy in spite of his arrogance. I guess we'll see."

Prudence added, "Hey, I don't know how this is going to affect your part of this thing with the DOJ, but Reverend Drummond, Theo, and I were talking earlier this afternoon. I think I put some other pieces of the puzzle together. You remember the fight Theo got in and the coin he found and gave to Reverend Drummond, right?"

"Yes, but what's that got to do with it?"

"I'll give you the short version; Theo gave the coin to Reverend Drummond, who confirmed with Reverend CJ that it was probably the UAK that burned down Tante Ju's house. What if it wasn't the UAK? What if it was the cousin of the boy that Theo beat up and it was just a coincidence that the cousin was *in* the UAK? We know that Oscar and Falke used the UAK as the money source for Project Azalea, right? And the UAK uses the gangs. Now, let's take a critical look at Reverend CJ. He's enhanced his lifestyle over the years, a lifestyle that a little community like the Cypress couldn't support. He also sends *troubled* boys to the city to hopefully get them on the *right* path—as far as anyone can tell, anyway. Jimmy, he has been feeding those boys to the gangs! Those boys peddle the drugs, and he's getting kickbacks!"

"Whoa, hold on now! That's quite a stretch," Jimmy replied in disbelief.

"Think about it, Jimmy. Reverend CJ took care of me and Theo the whole time we were at the Cypress. That's about the same time the Azalea Group started buying property and the KTL construction work started. He's a good guy, but he's also a bad guy," explained Prudence.

Jimmy rubbed his chin. "Okay, I can see that. Even if it's true, what do we do with that information?"

"I've thought about that. We're going to confront him today. We'll convince him to come clean, and hopefully we can convince your friend to grant him immunity for cooperating. He knows more than us and he can make it a slam dunk case."

"Immunity for Reverend Hill?! Prudence, you just said it yourself; he's a bad man. If what you are saying is true, he's as tied up in this as much as everyone else. He—"

"Jimmy, I need to clarify. Reverend CJ is a *good* man who has obviously done some very *bad* things, and for all the wrong reasons. He was good to me and Theo in our hour of need. He supported us for ten years, which allowed me to get my GED, and eventually led to my paralegal certificate. That brought me to you and where we are today, trying to take down a criminal enterprise. He's still doing things for his congregation, and he helped out at the Antioch after the cross burning."

"Yeah, a cross set afire by the very people he's working for. He might as well have set that fire himself. Prudence, I appreciate your loyalty, but he still did very bad things. He's a part of all of this. We can't reward him. He'll have to pay his debt to society," Jimmy said sternly.

"Well, what if his immunity deal was contingent on his ability to help the government get convictions?" Prudence pushed. "Even murderers get immunity when they have information that can bring a kingpin down, right? Reverend CJ will face judgment with his congregation and ultimately the good Lord himself. I think he needs a chance to redeem himself, don't you? Life is full of second chances."

"Well, you make a good point, but we need to confront him and explain the reality of the situation. He might not get an immunity deal. Hopefully, he'll see the light and cooperate just the same. I just hope he has enough probative information to help the case."

"Let's hope so," said Prudence sincerely.

"I think you're right. You get him down here, and I'll get with my friend. We're going to make this go down now."

# Chapter 76

## CJ Comes Clean

It was time to confront CJ; his day of reckoning had arrived. Reverend Drummond convinced him they should speak and suggested they meet right away at the Antioch. No time to waste, as both congregations and the entire surrounding communities were in grave danger. They could not allow the loss of another innocent life. What started as a cordial meeting soon escalated when CJ became quite indignant.

"I've done nothing of the sort! How dare you accuse me of consorting with criminals and hate groups! You can't prove that! You can't prove anything!" Reverend CJ was riled up. "You think for one moment I've sold my people out, Mr. O'Leary? I'm not going to sit down for this and dignify your questions with answers. Good day, sir." He then glared at Reverend Drummond. "Honoré, you're part of this... charade? You're the devil! May God have mercy on your soul!"

Jimmy took a stern tone and said, "Sit down, Reverend Hill! You sit down *right* now, and you listen to me good, ya here? You're right, we can't prove much of this, but the fact that you were so defensive and immediately cited a need for us to *prove* your involvement tells me you are either knee-deep in this fiasco, or at least have knowledge about it. We—"

"Prudence? You, too?" CJ cast his gaze onto Prudence, who avoided him by staring out of the window. "Girl, I took you in when you had nowhere to go. The Cypress raised you and Theo. You worshipped with us at the Redeemer, and we took care of y'all. This is how you repay me?"

Tears streamed down Prudence's face. Jimmy leaned across the table until he was just inches away from CJ's face, his jaw clenched so tightly that the reverend could hear his teeth grind. "Reverend Hill, I'm going to tell you one more time. We can't prove much of anything right now, but we know, and you know we know, and you're going to have to live with all that you've done for the rest of your life. You sent those boys to be drafted by the gangs. You sent them under the false pretense that they would be helping others. They come from a poor place, where the people there probably needed the help more than those in the inner city, and you convinced them that their salvation was in helping others. You sent those poor boys right into the lion's den. You, Reverend Hill, are the one who made the deal with the devil. The dominos are about to fall, sir, and you're in the middle of the row. I'm prepared to push the first one, so the question is whether you can jump out of the way before they crush you. Now, I'm going to give you thirty seconds so you can take a deep breath and tell me everything you know—from the beginning of your involvement until you arrived here today."

CJ looked around and took stock of his surroundings—all eyes were on him. While looking at Prudence, who was still avoiding eye contact, he spoke. "I don't think you understand, son. I don't have to tell you *anything*. You have the audacity to accuse me of unspeakable acts, and expect me to just admit to something I've had nothing to do with?" CJ started to rise from his chair, but before he could straighten up, Jimmy motioned for him to sit back down.

Jimmy thought fast on his feet and came up with a bluff. "Reverend Hill, I don't think you want to get out of that chair just yet. If you do, I won't be able to help you. You see, one of the boys you sold to the gangs is on his way to my office to give a sworn statement detailing how you promised him that going to the city would be good for him, how helping people would make him a better person. He's going to talk about the horrors he's had to endure, and what he's had to do to survive gang life. Do you see this phone in my hand? With one call, I can cancel his statement and have him taken back to the safe house. If you get out of that chair, though, I'll put this phone down on the table—right in front of you, as a matter of fact. And he's not the only one. We have others queued up and ready to go. So, you see, it won't be his word against yours. It'll be the words of several of them. Who do you think a jury would believe?"

CJ stared at the table in front of him for a moment, then looked out the window and seemed to say a little prayer before he looked up at Jimmy. "Alright, Mr. O'Leary. If I tell you, you're my lawyer, so you can't say this to anyone else, right?" implored CJ.

"No, Reverend Hill, I'm not your lawyer, and I wouldn't want to be. Everything you tell us is on the record and will go straight to the federal government. If you want a lawyer, then we have nothing else to say and you may leave. I'm not a cop and you are free to go any time, but I recommend you sing like a canary. Unless you have enough to get an immunity deal on your own and help the prosecutor put those animals away, you can consider talking to me as if you're talking to Wolf Blitzer in *The Situation Room*. But you have enough to bring them down, don't you Reverend? I can tell. I can tell by that smug grin. You have enough that the government doesn't need the information we already have. Am I right?"

The Reverend Dr. Cleophus James Hill V tried to muster as much dignity as he could. He sat upright, tugged on his coat, straightened his tie, and cleared his throat. "Alright, Mr. O'Leary, we'll do it your way. Jesus, please help me."

For the next hour and a half, CJ told all: the kickbacks, sending young men into the city, his involvement with Oscar, as well as the UAK. At the same time, in a small effort toward self-redemption, he talked about the good he'd done with his life, of which there was plenty: helping unwed mothers like Prudence, putting people in need together with people able to help, providing a shoulder to cry on in times of crisis, acting as an advocate for those who had been wronged. There was, indeed, a rose growing through the thorny filth.

# Chapter 77

## The Big Bang

It was 20:00 hours when Ti Pop pulled his Cougar into Aryan Cove, which was eerily quiet and pitch-black, save for a small fire set by a few Troops for warmth and light. The materiel was segregated into three packs. Ti Pop exited the ragtop, then pulled a rocket-propelled grenade launcher from the massive tank's trunk.

With a smile that displayed his laser-white teeth, he slung the RPG across his left shoulder and walked toward the two men as he said, in his best Tony Montana impersonation, "Say hello ta ma lil friend! Y'all can split up dat tird pile. I'm goin' all *Black Hawk Down* on dis."

A smile grew across Krieger's face. "Holy shit, Pop! Isn't that a little over-the-top?"

"Yeah," said Cerata in apparent awe of the master's methods. "Not even the mob was this hardcore."

Ti Pop waxed eloquent. "Fellas, in a few hours, when da pageantry begins 'n da sirens wale, when embahs have been doused 'n da plumes of smoke have been blownt away by da lake's balmy breeze, when all are beset wit disbelief, grief, 'n fear a da daylight, when providence has shone 'n da mission has been completed, I'm done wit all dis shit. I want ta top off Ti Pop's swan song wit a bang—a big friggin' bang da likes a' which are seen only in places like Baghdad 'n Bagram. In case any of ya rookies tink you're gonna take Pop down wit ya sinkin' dinghies, y'all got anothah thing comin'. *Betty Lou* is tied off in a secret location, 'n as soon as da echo of da big boom has faded, we're gonna sail away to parts unknown. If ya peckahheads tink you're gett'in away wit dis shit, ya foolin' yaselves. The feds are gonna be all ovah dis, but I'll be long gone. I'm not worried, though, y'all go through wit ya parts like clockwork, 'cause if ya don't, ya have two problems. Firs', Robertsen is countin' on it, and if ya back out, y'all prob'ly gonna wind up like Mr. Tyler ovah dere. 'N secon', I know where ya idiots live, 'n I also know where da friends of my lil friend here live. So, let's take a tipple or two, saddle-up, 'n get ready to light it up! As da oft-used sayin' goes: wine for my men, we ride at dawn!"

# Chapter 78

## A Federal Case

Jimmy convinced his friend, U.S. Attorney Camille Jeansonne, that there was enough evidence to obtain a warrant and convene a grand jury that would undoubtedly indict Oscar Brimley and BB on a variety of charges, including money laundering and RICO violations. There was not yet enough, however, to indict William Thomas Falke, Lawrence Robertsen, or any of the members of the UAK. Earl Tyler and Tyler Loomis were implicated in the burning of Tante Ju's house, but the trail on Earl ran cold and he hadn't been seen in some time, for obvious reasons. Tyler Loomis was sixteen and would probably be charged as an adult for accessory to arson and second-degree murder. Those indictments would come later.

Oscar was chosen first, primarily since most of the information they needed to go after the others resided in the law firm's files. BB was chosen since his files contained the ancillary evidence that tied the Renaissance to Oscar and KTL. Additionally, Jimmy and Camille thought the best way to secure BB's full cooperation was to have him formally charged and then offer him immunity. It was a simple proposition; secure the firm, secure the evidence. All that was left was to follow the money.

In order to get a warrant to seize the offices of the venerable law firm of LeRoux, Godchaux, Bouligny & Tooley, all Camille needed was the sworn testimony of those who knew anything and would turn witness for the prosecution, namely Jimmy, Rachel, Prudence, and Bernadette. Camille and her team then secured the conference rooms adjacent to the chambers of the Honorable Dwight McPhain, a federal district judge in senior status for the Eastern District of Louisiana and first-term Reagan appointee. Judge McPhain gave Camille until five o'clock in the morning to convince him to issue the warrant. Rachel was confident she would have it wrapped up by four.

Knowing that she'd be at the federal building on Canal Street all night, Prudence sent Theo to spend the night at the Antioch on a makeshift cot with some of the same ladies who looked after Chookie in his time of need. All Prudence told him was that she was needed for an all-night document review for a very high-profile case. The group arrived at the federal building at ten and settled in for the long haul. Camille trusted Jimmy, and gladly agreed to immunity deals for all present, subject to the truthfulness of sworn testimony and incontrovertibility of the content. Only CJ's was contingent on probative value leading to an actual conviction. If the case ended up being built on evidence not given by CJ, however, the deal would be dead, and he would be prosecuted for a multitude of crimes.

# Chapter 79

### The Sworn Statement
### of Prudence Jean-Batiste

"The time is 10:15 p.m." Kelvin Williams, U.S. Assistant District Attorney, was no nonsense and got straight to the point. "Good evening, ma'am. Please place your right hand on the Bible in front of you and repeat after me." Prudence looked nervously at the court reporter, who adjusted the microphone and recording equipment.

"Do you swear or affirm to tell the truth, the whole truth, and nothing but the truth?" Prudence nodded in the affirmative. Williams instructed Prudence, "Please verbalize your response, ma'am."

"Yes."

Williams continued, "Please state your full name and occupation."

"My name is Prudence Hope Jean-Batiste, and I'm a paralegal at the law firm of LeRoux, Godchaux, Bouligny & Tooley."

"Thank you Ms. Jean-Batiste. Do you come here tonight of your own volition?"

"Yes, sir."

"Have you been promised anything in exchange for your testimony?"

Prudence nodded in the affirmative.

Williams instructed Prudence again. "Please verbalize your response. I understand that you may be nervous, but the court reporter
needs to take your words down for the record."

"Yes, sir. I am very nervous. Sorry for that. Yes, I have been promised immunity in exchange for my testimony."

"No problem, ma'am, thank you for your cooperation. Now, Ms.
Jean-Batiste, does this promise of immunity have any influence on the
testimony you're about to give?"

Prudence responded with her voice quivering a little. "No, sir.
Whether or not immunity was promised, I'm here to tell the truth. I've
got nothing to hide."

"Ms. Jean-Batiste, you understand that this is not a court proceed-
ing and you are merely making a sworn statement here today? At
some point in the future, you may be asked to make additional sworn
statements both in and out of court. Any inconsistencies between your
sworn statements could be grounds for future investigations, vitiation
of your immunity arrangement, and perhaps legal action against you.
I am not trying to be dramatic and the U.S. Attorney's office has no
current interest in any investigation of you beyond what I am going to
ask you in this setting. I just want to be up front with you and ensure
you fully understand the potential impact of tonight's proceedings. Oh,
and one last thing—at any time, feel free to ask for a break or even call
a stop to these proceedings. Ms. Jean-Batiste, you have stated that you
are here freely and have waived your right to have counsel present,
and you understand that you may leave at any time. If you choose to
leave before I have finished my questioning, the U.S. Attorney's Office
reserves the right to ask you to return for additional questioning by

subpoena, if necessary. Do you understand what I have just said, and do you agree with this path forward as I have just described it?"

The gravity of the situation weighed heavily on Prudence, whose countenance grew increasingly sullen. "Yes, sir. I am here of my own free will. I understand that I'm giving a sworn statement. I have waived my right to counsel. And, I know I can leave at any time."

"Thank you for that, Ms. Jean-Batiste," Williams responded. "Again, sorry for the formality. We must ensure that these proceedings are beyond reproach. We are dealing with some potentially dangerous people, and if we choose to prosecute, we would not want to lose the case based on a technicality. We've spoken off the record already, so I'll give a quick recap of our conversation. You will have an opportunity to further elaborate or correct me, but for now I'd appreciate it if you allow me to give my summary uninterrupted."

"Yes sir, I understand."

Williams began his recap. "Ms. Jean-Batiste, you are a single mother of a fifteen-year-old boy named Theodore. Prior to your employment as a paralegal, you worked as a waitress at La Bonne Cuisine, where you first met Mr. Oscar Brimley, managing partner of LeRoux, Godchaux, Bouligny & Tooley. While at work one day, you waited on Mr. Brimley and his party and asked him, in passing, whether he thought someone like you could ever work at a law firm like his. He initially gave you platitudes, but then immediately offered you a job on the spot. Within a few days, you began working in the firm's pro bono section as a legal secretary and spent approximately half of your time preparing to become a paralegal. Once you obtained your paralegal certificate, your employment status changed, but you remained in the pro bono section and worked under the supervision of the managing attorney of the department, Mr. James O'Leary. Is this a fair summary, Ms. Jean-Batiste? Please feel free to correct me or elaborate."

"Yes, sir. Your summary is fair."

Williams continued, "Thank you for that, Ms. Jean-Batiste. Shortly after you began to work as a paralegal, you were provided various files on which you worked. I will not get into the details of those files, and you have not shared any details due to confidentiality reasons, but I will note that the firm was happy with your work and you were eventually presented with a file by Ms. Rachel DeRouen from the firm's real estate section. You told me that Ms. DeRouen was happy with your work and had plans to bring you into her group. Even though you were still officially in the pro bono section, Ms. DeRouen continued to give you files, some of which were for two of the firm's largest clients, Knight Trucking & Logistics and KTL Construction. Now, if it is okay with you, I'll skip ahead, but we can revisit anything at any time if you need to correct me or provide an additional explanation."

Prudence responded, "Yes, sir, that's fine. Everything you've said up to this point is correct."

Williams then got down to the point. "Ms. Jean-Batiste, you were asked to retrieve some files from Mr. Brimley's office to copy for a matter you were working on for Ms. DeRouen. While you were copying the files, you noticed that, mixed in with the matter files in light green folders, there were some files in light blue folders. These were marked personal and confidential and carried the name of one Oscar Brimley. Despite that marking, however, you chose to copy the files, and you knew—or should have known—that the light blue files were not meant for your eyes. We'll stop right there and give you a chance to confirm, deny, or elaborate on my summary."

Beads of cold sweat lined her forehead, and Prudence became nauseous. "Yes, Mr. Williams. Everything you just stated is correct and I would now like to take a brief break, if that's okay with you. May I speak with my friends during the break?"

"Of course. I could use a little break myself; it's been a long day. And feel free to confer with whomever you wish. Just know that I may question you about those conversations and I reserve the right to question those with whom you speak regarding the content of those conversations without your presence."

"I understand. Thank you."

Williams replied, "Thank you, Ms. Jean-Batiste. The time is now 11:37 p.m."

And with that, the court reporter turned off her equipment.

Prudence met Jimmy in the adjacent room. "Jimmy, I'm so frightened! I've never been through anything like this before."

"Prudence, you got this. The truth is on our side," Jimmy replied. "All you need to do is tell it exactly as it happened. I told you this wouldn't be easy when we started. We have to see this through to the end, otherwise some very bad people will get away with terrible crimes. Remember, we discussed how we'll be impacted by what we've done, as will our friends and family. This doesn't end after our interviews tonight. I've come to grips with that, and I hope that by now you have, too."

Prudence stared at her feet and nodded. "I know, and I blame myself for all of this. If only I hadn't gone poking around into Oscar's files! Something told me to do it, though."

Jimmy took a stronger tone, as if he could convey some of his strength to her through it. "You have to stop with this self-loathing *right now*. The fact is that you did it. It wasn't right, but the good outweighs the bad here. Just imagine what would have happened if none of this ever came to light. These people would continue to push drugs on our streets, and that's not the worst of it. They're involved with at least one murder, arson, political corruption, theft. Remember what Reverend Drummond told Theo; if not for your actions, we wouldn't be able to help put an end to all of this. We have to see this through. We have to finish."

"You're right. I'll just go in, tell the truth, and let the rest unfold," Prudence said. "Thank you, Jimmy. I needed that."

The break was over. Kelvin Williams nodded to the court reporter, who turned on her recording equipment. "Welcome back, Ms. Jean-Batiste. The time is now 11:49 p.m. We'll pick up where we left off, but before we do, I'll ask you a few questions. Ms. Jean-Batiste, during the break, did you confer with anyone about your testimony? And if so, with whom did you confer and what was the scope of those discussions?"

"Yes, during the break I spoke with Jimmy about what I told you and I asked him for some advice."

"By *Jimmy*, you mean James O'Leary, correct?"

Prudence responded, "Yes, James O'Leary."

"You noted that you asked Mr. O'Leary for advice. Is James O'Leary your attorney?"

Prudence stared at the microphone in front of her. "Mr. O'Leary is not my attorney. He is my friend and I asked him for some friendly advice. I've never been deposed before."

"Just to reiterate what I said during earlier questioning, Ms. Jean-Batiste, you are not being deposed," Williams said. "You are merely making a sworn statement. Do you understand?" Prudence nodded and Williams issued a gentle reminder. "Ms. Jean-Batiste, if you would, please verbalize your answer."

Prudence replied, "Sorry, Mr. Williams. Yes, I understand that I am not being deposed."

"Not to worry, and thank you, Ms. Jean-Batiste. Now, what was the scope of your discussion with Mr. O'Leary? What did you talk about?"

Prudence answered, "I told him that I was scared. He told me to just tell the truth. I told him that I felt terrible and that this was all my fault. He reminded me that we always knew that all of us, as well as our friends and family, would be impacted when this came to light. He also reminded me that the good outweighs the bad here, that if I hadn't done what I did, some very bad people would be getting away with murder, arson, and a number of other crimes. I told him I'd come in here and tell the truth, and that the rest would unfold."

"Let's talk about that, about the good outweighing the bad," Williams said. "What does *bad* refer to?"

"The *bad* is that I shouldn't have copied Oscar's files. They weren't mine. The *good* is just what we're doing here: finishing what we started so some bad people will be punished, and so those who have been wronged will receive justice."

Williams paused a moment before saying, "I think Mr. O'Leary gave you some good advice and perspective. I would like to personally thank you for helping us get to this point. Now, back to business. Just prior to the break, we spoke about the personal files of Oscar Brimley, files you copied and took home with you. You mentioned that while you were reviewing the files, you weren't comfortable with what you found, so you began your own investigation and eventually asked Mr. O'Leary to get involved. You both felt that there was merit to your concern and that it would be best for the two of you to work together. I realize that was a broad statement, but would you agree that it is accurate? Please, feel free to correct me or provide additional information."

Prudence shifted in her seat. "Thank you for those kind words, Mr. Williams. Your statement is accurate. I would add, however, that I initially reviewed the files while alone in my own home. I did not approach Jimmy until a week or so later."

Williams continued, "Thank you for that clarification, Ms. Jean-Batiste. I didn't mean to imply that you spoke with him right away.

Once you brought this matter to Mr. O'Leary's attention, however, you suggested to him that the two of you needed a place to conduct your investigation. You suggested to Mr. Brimley that it was a good time in the firm's history to bring pro bono services directly to the community, and requested that he allow you and Mr. O'Leary to establish a legal clinic at your church, Antioch Faith Church. Rather than rendering pro bono services, though, you and Mr. O'Leary used the clinic as a base of operations to conduct your investigation."

Prudence replied, "Yes, Mr. Williams, that is correct."

Like flipping a switch, Kelvin Williams turned aggressive and caught everyone in the room off guard. "So, Ms. Jean-Batiste, what you are telling me is that you deceived your employer into spending what was probably a great deal of the firm's money in an effort to investigate the managing partner without him knowing? That's tantamount to fraud, isn't it? In fact, without your immunity deal, the firm would be well within its rights to take legal action against you, both on a civil and criminal basis. It still might. If I managed the firm, I'd attack your immunity deal and try to prosecute you or sue you civilly. Did you think of that before coming here tonight?"

Tears welled in her eyes, but she defiantly replied in an uncharacteristically loud voice, "Mr. Williams, if you are implying that I wanted an immunity deal to simply get out of some things I've done, you are dead wrong! I'd be here even if I didn't have immunity. These people killed a sweet lady and my dog. They've stolen, paid off politicians, taken advantage of people in financial trouble by buying their homes at reduced values from crooked bankers. Proud people. *My* people. People who have to either move in with relatives or into public housing. Some will have to leave the city." She paused, then asked, "For what? Money, greed, power? The color of their skin? If for some reason the immunity deal is threatened or taken away from me, I'll deal with it, but I'm insulted by your insinuation."

In another surprising move, Kelvin Williams smiled and gently said, "Ms. Jean-Batiste, thank you for that. Your reaction is just what I hoped it would be. My apologies for the drama and theatrics, but I wanted it to be crystal clear that you're not here with us tonight just because of an immunity deal. I have no doubt that your testimony will be very helpful to us in getting as many of these people off the streets as we can. Thank you. Do you have any closing questions or statements?"

Prudence, still confused and hurt by the last round of questions, shook her head.

"Please verbalize your answer, ma'am."

Prudence simply replied, "No."

Williams then turned to the court reporter and said, "That concludes the sworn statement of Prudence Hope Jean-Batiste. The time is now 12:17 a.m."

With that, the court reporter switched off her equipment and Prudence ran out of the room without looking at or speaking to anyone. She ran down the hall, looking for an empty room. A federal marshal started to go after her, but Kelvin Williams waved him away.

For the next two and a half hours, James Ian O'Leary, Rachel René DeRouen, Bernadette Hazel Forrester, Reverend Dr. Honoré Alphonse Drummond, and Reverend Dr. Cleophus James Hill V were interviewed individually in separate conference rooms and spilled everything they knew about the UAK, Oscar Brimley, and his affiliation with Knight Trucking & Logistics Company, KTL Construction, Inc., O.B. Enterprises, LLC, and the procurement of the land and permits for the construction of the Renaissance d'Orleans.

After each interview, they were taken back to the main conference table and instructed to stay there until further notice. A federal marshal stood sentinel to ensure all remained quiet. Camille and her team wanted to ensure there were no inconsistencies in the witnesses' stories. Inconsistencies could jeopardize the case and potentially negate plea deals.

Bernadette gave her interview right after Prudence. Her face was swollen and her eyes were red from crying. She couldn't believe that the man for whom she'd worked all those years could be so evil, and that his selfish actions would forever impact the lives of innocent people. While glad she would be spared the expense and embarrassment of going through a criminal investigation, she feared she could never get another job, and she was in no position to retire.

The U.S. attorneys milled about the rooms. Camille excused herself around four that morning and returned thirty minutes later with a warrant in hand. Judge McPhain readily agreed to issue the warrant on the sole condition that the raid was to be held within the hour so that the innocent employees would be spared the embarrassment of having to be escorted out of the building by federal marshals. Any employees not under suspicion and in the office at the time the warrant was served would be allowed to leave unescorted to the freight elevator. Plainclothes marshals greeted them in the parking garage and saw that everyone who drove to work made it safely to their cars. Those who used public transportation or were dropped off by others were provided rides in unmarked cars to their chosen destinations.

The offices, including the floor on which the Clinic was located, would also be seized; no one in and no one out unless they were released by the marshals, and only after sworn statements were given to the U.S. attorneys. The businesses on the floors above and below the firm, as well as the church's clinic, would be closed for the day and perhaps longer. The firm's clients would suffer as court dates, deadlines for submission of briefs, and deal closings would be missed. Malpractice insurance claims would cost underwriters millions. As with many disasters, the lawyers on both sides of the equation would make out like bandits. The reputation of one of the city's most hallowed and historic law firms would be sullied forever, along with the reputations of all who worked there, regardless of their status—from the senior partner to the entry-level court runner. An investigation by the Louisiana State Bar Association would ensue for all lawyers, old guard partners, and associates. Most reviews would be quick, but special attention would be placed on those who worked in the corporate and real estate groups, the ones that had the most involvement with Knight Trucking and, perhaps unwittingly, the UAK. Some would, undoubtedly, be disbarred or at least put on probation. Not one of them would ever be able to retain the same type of job or social status they'd enjoyed at the firm, and whispers would follow whenever they attended parties or conferences.

Around five that morning, Camille amassed a team of twenty-five U.S. marshals, who entered Oil Centré Tower via its receiving dock. They were simultaneously dispatched to the houses of Oscar Brimley and Brian "BB" Brady to ensure they were picked up before getting to the office, lest they be tipped off and try to evade arrest. One of the marshals tipped off a local TV station to ensure they would not escape a perp walk for the cameras. If they couldn't be led out of the office in handcuffs, they would at least be seen entering the federal building in shame, and during the morning news for the world to see.

# Chapter 80

## Armageddon Time

It was as if Armageddon had arrived.

While Reverend CJ was being interviewed, his historic house of the Lord, with its beautiful centuries-old woodwork, erupted into a fiery inferno. The volunteer fire department from the next town over was too far away, and ill-equipped to handle a fire of that magnitude. The Redeemer burned through the night. By daybreak, all that was left were a few charred hardwood beams and smoldering embers. The light gray smoke rose to kiss the morning fog, creating a moribund scene right out of a Poe story. The congregants stood and wept silently at the sight of their beloved church, which had been the fabric of the community for more than a century and a half. Ironically, as if it was a message from the good Lord himself, a scorched, but intact Bible was found tucked under a pew and open to Proverbs 10:9. *Whoever walks in integrity walks securely, but whoever takes crooked paths will be found out.*

In furious contrast, it took mere seconds for the small, thinly insu-lated, yet immaculately clean clapboard house with a postage stamp of a yard to explode. The concussive effects of Ti Pop's rocket-propelled grenade sent shock waves through the neighborhood, breaking windows and setting off car alarms as far as seven blocks away. Ti Pop looked on from his vantage point and smiled at his handiwork. The explosion was necessary, given the close proximity to the fire department. He wanted it to be erased from history. It wasn't personal, just business.

Miraculously, the Antioch was spared. Ti Pop called off the attack at the last minute. It wasn't because he had a particular affinity for the historical significance of the place as a founding site of New Orleans' civil rights movement. He just didn't want to take an undue risk and believed that, because of the cross burning, the feds likely kept the property under constant surveillance.

During the interviews, one of the U.S. Attorneys whispered the news regarding Prudence's house in Camille's ear. She chose to wait to tell her until after she obtained the warrant. It proved to be the right thing to do. If she had delivered the news immediately after the horrid events, the meeting would have been over, and Judge McPhain's dead-line would have expired. Keeping the information close to the vest was best for all concerned since there wasn't a thing that could be done to change what had already happened.

After the warrant was issued and everyone was dismissed, Evie drove a distraught Prudence to pick up Theo at the Antioch. They arrived at Mamaw's house just as the fire department was reeling in the hoses. The lights of the ladder trucks were still turning with a disorienting strobe effect to signal to all that they should keep their distance. Finding no bodies, the paramedics had been dismissed and the firemen combed the rubble and canvassed the scene, looking for evidence and any remaining ignition sources. Theo fell to the ground, sobbing and inconsolable, with his face cradled in his hands. Despite all the good work he had done after the fight with Tyler Loomis, he still felt responsible for the horror.

Reverend Drummond took Prudence gently by the hand, and together they walked through the ruins to see if any remaining family heirlooms, photos, or mementos could be salvaged. Then, poking out from under the charred remains of Theo's bed, Prudence spotted it: a small patch of royal blue yarn interwoven with shades of green and black. Though wet, singed, and dirty, the afghan was in remarkable shape. Out of the misery there was a little joy, something of Mamaw's to hold on to and honor her memory. Prudence clutched it in her hands and brought it to her face. Underneath the smell of the smoke was a hint of lilac. She looked up, searching as if Mamaw would at any moment appear and take her by the hand to reassure her that everything would be alright.

It was all too much for Prudence to process in the moment—the upstanding businessmen who held evil in their hearts, the esteemed lawyer who was blinded by his greed and cared not for his legacy or the innocents whose lives would be forever destroyed. The acts of these men paled in comparison to those of the leader of the historical community that supported her and helped raise Theo—a community, as it turned out, that was led by a fallen man of God. In the midst of the sadness, however, Prudence's faith showed her that better days were ahead. Newfound friends shared life-changing experiences, the Antioch was spared, and Reverend Drummond could resume tending to the needs of his flock. Finding the afghan gave Prudence a sense of closure, which allowed her to turn her attention to a new day.

## The End

# Epilogue

The trials ended quickly. There was not enough evidence to directly link Falke and Robertsen to the UAK or the fires, and Knight Trucking and KTL Construction were clean. With their wealth and stable of lawyers, they decided to play the long game by stretching out the investigations and trials as long as they could. They would never spend a day in jail.

Krieger and Cerata flipped quickly and turned states' witnesses against Oscar in exchange for one-year sentences in an unnamed, minimum security federal facility. They would enter the witness protection program when they finished their sentences. Feeling as if he had been betrayed by Judas, the chair of the disciplinary committee of the Louisiana State Bar Association recommended that Oscar be permanently disbarred, and the committee unanimously agreed.

In an effort to preserve his wealth for his family, Oscar entered a quick guilty plea in exchange for a five-year sentence and subsequent five-year probationary period. He knew turning against Falke and Robertsen would be tantamount to a death sentence, so he opted to pay his debt and reenter society, albeit as a pariah.

The venerable law firm of LeRoux, Godchaux, Bouligny & Tooley was dissolved. Those who were able to disassociate themselves from Oscar and prove they knew nothing of Project Azalea were permitted to keep their law licenses and quickly set up boutique firms in the hopes that their main clients would follow them. There would forever and a day be a shadow cast over their careers.

Camille agreed to hold a prime time press conference to ensure that Jimmy, Rachel, Prudence, and Bernadette would be heralded as heroes who were willing to risk their lives, careers, and reputations to pursue justice. The world was now their oyster, and all they needed to do was decide their new direction. An opportunity to do just that would arise, and in a manner unforeseen by any of them.

Prudence wanted to maintain a low profile so as not to bring unwanted attention to Theo. Fortunately, Mamaw had maintained insurance on the house, and because of Prudence's selflessness, the insurance company was quick to take advantage and promote themselves alongside the city's new, unsung heroine. They paid the full amount of the policy in record time, and the communities of the Antioch and the Redeemer stepped in to help her keep most of that insurance money by offering their time and talents. They soon built a house of which Mamaw would be proud.

During the rebuild, Jimmy moved in with Rachel and offered his condo to Prudence and Theo, which they reluctantly accepted. She took that time to reconnect with Theo and to reflect on their future. In a moment of clarity, she had an epiphany and requested the presence of Jimmy, Rachel, and Bernadette to share a simple meal and offer a simple plan. After a few bowls of red beans and rice, complemented by a nice Malbec or two, it was decided that in the coming months, the four of them would revive the pro bono clinic and christen it the Antioch Legal Clinic. It would specialize in helping women, children, and the disabled. Jimmy would ask Camille to call in favors from her friends so that seized funds from Project Azalea would be subtly directed to the clinic's establishment via federal grants.

The clinic opened for business about the same time that Mamaw's house was rebuilt. After its first day of business, Prudence came home tired, yet exhilarated, and took in the beautiful calm and silence of her new home. Theo was at the Antioch helping Reverend Drummond finalize the upgrades to the clinic. Prudence sat in her new chair with a sleeping puppy at her feet and continued to repair the afghan. Knit one, purl two.

What does an author stand to gain by asking for reader feedback? A lot. In fact, what we can gain is so important in the publishing world, that they've coined a catchy name for it.

It's called "social proof." And in this age of social media sharing, without social proof, an author may as well be invisible.

So, if you've enjoyed *Project Azalea*, please consider giving it some visibility by reviewing it on Amazon or Goodreads. A review doesn't have to be a long critical essay. Just a few words expressing your thoughts, which could help potential readers decide whether they would enjoy it, too.